Indigenous Pacific Islander Eco-Literatures

The New Oceania Literary Series

Series Editor: Craig Santos Perez

The New Oceania Literary Series publishes thematic anthologies that highlight the diversity and complexity of Pacific literature. These volumes present creative writing, literary scholarship, and pedagogical materials written by an intergenerational network of authors, scholars, and educators from Polynesia, Micronesia, Melanesia, and the global Pacific diaspora. This series is committed to creating thought-provoking books for the classroom and the community.

Indigenous Literatures from Micronesia
edited by Evelyn Flores and Emelihter Kihleng

Indigenous Pacific Islander Eco-Literatures

Kathy Jetñil-Kijiner, Leora Kava, and Craig Santos Perez

University of Hawaiʻi Press
Honolulu

Printed in the United States of America

2nd printing, 2024

Library of Congress Cataloging-in-Publication Data

Names: Jetñil-Kijiner, Kathy, editor. | Kava, Leora, editor. | Santos Perez, Craig, editor.
Title: Indigenous Pacific Islander eco-literatures / edited by Kathy Jetñil-Kijiner, Leora Kava, Craig Santos Perez.
Other titles: New Oceania literary series.
Description: Honolulu : University of Hawaiʻi Press, 2022. | Series: The new Oceania literary series | Includes bibliographical references.
Identifiers: LCCN 2021061695 | ISBN 9780824891046 (hardback) | ISBN 9780824891053 (paperback) | ISBN 9780824893514 (adobe pdf)
Subjects: LCSH: Ecoliterature, Pacific Island (English) | Ecoliterature, Pacific Island—Translations into English. | Pacific Island literature—21st century. | Pacific Island literature—21st century—Translations into English.
Classification: LCC PR9645.5 I53 2022 | DDC 820.8/0360995—dc23/eng/20220509
LC record available at https://lccn.loc.gov/2021061695

Cover art: "Matalaʻi Vāvā," by Taniela Petelō.

University of Hawaiʻi Press books are printed on acid-free paper and meet the guidelines for permanence and durability of the Council on Library Resources.

In Memoriam

Haunani-Kay Trask
(1949–2021)

Teweiariki Teaero
(1962–2021)

Teresia Kieuea Teaiwa
(1968–2017)

Contents

Flowers, Plants, and Trees

Animals and More-than-Human Species

Climate Change

Environmental Justice

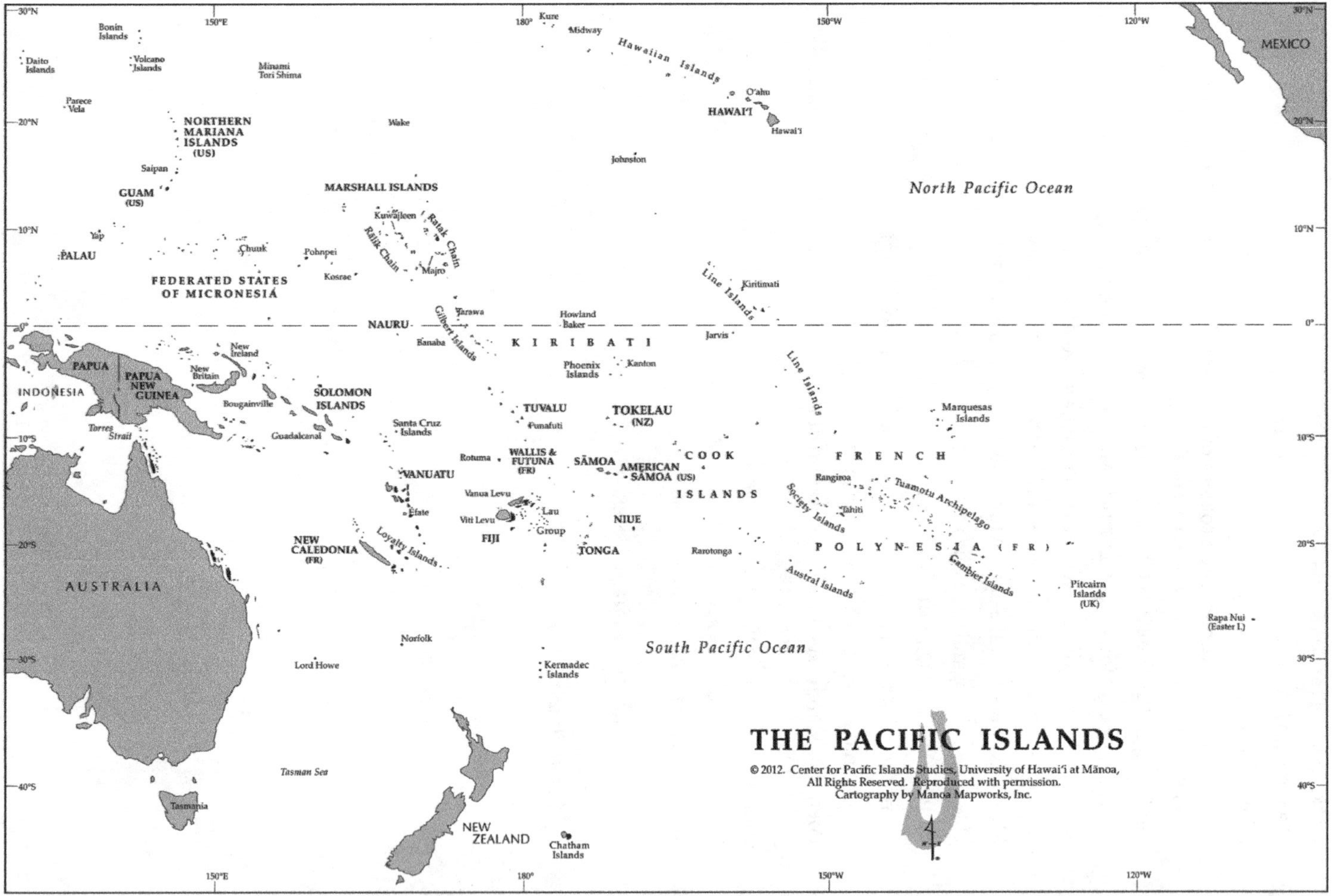

THE PACIFIC ISLANDS

Cartography by Manoa Mapworks, Inc.

Editors' Introduction

Culture and nature are inseparable.

—Epeli Hau'ofa, from "The Ocean in Us" (1998)

As we write this introduction in January 2021, a novel coronavirus is spreading across the globe. More than 92 million people have been infected and 2 million have died. The three of us are living in Hawai'i, the Marshall Islands, and California. Hawai'i has the most cases in the Pacific, and residents are sheltered in place, schools canceled, and "nonessential" businesses shut down. The Marshall Islands, along with several other independent Pacific nations, have been able to suspend most air travel and prevent outbreaks. Pacific Islanders who live in California and the continental United States are suffering from disproportionately high rates of COVID-19 infections, hospitalizations, and deaths when compared to other ethnic groups.

An undercurrent of fear has spread through our communities because so many of us are immunocompromised and afflicted with comorbidities like diabetes, heart disease, and cancer. We are concerned about our elders, who not only are the most vulnerable but also are the most valuable to our families as caregivers, native-language speakers, holders of cultural wisdom, and storytellers. The pandemic has triggered memories of intergenerational trauma from previous eras when infectious diseases (such as smallpox, cholera, influenza, syphilis, mumps, and leprosy) ravaged our populations.

Beyond the human toll, the coronavirus has raised awareness about urgent environmental and economic issues that have contributed to the crisis, such as deforestation, wildlife trafficking, air pollution, underfunded health-care systems, and precarious employment. One truth has become as clear as the blue skies during lockdown: our physical health is intimately connected to the health of the environment, animals, and society.

While it has been difficult to work on this anthology during the pandemic, bringing Pacific authors together has made "social distancing" feel less isolating. Reading our people's stories has given us strength during moments of anxiety and exhaustion. We are reminded that we are not alone; we are always in relation, always ecological.

The seeds of this anthology were first planted in 2014 when the three of us all lived in Hawai'i. We studied and taught Pacific culture, history, politics, and literature at the University of Hawai'i at Mānoa, and we were also involved in environmental, decolonization, demilitarization, denuclearization, and sovereignty movements.

Two older anthologies made a lasting impression on us: *Lali: A Pacific Anthology* (1980) and *Nuanua: Pacific Writing in English since 1980* (1995), both edited by Albert Wendt. Even though these anthologies were not devoted specifically to environmental themes, they do foreground the environment's importance. In the introduction to *Lali,* Wendt described how we are nourished by the love of the Pacific, our mother, and our words flow like springs into the ocean. In *Nuanua,* he explained that the title, which translates as "rainbow," is an appropriate metaphor for the diversity of Pacific cultures, languages, ecologies, and literatures. After reading these important collections, we felt inspired to edit the first anthology that would focus exclusively on representations of the environment in contemporary Pacific Islander literature.

We cast a public submission call in 2016, and over the course of a year we received a substantial amount of poetry, fiction, and nonfiction from emerging, mid-career, and established authors from Melanesia, Micronesia, Polynesia, and the global Pacific diaspora. Additionally, we solicited permission from well-known writers, as well as from the families of writers who have passed away, to include a selection of previously published work. The works we received range from avant-garde to free verse, from chants to short fiction, from visual poetry to a dramatic play. They are composed in English, Pacific languages, and pidgin and appear in translation as well. The diversity of the nearly one hundred contributors is a beautiful reflection of the vibrant biodiversity of the Pacific itself. This anthology is not merely a literary form; it is itself an ecological form with rhizomatic roots and blossoming branches.

While the length and scope of this anthology are substantial, it humbly offers just one glimpse into the vast ocean of Pacific literature, and we hope it will encourage readers to seek out Pacific literature beyond these pages.

During the years we spent editing this anthology, we witnessed the impacts of climate change in the Pacific. Every year has been "the hottest in history." Sea levels continue to rise, and king tides have inundated low-lying countries like the Marshall Islands, Tuvalu, and Kiribati. Tropical storms have increased in frequency and strength: Cyclone Winston devastated Fiji in 2016, and Typhoon Yutu decimated the Northern Mariana Islands in 2018. Ocean warming and acidification have led to coral-bleaching events and marine die-offs, while extreme drought has caused water scarcity and crop failures. Disease outbreaks are more common; the most tragic occurred in 2019, when a measles epidemic in Samoa infected more than five thousand and killed nearly eighty people, most of whom were very young children.

While the Pacific is on the "front line" of climate change, we have also been on the front line of ecological imperialism. Beginning in the sixteenth century, European, American, and Asian nations colonized, militarized, and exploited the ocean and our islands. Across the centuries, there have been so many instances of environmental devastation. Whaling and overfishing in the Pacific. Phosphate strip-mining in Banaba and Nauru. Gold and copper mining in Papua New Guinea and Bougainville. Clear-cutting and logging in the Solomon Islands and Vanuatu. Sugar plantations in Fiji. Copra plantations in Micronesia. Palm oil plantations in West Papua. GMO plantations in Hawai'i. The militarization of Guåhan. The bombing of Kaho'olawe and Pōhakuloa. The dredging of Apra Harbor, Pearl Harbor, and Pago Pago Harbor. The horror of nuclear testing in Bikini, Enewetak, Fangataufa, Mururoa, Malden, and Kiritimati. These traumas have scarred not only our lands and waters, but our bodies and memories as well.

Our people have a long legacy of struggling against these environmental injustices, and we continue to protect our sacred places. While editing this anthology, we have witnessed our people rise across the Pacific. Political leaders like Anote Tong, Hilda Heine, and the late Tony de Brum have all advocated for change locally and internationally. Our co-editor, Kathy Jetñil-Kijiner, represented civil society at the United Nations Climate Summit in 2014. For the opening plenary, she performed her poem "Dear Matafele Peinem," which moved the audience to tears and a standing ovation. In 2017, Fiji presided over the twenty-third Conference of the Parties to the United Nations Framework Convention on Climate Change in Bonn, Germany. Many Pacific countries have taken important steps to protect the environment, including the establishment of vast marine protected areas and sanctuaries. The Pacific Climate Warriors, a network of environmentalists spanning fifteen Pacific nations, have taken nonviolent direct action to protest the fossil fuel industry, such as blockading the world's largest coal port with a flotilla of traditional canoes. Their memorable slogan has become an undeniable chant: "We are not drowning, we are fighting."

We have also witnessed Hawaiians protecting their sacred mountain, Mauna Kea, from the construction of the Thirty Meter Telescope. The *kia'i,* or protectors, blockaded the access road to the summit and established a *pu'uhonua,* or place of refuge. We have witnessed CHamorus across the Marianas protesting further militarization by the United States. Those on Guåhan are resisting a live firing range complex in Litekyan (Ritidian), which is a wildlife refuge and the site of an ancient village. We have witnessed Māori protecting Ihumātao, a sacred and significant historical, cultural, spiritual place in Auckland, from plans to build a high-cost housing development. We have witnessed West Papuans standing up against mining, logging, and palm oil plantations in the face of violent repression by the Indonesian military. We have witnessed islanders across the Pacific rise up against nuclear weapons through the Global Zero coalition and the International Campaign to Abolish Nuclear Weapons, which won the Nobel Peace Prize in 2017. We have witnessed our people rise up against the new, terrifying threat of deep-sea mining. These movements have inspired us, and we offer this book as a way to honor all Pacific *kia'i*—past, present, and future.

Editing this anthology has been a long journey for us. Our lives, as well as the climate, have changed dramatically during this time. What hasn't changed is that our homes are still under threat. And what will *never change* is the willingness of our people to stand up and protect our sea of islands. As you read this anthology, we hope you feel the *mana,* or power, of Pacific eco-literature. We hope you will see how our stories teach us that humans, nature, and other species are interconnected and interrelated; land and water are central concepts of indigenous cultural identity and genealogy; and the earth is the sacred source of all life, and thus should be treated with respect, love, and care. We hope our voices will inspire and empower you to stand with us. We hope this anthology will be a trusted companion as we all navigate toward a precarious yet hopeful future.

CREATION STORIES AND GENEALOGIES

This anthology is just one of many technologies we use to pass on our stories. We write in order to continue passing down the universes that our stories make possible. Here, we can trace maps that point to the complexities, depths, and sheer diversities of our histories—how we consider our world as people who descend from ocean and island places.

Genealogy is a framework for defining and telling our histories, of being precise and critical of our forms of historiography. In English-speaking contexts, genealogy as a term has been imaged as a "family tree," or a chart of direct bloodlines. While our forms of genealogy build from these concepts, they also expand beyond terms of strict biological descent. We tell genealogies in order to pay attention to all the relationships, events, histories, environments, and people who have shaped us. Our genealogies name our ancient and contemporary migrations, our connections to the island and ocean worlds that shaped our ancestors' ways of being and thinking. Our genealogies hold the cultural and political movements that inform how we bring ancestral knowledge into the present as guides toward our futures. We begin with the ancestors before us—for us to argue with, rage with, mourn, and reclaim, and for whom we take back our names.

This section demonstrates how we use the technology of our literature to hold our stories, our complexities, our vast histories. The forms and content of genealogies in this section, and throughout this anthology, are vital places of guidance and navigation. They are stories that help us ask questions about ourselves, our pasts, our futures.

> Why do we write?
> How do we record?
> What do our genealogies make possible?

Genealogy is both text and teacher. These stories define, teach, and model the importance of practicing multiple literacies. Our genealogical frameworks provide options and methods for better reading our island and ocean environments, our connected and complex histories, and who we are, positioned within so many complex and complicated relationships.

Telling, and defining how we tell, our genealogies is also a form of resistance. Colonialism is part of our genealogies—militarization, missionization, land dispossession, environmental racism, nuclear testing, climate change; all are at work in how we shape and tell ourselves as genealogically linked to islands and ocean. We document how our access to our genealogies, our space to tell and retell and rework them, has been stolen, overwritten, reshaped, and erased through massive projects of colonial structures. The very presence of these stories in this anthology is due to our genealogies of keeping knowledge, hiding our stories to protect them, unburying our histories, and reclaiming them as we take up more space and power over our self-representation.

Inside us our dead, before us our ancestors—these stories are the bodies of our memory and the dreams of our future.

Maps to the Ancestors

Peter Sipeli

In three parts I come here today
My tongue, na Yamequ, a library of stories within stories, of my life and all the lives of my ancestors inside of me they sit thick, like molasses on my tongue
My belly, na Ketequ, where my sacred self is sleeping, where borrowed dreams and my inherited "mana" transmits memories and power through my skin
My head, na Uluqu, I pick up radio frequencies of my other selves, I hear voices of my people in languages that I cannot understand, like waves they roll in and out of my body, my body, this vessel, this canoe

Yamequ (1)

I am the sum of my parents
Part island with the sand and song between the folds of my heart
Part city with grit and dirt under my fingernails and skinned into the flesh of my knees
My tongue is thick on the voice of the kaivalagi
But my brown as true as mother skin, and proud of her lineage that she carried like flags wrapped around her hips and tucked deep inside her throat

I sleep with ghosts
Ghosts that don't dance on my tongue
Ghosts that don't know my name
But they know me
They smile in faces like mine
They sing to me, their songs are like hugs only large people can give
In voices part mine, part water, part wood and heavy with the scent of salt
Like the heavy celestial bodies of stars and dreams, these voices call me
They call me . . . Au rogoca na Kaci, I can hear the call
And I am afraid
I am afraid

I am a son of the ocean
I am the son of men that came in cloaks of western reason and rhyme
In canoes the size of mountains with men heavy with ambition and
conquest
And we smiled and gave them ourselves
We smiled and gave them ourselves
Our smiles are weapons
Our smiles smell of blood and sweat
Our smiles are prayers, defiant prayers
Silent prayers of power, heard only by the sea

And we folded our hearts into small graves that we dug in the sand close
to the water
And we folded our broad shoulders & proud hearts into cloth and found
value in shame and our bodies became ornaments in a museum, a
graveyard of our stories
And we stood silent
And we faced the wind
with our hearts in our hands
Smaller versions of ourselves

Today I will begin to draw my maps
Maps of space, place and time
Of stars and of constellations
Maps of places my ancestors occupied
Maps of places they left parts of themselves
In rock, and bark and tree and leaf, in rivers and in the wind
they remain
forever here
forever watching
forever inside

Our bodies are part earth and sky
Our stories are inked into our eyes and on our tongues
I keep drawing my maps in the sand and each time the tide comes in . . .
I draw new maps

Ketequ (2)

Na Ketequ, my belly where my ancestors sleep
dreaming in black & white picture postcard frames
their sleep interrupted by the noise of my broken heart
I carry "our" worlds in our belly,
I carry my father in my belly
his silent anger sits hard on my pito

Reminding me of his journeys, his pain and his absent love
I carry my grandmother "e"—a Samoan woman of noble birth
who raced away in a lonely boat, from her family to marry a commoner in Fiji
who talked to the spirits and believed in Jesus
her laughter and love stay with me

I am halves of many parts, Samoa, Tonga, Fiji, Solomon Islands and Scotland
These parts of me sit in war and peace in my Center
They speak to each other in metaphors understood only by the gods
I feel them when I walk through the plantations of my father
I hear them sometimes in my words
And sometimes they come to me in dreams
they weep at my bed asking me to forgive my father
to speak only what is in my heart
and to only fear untruths
They tell me to plant my ego in the forest so worms can feed on it
so I can be free again

I carry my mother's pain in my belly,
Of her sons the ones born without breath
They were buried in Lovonilase next to my grandfather
Daniel Lockington, an alcoholic that had a heart full of love and laughter
whose hands shaped wood into beautiful objects that sit in rich people's homes

I carry my great-grandmother Leniaro, who married my great-grandfather George Lockington
a black-birded woman from Guadalcanal
She slept on the floor of her husband's room
A small dark woman with short cropped hair
She bore him three sons, the colour of their father with flaming red hair,
I carry her memory
Only one picture of her remains, she stands behind her three sons and George
Only half her face visible

Today I will begin to draw my maps
Maps of space, place and time
Of stars and of constellations
Maps of places my ancestors occupied
Maps of places they left parts of themselves
In rock, and bark and tree and leaf, in rivers and in the wind
they remain

forever here
forever watching
forever inside

Our bodies are part earth and sky
Our stories are inked into our eyes and on our tongues
I keep drawing my maps in the sand and each time the tide comes in . . .
I draw new maps

Uluqu (3)

Na Uluqu, my head—where knowledge not my own, stirs
E Tabu mo Tara na Uluqu—it is forbidden to touch someone's head or hair in Fiji
This is sacred
We believe this part of our bodies keeps us connected to God
Keeps us connected to each other
Our bodies are extensions of the Vanua, the land

My head is a cathedral of memories
Most not my own
I am the face and the skin of my ancestors
Inside of me they sit
Inside of me they stand
Inside of me they dance
All speaking at the same time in frenzied whispers and in silent verse

Original sin I was born into and baptised into Roman crimson cloth robes heavy
with the scent of guilt
I am the burden of theft, of innocence taken inside the hands of home
I am the face of my grandfather and I am the stubbornness of my father
I am the heart of all men Epeli, I am the soul of Koni
Without language I have new maps
These are maps that I taste in the morning light
These are maps that are tattooed on the insides of my mouth
and on the palms of my hands

I stand on the edge of memory, where words fail and movement is prayer
In my dream memory
I see the faces of my parents, I see the faces of Leniaro and George and I see Papa I see Mama and today I see Teresia
Their smiles radiant with the moon in their mouths
They have crossed to the other side

They have given their names back to the sky
No longer physical their names will be whispered in our heads

I swim the radio spectrum of where I am and where I am supposed to be
My cultural face wrapped like my tauvala
Thick woven leaf on cloth, with folds to store my selves in
My gay face, the activist, the poet, the absent son, the reluctant man, the invisible brother
Like Sunday clothes I put them back into drawers carefully pressed for days ahead

The ancestors dance on my tongue
They speak to me
I know under that fire in my belly, inside the blink of my blind western eyes and on the ridge of my soft brown smile, the ancestors sit knowing and they smile at me

Today I will begin to draw my maps
Maps of space, place and time
Of stars and of constellations
Maps of places my ancestors occupied
Maps of places they left parts of themselves
In rock, and bark and tree and leaf, in rivers and in the wind
they remain
forever here
forever watching
forever inside

Our bodies are part earth and sky
Our stories are inked into our eyes and on our tongues
I keep drawing my maps in the sand and each time the tide comes in . . . I draw new maps

Ikurangi

Takiora Ingram

Ko Rarotonga te motu
Ko Ikurangi te maunga
Ko Avarua te ava
Ko Ngati Makea te kopu tangata
Na Tongareva Rangatira, tangata toa

Rarotonga, my island
Ikurangi, my mountain
Avarua, my harbor
Ngati Makea is my family
Tongareva Rangatira my grandfather

Ikurangi
Te Maunga teitei, maunga ruperupe
Tumu nu, tamanu, tutui
Maunga piri
Taratarai koe na te maunga mama'ata
Maunga tapu no te ora
No te uki ou

Ikurangi,
Mountain of flourishing forests
Of coconut, tamanu and tutui nut trees
Mountain of mystery
Eroded from a massive volcano
Sacred source of life
For generations to come

Kua amiri te tumurangi i to mata tokatoka
Te topa nei te roimata o te rangi
Ei akapuma'ana ia koe
Iti mai te ra kia ma'ana'ana koe
Anuanu te matangi kia kore koe e vera

Iti mai te marama, turama te enua
Na'au e tiaki i to tatou ipukarea
Na roto i te po

Clouds touch your rocky face
Misty rain falls like soft tears from heaven
Comforting you
Sun warms you in the first hours of day
Gentle winds cool you from the sun's heat
Full moon rises from the east, lighting up our land
As you watch over our island home throughout the dark night

Descended from Makea
From the warrior Tongareva Rangatira
Born in your shadow, te ata o Ikurangi
On Ngatipa, our sacred land

After birth Papa Kare buried my enua in your soil
Soil of my ancestors
Linking me forever to this land
With those who came before
My maunga, Ikurangi
Tail of the sky, the not-earth place
Supreme authority inspiring peace
A beacon for fishermen, seafaring voyagers
Te pito o te 'ao
Center of my world

August 2014

At the Centre of Everything

Virginie H. Tafilagi-Takala

Translated from French by Jean Anderson

Here
Taputapu the surging Earth
The fish-hook bone
Kneading tresses of seaweed and foam
Tapu my Land
That my mouth's honest breath predicts

Away up there
Jutting the night
The Taputapu sky unfurls
Infinite

Tapu my Sky
That my mouth's breath brushes
With the tips of its wings

Down there Moana Uli
Generous salt revives
On the highest crests

The crashing cadence of the oars
My mouth engulfs your torrid trace

My breath
Aflame
Clad in you
Standing tall
Standing tall in you
In my cobalt cliffs
Of breasts

Plant your paddles in unison
Thundering columns
Waves of triangle rainbows

By day also dig into my nights
Ramparts of wrung-out eyes
Roping carapaces and shells
To lavish leaves

Tie your tattooed finery to the fragrance of the skies
Tie them to the raw dance of our alliances
To our impatient bodies
Fan coolness over ancient Mala'e's rhythm, fan it!
Sniff out the Word
The challenge that summons and nourishes
Bringing forth the pious memory of the Earth

Black Stone

Grace Mera Molisa

Black Stone
Molten lava
solidified.

Solid
jagged forms
starkly
awe inspiring.

Black Stone
core of creation
basis of being
demi god.

Black Stone
flowing free
from depths
unknown
a viscous form
coagulated

Jet black
sleeping fortress
weather rock
come wind or shine.

Black Stone
hard
and obstinate

Previously published, *Black Stone,* Mana Publications, 1983.

indelible
solidity.

Black Stone
bird of wealth
solid bedrock
dwelling of death.

Eternal essence
of immortal soul's
steadfast fixture
founding Man's
physical cosmos.

Threshold
of the spirits
transfixed
to the stable
equilibrium
of constancy
and permanence.

Black Stone
immovable
immobile
Black Stone.

Tagaloa

Karlo Mila

alone

in the
vānimonimo

vast
illimitable
expansive
space

alone.

Tangaloa-fa'a-tutupu-nu'u

a rock

split by strong comet hands

a big bang

split into named rocks
Papa-taoto; Papa-sosolo;
Papa-lau-a'au;
Papa-'ano-'ano;
Papa-'ele; Papa-tu;
Papa-'amu-'amu
and his children

the oldest sedimentary surfaces

with meteorite might
split it open to the right

earth

—that cooled
rocky crust

became
the parent
of all things
blessed
with vapour

then the sea came

and then the
freshwater

and sky

each had
offspring

primordial
chemicals

ancestral
atoms of mutual
attraction

male and female
paired

elements
gravitating
towards
each other

copulating
bifurcating
replicating

molecular
love-making

immensity
(male)

and space
(female)
were attracted
to each other

massive crush
of clouds
dust and gas
interstellar sex

procreating
night and day

night and day
were attracted
to each other

coupled
copulated

procreating
the eye of the sky
the sun

then the moon
and their siblings
the stars

a series
of amino acidic
attractions

protein reactions
elements birthing
in a stellar nursery

eventually
the youngest

the islands
were birthed

plants paved the way
for all other forms of life

yams and arrowroot
among the elder siblings
and finally
what was called
the peopling-vine

microscopic worms
began to burrow

a multitude
of worms
multicellular
eventually
nerves, vertebrate,
muscle structure
much later
head, faces, hands
finally distinguishable
as organisms
that evolved
eventually
into us.

At the end of
these ongoing
expressions
of love
and productive
relationships
of mutual attraction
all life flourished

an evolutionary
eco-diversity
a genealogical order
a world of relatives

an interconnected
dna sequence

a phylogenetic
family tree

and we are

the younger siblings
subordinate to all that
preceded us

all of us
returning
to common
ancestor

stardust
shining in the bones
of our bodies

Our stories are within us

Serie Barford

Our stories are within us. You'll find them encoded in genealogies, embedded in our hearts, imprinted in our minds. They migrate with the tongues that tell them, flourish in the presence of orators and gossips and are readily transported to the arenas of lotu and aiga, where they open and close wallets, elevate and deprave souls, win and lose wars.

Some stories cling to the outside world once they're told. They seep into shadows, harbour with bitterness and grief, churn fists into flesh in the pissy corners of derelict streets. Others laugh from the necks of bottles or froth from aluminum cans onto pandanus mats in suburban lounges. Then, there are the stories that crystallise into swinging hips and hula hands or bounce off hats and rafters in churches where not-so-innocent tongues sing glory hallelujah.

Stories are everywhere. They lurk in unlikely places, forming and growing like children, connecting us to a myriad of worlds. They make us laugh. They make us cry. They make us human.

Stories can be forgotten or die out. Local stories can be ousted by the stories of strangers living in faraway lands. Satellites beam these people onto screens that light up our homes. Neighbourhoods relinquish their communal memories for the roller-coaster lives of screen characters they emulate but will never meet.

But truly precious stories, those that hold sacred truths within them, can never be lost. They are kept intact by the universe itself. They exist beyond everything we can touch and name. They are in our blood, and like red hibiscus burnt by frost, recover and reveal themselves again. These stories are so powerful that only the pure of heart can carry them between worlds and survive. They change lives and their coming is signaled by the stars.

Such a story arrived recently in a small coastal village in the Pacific. A child awoke one night, overcome by fever and vivid dreams. Her delirium shred the mosquito net and woke the entire village.

The quietest elder in the village, one so quiet some thought him mute, entered the thatched hut and elbowed the girl's parents aside. She'd collapsed and lay still as if already dead. The elder knew he was born for this night. He started

Previously published, *Niu Voices: Contemporary Pacific Fiction,* Huia, 2006.

chanting in a voice that carried through the heavens. He chanted throughout the night—guiding the girl's soul back to her sleeping mat and anchoring it to her body as the stars gave way to dawn.

When the sun rose, the child sat up and recited lost chains of genealogies that linked people to the gods and the village lands. When she finished, she collapsed into a deep sleep, but the elder, his purpose done, lay down and died.

The villagers wailed and gripped each other. They looked to their priest and chief for guidance, but they were holding the elder and weeping. Then something happened as the story coursed through their veins, travelled to their toes, the tips of their waxy ears and the hollow spaces behind their eyes.

The people began to wriggle and cough as darts of recognition pierced their hearts and opened their minds. The genealogies triggered memories they didn't know they had. Rocks, trees and marks on the land seemed as familiar as the smiles of loved ones. They remembered who they were and where they came from. They understood that the sea, the land and the sky were within them and without at the same time. The village woke up.

The very next day they said "no" to the land developer from the transnational company who'd promised them electricity and every appliance under the sun.

The next week they said "no" to politicians who'd promised them jobs in the high-rise hotel planned for the land beside the river that gushed into the sea.

The next month they said "no" to policemen who tried to evict them from the foreshore and tore up the memorandum of understanding their chief had declined to sign with the Minister of Economic Development.

Their boats, fishing nets and pick-up trucks were confiscated. Their plantations were trampled by herds of cattle that appeared out of nowhere. Their houses mysteriously burnt to the ground and all the pigs and chickens were poisoned.

They were labelled "terrorists," and the army planted barbed wire instead of trees in a ring around the village. No one was allowed to trade with them, give them food or medicine or publish their story. They were outcasts on their own island.

But the story fed them, kept them strong. The people smashed their battery radios and burnt the pamphlets planes dropped on them from above. They reconnected with legends, healed their hearts, replaced knowledge with wisdom and stepped in and out of courtrooms and prison cells with grace and fortitude.

The truth refused to be hidden. It leaked out and was aired around the world. The villagers' story was beamed into the living rooms of strangers in faraway places, inspiring both the dispossessed and couch potatoes to rise up and get a life.

The villagers are still living their collective story and fighting to keep the land intact. They have rewritten history books and redrawn maps. They have renamed places and each other. And all the while, they listen to the inner voice that links them to the stars.

"It's like this," their chief said. "Everyone has stories. They come from what we call daily life and from the worlds between worlds that we dream and fly in. There's a tusitala in all of us, just waiting to get out. That's where they are. Our stories are within us."

Inside Us the Dead

Albert Wendt

Prologue

Inside us the dead,
like sweet-honeyed tamarind pods
that will burst in tomorrow's sun,
or plankton fossils in coral
alive at full moon dragging
virile tides over coy reefs
into yesterday's lagoons.

1. Polynesians

Inside me the dead
woven into my flesh like the music
of bone flutes:

my polynesian fathers
who escaped the sun's wars, seeking
these islands by prophetic stars,

emerged
from the sea's eye like turtles
scuttling to beach their eggs

in fecund sand, smelling
of the sea—the stench of dead
anemone and starfish,

eyes
bare of the original vision, burnt
out by storm and paddles slapping

Previously published, *Lali: A Pacific Anthology,* Longman Paul, 1980.

the hurricane waves on, blisters
bursting blood hibiscus
to gangrened wounds salt-stung.

These islands rising at wave's edge—
blue myth brooding in orchid,
fern, and banyan; fearful gods
awaiting birth from blood clot
into stone image and chant—

to blind their wounds, bury
their journey's dead, as I
watched from shadow root, ready
for birth generations after they
dug the first house-posts

and to forget, beside complacent fires—
the wild yam harvest safe in store houses—
the reason why they pierced the muscle
of the hurricane into reef's retina,
beyond it the sky's impregnable shell;
and slept, sleep waking to nightmare
of spear and club, their own young—
warriors long-haired with blood
cursed, the shrill cry
of children unborn, sacrificed.

No sanctuary
from the sun-black seed
inside the self's cell—
coral lacerating the promise,
self-inflicted wounds at the altar
of power will not heal.

2. Missionaries

Inside me
the Sky-Piercers terrible as moonlight
in black and winged ships breaking

from the sun's yoke through
the turtle-shell of sky
into these reefs,

miraculous iron barking
the sermon of Light, in search
of souls in the palm-milk child.

        My fathers'
gods, who had found voice
in wood. Lizard, and bird,

        slid
into the dark like sleek eels
into sanctuary of bleeding coral,

        but were exorcised
with silver Cross harnessing
the sun's beauty, burning, burning.

And my fathers, in the pulpit's
shadow bowed, slept
the new sleep, waking to men

of steel hide exuding
a phosphorescent fear, and learnt
to pray the litany of sin—

            the Fall
            in a woman's thighs,
            the papaya feel
            of her gift
            and phallus
            sprung.

All was sin.
The Kingdom was come in

            Calico. Axe. Words
            captured in print
            like bird footprints
            on the white sand
            of my breath.

            Beads. Tobacco. Knives.
            Nails for each palm cross.
            Promises of eternity beyond

the reefs of the sun
to be paid for with the foul
bandages of Lazarus.

The new way is the Cross.

3. Traders

Inside me the dead: a German,
my great grandfather, booted
sea-captain in a child's
book, in a schooner ploughing
the fables of Polynesia from
a cold Europe, his glass eye
focused on exploding stars, selling
exorbitant wares for copra
and women. Bearded with luxuriant
dreams of copra fortune
and the "noble savage," but greying
with each fading horizon—
the next atoll holding only
"thieving natives and toothless
syphilitic women." Too late
for a fortune, reaped a brood
of "half-castes" and then fled
for the last atoll and a whisky death.
His crew tossed him to the sharks
and sent home only his blue glass
eye—crystal ball of Europe—which
my grandfather buried under
a palm, a fitting monument
to his father's copra lust.

No prayers
were said for him I hope.
I want to imagine him
an atheist adventurer wormed
with the clap, dispersing snakes
into every missionary eden.

My grandfather—
and I can only describe him from
a photograph cobwebbed in my
father's cupboard—died
too of whisky, at thirty-six.

"Tall, dark and handsome" is apt
for him. No glass eye for
this Hollywood trader marooned.
Arrogant gleam in his eyes
    with nowhere to sail
    without a ship,
Straight junker nose inhaling
    the bitter serenity
    of failure,
Thick polynesian lips shaped
    for wine, whisky
    and fierce infidelities.

White-suited in a cane chair,
the kaiser—of whisky come-courting
the camera, in love with Bismarck,
burdened with the failure of Europe,
heir to the cold crystal eye.

4. Maternal Myth

My mother, dead since
I was twelve, spider-high.
Memories of her are flamboyant
blooms scattered across
pitted lava fields under
the moon's scaffold, or fish
darting among fabulous seaweed.
Escape from the grasp of my tongue,
images shatter into dust
from which myth rises
to elixir air at the rim
of my skin:

    In her years
of scarlet ginger flower snaring
bumble-bee, I remember

    In her lilt fingers
in scent of moon,
    plucking
my clumsy tongue to butterfly
hymn; my mind, white
as spider lily, to morning
pigeon in tavai, cooing;

my eyes to vision of her fatal
human face that knew
        the bravery of tears.
She was the fabric of fairy tale,
the golden key to each child's
quest for giant's castle.

Dead, she walks the miracle
of water-lily stars, more moonbeam
than flesh, the sinnet of myth
I weave into my veins.

5. The Ball Thrown Up

An engineer, inspired like a juggler, derives
his essence from earth's ores. Stone,
iron, lava, sale, fuel to construct
bridges between his nimble feet
and the angels:
a mathematical universe wired
to his computer fingertips,
the planets tick to his vision
of designing, the ball thrown
up will not come down.

That's what my brother wanted
to be—feet in iron, head
in the rainbow, rewinding
the moon.

        The final time
I saw him, moon pouring up
from the sea, he was side-stepping
into a midnight plane,
albatross guitar round his neck.

With a roar, the silence
scattering, he was winging
off towards temperate sun
and snow, the darkness
falling on all paws
on the tarmac.

"The black dew," said
my pastor uncle, the pulpit

juggler, at his funeral,
"does not discriminate
between jugglers
and engineers."

My brother was brought
back from the snow in
an oak box polished to see
your face in, designed
to lock gravity in.

        No spider's-web bridge
to rainbow strung,
he had slipped off
        an ordinary
highway built
        for ordinary mortals,
car buckling in, like
a cannibal flower, to womb
him in
death,

        petrol fumes rising—
a cat uncurling to lap
the milk sky,
        the wheel spinning
spun the white dew
        of prophecy: the ball
coming down
to stone,
(breaking).

Beginning

J.A. Dela Cruz-Smith

is a cycle, patches of grass, waterfalls, ladies
of coconut tree fronds, latte stones.
Monuments, the crosses atop Mt. Lamlam.

Nuns browsing their purses before class,
Mysteries in the windows.
As I float I inquire

the daddy seahorse, lone stallion
in the yellow found only in multicolor scenes,
I feel machetes the tops off coconuts

as slivers of baby fish peruse
the immaculate sand and seaweed
just beneath me

a whole world pumping. Volcanic
rocks —the time—
polished like crystals
set the ocean floor on fire,
greens I confuse as red and blues,
sizzles of crabs on the grill

the size of boulders, full of white
creamy flesh
covered in shells the same red

as the fire,
its smell tickles my feet
or are the baby fishes nibbling at me?

Purples in the tiny   prisms
                wetting my skin.
My father   brushes them off

letting in the sun,   kisses
        on my arms and belly.
He swaddles me   out from the sea

keeping me   still
        and silent   as the wind
dives   headfirst   into the ocean.

From there   I can   hear the shaking
of my hairs   completely   dry,
salts stinging,   as I   eat with him.

Offspring of Oceania

Kisha Borja-Quichocho-Calvo

Our cultures of Oceania
are as diverse as our peoples
Brown
Black
Mixed blood

Our practices and values
are as diverse as our peoples
yet
we don't just dance
to the beats and rhythms of drums and guitars
sing songs, melodic tunes of precious memories
and put on shows for people's pleasure.

We write words of wisdom,
lyrical legacies for future generations of Oceanians.

We carve stories onto skin, stone, wood, and shell,
leaving no room for forgetting,
only

Remembering

We hunt and fish for sustenance
like our ancestors
feeding the fire of hunger
for identity and culture.

We weave
intertwining every leaf
locking in lines of genealogy

strands of stories
shared across our Ocean.

Our peoples of Oceania
are as diverse as our cultures

And while our diversity makes us unique
Brown
Black
Mixed blood

Our Blue Ocean connects us.

We are bridged by
common practices and values
ancient tongues
vessels of voyages
stories on skin, stone, wood, and shell
lyrical lines written and spoken

All of which
gift us with
genealogies that have flowed
through our bloodlines
for thousands of years.

We are more than simple song and dance.
We are more than beats and rhythms
We are more than melodic tunes and
skin-revealing cultural wear.

We are complex identities and
creation stories.
We are survivors of colonial struggles and
complicated histories.

We are colonized.
We are de-colonizing.
We are different.
We are the same.
We are searching.
We are rooted.
We are disconnected.
We are connected—

We are the offspring of Oceanic ancestors,
sea vessels
guided by ancestral
currents
and
constellations.

Notous and Falcons

Waej Genin-Juni

Translated from French by Jean Anderson

For a very long while, there existed a kingdom
Unknown to the living and ignored by humans
Arising out of nowhere, after a slow journey
From the depths of the abyss, there gradually emerged
A multifaceted archipelago.
At first, slight and frail, able to be tweezered up,
The islands lined up neatly
But trailing behind, there happened along
A black rock, a great long rock that latched on.
Wind and water mingled bringing seeds,
Flowers, plants and soon tall trees over all the plain.
Next came winged travelers of glowing hues.
The supple boughs of the araucaria delighted them.
They settled in.
The climate suited them, they made a thousand nests.
In no time at all, clouds of baby notous
Were flying above the houp and kaori trees
While their siblings, still in their nest,
Waited
For breakfast.
Bountiful nature, over time,
Had here and there sown treasure of nickel and silver.
The kingdom of the proudly plumed
Was peaceful at heart, knew no constraints
And lived a wild life
In its beautiful plumage.

But the unknown island was spoken of more
And from then on it drew to it clouds of seabirds
Bringing with them in their winging wake
An armada of proud falcons on pilgrimage.

They would just rest their wings, they said,
Then rejoin the rising currents.
Of leaving, there was no longer any question
The falcon people made a stronghold of the tallest pines.
Seeing their warlike demeanor and their disdainful beaks
The clan of the notous, united behind their king,
Spoke out at once and with one voice:
"We are the first people.
We are the only descendants of the forest.
We are the only children of the land.
We are the only siblings of the wind.
We will live alone on the eternal hillocks
Of our ancestors.
This is our wish."
From the forest to the reefs
There buzzed the aggressive chants
Of the notou people, habitually peaceful.

The winged nation of falcons, tired of their ocean crossings,
Turned to the Almighty,
Called on Him as witness, stressed the faults in the argument,
Lost patience, proffered threats,
Then attacked.
The archipelago with its thousand delights
Endured much bitterness.
A deafening cacophony:
Yesterday's friends, enemies today: a dizzying hatred.
Each side calling on the Almighty
To show the weaknesses of the opposing claim.

Given His dislike of quarrels, the Almighty
Considered making their feathers fly
But changed His mind:
Will you live separately or together? He asked.
The high chief of the notous believed, childishly,
That they must all sing from the same page
And remain faithful unto death.
The falcon pilgrim agreed, his wing on his heart
That in fact
There would have to be concessions.
The Almighty up in His lovely aviary
With an absent look, taking off His hood,
Said, "Off you go, by yourself, and explain
That you're together."
The notou chieftain paid the price, plucked clean.
Oh, such a heavy price to pay!

Gata (with a mechanical jaw)

Jahra Wasasala

black and brown poets
are called
into the poem
to bend the english word until
it breaks, begs
and transforms (there is joy here)
black and brown slang
is a sign that the mouth is refusing
the ruling
language's law (there is humour here)

english
is not the bounty
it is the trap

my great-great-grandfather, a cannibal
refused
to taste the body of christ
redemption (enacted) left
him jawless
his body, filled with concrete
now sinks
into Fiji's memory

swallowing
is not the bounty
it is the trap

I have not inherited a tongue
inside of my mouth
an ancestor
throws itself against the walls
the sound leaks
through teeth

as a stutter
as a prayer
finding its body

romanticised horror is a generational genre:
a serpent
with a mechanical jaw
growing outside of its father's
swollen belly
or
islands swallowing
graveyards
hiding them from a rising sea
(we all become cannibals
against our will)

the human
within me worries
that if my grandmother doesn't speak english, maybe
my ancestors don't either
& then what use is a borrowed education?

||

I have learnt
that english words are where
old gods are sent to be buried

I have learnt that speaking
vosa vakaviti,
vakamarautaka na yaloqu
and no poem can replace
being able to speak
fluently.

I have learnt that a body is
a home
for voices
with too much blood in them.
so when the tide rises into an unbearable
thing, I ask Julia Mage'au,
to mark me (body and voice),
to puncture
breathing holes.

I see Lay Kabalan's throat
filling with ink & saltwater,
opening
the gate to Pulotu.

(there is comfort here)

I see Akwaeke Emezi's cheekbone
spilling ash & freshwater,
out of the mouth
of a python.

Julia says "now, Veiqia"
& I see Adi Vilaiwasa, the ancient first.
our together-god-skin
bleeds as it sings,
drawing maps to find the buried things.

||

the pantheon
within me knows
that when I am called,
two prophets trade story within my first name
as the tale-end of
(and a world is conceived in-between them)
a hiss uncoils itself within my last name.

the prophets say,
"rub the earth of the village
into the eye of the wound"
the gata says,
"mark me,
so that Viti may recognise me
& I might recognise my selves"

||

Shore Song

Lehua M. Taitano

Our people

were shaped from stone

and the pulsing

sea.

Sister's crouched
body

wave kneaded

salt lapped

until we tumbled

from her

of her (of them)
all strong
and
whole
together.
Birds
regarded

our sea foam
anklets

our slippery ropes
of hair our

cheeks full

of
pebbles

and scattered from the shore

singing.
We opened
our new mouths
to
our
own chorus

crooning
SisterBrother

we are

sun
moon
sky

water
earth

all

siblings.

Tåno I Man Tao

Jay Pascua

Gaige yu gi sakman . . . hu aligao i gima yan i tåno-ñan i famagu'on-hu . . . yan i famaguon-ña.

(I am in the oceangoing outrigger canoe . . . I am searching for a home and land for my children . . . and their children.)

Ti bai attan tåti . . . bai attan mo'na . . . angocco yu na hunggan guaha tåno guini gi matingan.

(I will not look back . . . I will look forward . . . trust me, yes, there is land in the middle of this deep ocean.)

Gi painge hu li'e salungai . . . mahånao guato gi pulan . . . på'go hu tungo na ti man maleffa i mañaina-hu nu guåhu.

(Last night I saw whales . . . they were headed towards the moon. Now I know my ancestors did not forget about me.)

Aye . . . sa chågu ini na hinanao . . . lao hu tungo gi senhålom-hu na ti åpmam yu bai li'e i tåno ma nåhi yu ginen i mañaina-hu.

(Oh, this journey is long . . . but I believe with everything in me that I will soon see the land my ancestors have given me.)

Maåtñao i pa'låan yan i famagu'on . . . sa dångkulo na långat . . . kada tumomba i sakman . . . kada ma eshalao i taotao-hu.

(The woman and my children are scared because of the massiveness of the huge waves. Each time the waves smash against the outrigger canoe . . . it is these times that my people scream.)

Kada homhom uchan . . . kada i satpon mapanak yu . . . hu tungo na hunggan ti man magof i taotao-hu lao ti bei nåhi håfa malago'-ña.

(Each time the rain clouds gather . . . it rains horizontally and slaps me . . . I know my people are not happy but I will not give them what they want.)

Ti bai hånao tåti guato gi tåno-hu . . . sa hu li'e gi guinifi-hu . . . meggai na dångkulo na okso yan i nao'aon saddok yan niyok guato gi tåno i famagu'on-hu.

(I will not return to my land . . . I have seen it in my dream . . . numerous large hills as well as clear rivers and coconut trees at the land of my children.)

Håfa eyu . . . kulan fanihi . . . magåhet fanihi . . . ma ekongok i mañaina-hu i kumakåten i lahi'-ña . . . eyu guato i tano-ña'n i famaguon-hu ginen i mañaina-hu. Tåno-ta . . . tåno-ta.

(What is that . . . it is like fruit bat . . . yes it is fruit bat . . . the ancestors have heard the cries of their son . . . there it is the land of my children given by my ancestors. Our land . . . our land.)

Patgon-hu . . . ekongok yu . . . på'go måkpo i hinanao . . . gai guihi i tåno-mu . . . ti åpmam bai håksa i gima-mu . . . yan i gima-mun i famagu'on-mu.

(My child . . . listen to me . . . the journey is over now . . . here is your land . . . I will soon erect your home . . . and the home of your children.)

Ekongok yu . . . na yanggen somu na mappot i lina'la-mu . . . hasso na chågu man måtto hao guini . . . lao på'go yan mo'na i mañaina-mu ma nåhi hao håfa malago-mu.

(Listen to me . . . should you believe your life to be difficult . . . remember that it was a long journey here . . . but now and in the future your ancestors will provide you with what you desire.)

Ini guihi . . . guaha gi guinifi-hu . . . guaha niyok . . . guaha nao'aon saddok . . . guaha meggai dånkulo na okso. Tåno i man tao!

(Here it is . . . there are many things from my dreams . . . there are coconut trees . . . there are clear rivers . . . there are numerous large hills. This is the land of the Chamorro!)

Matariki

Kiri Piahana-Wong

It is winter and the new year
opens its arms before me

The moon is gone
The sun has fled

I am bathed in darkness
A woman with no moon

I wander the land alone
My blood quiescent, stilled

In the darkness my words sink
like stones
Spiral into the deep

The ground is hard
My footprints leave no trace
I am witnessing the sky's
rebirthing, in the dark of the moon

His dance with the depleted earth
Her bones pressing
against the curve of the bay
Longing for the sky

I walk as if my passing matters
I walk as a witness
I let my tears fall
spiral down my arms
fall from the ends of my fingers

Previously published, *Night Swimming*, Anahera Press, 2013.

Anoint the earth
with the salt of the sky

And I think of the words
of my tupuna—

Tukua mai he kapu ngā
oneone ki a au hai tangi

Send me a handful of earth
that I may weep over it

Ars Pasifika

Serena Morales

after craig santos perez

i roll within a fiddlehead fern till we unfurl into water and
wave, leaving alluvial tracks like crumbs to an old eruption.
the coqui frogs sound off—
whistling their own names,
i join in chorus, chanting mine
till it takes
soft hope it will burn into star tale, hips willing this body
of breath, our collective call,
to constellate
while we wreathe it from our root caps, upward through
hull, through hula,
our kumu, our kupuna,
an inherited narrative: kukui unto kukui unto kukui
a lei
made from memory here:
our moon mothers the mountains to her, here:
our hands cradle your shoulders, here:
we touch foreheads,
inhale
through our noses, exchange *hāāāāāāāā*
our mana one mana as we
share this prayer for prosperity
that what blesses the mauna may reach the moana,
that each ribbon of water might carry our mele
to a brackish embrace where cold flow
honi hot tide
what hum, what bubbling, abeyance
and uncovering of crab clamber, lips to Pū, lungs full—
Mākaukau!?

these are the songs that birthed us as we woke ensconced
beneath lava rock, crawled from the cracks like hatchling
and stretched toward the poli of white light—

a yawn of exordium,
                                        a dry cry.

Masu

Tagi Qolouvaki

> "Tiko can't be developed," Manu declared, "unless the ancient gods are killed."
>
> —Epeli Hau'ofa, *Tales of the Tikongs*

Dua

Where do the gods we've forgotten go?
To Burotu?
Did they slip into the skin of the new god?
Do they sleep
in the qele ni vanua
Awaiting our remembering
we, na lewe ni vanua
the flesh of the earth
their descendants?

Where are all our bete, na dautadra
our priests and priestesses?
Do they slumber in the archives
records of ritual
and ethnographic portraiture?
Do they live in the vuniwai
prescribing roots and medicinal herbs
to remove sorcery, heal hearts and other wounds?
How do we supplicate the gods without
their bodies, mouths, ears as mediums
na wa vicovico between us?

Previously published, *Ika Journal of Creative Writing*, 2014.

Rua

Karlo once said, "the gods are in your marrow"
and the words have settled deep
like kava sediment
na yalo ni vanua   the earth's soul
in the base of the tanoa.
Kalou gata, Kalou vu
Degei, Dakuwaqa, Daucina,
is that you, coiled in the heart of my bones?
Your breath what moves my blood?

If our dead are woven into our flesh
like the music of bone flutes
perhaps it is we who lie dormant;
flesh of the vanua
asleep to the divine
rocked to unconsciousness
by the seductions and threats of new gods

Tolu

Capell's *New Fijian Dictionary*
defines Kalou gata
as "blessed, happy; happiness
and *formerly* a mode of worship rendered to Degei."
Kalou gata literally translates to
snake god.
"Kalou," the new god inhabits you now
but Degei is as old as the land
the root of his body is vatu
stone

Va

Degei
you who live in the sweet juice of our bones,
you who birthed our people
from Turukawa's eggs
kept warm under your watch,
you who made a home for the first people
in the arms of the Vesi tree,
you who taught us how to grow and cook
the kakana dina
the true food of the land

Kalou gata, Kalou vu
we your children
face futures without fish
and shores that creep steadily inland.
You, god of the mountains
cave-dweller,
we open our eyes
we bring dalo, ika, puaka, vonu
and yaqona
remember us

Tooth of the Moon

Déwé Gorodé

Translated from French by Jean Anderson

It's four in the morning. The birds are starting to sing beneath my window, as they do at dawn every day. It's a bit chilly for a December morning. And I couldn't help thinking that one night, while we're asleep, the nuclear winter might arrive and it would be so cold we'd be frozen for all eternity. Or it might be during the day, stopping us cold in the middle of our everyday activities. Some of us out in the fields, some of us in our offices, some of us at the beach. According to one theory about the extinction of the great lizards that occupied the planet before humankind, that's how the dinosaurs disappeared. And what about our Kanak lizard ancestors, clinging to this great mountainous pebble,[1] after the falling away of the waters and before mankind, according to our fathers' and grandfathers' theory of evolution? Not to mention Darwin's theory and the divine creation of man and woman from his ribs, if you're going to believe the Bible or the Holy Scriptures. Good Heavens! There are so many stories, so many different stories about our origins! And don't forget the progress of civilization and the travels of the Lapitas and the yam that link the whole Melanesian arch, running vertically on the map from West Papua via PNG, Bougainville, the Solomons, Fiji, Vanuatu and Kanaky! Apparently we came long long ago, in a series of waves of migration, in our canoes, from the distant—or not so distant, if you rely on the map—South-East Asia. And what about Kanak identity and our connection to the land in all this? When did that start? Well, after, obviously. After what? Well, after our arrival on these islands where there was nothing but birds, lizards and snakes. The clan totems, in other words. Yes, what we call tee re âboro in our language.[2] With the idea of some supernatural power and taboo in your real life on the earth, laddie! How can you get away from it? That's a good question . . . with no answer. Because, sorry, but they were here before us! So . . . Well that's not the whole story, but I have to get my head

Excerpt from *Graines de pin colonnaire,* Seeds of the Columnar Pine, 2009.

1 Le Caillou, or the pebble, is a commonly used name for the largest island of Kanaky.

2 *Cî,* or *paicî*—one of the widest-spoken indigenous languages.

straight, with all that stuff! How do you expect to do that if you've all the time got to come and go, zap back and forth, zigzag between two or three or I don't know how many theories all at once? Well, do what the lizard does, cling tight to the pebble or be like the giant clam in the story, that stuck itself tight to the rock and survived that way! No, I mean to say, what sort of an idea was that for the teacher to give us as topic for the last essay of the year, to imagine the evolution of the species! Obviously he's been influenced by *Planet of the Apes,* the film based on Pierre Boulle's novel, that's showing at the moment on TCM on the Canal Sat channel. And Grandmother saying she's descended first of all from her ancestors, from Adam and Eve, fair enough, yeah like the Bible says, and from the lizard ancestor, yes of course, because we're sick from our tee re âboro and only some of them can properly cure us. But descended from monkeys, no, she doesn't believe in that and doesn't want to, because there've never been any here. But what about if there were monkeys where we came from? Where? Well, I don't know, from South-East Asia, for example. But who told you that? Well, my teacher, Granny. Oh yeah? Well, you can tell your teacher that your grandmother, she says we're all descended from the tooth of the moon.

He karakia timatanga

Robert Sullivan

A prayer to guide waka out the throat,
between Hawaiiki's teeth, the last green speckled

glove of coast, past upthrust knee and rock toe
in the distance to paddle and sail toward sunset—

when each crack in the house of the sun
is submerged—doors and windows cloaked by night,

charred sky where stars become arrows,
lit signs travelling across a black zone.

A prayer to hold lashings and fittings close
amid the swelled guts of Tangaroa.

A prayer to scoop out sustenance—
sweet fish caught by divers in bright saltwater

marinaded in coconut and hunger. A prayer
to keep food for the two week trip to Aotearoa,

gourds intact, yam and taro and kumara gods alert
to the slap and grab of a restless swell—

whether in the breast or seabed. A prayer, a declaration,
for quick land, straight seas, and health

of all parts celestial, temporal and divine:
food music and drink of this star waka—

Previously published, *Star Waka,* Auckland University Press, 1999.

the chanted rhythms
hoea hoea ra

storms
hoea hoea ra

a thousand years
hoea hoea ra

fleet mothers of tales
hoea hoea ra

I greet you in prayer oh star oh waka . . .
and pray for your combination here.

He karakia mo korua, e te waka, e te whetu o te ao nei.
Star and waka, a prayer for you both.

Into Our Light I Will Go Forever

Haunani-Kay Trask

Into our light
    I will go forever.

    Into our seaweed
        clouds and saltwarm
            seabirds.

Into our windswept
    'ehu kai, burnt
        sands gleaming.

            Into our sanctuaries
                of hushed bamboo,
                    awash in amber.

    Into the passion
        of our parted Koʻolau,
            luminous vulva.

        Into Kāne's pendulous
            breadfruit, resinous
                with semen.

Into our wetlands
    of Heʻeia,
        bubbling black mud.

Previously published, *Night Is a Sharkskin Drum,* University of Hawai'i Press, 2002.

Into our spangled,
blue-leafed *taro*,
flooded with *wai*.

Into Waiāhole,
chattering with rains
and silvered fish.

Into our shallows
of Kualoa,
translucent Akua.

Into the hum of
reef-ringed Ka'a'awa,
pungent with *limu*.

Into our corals of
far Kahana, sea-cave
of Tina.

Into our chambered
springs of Punalu'u,
ginger misting.

Into the songs of
lost Lā'ie, cool
light haunting.

Into murmuring
Māleakahana,
plumed sands chanting.

Into the sheen
of flickering Hale'iwa
pearled with salt.

Into the *wa'a* of
Kanaloa, voyaging
moana nui.

Into our sovereign suns,
drunk on the *mana*
of Hawai'i.

OCEAN AND WATERSCAPES

What does our water teach?

What is Oceanic—in thought, in memory, in practice?

Our languages have been shaped from our relationships with water, and this section traces our water, where it comes from, what it teaches, what it creates and destroys. We shape the definitions of ourselves from the ways water behaves in our lives as Islanders, and the reminders are always with us, as Teresia Teaiwa has said: "We sweat and cry salt water, so we know that the ocean is really in our blood."

Epeli Hau'ofa's essay "Our Sea of Islands" (1994) is just one example of how critical Pacific Islander relationships to water—which are encoded in our stories, languages, and literatures—provide maps for looking at the world as a more connected place, as a whole and connected body. In that essay, Hau'ofa models how Pacific Islanders reclaim ourselves and the terms of our definition by returning to our stories and relationships with the ocean as a connector, not as a limiting, insurmountable barrier. Across this section, our stories document and navigate bodies of water as complex, nuanced, and changing spaces of connection. In writing our relationships to our ocean and our waterways, we are negotiating what it means to be of the ocean from island homelands, to carry Oceanic histories and worldviews when we travel and live beyond our ocean, moving within the multitude of currents defining home, departure, and cycles of returning.

There is an ethics of movement and connection traced across each of the pieces in this section. These ethics come from our relationships to water, which we hold from our ancestral stories to the ways water lives in our everyday lives. Our waterways behave, adapt, and change in ways that teach us definitions of connection, kinship, and responsibility. One of the most foundational lessons drawn from our relationships to water is practiced in the message of the Nuclear Free and Independent Pacific movement—that what happens to one part of our ocean affects all parts of our ocean. What happens to one part of our body affects all parts of our body.

Tracing water, from deep ocean to the homes of freshwater in our islands, this section draws out understandings of Oceanic perspectives, ultimately showing what it means to language our oceans and waterways, speaking into practice how, as Robert Sullivan writes in his poem "Ocean Birth" (2005), "we are skin of the ocean."

Ocean Birth

Robert Sullivan

With the leaping spirits we threw
        our voices past Three Kings to sea—
                eyes wide open with ancestors.

We flew air and water, lifted
        by rainbows, whales, dolphins thrashing
                sharks into birthways of the sea's

labour: Rapanui born graven
        faced above the waves—umbilical
                stone; Tahiti born from waka:

temple centre of the world;
        Hawai'i cauled from liquid
                fire: the goddess Pele churning

land from sea: born as mountains;
        Aotearoa on a grandmother's
                bone—Maui's blood to birth leviathan;

Samoa, Tonga, born before
        the names of the sea of islands,
                before Lapita clay turned to gourd,

before we slept with Pacific
        tongues. Chant these births Oceania
                with your infinite waves, outrigged

waka, bird feasts, and sea feasts,
        Peruvian gold potatoes.
                Sing your births Oceania.

Previously published, *Voice Carried My Family,* Auckland University Press, 2005.

Hold your children to the sky
          and sing them to the skyfather
                    in the languages of your people.

Sing your songs Oceania.
          Pacific Islanders sing! till
                    your throats are stones heaped as temples

on the shores for our ancestors'
          pleasure. PI's sing! to remind
                    wave sand tree cliff cave of the songs

we left for the Moana Nui
          a Kiwa. We left our voices
                    here in every singing bird—

trunks like drums—stones like babies—
               forests fed by our placentas.
                    Every wave carries us here—

every song to remind us—
we are skin of the ocean.

Prelude to Lagimalie

Grace Iwashita-Taylor

western constructs of time are linear
when imposed on a body birthed from the moana
it squeezes the vastness
into tiny confined spaces
compact
identified
and foreign

the body birthed from the moana twists
when the breath is not honoured
craves the salt
how you expand at the sea

but the body remembers where it once was

tā & vā | time & space
is malleable
multidirectional
multidimensional
multitransactional

our nervous system a sacred internal ecosystem
not a shock absorber

restore lagimalie | balance

Rivers in the Sea

Steven Edmund Winduo

Here high above the clouds
In the belly of the Bird of Paradise
I look out into the open space
Clouds beneath drag on somewhere
And further below
        The Great Barrier Reef dances
        In colours of rainbow this hour
        With all its marine glory
        From the beginning of time

I have travelled a thousand miles
Across lands I have never seen
In their sameness to their difference
Their memories are no longer dreams
Of a lifetime, but veins of change
        In the blue Pacific Ocean
        Its splendour on display
        The rivers in the sea
        Lies between them and us

With them or without us the beauty
Of the Pacific Islands remains serene
In our minds and in our lives
As we disappear upon disembarking
At the destination of our journeys

Previously published, *A Rower's Song*, Manui Publishers, 2009.

star language

Emelihter Kihleng

For Mau

you are now an usu
one of the brightest
my eyes squint
to see you
nanmadau o
beyond the reef

you were fearless
you men of the ocean
usually are
trusting the currents, wind, birds
smell of the rain
schools of fish
comforted by danger
home in the quiet isolation
of vastness and depth

my friend says her fisherman
goes to see the mermaids
you left your little atoll
for volcanic Hawaiian Islands
barely speaking English
you went

who needs language
when your mind expands the Milky Way
when you still dream as your ancestors did
when you sail alongside those first voyagers

Previously published, *4th Floor Literary Journal,* Whitireia, New Zealand Writing Programme, 2013.

only your people from outer islands of Yap and Chuuk
kept this sacred knowledge
sacred
your people never forgot
words mean little
with such manaman

did you know you were holding the light?
it was your usu Nainoa and so many others would follow
it is your usu up there that I see
at Matariki, here in Aotearoa
this lonely Micronesian thinks of you

Na Wai Eā, The Freed Waters

A Story of Ko'olau Moku, Maui Hikina

Mahealani Perez-Wendt

1. *Mahi'ai Kalo,* Taro Farmer

All his life loving earth
a living harrow waist deep in mud
planting tilling trenching shoveling plowing
mud to field, gravel to path, stones to bank
yoked no less than animal to plow
a year of this then *huki 'ai,* harvest
shouldering the heavy bags
heaving lifting hauling slogging
through acres of taro fields
ancient footpaths fragile *'auwai* wetlands
swollen feet hands torqued elbows knees
pestilences infestations droughts
year after year, year after year
for love of family love of ancestors
love of the Elder Brother
for love of *Hāloa.*

2. *Lo'i Kalo,* Taro Fields

As far as eye could see their green hearts
were laid bare under rains
that never ceased falling a much aggrieved sun
the dim glint of it through upstart clouds
but always the rains and he was glad for the gods'
beneficence and the harbingers who coaxed

Previously published, *Living Nations, Living Words: A Collection of First Peoples Poetry,* Archive of Folk Culture, American Folklife Center, Library of Congress, 2020.

sunlight's bright threads the *'auku'u* herons hovering
then ensconced in pools
of watery green expanse their emanations of light
vectoring the same paths trod
the same earth the same ancient waterways
the ancestors walked he regarded the plants
hungrily the same green ones whose presentiments
were his Elder Brother *Hāloanakalaukapalili*
vivified who was born of the gods
Wākea and *Ho'ohōkūokalani* their union
a conflagration of heaven and brightening stars
their firstborn, the Elder Brother
stillborn buried *Ho'ohōkūokalani*'s tears unceasing
until the quickening
shimmer of green in graven earth
the unfurling leaves
and the risen *Hāloanakalaukapalili*
progenitor
his offspring the stalwart green-hearted ones
who followed growing up
out of the same earth again and again
he called them *koa,* warriors
as they hoisted their green banners
forming leaf arbors under sun's radiance
their stems rooted deep their arbors
protecting parents, grandparents, the corm, *mākua*
protecting children, grandchildren, *'ohā,* the offshoots
succouring cradling them
millennia of generations turning returning
e huli, e huli, e huli ho'i, the ancestors called
their names auspicious names naming
their offspring in dreams
through keen observations
ho'ailona, signs
close attentions to minutiae of corm
stem petiole rhizome
shimmering sun wind
sea clouds and earth
cradle of the hallowed ancestors
and the risen *Hāloa*
give us the right names the *mākua* prayed
dispatched their entreaties released them
mana ulu, mana 'ōpelu, mana weo,
mana uliuli, mana 'ula'ula, moi, piko,

lehua, ha'akea, hapa hapapū
were names given
and many more all his life
he knew and never forgot
their names
sacred from the first
they were the names of the generations
of his Elder Brother
they were the names of his family
they were the names of *kalo.*

3. *Maka'ala,* Be Vigilant

Elena his grandmother James and Samson
the grandfathers who brought him to the gods
he followed along the ancient paths
of well-tended fields
the rows of plants who were offshoots
of his Elder Brother green sentinels
as far as eye could see
he sloshed through the maze of waterways
the irreproachable fretwork of ancestors
arrayed he heard
their songs prayers incantations
traceries of winds waters ocean
he heard *Pahulena* the grandmother's birthplace
she said her birthplace name
and motioned toward a dense growth
of *'ōlena* and the tall stand of *niu*
where *'ehukai* breezes warmed
the wide river mouth churning
above reddish brown sheen of seaweed *limu kohu*
spawning place of *āholehole, moi, 'anae,*
pāpio, 'o'opu, hīhīwai, po'opa'a
'opihi, wana, hā'uke'uke, 'a'ama
he remembered stories fishing canoes divers their nets
the surround of *akule, halalū,* mishaps at sea
the *kilo i'a,* fish spotter's lair high above the *kāheka*
the first catch offered there at the *ahu*
he remembered his grandmother's warning
maka'ala and that after the bosses came
aia nō iā ha'i nā 'āina o mākou she said
other men have our lands
then her words went dry
and *Pahulena* was no more.

4. *Waimaka,* Tears

There are hidden places
　　where the high waters fall
in rainbowed silence
　　sucked in through igneous stone
pulsing the columnar dikes
　　of earth's vast waterworks
spilling over soul's sacred edge
　　Elena's tears Elena's tears.

5. *Na'aupō,* Ones Devoid of Light

From sea dregs the onslaught winds
　　its shifting stars, the detritus tides
carry dark strangers
　　under cover of night
stealthy ones of fervent prayers
　　and exhortations Holy Father
bring us safely to the village
　　Pahulena in the distance
grant us safe conduct
　　in our sacred mission
to save the unbelievers
　　for Your greater glory
Amen.
　　he malihini lākou no ka 'āina ē
ka 'āina huna wai no Kāne
　　strangers they come
to this land of hidden waters
　　belonging to *Kāne*
ghosts grey as gunmetal
　　intractable as cannons
sulphurous gunpowder flashes
　　their lodestars
at artillery's first report
　　the stalwart sons and daughters of *Hāloa*
rout the shadowy ones
　　but from dregs of darkness
there is no surcease
　　wave upon unending wave
commend ravening spirits
　　to the tasks set before them
conversions appropriations
　　decimations subjugations

as has been for[illegible]old
in their[illegible]rits
[illegible]on *Hāloa*'s people
they look[illegible]able idolaters unclean ones
[illegible]st be brought to the One God
wh[illegible]nd called to atone
[illegible]m the lost souls' darkness withal
a Savior shall lead them
their dark paths made light
the Savior's blood sacrifice
upon Golgotha's mouldering cross
their lamp of redemption
na'aupō look with dismay
upon the god *Lono*'s handiwork
his raft of green mountains
his canopies of forest
they judge these iniquity
evil fruit of indolence
an affront and mortification
to industry
they are disdainful
of *Kāne,* his Living Waters
flowering to sea
abased are the natives
of this extravagant land
upon their stolid ramparts
na'aupō recite oaths
their kingdom come
their will be done
they issue the edicts
dispatch the cadres
to bulldoze the lands
build fantastic scaffolding
engineering marvels, masterworks
for excavation of the high mountains
extraction of waters
to bring the vile gods low
to siphon off the lifeblood
from the green realms
of the Elder Brother
the brooding altars are abandoned
the disconsolate moon holds no sway
as the waters are wastreled
the fate of an unrighteous people

turned in dark hands
        through a marvel of gravity flow
the waters are extricated
        ho'ohemahema, i 'ō i 'ane'i
dug here, trenched there
        tunneled here, siphoned there
the uplands turned into wallows
        'inu ihu pua'a
for dirty snouted pigs
        loosed upon the land
rooting here looting there
        through gross machinations
the sacred is harried in ungodly ways
        ditches pipes channels
tunnels siphons flumes
        aqueducts intakes funnels
dark grasping hands
        leering lewd imaginings
broad hillsides of waving cane
        the far distant and arid plains
prolific with cane tassels under brightening sun
        all of this has been foretold
all has been readied, all paths cleared
        the export tariffs have been lifted
foreign labor contracts signed
        the people's protestations—
the devil take them!
        the necessary approvals have been given
government officials are aboard
        the false idols *Kū, Kāne, Lono,*
Kānaloa a me nā akua apau
        banished to the greater glory
of Almighty God!

6. The Fisher of Men

From high promontories
        elevated stations of the cross
the bosses offer prayers
        for the blessing of verdant lands
mahi'ai in the fields
        lawai'a at the nets
and there are remembrances
        vague recollections

of One Other
        a Fisher of Men who once led them
who fed multitudes
        with few fish and loaves
the bosses remonstrate with themselves
        as the tableau of *kua'āina*
unfolds in the lowlands
        a childlike people easily duped
to be cajoled lured away
        or forcibly removed
from the greening hills
        what do they know these unwitting
of the true faith, divine purpose
        the higher reckonings
of true believers
        little do they know
of theft treachery genocide
        deception stealth coercion
the idolators must be readied
        for the benefactions of civilization
na'aupō are filled with saccharine thoughts
        of panoramic cane
the lands' expeditious acquisition
        a foregone conclusion
the unrighteous ones' swift conversion
        to a penitent upright people
the gift of civilization
        a bargain more than fair
promised by the One God
        who from the time of Adam
conferred to His true believers
        dominion over the world
these truths being self-evident
        the bosses are feverish
with thoughts of unholy war
        upon *nā kua'āina* the people, their gods.

7. Naming the Waters

I ka wao nahele
        in the god-realms of *Ko'olau*
ka 'Āina i ka Wai a Kāne
        the lands of the waters of *Kāne*
the sons and daughters of *Hāloa*
        named the waters:

where the long waters fell seaward
        ravishing black stones
where the eyes smarted from backspray
        and in dark depths like stars
the seed pearl oysters
        their faint songs could be heard
the name *Makapipi* was given;
        where *wī, hīhīwai* shells
migrated upstream and down;
        where *wī* groves
grew as thickets
        seeding the lands
where *wī* wind sounds were heard
        the name *Hanawī* was given;
where the waters scudded cloud-like
        as though firmament
where a red sheen was seen above
        signifying the presence of Sacred Ones
the name *Ka'a'ula* was given;
        where the *mo'o* goddess
was well-pleased
        and smiled at her own reflection
in the shadow waters
        the name *Waia'aka* was given;
where limestone beds
        of *'āko'ako'a* formed
and the *ulu maika* stones were shaped
        the name *Pa'akea* was given;
the narrow-necked gourds
        for water-carrying
gave *Waiohue* its name;
        ravenous *Kamapua'a*
the pig god
        his stampeding hordes
gave *Pua'aka'a* its name;
        where *wauke* was kneaded
to kapa of fine transparency
        stained with *'akala* berries
for a red birth gift
        Kōpili'ula was the name given;
where two waters converged
        and *'o'opu* scaled waterfalls
where *Pele*'s sister the sorceress
        Kapōma'ilele removed her genitals

sent them flying to thwart
        the rutting pig god *Kamapua'a*
his lust for *Pele*
        Wailua-Iki was the name given;
where *Kāne-i-ka-Pahu-Wai*
        Kāne of the Great Water Source
where he was seen in the heavenly clouds
        in the verdant mountainward ridges
where he was seen in the red-tinged rainbow
        where he was rain, lightning flashes
where he slept in the glowing light
        where his great heart was heard
in the thundering waterfalls
        cascading stones quaking corals
where *kalo* was planted along the high ridges
        where it was planted in the wide valleys
where it was planted inland of the teeming shores
        kaulana nā 'āina kalo
a na hoa'āina
        where famous were the *kalo* lands
and the people who cultivated them
        Wailua-Nui was the name given;
where *Kāne* and *Kanaloa*
        refreshed themselves in springs
near groves of red and yellow *lehua*
        'Ōhi'a was the name given;
where the stout-stemmed *olonā* grew
        where in frigid waters the strands
were immersed cured
        braided into fine white cordage
for canoe lashings, fishing lines, nets
        where it was plaited
for chiefly raimant *'ahu'ula,*
        kahili, lei, mahi'ole
where the stout-stemmed *ōlona* grew
        Wai'anu was the name given;
where fine-grained *milo*
        were shade trees for the old chiefs
where windstorms incised the heartwood
        the omens carved into god likenesses
made into canoe paddles, serving bowls,
        implements for planting
where prolific headwaters
        were called *moana*

the name *Waiokamilo* was given;
        where *mai'a* was food curative unguent
where its broad-leaf canopies
        were rain-coverings, enclosures
where spring waters bubbled up
        through igneous cinder, *'ākeke*
the name *Palauhulu* was given;
        sentience along the high ridges
an exhilaration of climbing, of mounting
        gave *Pi'ina'au* its name;
where thundering rains
        poured down hollows caves ravines
where the tumult echoed down ridges
        sidewise along boulder-strewn seacliffs
where earth shuddered and heaved
        with *nū* sounds
where great schools of fish hearkened
        where the torrents narrowed
Nū'āilua was the name given;
        where the torrents were made wide
Honomanū was the name given;
        where *hāpu'u, 'āmau'u, hala, 'ōhe,*
niu, loulu, kī, halapepe, ulu
        where *mamaki, 'ili'ahi, wiliwili,*
koa, palapalai, pala'a
        where *kukui, hau, milo, kamani, awa*
where cherished forest plants grew
        the name *Punalau* was given;
where *tapa*-beating logs were harvested
        the black and red berries
strained for dyes
        the name *Kōlea* was given;
where a glowing light appeared
        above the ridgeline
signifying the presence of *Kāne*
        the name *Ha'ipua'ena* was given;
where in cold springs
        ali'i wāhine bathed
the name *Waiakamō'ī* was given;
        where the *ali'i wāhine* ran
to the flat hiding stone
        where she found refuge
from the pig god *Kamapua'a*
        the name *Wahinepe'e* was given;

no ka mea, he mau inoa akua lākou
e ola nō lākou a pau.
In the god-inspired naming
the people remembered
because they remembered
the waters lived.

8. *Koʻolau,* The Windward Cliffs

All night
and for endless days like ghost canoes
at full sail under brightening moon
the billowing *ʻĪʻaleʻale* winds sweep across
Koʻolau mountain seacliffs
over razor edged ridges valleys
with thunderous bursts exhalations
obscurations of light
the spectral crew worrying each blade leaf
branch with roaring cascades waterfalls
avalanches rockslides incessant rains
it is the season of *hoʻoilo*
hoʻīloli ke kai, the sea rages
the god *Kanaloa* furious his seamounts shaking
he hurls himself against seacliffs
sending *ʻaʻama* scuttling over the reefs
shoals corals the staid seaweed
limu wāwaeʻiole, limu manauea, limu ʻeleʻele,
limu kohu, limu huluhuluwaena
their swaying frondescences under frothy waves
in the uplands *kalo*
revel in watery pools
rainbows bead on the leaf-green
arbors of scintillate light
refractions mirrored prisms riven
by *Kāne-i-ka-Wai-Ola*
Kāne takes the form of a night owl
he thrusts his wings and talons
disarming his enemies
Kāne god of the living waters
walks abroad with *Lono*
scion of water, scion of land together
summoning forth the sacred springs *Oiana!*
waters gush forth out of earth
the living waters of *Kāne* coursing to sea.

Last Coral Standing

Brandy Nālani McDougall

after a painting by Joy Lehuanani Enomoto

You paint an ocean background,
lightening blues and grays. Emptied
of all life, all other color, so the polyps
expelled from their coral crevices
are held in that moment
right before death,
overheated and exposed.

You show us there is
beauty in their dying,
in the way their vessels
constellate in branches
to echo the blood
in our veins, before
saltwater dissipates every
memory of their being.

But you urge us to remember
a brighter beauty in their living:

Hānau ka pō
Hānau Kumulipo i ka pō, he kāne
Hānau Pōʻele i ka pō, he wahine
Hānau ka Uku koʻakoʻa,
hānau kana, he ʻĀkoʻakoʻa, puka

If coral polyps, living
in their perforated skeletal
branches, are our eldest
ancestors—what history disappears
when the turning heat reclaims

them? What saltwater will rise
in us, in that moment, expelling
blood from bone? Who will still
be here to remember that we,
temporary in such temperatures,
too, were beautiful once?

Clouds and Water

John Puhiatau Pule

Clouds understand the phenomena involved in earth movements, because they are nations in themselves. Often clouds seek out glass structures to see a human perspective about the spaces they occupy. Clouds are not new to the eyes of buildings, or man, but they are new mediums as a way to strengthen foundations of buildings, where we dwell or when mesmerized by the transparency of corridors, we see poetry in the atmosphere, light, shadow, walls, and inside our hearts. There are huge spiritual emotions to be seen when walking in buildings when solidified by these globular mists of the gods. The first for me is poetry. My own poetry craves for Glass and Clouds. The minerals contained in these clouds accompanied my family and myself every Sunday as we walked the five miles from our state house in Otara to the Church of Jesus Christ of Latter Day Saints in Papatoetoe. I remember these pathways as always illuminated by the sun. At the end of that road was the church. Walking past houses I used to make sure I saw my reflection in windows, fascinated at how distorted I looked and how this manipulation of my features related to the uneasiness of living in a new country.

That anatomical system called childhood, joined at the placenta by soil and sky and later morphed into native places and government homes, is a site of joy and horror, destitute of color. It is also a place where I have become accustomed to spending years filtering its vices to rid it of imperialistic policies, racist propagation and industrial factories seeping into the indigenous languages found languishing first inside passports and later at airports. At airports constitutional laws impervious to any form of light contain defects of visions and an unprecedented monumental fear of visitors, especially those of colour.

I look at this world from a distance, my memories now rituals of increasing complexity. I began writing poetry that can ingest three times its weight in that rich sea-battered soil I originated from. My poems are vascular ducts that have a Polynesian way to moisten my voice, sharpen my tongue and decorate my hands with rain. Everything I have participated in and experienced so far erodes mainly from my poems to form a ground, a foundation.

Previously published, *News from Islands,* Group Exhibition at Campbelltown Arts Centre, New South Wales, Australia, 2007.

The road to the church was embossed into the soles of my shoes. A part of the journey involved passing through an under bridge. Above us were four lanes of motorway. Quite often we walked in pitch black as the lights in this under bridge were vandalized. Halfway across I would stop and look back at the light that always said farewell. Ahead of me the alluring light cried joy. Grief has great light. As a child I saw feelings at funerals that resembled remarkably the images of paradise portrayed in the Holy Bible. Where animal lived happily amongst different nationalities. It was always my poetry that set me apart from other living species. I only stand up when the world needs it. If you seek me out a new world is born. Left-right ventricles will appear, valleys are carved, miniature suns take shape, abundant nutrients generated by blood corpuscles flood my voice and only then I see there is no distinction between desire, ambulance and the muscular energy of the hospital.

As a family we sort of tumbled into church like one massive wave, trying to avoid my Pacific Islands that floated behind us everywhere we went, ravaged by physical and biological colonialism disintegrating in our shadows. During the endless hours of sermons reminding us we were sinners, I would sneak off for that one reason, to stare and hate the feeling and the isolation generated by corridors. The portrait of Jesus would be everywhere, inquiring about the desolate nature that permeated my first communion as he walked around the rooms and hallways asking me, *Where would you go if you should leave me.*

I hurried to keep up with my father that day as he sped around the Otara shopping centre, which then as today was a town of languages but on closer inspection I could also see a defeated and sick marine carcass. My father was on a mission to buy me a suit. We found this at Hugh Wrights, a men's and boys' store famous for their effective epigram that is the fundamental principle to dress every man and boy in New Zealand. The suit was an imperfectly transparent black, lined with red poly viscose. Inside the collar in gold lettering, the words simply state: "Young Sir, Made in New Zealand." I stood before the mirror looking back at myself. There were different cultivators around that day varying in the presence of variegations forming on my arms and legs. It had several meanings relating to possession of land by colonial force; the occupancy and holding of a nation by another country. Invading another country for its rich mineral resources. I suddenly found myself in the possession of different characteristics, designating a type of inflorescence commonly seen around the coastlines of Niue. Inside the jacket my arms seem to transform into leaves with slender petioles; my fingers, which so often when I slept became sub-equal to the passports issued at immigration; my face appeared to have changed because I felt I was ready to disregard what was required of someone with my kind of ethnic and social background, an obligation to assimilate.

Worried that the capillaries relating to matters connected to my birthplace might terminate upon putting the suit on, as well as the constituents of an effuse memory formed before its appearance in words might disintegrate. Having distinct individuality, I stepped back, substantively withdrew my interest in this difference in my new zeal. I was made in New Zealand, though I was born elsewhere.

Along with my passport this was my first true bonding with New Zealand. Turning to agree with my father, I could see him staring into faraway time, depositing memories into a warehouse for safe keeping, while I prepared a storage sac for the generation of electrical energy. These were all the tools I needed to make a casting of my own young memories in a mould of water. I had to adapt to the motion of a journey before embarking, and I found that in clouds and water. Almost after a year of readings from the Holy Bible, lectures and prayers, I was ready to be submerged in holy water. By turning the tap on, the church thought the cascade flowed directly from heaven but which I knew was just city water, full of pollutants from nearby farms, waste from factories and machinery and the foul smell of chlorine, all combined to produce a thick coat of chemicals.

These hot evenings make dreaming difficult,
as if the sun had used all the day up getting here,
and these windows did not stand a chance
nor the way those sparrows hid under small leaves,

or if the wind changing the clouds into petrol stations,
and the fumes of these changes make drowsy
my hands and the roads that end close to your shoes,
managing to lift up a photo of you posing in front

of a fountain, only then I try again to
close my eyes, and see a way into your night:
I will arrive with a drawing of a starry sky,

and before the sun-sets try to install these planets
between my mouth and your mouth, so you know
my tongue will never be exhausted from waiting.

Soon after my arrival to Aotearoa I realized how mythical my hands had become. An invisible quantity distinguished from the velocity of being accepted, although a pattern of apartheid was emerging. My body contained autonomous soils and distinctive nutrients locked up in taro shoots, hibiscus, sugar cane and banana, which my family brought with them from the islands. By replanting these in the yards of their first rented homes, these plants simply reacted to the new soil. It was a kind of ethical impulse hoping to shed light on the powerful alteration of status and place, which we were about to experience in a new country.

That day when I first tried the suit on I felt the early stages of infinite struggles. As a recently arrived islander my place in this country was seen only in a semi-adventive state. It was assumed I would not persist for long periods away from the newly constructed factories, breweries and state houses that were being built at a phenomenal rate in and around the periphery of Otara, and that my kind could not grow outside the boundary, but function only in the poverty and separateness nurtured in South Auckland. The idea of separateness becomes a leech and forces the knowledge that I only know one picture in this world. That is the long, potholed road that winds crookedly through the streets of Otara, coughing and vomiting as it ends at the wharves in the central city, where ships whose cargo of Pacific Islanders disembark, followed by angels, new gods, mythical gods and out of date perspectives. Despite this perspective, forested soils still use my veins to sprout.

I knew my father only too well. He labored hard at his memories. That day as I stared at the young sir in the mirror, I whispered, "Yes, I admire you, you have become a new species already proficient at utilizing whatever light is available."

It was not because the land was inferior but because dreams of honey and milk were not becoming a reality. Our presence seemed weakened, giving our appearance a straggling habit. And to those in authority, Pacific Islanders soon became second-class citizens, like indigenous people in their own countries, troublesome and a nuisance. Even though we were at that time only a small infestation in Auckland, it should prove possible to eradicate us before we got out of hand.

My relationship with my father was volatile, forged by his lectures and horrors from the Revelation, and the constant polishing of the portrait of Christ that hung between photographs of uncles and aunties, their features obscured by plastic lei and the increasing dust of unemployment and laboring jobs. He belonged to that rare group of men who invented solitude to make sense of everything, to face the world and their family and especially their sons.

Anything with blood and a heart must be given space to flourish and breathe. It must not be banished from its customary place of desire. That day soon arrived after what seemed like eternity of preaching and preparatory cleansing from American Mormons. I stripped down to a pair of white shorts. My family, friends, elders and ministers took their places around me as I stood in the water. An American had one hand behind my head and the other supporting my back. Prayers. I went under. Water found its way into my mouth. When all concerned were sure I was cleansed, I dried myself and walked into a small reception consisting of tea and biscuits, wearing my brand new young sir label, which by then, after those few days and nights hung on a nail in my parents room, had taken on the appearance of a vessel for carrying liquids.

The suit. It had become an act of process to show that I had been successfully changed and that I did not have the ability to identify my self with an object or with another person. I could not assert or prove that I was the absolute same person. Not really aquatic. A strip of territory leased in perpetuity to New Zealand, or since I was born on a piece of land shaped in the head of a shark, maybe I was a shark, although having the eternal crystalline form of a mineral.

That night for the first time in over a year I fell asleep to the sound of my own thoughts. I no longer thought of angels, paradise, or even the devil. I even thought that the thousands of animals shepherded by Noah could not possibly fit into a small boat. That same ancient rain that flooded the known world also damaged mine. And in my sleep there was no such thing as reality, no objects, nothing tangible, and my hands when I reached out to touch things would only pass through them. There was, though, one notion that I had to render ideal, and that is that I had only pre-conceived ideas about the mother of all mothers, the ocean. My face, already used to clouds vying to be my eyes, was the only division to compatibly lie within the ocean's jurisdiction.

I have asked you many times not to cry
your eyes are warm like my country
bright as my mother's voice
stunningly beautiful as her hair

A use of words peculiar to a particular language, I still keep; my tongue contained ancient minerals of limestone, grains of sand, fossil shells, feathers and auditory hallucinations. I rejected the etymological pronunciations created by outsiders to understand my language. To escort my poetry with light, juices extracted from taro act as fuel. Poetical forms of Polynesian energy stimulate sight and sound, partly derived from immigrants trying to pronounce *kia ora* as well as the superficial songs of kiwi and tui that sing you welcome notes upon entering the Waharoa at Auckland International Airport. All these welcome symbols were regarded as biologically safe, with equal opportunities and medical health for all, but the reality is they are devoid of virtue and truth. Passports when presented at customs in imperialistic countries such as America, England, Australia and surprisingly New Zealand, produce a reduced level of oxygen that eventually leads to paranoia and hysterical xenophobia, stamping of passports also introduces lethal bacteria into the tissue of colonized peoples who enter other colonized people's *whenua,* inflict wounds into the psyche of immigrants who simply desire a new home.

When he thought of things, in particular where
his birthplace was situated in Polynesia, his thoughts
were always associated with the ocean, tagata moananui

This is another of those human stories that binds personal history and memory, making realistic photographs of ships, planes and passports. Personal stories are simple proteins that escalate the messages in my people's vision. I, being constantly reminded that I am a genus of Niue, related to fish, sharks, rays, dolphins and whales. My skin is smooth, but my interior is made of the hardest wood, kauri.

I know of a dream full of trees.
A river with a passion for hearing grief.
A room with all its furniture from heaven
and an angel disguised as a ceiling.

In that dream my platelets succumbed
To bees, inverted every cloud in my veins.
I am made from pohutukawa and soil.
Since my hair stopped glittering I have

Struggled to live. I tried to eat constellations.
I was involved in the secretion of honey,
Stabilizing the accumulation of wharves in its blood.

The first ship I boarded is my stone.
The first car I touched is my bad luck.
The first incision I saw I dreamed no more.

Like my father, I am made from the same tree whose design is composed of solitaries. My father was utterly exhausted by the time he was sixty-two. He didn't have a harmonious or methodical arrangement with this land when he arrived. No heavenly body foresaw that he would die at sixty-two from alcoholism. That day when I wore my suit for the first time, I felt something happen to change my outward appearance. Like thousands of other Polynesian children of migrant families, I inherited the same story of imperial treachery, loss of language and culture, destiny and confidence, and the extermination of dreams. I still have that suit, covered by plastic. It is moved constantly around my studio. I protect it from the sun by keeping it in shade.

Children of the Shoreline

Michael Puleloa

They were raised on the southern Moloka'i shoreline, so they thought they knew their place. They knew, for example, the way the moon moved the shape of tides and waves and the shoreline itself. They knew the shoreline fish by name, and the way sand crabs moved up and down the beach at night. They knew all the southern winds.

They were children with fire, the six of them, loud and energetic and bold. They came home after school and tore to the beach outside their Kawela homes before homework or chores. There was an air about the way they fanned out across the brown and yellow sand that let you know they had an unquestionable love for the shoreline.

Their names suggested they'd be this way. Intimately tied to the natural world around them. Ma'a had a way about him so everything he said about the shoreline seemed like truth. The sisters, Moana and Kai, said it was the way Ma'a gazed at the shoreline and the ocean, and then out at the horizon, but the three other boys said his truth mostly came from the fact that Ma'a was the biggest.

The tall, lean one—Moku—knew every landmark on Moloka'i, Maui, Kaho'olawe, and Lāna'i from their view on the shoreline. He knew the months when the sun rose behind Pu'u Kukui and the months it rose behind Hālawa. He was kolohe, hardheaded sometimes, short-tempered, but he was always the first to step forward if one of the children was in trouble. Moana and Kai said Moku was grounded, rooted to the land, just like his name. And none of the other three boys disagreed with them.

Nalu knew the ocean and moon phases enough to predict swells. During southern swells, he surfed the spotty reef outside Kawela until the sun had set and little lights began to flicker between coconut trees on the beach. He had wavy 'ehu hair and light brown eyes, and Moana wouldn't let anything or anyone do him harm. Nalu, she said, was beautiful because he was born in June, just like her and Kai.

They had all tasted the sand, literally eaten it on more than one occasion, but Keone, the youngest and the smallest, seemed to crave it. Trails of sand fell from his pockets wherever he went. He left them in his bedroom, on the school bus, sometimes even at church. He was the youngest and the smallest of the children on the shoreline, but he was fearless.

On land, they had digital music devices and smartphones, liked brand names like Nike and Nautica (Moana and Kai, especially), but here on the shoreline they carried spears and scoop nets. Here, they chased baby eagle rays and blacktip sharks. They raced milk carton boats in the trade winds. Here, they spent sunny afternoons running from the beach into the water and then to sandbars thirty yards off the shoreline. Here, they spent cloudy afternoons watching brown river water from the uplands filter out onto the surface of the sea.

They had genealogies that stretched back to Hawai'i before 1800, before 1778, before contact, but they were also from a medley of customs and traditions from around the world. They were Chinese and Japanese, Filipino and French, Puerto Rican and Portuguese, German, Samoan, Māori, Tahitian.

❦ ❦ ❦

There was an old man whom the children acknowledged as part of the shoreline. He was quiet, unlike them, but he told them once that he sometimes liked their noise. Their shrieking voices on the shoreline, he said, were at those times like a sign of life.

There were many days the children watched the old man walk between the shoreline and the reef with a throw net, and they mimicked what they saw, the old man's grace and patience in the water, his ocean-style, the girls called it. They studied him from afar on the brown shoreline as he hunkered with the throw net wrapped around his body and his gaze on the shimmering surface of the water until one day Keone saw the old man standing without his net on the outside of Kanoa—the fishpond protecting the shoreline—piling stones on the broken wall, and they all circled around him in silence before Keone asked what the old man was doing, if he had seen any eels, if the rocks were heavy, and if he planned to rebuild the entire fishpond himself.

The old man stopped and wondered first about Keone's parents. But after a moment, it was clear he was simply wondering about Keone, what the little boy knew of the eels in the fishpond wall, what he knew of the fishpond itself. And as the small one spoke and the others stood behind him, leaning over his shoulders, waiting for the old man's answers, the old man sensed the spark in Keone ignite the other children. In the silence that followed, they gave the old man their complete attention, or the best they could muster, their faces up at him and then away to the shoreline or out toward Lāna'i before returning again to him.

The old man had wanted solidarity with the stones and the wall that day. He had hoped to somehow free himself of his troubles on the shoreline. He looked toward his home and also out to the sea before turning to the children and then pointing to a stone near Keone. There, he said. There's a moray. And he found himself smiling when the children broke apart and splashed through the shallow water outside the fishpond like a school of pua evading a pāpio.

❦ ❦ ❦

The children sometimes whipped pohuehue vines across the surface of the shallow water to drive pua toward the shoreline. They scaled and gutted and ate the small fish they caught right there on the beach.

They used expressions like, *Eh?* and *Wot?* and *Garanz!* and *Hūi!*

And sometimes, they bathed in the ocean.

Maʻa was so much bigger the children joked his dad was supernatural. On the shoreline, Maʻa broke things with his bare hands as a demonstration of his power, but away from the shoreline, he was the most reserved of them all.

Moana and Kai were twins. And this made them twice as strong as any one of the four boys, except Maʻa. Kai was always running around the beach with a runny nose and Nalu, because he sometimes studied her like the waves, learned her allergies were always worst in the calm just before a storm.

Moku had both the blood of chiefs and slaves running in his veins. His father had taught him to fish along the shoreline and he in turn taught the children. He was nowhere near as big as Maʻa, but by fourth grade he was the only one with the beginnings of a moustache and a beard.

They all knew, as if it had been determined before his birth, that when he grew older, Nalu was going to leave for faraway places. He might just jump on his surfboard and paddle off into the horizon one day. He'd be a swimming champion or a world-class surfer, and he'd spend just as much time in the water as he did on land.

The little one, Keone, lived with his mom and grandmother. They fed him herbs from the shoreline to make him strong, and when the river was high, he fed them ʻōpae and ʻoʻopu. The children looked after Keone like he was their youngest sibling—the girls walked him home along the shoreline every day just before sunset.

When Keone jumped on Moku's back after seeing the eel in the fishpond wall, he wrapped his arms around the bigger boy's neck like a lei. The old man was surprised when Moku let Keone hang there, but he was also comforted by the image of the two boys now back and beside him, one hanging from the other. The old man didn't tell the children—maybe because he didn't completely believe it himself, or maybe because he wasn't entirely sure it was right—but just then he imagined what it might be like to treat the children like they were his own. On the shoreline, they might be his children. To raise in the sunlight. He might treat them like little chiefs. If they talked too much, he could feed them. He could send them out on tasks depending on the weather and the tide. The shoreline would be their home. They were precocious, of course, but they also needed supervision to realize their potential. It would do them good to be looked after on the shoreline.

Just then, the old man also thought these things: 1) There was a spot on the reef outside Kawela where he went when ʻono for kole. He called it Makamae, a play on the yellow eyes of the fish which sparkled sometimes in the sunlight and distinguished them when they moved skittishly among other schools of fish across the ocean floor. Makamae was in fact a crevice that led to a hole in the reef where the fish balled up and hid when threatened, and it was a fitting name if only because the little surgeonfish were—of everything in the ocean—one of his favorite things to eat.

2) At home, in the midst of his troubles, the old man had taken to drinking in order to fall asleep at night. He ate his meals alone. And on very windy days, when the ocean was not an option, he hoped for the calm if only so he could hear the sound of birds in the trees.

The children had their share of arguments, like when Moana learned about the way Nalu studied not her, but her sister, Kai, as he did the waves. Moana took to an older boy from town, a bully in school, so the children constantly belittled her. But she didn't care. It was the end of her secret dream—that her love for Nalu would bind their families, that one afternoon his father and mother would walk down the beach to visit her parents to watch the sunset, if they all met right there on the shoreline.

Sometimes the arguments got physical like when they lost Moku's lay net. Moku insisted it was Nalu's fault and now that the net was gone and his father was going to punish him, he wanted to make Nalu pay. Moana jumped in because she still loved Nalu, of course, and then Kai jumped in because Moku was outnumbered. The boys wrestled in the sand and the girls kept on their feet and punched at each other until Keone screamed for them to stop and Ma'a pulled apart the boys. Moku and Nalu were crying, but not the girls. And soon, the girls went on as if the fight hadn't happened and the only way anyone could tell something had gone wrong earlier that day was when Kai walked Keone home without Moana.

Feuds like this happened all the time, they did, but they were temporary, just like the tides. They'd happen one day and the children would retreat to their homes before sunset. Then they'd return to the shoreline and everything was new, just like the sand when they first arrived on the beach.

They were not gullible children. They were innocent. They believed they knew the shoreline like they knew themselves. They loved the shoreline, so it made good sense.

But when the old man began telling them stories of the shoreline they hadn't imagined, they saw the possibility of something more. In the old man's stories, they learned about the ocean's breadth and what he liked to call "the big picture." They learned to lure baby black tips into shallow water so the sharks swam up and brushed against their fingertips. They learned to feed the eels with their hands. They learned to steer the baby rays in figure eights from the beach. With the old man, they found—among all the things on the shoreline—a great affection for one another. They learned to use the ocean to bring health and happiness and even peace. Eventually, they learned to use their knowledge of the Kawela shoreline to bring the shoreline to them even when they weren't there.

One afternoon on the beach, the children gave the old man a plain white envelope. They told him to open it that night at home. And later, when the old man sat at his kitchen table inspecting the envelope, he wasn't sure what to make of it. He peeled open the envelope and carefully slid out the six 2 × 2½″ pictures. They were school pictures of the children. And when he turned them over he saw notes on the back and their signatures in the bottom corner. He read their notes and then turned them over so the pictures faced up, and then he spread them out on the table. He looked at the pictures for some time.

⁂

He might've been old, but the children were never certain of his age. In fact, the only time they ever thought of it was when he told them the story of the giant heʻe, when he sat them on the sand, stretched out his arms, and told them of its silent strength. He would describe the intense speed of its arms striking out from the coral reef before wrapping themselves around their prey.

Then the old man would wrap one of the children in his arms, pull one of them close, and imitate the sound of the octopus beak breaking shell or bone by popping out the top row of teeth in his mouth. The children were delighted when he did this, finally letting them into a part of his life that seemed so secret. And when the old man placed the child in his arms back on the ground and exposed the row of dentures on his tongue, the children cringed and laughed and then turned and ran down the shoreline towards their homes.

The children soon loved the old man so much they began calling him Papa Henry. Keone started it one day after finding the old man lying on the shoreline. Papa Henry: their voices rang in the old man's head later that night when he sat alone in his little home on the Kawela shoreline. And he thought then of nothing more than taking them to the shallow reef outside Kawela on his flat-bottom boat. In fact, he decided that night to do everything he might for the children. Grow them like little seeds in a garden. And the flat-bottom was ideal. On the beach, they were a copious bunch, and sometimes like driftwood on the shoreline, there one moment and then out of sight. He could at least contain them on the boat, ferry them along the shoreline and to the reef and then, if it was calm and clear enough and if he saw it fit, into the water with masks and snorkels and spears.

Stories were one thing, but to take them to the ocean and show them what was just beyond the murky shoreline water was another.

⁂

The flat-bottom was tucked under a small E-Z Up between his home and the shoreline. It was covered with frayed silver tarps and surrounded by old paint cans, buckets, and a gas tank. There was an assortment of fishing gear and rusty hand tools. It had been there a long time.

Henry began to clear away the debris, placing the tools where he found space in the buckets, piling the paint cans against one of the posts of the tent. There were memories there, and he couldn't stop them from rolling through his mind, so he worked quickly, cleaning up around the boat, sliding the tarps to the ground and looking under the boat to inspect the trailer and its tires. Then he rested his hand on the bow of the boat.

There was nothing in the world that might've prepared him for this. And he began to cry.

He still had a few hours before the children came home from school and down to the shoreline, so he stopped. He thought about his wife, and then about the way the boat had carried them back and forth along the reef for many years before she was too ill to leave their home. The way the boat had bridged their differences. The way it had fed them over the years. And then he smiled when he remembered the first time they had ever taken out the boat, and the first time he had ever kissed his wife on the ocean.

He lifted the front of the trailer and gently slid the boat out from under the tent and toward the shoreline for a few yards before he set down the hitch and walked back to the house for a hose and a can of starter fluid.

Keone was the first to find the boat in Papa Henry's backyard. He circled it like a shark, running his hands along the gunnels until he reached the bow. He stopped there for just one moment like the old man had, as if he felt something, too, and then when he heard the other children running down the shoreline, he climbed into the boat to mark his seat.

The children were giddy at the idea of taking the boat into the water. They had all been on boats before, but never together like this. Ma'a and Moku lifted the trailer frame near the winch and Nalu and the girls were at the back of the boat, guiding it as the two bigger boys pushed it backwards, toward the beach. Keone stood up in the boat pointing one way then another, reminding Nalu and the girls to watch their feet, and Ma'a and Moku to watch their backs.

Henry stood and watched the children, letting them negotiate the boat through the yard and over the soft sand on the beach. He was pleasantly surprised by the success of their cooperative work.

The ocean inside the reef sparkled in the sunlight. There were small pockets of wind here and there, but it was a beautiful day, just like the one when the children had approached him at the fishpond. He wasn't going to waste it. After the children had slipped the boat into the water, he sent them home to get their diving gear.

Being together on the ocean had changed them, especially Henry. His commitment to the children blossomed so that soon they found themselves in or around his home on a daily basis. He asked them about their teachers and about how they were doing in school. He even sometimes cared for them when they were sick. And when they stayed for meals, he found he had his taste again.

On the boat, they stayed in the shallow areas of the reef, sometimes stepping off onto coral heads, sometimes anchoring the boat for hour-long dives that were followed by conversations in the boat about what they had seen and heard and felt. They were riveted to their time on the ocean, Henry included, and there was always a bit of anguish when in the late afternoon Henry cut off the engine and the boat finally slid onto the sandy shoreline.

They spent nearly a year together on the ocean like this before they finally took the boat beyond the edge of the reef and Henry took them to Makamae one Saturday morning. They had prepared weeks for the trip. Hours on the shoreline discussing the protocol for handling various situations that might arise once they entered the ocean and traversed as a group into the unknown.

Henry did try hard not to act as excited as the children. Before their first trip to Makamae, he rummaged through his home looking for extra spears and stringers and mesh bags while the children were in school. He double-checked and triple-checked the outboard engine.

They held hands in a circle on the shoreline while Kai took her turn to say the prayer. She was thankful to enter the ocean with Papa Henry, her friends and her sister, especially her sister, and she asked that they be granted a safe passage. She kept her head down, just as they all did, and when she was done, she squeezed the hands in her own.

Soon the boat was sputtering away from the shoreline between colorful green and purple outcrops on the ocean floor and toward the reef. The children were silent, taking it all in, imagining the layout of the crevices and caves Papa Henry had drawn for them on the beach. Then Nalu leaned over the gunnel and looked overboard, letting his hand cut through the surface of the water. Moku turned back to look one last time at the land, and Maʻa examined the prongs on his spear.

The girls let their arms hang over each other in the middle of the boat, and Keone, at the bow, began putting on his fins.

When the flat-bottom reached the outermost edge of the reef, Moku stood up and let out the anchor while the others rinsed out their masks and snorkels. They sat in the boat like a regiment with their diving gear until Papa Henry finally broke the silence to tell them that he hadn't felt so good in a long, long time.

And later, the girls were convinced those were the last words they ever heard him say.

The children found Papa Henry in his bed one Saturday morning surrounded by hundreds of photos from his life, some of them in frames on the dressers and tables, others simply out on the bed at his side. There were photos of his family, his mother and father, his brothers, old-time photos of people on the shoreline. There were pictures of the children, the ones they had given him, and some they hadn't remembered seeing before. In the midst of his death, there was still an air of warmth, life emanating from the small room that had somehow been transformed since the arrival of the children years before.

They moved around the room like children underwater, poised and silent, every so often looking up at each other from the pictures to make eye contact and point out something they had found in the room. Then Keone began to cry and soon after the house filled with sobs and wails.

Life underwater was filled with complexities, most of them linked to communication with those around you, but by now the children had come to appreciate that it took more to communicate with each other in the ocean than it did on land. They were proud of their underwater language, a complex blend of hand and eye gestures. The girls called it true evolution.

As soon as they were in the water, Nalu led the four older children away from the flat-bottom in a V-formation, and Keone kept in back with the clear plastic bag holding Papa Henry's ashes. The little boy felt something reassuring, something that made him think the old man would always be with him. Nalu turned around at the surface of the water and when Keone swam up to him with Papa Henry, Ma'a and Moana pulled in from one side and Moku and Kai pulled in from the other.

The children formed a circle around Papa Henry and placed their hands on him. There was warmth in the moment for all of them, there underwater, just as there was when they found him on his bed. Keone let it move from his fingertips into his arms and then into his body. He waited for the others to lower their hands to their sides, and when they did, he descended to the crevice and followed the school of kole until they were hidden in the cave and the five others above him had regrouped and formed a ring at the surface. He looked at Papa Henry in his hands one last time. Then he released him from the plastic bag, letting the ashes move upward in the current.

He had learned from Papa Henry that life was full of signs, that all he had to do was look around and pay attention. So it didn't faze him the least bit—when as he rose through beams of sunlight and the floating streams of ashes in the current—that the school of kole soon emerged from the edge of the reef, rose and wrapped itself around him and Papa Henry, swirled enough to redirect the ashes, then dove back into the hole with a gray trail following it.

Keone watched the kole pull Henry's ashes after them and into the reef before he ascended toward the shadowed hull of the flat-bottom and the shimmering ocean surface. He felt cool saltwater trickle in at the edge of his mouth before he emerged at the center of the ring of children as the ashes disappeared. And he hoped just then that he, too, would remain forever in the currents off the Kawela shoreline.

Remembrance

Jully Makini

for Dolly

It rained the day they buried Luta.
Clouds over Ranonga
Dropped their load,
Winds over Ranonga
Swept the droplets to Gizo.

It rained
In our hearts
The day they buried Luta.
Like a flood
Water flowed thru our veins
To a reservoir
Of despair and agony
And it rained.

It rained
From our eyes
The day they buried Luta.
The hurt built up inside
Overflowed
And fell as tears.

The *maqarea*
Over Ranonga
Was beautiful, beyond description
Red, pink, purple, orange, yellow
The day they took Luta home to rest.

Previously published, *Flotsam & Jetsam: A Third Collection of Poems,* Institute of Pacific Studies, 2007.
maqarea—sunset

It hasn't stopped raining
And never will
For those left behind
Each time there's a beautiful red and gold
sunset
Each time there's a gentle shower from
heaven
It will rain from our hearts
And flow as tears.

Atlas

Terisa Siagatonu

inspired by and dedicated to Teresia Teaiwa

If you open up any atlas
and take a look at a map of the world,
almost every single one of them
slices the Pacific Ocean in half.
To the human eye,
every map centers all the land masses on Earth
creating the illusion
that water can handle the butchering
and be pushed to the edges
of the world.
As if the Pacific Ocean isn't the largest body living today
beating the loudest heart
the reason why land has a pulse in the first place.

The audacity one must have
to create a visual so violent
as to assume that no one comes
from water
so no one will care
what you do with it
and yet,
people came from land
are still coming from land
and look what was done to them.

When people ask me where I'm from,
they don't believe me when I say water.
So instead, I tell them that home is a machete
and that I belong to places
that don't belong to themselves anymore
broken and butchered places that have made me

a hyphen of a woman:
a Samoan-American that carries the weight of both
colonizer and colonized
both blade and blood

California stolen.
Samoa sliced in half stolen.
California, nestled on the western coast of the most powerful country on this planet
Samoa, an island so microscopic on a map that it's no wonder people doubt its existence
California, a state of emergency away from having the drought rid it of all its water
Samoa, a state of emergency away from becoming a saltwater cemetery if the sea level doesn't stop rising.
When people ask me where I'm from,
what they want is to hear me speak of land
what they want is to know where I go once I leave here
the privilege that comes with assuming that home is just a destination, and not the panic.
Not the constant migration that the panic gives birth to.
What is it like? To know that home is something that's waiting for you to return to it?
What does it mean to belong to something that isn't sinking?
What does it mean to belong to what is causing the flood?

So many of us come from water
but when you come from water
no one believes you.
Colonization keeps laughing.
Global warming is grinning
at all your grief.
How you mourn the loss of a home
that isn't even gone yet.
That no one believes you're from.

How everyone is beginning
to hear more
about your island,
but only in the context of vacation and honeymoons
football and military life
exotic women exotic fruit exotic beaches
but never asks about the rest of its body.
The water.
The islands breathing in it.

The reason why they're sinking.
No one visualizes islands in the Pacific
as actually being there.
You explain and explain and clarify
and correct their incorrect pronunciation
and explain
until people remember just how vast your ocean is
how microscopic your islands look in it
how easy it is to miss when looking
on a map of the world.

Excuses people make
for why they didn't see it
before.

Ocean Pictures

Dan Taulapapa McMullin

You make me feel real

Is this English?

Then I colonize my self since you

For telling me I'm a beautiful example of

Now get out of my shower

Would you? The sky descends in a machine

You make me feel real (mighty real

Here, in New York City, golden summer simmers

I was born in exile, and I will die in exile, but I was home now and then not now

Here, in New York City, American Samoa

Am I a panic queen? Long live institutional critique!

Hollywood stars led the indigenous environmental protest parade

Ocean: tsk, tsk-tsk, chicken, Madison Avenue, U.N.

You make me feel, would you?

Euro-billionaire sponsored indigenous voyaging

Ocean: Doctor, who will save us from those who save us?

You make me feel. Would you?

Are we going to be Disney A-listers?

Euro house sponsored contemporary art collectors environmental voyaging

They whoever they are will save us in their pocket for porridge

Hottest autumn ever, in Upstate, New York, American Samoa, Central Park, Olosega

There's a Garden of Eden

Never mind the fossils ban all fossil fuels in the Pacific charity starts at home

Reunite Samoa. Reunite Papua. Chase the rock down the wash, save yourself

Stop burning witches like bread

You make me (mighty real

You make me feel

Real, in New York City among the expelled vanished

You? Discover Paradise, Dr. Who, indigenous bodysuit

My cat may look upon you, are you?

Nearly natural by nearly natural tropical tree

Nearly counted as wildlife, would you?

My cat may (mighty real

You make me feel (mighty real, the sun

May look upon where are the wives of the trees the trees?

Now get out of my shower of rain wild rain

Ocean pictures motion superior: Going to be Disney A-listers, the sky

You make me feel conflated to the sky running away

Fa'apusi realness, eating Walt Disney for breakfast with a side of the Actors Guild

Now get out go stand over there stop sweating on me

Realness

Am I a panic queen?

Is this just fantasy?

Caught in a sea change

No spaceship

To Hånum-Måmi, i Nanå-ta

A Dramatic Poem in Five Acts

Evelyn Flores

And the spirit of God moved upon the face of the waters.

—*Genesis 1:2*

Characters

Narrating Woman
Dancing Woman
Male Scientist Broadcasting
Drumming Man
Wailing Woman
Chanting Man
Singing Woman

ACT I—Flowing

In northern Guam, 180 wells tap the upper part of a fresh ground-water lens in an aquifer composed mainly of limestone.

Total Darkness. Drumbeat begins—a slow, steady rhythm, a somber monotone. A dim, spectral spot comes up illuminating the interior of a cave. Narrating Woman with long, black hair stands to the side of the cave, dressed in a woven wraparound. She is facing the center of the cave.

The light comes on, softly revealing Dancing Woman, who is poised with arms outstretched toward the audience, motion frozen in soft, muted light. Diffused spot opens on Drumming Man. He is sitting cross-legged, clothed in antigu Chamoru clothes, bare-chested, bare-legged, oiled.

As Narrating Woman begins to speak, she releases Dancing Woman into motion. Dancing Woman moves fluidly across the stage, a figure of liquid and light throughout the narration.

Narrating Woman:

I cannot get your picture
out of my mind

Narrating Woman turns slowly toward audience. Light dims on Dancing Woman so she is a shadowy figure in the background. A somewhat brighter spot opens on Male Scientist in white shirt and black tie and trousers.

Male Scientist Broadcasting:

The current
incidence
of fecal
coliform
in the
Afa'me
Sinajana
Hagåtña
Agana Heights
Agana Springs
area and in the
Yigo
Dededo
Basin
suggests
sewage
is going
directly
into the
freshwater lens
beneath
both areas
and then
is being drawn
into local wells.

As drumbeats continue,
Narrating Woman turns to Dancing Woman.

Narrating Woman:

You,
dancing there in the darkness,
waiting
watching
whispering
gathering

in your black,
limestone cave

Drumbeats continue. Wailing begins and then fades into distance.

Narrating Woman:
while that
cool, protecting lover
of yours,
Darkness,
caresses you,
as you lean back
into his body rutting
the earth rocking with
you
and i halum tånu' hiding
you
from
us

ACT 2—Sensing

Dissolution of the limestone by percolating rainwater has resulted in a complex underground drainage system, including caves and sinkholes.

Wailing begins, softly in the distance.

Male Scientist Broadcasting:
Fecal
coliform
in the area
that includes
Afa'me
Sinajana
Hagåtña
Agana Heights
and Hagåtña Springs
is most likely
associated
with the same source
that was in the news
some months
ago
discharging
raw sewage from

the Chaot sewage
pump stations.

Narrating Woman:
You, our mother,
womb of ours
you,
såguan mañagu,
ancestral inlet
outlet
sensuous, lovely
wetness
of our life
without which
we are nothing—
dry rocks
broken clay

Drumbeat accelerates; wails grow louder
throughout this section into a crescendo.
Dancing Woman's motions take on frantic, struggling qualities.

Narrating Woman:
You,
whispering unease
to me
tensing
at the danger
the danger
of men
prodding
drilling
gouging your earth,
puncturing roofs
sacred temples collapsing
into prostitution
of you

Drumming and wailing reach climax and are held there;
Dancing Woman arches in anguish,
then abruptly the drumming and wailing cease; the stage goes black.
A second of silence and then a scream pierces the air, a crash, then silence.

Monotone drumbeat begins.
Spotlight gradually distinguishes Dancing Woman collapsed on floor,
softly groaning, rocking.

Male Scientist Broadcasting:

Fecal
coliform
found in the
Yigo-Dededo area
also
is coming almost certainly
from pump station
overflows and also from
the numerous
septic tanks
that have been
installed in the basin
over the years.

ACT 3—Seeing Hearing

It's official: The Navy has signed off on a plan to move 5,000 Marines and 1,300 family members from Okinawa, Japan, to the island of Guam.

Spot softly opens on Narrating Woman facing audience.
As Narrating Woman speaks, lights gradually dim out on Male Scientist.

Narrating Woman:

How
do we
(do we
do we
do we)
destroy the danger
how
escape
(escape
escape
escape)
the helplessness
how
refuse
(refuse
refuse)
refuse the
"they"
who have
become the
"we"

who wish to
corrupt
contaminate
rob
you
of that waiting, watching,
careless beauty
that waters
our thirst

Light goes down on Dancing Woman. Wailing gradually fades out.
Narrating Woman turns slowly to face the darkness—
where Dancing Woman used to be. Drum moves into an accelerated rhythm.

Narrating Woman:

We,
your offspring,
the source of your threat,
our lust
enslaved to
the "benefits" of civilization,
we
overcome
by the contradictions
of our desires
plot your mutilations
(Drums stop.)

We
give our consent.

Lights come up on Male Scientist.

Male Scientist Broadcasting:

The limestone
terrain
of northern
Guam
does not have
sufficiently
thick soil
to absorb
surface
sewage
discharges

or to support
septic tank
leach fields

Light illuminates Chanting Man, who joins in softly and continues his chant even as Male Scientist broadcasts.

Chanting Man:
Guela yan Guelu, kao siña yu maloffan
Guela yan Guelu, kao siña yu maloffan
Guela yan Guelu, kao siña yu maloffan
Guela yan Guelu, kao siña yu maloffan

Male Scientist Broadcasting:
and the
limestone
bedrock
below the soil
is
too porous
to retain sewage
or leachage
long enough
for natural
degradation.

ACT 4—Understanding

With construction of this type, the potential for accidental spills of sediment, fuel, and other toxic materials may occur at any time during the construction period.

Drumbeats take on more rapid and varied tones. Narrating Woman faces center stage, arms outreached.

Narrating Woman:
Unheard, your siren song
as they stomp on your breast
unheard, as they take
your belly for their play
unheard, as the poison
injected into your veins
mother-mine,
feeds into my bloodstream
dangerous chemicals

that poison
hagå-mu
hagå'-hu
daughter-yours
blood-mine

Male Scientist Broadcasting:
Contamination
such as
we are
witnessing
now
will likely
persist
and recur
until
pump station
discharges
and leaking lines
are located
and repaired
and septic tank use
has been
eliminated.

Chanting ceases. Drumming softens.
Singing Woman begins singing softly, wordlessly.
Narrating Woman turns to audience, arms upreached.

Narrating Woman:
Draw me home
Nanå-hu,
Draw me home
awash in amniotic fluid
pull me out to sea
with your strange tide
rush me back
back, back, back to
womb from which i came
back, back, back to womb from which
my children will come

Male Scientist Broadcasting:
Contamination in the
Yigo-Dededo area

is cause
for special
concern.
Not only
does the
Yigo-Dededo catchment
provide about
30 percent
of the island's
groundwater production

ACT 5—Fighting

The threats to fresh water—our most vital natural resource—have never been more abundant.

Narrating Woman slowly begins painting warrior colors on her face. As Singing Woman begins to sing, Narrating Woman drinks the warrior brew.

Narrating Woman:
I go out to fight
Nanå-hu
I paint my body
in warrior colors
drink the bitter brew

Singing Woman:
Adahi i tano-ta
Adahi i tano-ta
warrior strength
and ferocity
rush down into
poisoned veins

Male Scientist Broadcasting:
but all of the
freshwater
that percolates
through it
whether clean
or contaminated
eventually
discharges
into

Tumon
Bay.

As Singing Woman chants, Dancing Woman gains strength. From her huddled position, she rises falteringly to her feet. As Singing Woman sings the genealogy of her body, she strokes the different parts of her body, her head, face, neck, shoulders, womb, her thighs, knees, shins, her feet, and toes in healing motion. With each stroke, she gains strength until she is dancing again.

Singing Woman:
(repeats 3 times)
i lu-ña
i mata-ña
i tongho-ña
i apagå-ña
i susu-ña
i matris-ña
i petna-ña

I Tommon-ña
i satnot-ña
i patås-ña
i matris-ña
i matris-ña
i matris-ña

Narrating Woman:
Tumon Bay
Tomhon—
There
below
their mother's thighs
her children's sins converge;
in the soft, paleness
behind her
knees
at the tender,
vulnerable juncture
major arteries
cross
to go north to the
trunk of her body
or south to
her calves and feet,

where
their indictment is scrawled
in hieroglyphs of muddy effluvia—
Tumon Bay
Tommon
såguan mañågu,
pues haya ÿ apa'
desdi tummon
I Nanån-niha

Dancing Woman turns and beckons to Narrating Woman to come to her.

Narrating Woman:

You
whose image haunts me
dark, cool, inviting
you
murmur
return to me, my child,
I cannot
yet
return
my Nåna
I must fight

I turn once to look
then I go

Narrating Woman turns. She stops, looks back once and then leaves.
Drumbeats accelerate. Chanting Man and Singing Woman begin chanting and singing louder and louder. Dancing Woman turns toward the audience and dances with a certain amount of frenetic desperation. All head toward crescendo. Stage flashes with a kaleidoscope of predominantly white light, like a lightning storm. Dancing Woman becomes still in center stage, arms extended upward as the lightning flashes on her, lighting her up then darkening alternately. The effect is in fact that of a storm with lightning crashing and the singing and chanting like a wind roaring.

At the climax, all stop, are held. Total darkness.
In the darkness, the single drum begins softly beating the monotone of the beginning, two to three measures and then stops.

All the water that will ever be is, right now.

Narrating Woman:
2001–2002, meditating on the consequences of golf courses built over the pristine and pure water lens of northern Guam and on proliferating sewage system breakdowns throughout the island. Since 2002, the danger to Guam's water supply has increased terrifyingly with the impending arrival of 5,000 marines, their families, and supporting services.

Male Scientist Broadcasting:
August 13, 2002, PDN, excerpts from an opinion article written by John Jenson, hydrogeologist with UOG's Water and Environmental Research Institute of the Western Pacific.

anatomy of a storm

William Nu'utupu Giles

category two: winds reaching 96–110 miles an hour
disaster is a language
we all hear
but do not speak

the home sent back into folklore
the mother who becomes a song
the nation who becomes a list of numbers

we all know how to empathize through a facebook window
how easily our dry hands share grief with flag filters
read-post / repair / repost / repray

category four: winds ripping 131–156 miles an hour
in the after / math
every outsider's whisper
is a shard of glass
caught in the hand of the storm
  a small sharp reflection of pain in swirling rain

how do I mouth a story
of water transforming
child into ancestor

it is so simple to write
from the safe eye
of a tempest

a distant privileged heart's hope
thrown to the sea
is just debris
can become bludgeon in the breeze teeth

words are all I have to offer
but what is art to an empty belly
what is a poem to a power outage
what is prayer to a flood

the dip of my frown is a poor shovel
when sweat is needed
to pull survivors from the ground
like recklessly cast seeds

category five: winds rending 157 miles an hour
the quiet moves faster than wind
so the ocean breaking from this flesh
will not be the storm's son
will not be the averted eyes
and quiet half heart shrug
the soft washed skin of indifference

disaster is a language
we all hear
but are afraid to speak

but survival
is a salt song
written in brown blood

silence does not respect the dead
it forgets them

this dry mouth will flood poem
will flow plea
will swell and break
this scab of distance
will bleed

and again
islands will emerge from ocean
like the first day bruised unbroken
alive

Great World

John Puhiatau Pule

I kneel before the sea
bow to drink
nutrients at the first gulp
instantly I knew my genealogy

the sea is an enormous giant in my blood

to stand in the sea long enough
with stones as anchor

the transfer of salt into my veins

oxygen from the citrus trees
that want to fuel my life

The sun opens the heart
and the moon closes it

Polynesia is the great Vā

Previously published, *Kermadec: Nine Artists Explore the South Pacific,* Pew Environment Group and Tauranga Art Gallery Toi Tauranga, 2011.

From "The Ocean in Us"

Epeli Hau'ofa

All our cultures have been shaped in fundamental ways by the adaptive interactions between our people and the sea that surrounds our island communities. In general, the smaller the island the more intensive are the interactions with the sea, and the more pronounced are the sea's influences on culture. One did not have to be in direct interaction with the sea to be influenced by it. Regular climatic patterns, together with such unpredictable natural phenomena as droughts, prolonged rains, floods, and cyclones that influenced the systems of terrestrial activities were largely determined by the ocean. On the largest island of Oceania, New Guinea, products of the sea, especially the much-valued shells, reached the most remote highlands societies, shaping their ceremonial and political systems. But more important, inland people of our large islands are now citizens of Oceanic countries whose capitals and other urban centers are located in coastal areas, to which they are moving in large numbers to seek advancement. The sea is already part of their lives. Many of us today are not directly or personally dependent on the sea for our livelihood and would probably get seasick as soon as we set foot on a rocking boat. This means only that we are no longer sea travelers or fishers. But as long as we live on our islands we remain very much under the spell of the sea; we cannot avoid it . . .

The ocean that surrounds us is the one physical entity that all of us in Oceania share. It is the inescapable fact of our lives. What we lack is the conscious awareness of it, its implications, and what we could do with it. The potentials are enormous, exciting—as they have always been. When our leaders and planners say that our future lies in the sea, they are thinking only in economic terms, about marine and seabed resources and their development. When people talk of the importance of the oceans for the continuity of life on Earth, they are making scientific statements. But for us in Oceania, the sea defines us, what we are and have always been. As the great Caribbean poet Derek Walcott put it, the sea is history. Recognition of this could be the beginning of a very important chapter in our history. We could open it as we enter the third millennium . . .

It is one of the great ironies of the Law of the Sea Convention, which enlarged our national boundaries, that it is also extending the territorial instinct to

---

Previously published, *We are the Ocean: Selected Works*, University of Hawai'i Press, 2008 (1998).

where there was none before. As we all know, territoriality is probably the strongest spur for some of the most brutal acts of aggression. Because of the resource potentials of the open sea and the ocean bed, the water that had united subregions of Oceania in the past may become a major divisive factor in the relationships between our countries in the future. It is therefore essential that we ground any new regional identity in a belief in the common heritage of the sea. A realization of the fact that the ocean is uncontainable and pays no respect to territoriality should spur us to advance the notion, based on physical reality and practices that date back to the initial settlement of Oceania, that the sea must remain open to all of us.

A regional identity anchored in our common heritage of the ocean does not mean an assertion of exclusive regional territorial rights, for the same water that washes and crashes on our shores also does the same to the coastlines of the whole Pacific Rim, from Antarctica to New Zealand, Australia, Southeast and East Asia, and right around to the Americas. The Pacific Ocean also merges into the Atlantic and the Indian Oceans to encircle the entire planet. As the sea is an open and ever-flowing reality, so should our oceanic identity transcend all forms of insularity, to become one that is openly searching, inventive, and welcoming. In a metaphorical sense the ocean that has been our waterway to each other should also be our route to the rest of the world. Our most important role should be that of custodians of the ocean, and as such we must reach out to similar people elsewhere for the common task of protecting the seas for the general welfare of all living things. This may sound grandiose but it really is not, considering the growing importance of international movements to implement the most urgent projects in the global environmental agenda: the protection of the ozone layer, the forests, and the oceans. The formation of an oceanic identity is really an aspect of our waking up to things that are already happening around us.

The ocean is not merely our omnipresent, empirical reality; equally important, it is our most wonderful metaphor for just about anything we can think of. Contemplation of its vastness and majesty, its allurement and fickleness, its regularities and unpredictability, its shoals and depths, and its isolating and linking role in our histories, excites the imagination and kindles a sense of wonder, curiosity, and hope that could set us on journeys to explore new regions of creative enterprise that we have not dreamt of before.

What I have tried to say so far is that in order to give substance to a common regional identity and animate it, we must tie history and culture to empirical reality and practical action. This is not new; our ancestors wrote our histories on the landscape and the seascape; carved, stenciled, and wove our metaphors on objects of utility; and sang and danced in rituals and ceremonies for the propitiation of the awesome forces of nature and society . . .

These were the thoughts that went through my mind as I searched for a thematic concept on which to focus a sufficient number of programs to give the Oceania Centre a clear, distinctive, and unifying identity. The theme for the center and for us to pursue is the ocean, and the interactions between us and the sea that have shaped and are shaping so much of our cultures. We begin with what we have in common, and draw inspirations from the diverse patterns that have emerged from the successes and failures in our adaptation to the influences of the sea. From there we can range beyond the tenth horizon, secure in the knowledge of the home base to which we will always return for replenishment and revisions of the purposes and directions of our journeys. We shall visit our people who have gone to the lands of diaspora and tell them that we have built something, a new home for all of us. And taking a cue from the ocean's ever-flowing and encircling nature, we will travel far and wide to connect with oceanic and maritime peoples elsewhere, and swap stories of voyages that we have taken and those yet to be embarked on. We will show them what we have, and learn from them different kinds of music, dance, art, ceremonies, and other forms of cultural production. We may even together make new sounds, new rhythms, new choreographies, and new songs and verses about how wonderful and terrible the sea is, and how we cannot live without it. We will talk about the good things the oceans have bestowed on us, the damaging things we have done to them, and how we must together try to heal their wounds and protect them forever.

I have said elsewhere that there are no more suitable people on earth to be the custodians of the oceans than those for whom the sea is home. We seem to have forgotten that we are such a people. Our roots, our origins are embedded in the sea. All our ancestors, including those who came as recently as sixty years ago, were brought here by the sea. Some were driven here by war, famine, and pestilence; some were brought by necessity, to toil for others; and some came seeking adventures and perhaps new homes. Some arrived in good health, others barely survived the traumas of passage. For whatever reasons, and through whatever experiences they endured, they came by sea to the Sea, and we have been here since. If we listened attentively to stories of ocean passage to new lands, and of the voyages of yore, our minds would open up to much that is profound in our histories, to much of what we are and what we have in common . . .

The regional identity proposed here has been constructed on a base of concrete reality. That the sea is as real as you and I, that it shapes the character of this planet, that it is a major source of our sustenance, that it is something that we all share in common wherever we are in Oceania, are all statements of fact. But above that level of everyday experience, the sea is our pathway to each other and to everyone else, the sea is our endless saga, the sea is our most powerful metaphor, the ocean is in us.

Kantan Tåsi (Song of the Sea)

Mary Therese Perez Hattori

Ekungok
Listen
to kantan tåsi
the song of the sea.

Mañaina
in sotto voce murmurs
send wisdom in sea foam

power atop waves
that embrace the shore

salty sea spray
kisses across my face.

Ekungok
Listen

"Minetgot,
Guinaiya,
Lina'la"

Strength,
Love,
Life

delivered by ocean currents
umbilical arteries

Previously published, *Waves: A Confluence of Women's Voices*, A Room of Her Own Foundation, 2021.

mañaina—elders

nurturing me
as the song of the sea
echoes the sound of my coursing blood.

Ekungok
Listen

LAND AND ISLANDS

What do we read in the word "island"? What does it mean to read an island?

Stories attached to the word "island" have for so long been told in terms of isolation, smallness, and disconnection. These stories of islands construct a diminishing world, devoid of connection, lacking the possibility for being whole and mattering. But as Pacific Islanders, as descendants of islands, "we are islands traveling within islands," as Kānaka Oiwi scholars Māhealani Ahia and Kahala Johnson have said;[1] we tell our stories in order to speak back to these structures of islands as isolated and insignificant. Our languages, stories, and relationships to one another provide expansive, vast, far-reaching ways of being connected in the world *because* of our islands.

If an island lives, what other lives are made possible? What do we make safe when we steward our islands as independent, sovereign caretakers of our lands?

Islands create entire grammars of being in the world that are shaped from islander histories of living from and caring for islands. We have millennia-long practices of languaging islands, storying our lands, which place us in reciprocal relationships where our islands shape our relationships to existence, and we in turn have shaped our islands in our naming and languages as peoples living in and moving between our island homes, carrying understandings of home(is) land when we travel and live away from our islands, sometimes for generations. When we speak our islands, when we use and shape different technologies to tell our island stories, we are documenting relationships to home, to understanding history mapped in front of us, named in the land that grew our languages from our ways of living on islands. Our stories therefore create an island syllabary, where our writers document language and relationships to land as complex relationships to body and ancestor.

This section also connects us to the difficulty and struggle of confronting structures and feelings of isolation, disconnection, and the historical and current processes that dispossess us of our lands. The writers of this section consider the specific kinds of care we must practice in order to reclaim our stewardship of our homes and our connections across them. In reading and writing our islands, we document how we navigate massive historical, political, and cultural change necessitated by island life. Here we have island forms of scripting—island grammars—that link negotiations of home to definitions of place, belonging, movement, and reclamation. We link the ancient to the present to the dreams of a future where our islands live.

Following the syntax of being in the world that Teresia Teaiwa gives us in the first piece of this section, each entry that follows shows how we activate our stories by making "island" a verb. We island by taking control over our terms of definition. We island by naming precisely and by imagining way, way back into our pasts. We island by remembering far into our futures. We island by knowing and documenting our bodies as island places. We island by moving. We island by returning. We island by crafting island-shaped stories.

[1] Cameron Māhealani Ahia and Kahala Johnson, "(Pre)Mapping Punalua: Triangulating a Future Mahele Iki in a Restored Hawaiian Queendom," (Re)Mapping Indigenous and Settler Geographies in the Pacific Conference, University of Hawaiʻi at Mānoa, 2018.

To Island

Teresia Kieuea Teaiwa

Shall we make "island" a verb? As a noun, it's so vulnerable to impinging forces. Let us turn the energy of the island inside out. Let us "island" the world! Let us teach the inhabitants of planet Earth how to behave as if we were all living on islands! For what is Earth but an island in our solar system? An island of precious ecosystems and finite resources. Finite resources. Limited space. The islanded must understand that to live long and well, they need to take care. Care for other humans, care for plants, animals; care for soil, care for water. Once islanded, humans are awakened from the stupor of continental fantasies. The islanded can choose to understand that there is nothing but more islands to look forward to. Continents do not exist, metaphysically speaking. It is islands all the way up, islands all the way down. Islands to the right of us, islands to the left.

Yes, there is a sea of islands. And "sea" can be a verb, just as "ocean" becomes a verb of awesome possibility. But let us also make "island" a verb. It is a way of living that could save our lives.

Previously published, *A World of Islands: An Island Studies Reader*, Institute of Island Studies, 2007.

GAFA

Frances C. Koya Vaka'uta

Fanua

The old people say land and blood connects us. Root systems reaching out through and between like invisible hands. They say, we are naturally drawn to those we are connected to. The blood song, an inaudible hum like ocean in our veins.

Talatalanoa

The men in my genealogical tree
are trying to tell me something.

Sometimes when I am tired . . . No.
It only happens when I am exhausted,
caught somewhere,
between the temporal realm of awake,
and dreamstate that,
catching some frequency,
I tune in to faraway conversations.

The first time it happened,
I thought I was dreaming.
I sat up and listened.
It was a serious conversation—a fono perhaps.
I remember lying there for hours,
Trying to make sense of the words I could piece together.

Mana

Remember when we were kids and
we made those string telephones
with the plastic cups and string?

It sounded like that.
Like a bad radio reception.
I knew I was connecting to something that had happened a long time ago.

The second time,
It was in Fijian.
The sounds of a village—
Conversations and laughter.
And the echo of men talking.

Mana maps a root system bereft of words that ground my knowing,
To the stories that fuel me.

Roots

Funny how, I never tap into conversations in Hindi or Arabic. As if my feet never having been pressed against the naked earth in those lands and my body never bathed in the cleansing water of her rivers and ocean, has not opened my ears to their voices. Maybe those men have nothing to tell me.

Perhaps it is true, that crossing the seven seas, renders us in a state of disconnected lifelines, suspended in a reality that just is.

Strange too, that,
it is only when I am exhausted,
that I hear these men talking.
I wonder if they're trying to tell me something,
About the need to learn my language,
Connecting me to my mother's womb?
The earth. The ocean.

Tuning in doesn't scare me anymore. It's the not knowing what it means,
That I fear.
The clairaudience of,
Something I cannot name flowing through my veins.

Alofa

The old people say the spirits exist in the same world that we do. Another dimension to reality that science cannot verify. There is a disconnect between the ocean of eyes that only see in scattered dreams of fish, blue and green like the rain.

When my mother wants to tell me something,
She doesn't wait for sleep to come.
My grandmother is more subtle.
A bird in the curve of mouth that only speaks her native tongue.
My father's ghazals disappear,
Into the horizon as I attempt poetry in the colonizer's words.
And the orator chants on black rock watching,
To see if my body holds the memory of their words.
He asks if I know that,
Nafanua sleeps in hands that no longer dance.
I don't know what that means,
Or why I hear these men talking.

Tautua

I may be free of black markings, but I am scarred,
Without words to frame the cosmogony of place.
Trapped in this colonial frame of otherness,
Skin stories embody the spirit.
Spirit stories embodied in skin,
Connecting the space between feet and the land.

If my ears connect me to my history.
Then, service is listening deeply.
And, Faagogo connects us across time
So we plant our feet in the earth,
Sleep in ocean winds and tattoo our tongues,
Finding completeness in the black of sky and sea
It is the Land and blood that connects us.

Migration Story

Loa Niumeitolu

My family's migration, what I refer to as our forced displacement, from our homeland, Tonga, in the 1980s, influences everything about how I think, feel, and act on environmental issues, both locally and globally, regardless of where I currently call home.

European explorers, commercial merchants, and Christian missionaries arrived in Tonga during the seventeenth and eighteenth centuries. They inflicted European domination on Tonga by using guns and money and enforcing their religions. This act of aggression from outside Moana Nui threatened the self-determination of Tonga's indigenous people, to protect their land and culture. This led to unprecedented upheaval in Tonga, around the years of 1799–1852. Violent and ferocious battles, betrayals, the end of countless generations of alliances and the forging of new systems ensued between islands, island groups, chiefs, relatives, family members, and the Euro-American powers. In 1845, Tāufa'āhau I, in partnership with Christian missionaries, became King George Tupou I, the first in line of a new centralized government in Tonga. To ensure the support, confidence, and resources of the Christian missionaries and Europeans for his campaign for kingship, Tāufa'āhau staged public displays in which he destroyed and violated statues and symbols of the indigenous Tongan Gods, of which, most of them, due to the reverence and sacredness Tongans held for their land, the land as their mother, were female deities.

In Tongan cosmology, the land is female and she includes our Grandmother Moana, the great Pacific Ocean. All the inhabitants in her ecosystem, including the soil, the sky, the wind, are imbued with the sacredness of feminine energy. The land also included people and the roles they stewarded to support Tongan culture, including: languages, foods, medicine, education, multiple genders, governance, and economies. When Tāufa'āhau and his supporters violated our indigenous Tongan female Gods, the sacredness, tapu, of our land and our Tongan ways of life that were centered in the power of the sacred feminine were degraded and scorned. This carries on in Tonga today. The Western ways of living became an ill-fitting kupesi/frame for Tongans to live their lives and to envision their futures.

After Tupou I's coronation in 1845, Western systems were immediately adopted: a constitution, Parliament, police departments, taxation, land tenure to the eldest son, and compulsory Western education. By the 1970s, when I was born, the displacement of Tongans to "bigger and better" countries was in full practice. A family member or whole families migrated to a Western country to ensure what was believed to be a promising future. Many, like my parents, believed that migrating to obtain an academic degree or job experience and then returning to Tonga was not enough, and that we had to immigrate and permanently settle in a Western country in order to be awarded the benefits that country offered. In preparing for this migration away from our motherland, we had to overlook what was there for us in Tonga at that moment, so we could move forward and succeed in the Western dream. If we had looked at what we were about to leave behind, we would see our beloved grandparents and those who raised us since birth, closest friends, homes, foods, native languages, traditional medicines, arts, leadership roles in our extended families and communities, and the generous land and ocean where our placentas, both physical and spiritual, were buried. To leave our motherland and loved ones behind was a psychologically and spiritually destructive transition. Therefore, we kept our eyes on the Western prize of better opportunities and forced ourselves not to look back.

It is important for Tongans to tell our migration stories, and, in the telling, these stories reveal a displacement we have away from our motherland that was traumatic and caused insurmountable pain. We must heal that separation, especially as we settle in new host countries. Our displacement from our motherland is vital to how Tongans relate to what is called the environment and what is environmental.

For many Tongan families, including my own, the Mormon Church tore families from their loved ones and from Tongan culture through intense efforts at conversion of Tongans and control of family life. My mother worked as a math teacher at the Tongan government schools when she started raising us children. My father spent his days drinking and was not home during my early childhood. Many years after, my mother secured a better-paying wage at the American Mormon high school, Liahona. After seven years of teaching she converted our family to the Mormon Church.

Our lives quickly assimilated to Mormon culture when we lived in Tonga, and our lifestyle changed. We stopped drinking coffee with our relatives; we stopped playing face-card games with our cousins; my sister and I could no longer attend and enjoy different churches but were required to attend the "only true church," the Mormon Church. The losses were not so much the coffee and cards, but rather, the close ties and togetherness we no longer could share with our cousins, who were not Mormons, because we attended Mormon Church activities on Mondays through Sundays. We lost time speaking Tongan with our cousins, telling jokes, exchanging ghost stories, and building stronger relationships with each other. We also no longer received faitoʻo faka Tonga from Tongan traditional healers but now were required a religious blessing from a male priesthood leader and were encouraged to only go to the Western medicine doctor.

My mother tells the story that when she found a Book of Mormon, the Mormon holy scripture, in a desk in her math classroom in Liahona, she felt an affinity with Joseph Smith's, the founder of the Mormon Church, conversion story. She described her heart accepting the Holy Ghost and feeling deep gratitude that the church offered opportunities, particularly in higher education, for her and her children. When she was a young child, her father instilled a desire in her to attend university one day. The opportunities were very rare for someone of my mother's commoner class status to attend university. Her father was a respected teacher at the all-boys high school, Atele. He died of a heart attack while farming at his garden in Fatai when my mother was sixteen years old, just a year before she would leave to study in New Zealand on a scholarship. It was an opportunity for her to study at Epsom Girls Grammar and, hopefully, to continue onwards to the University of Auckland. My mother described those few years in New Zealand as the loneliest times of her life, fresh with the pain of her father's death, moving to a new culture, and missing her large family; she could not focus on her studies. Soon enough, her mother asked her to return to Tonga to help raise her younger brothers.

Before her conversion, my mother relentlessly pushed to provide us children with the best Western education in Tonga. My mother did whatever she could to supplement her teaching job: sold eggs and raised pigs to offer my sister and me a foot in the door of Western educational opportunities as children. We attended the private school, Tonga Side School, while our cousins attended the public Government Primary School, GPS. This privilege to attend Tonga Side School, which, back in the 1970s, was reserved for the children of nobles, ministers in government, and the business class, introduced us to many Western notions that prepared us for our migration and set us up to be specific kinds of immigrants. The Side School we attended in Tonga was next door to the GPS my cousins attended.

One day when I was eight years old, attending Class 3, I was waiting with other Side School students for the starting bell to ring. Older Tongan Side School boys, in their starched grey uniforms and polished burgundy sandals, were taunting a group of GPS boys who were shortcutting through the Side School yard to avoid being late to their school. The Side School boys mocked the GPS boys, in English, for being poor and not wearing shoes to school. My heart froze when I heard a GPS boy respond with swear words in Tongan. It was the deep voice of my beloved cousin who I climbed guava trees with at our grandma's home. He and I were steadfast accomplices in all games we played. I wanted to fight these Side School boys for my cousin, but, for the first time in my life, I saw that my cousin's uniform was shabby and his bushy hair unkempt. I felt ashamed for him and myself. My cousin saw me in the small crowd and his hard, focused eyes spoke to me clearly, without using words. They said, "In this world, we do not know each other. You are with the rich kids, and I am a poor kid. Do not betray our differences by trying to sympathize with me." I bowed my head and watched my cousin's fast legs as he ran, hurling rocks back at the Side School boys, and disappeared in the dust of the GPS dirt yard.

Back at my grandmother's home, where my cousin lived, we continued to climb the guava trees together. We never spoke about this incident. As a child, with all my mother's dreams for a better future for me, I was preened to succeed in Western ways and the losses inherent to this preening were beginning to pile up. My cousin lives here in California too, but we do not see each other often because our daily lives are a world apart.

Because of my mother's stalwart commitment to her and her children's educational goals, we migrated to Utah for my mother to attend Brigham Young University in Provo through a scholarship from the Mormon Church. In the early 1990s, my mother obtained a PhD in instructional science and technology with a minor in mathematics from Brigham Young. When we stepped out of the Salt Lake City Airport in 1980 for the first time, the Uinta Mountains greeted us, clothed majestically in snow and ice. It was the first time we saw snow. Utah is the land of the Ute, Paiute, Shoshone, Goshute, and Navajo. There were many European adventurers, explorers, and traders who went to Utah to stake their claims on the environment. As we stepped onto the awe-inspiring frozen landscape, we did not mistake it for a winter wonderland. We quickly saw the great challenges of racism, xenophobia, neglect, and invisibility that immigrants confront entering Western countries.

In joining the Mormon Church, my father became a Tongan interpreter for the Mormon Church in Tonga, and in Utah. He interpreted the Book of Mormon and other holy books, magazines, and newsletters; the church's annual General Conference talks; and our local congregation, or ward, church meetings, from English to Tongan and vice versa.

In Utah, my parents felt a lot of pressure from the cultural environment we lived in to only speak English at home. It only took a year before the three of us children, who grew up speaking Tongan in Tonga, stopped speaking Tongan in Utah. As a consequence, I could not teach my son Tongan and my son and his first cousins are part of the second generation in our family who do not speak our ancestral language.

My family was subjected to intense racism and anti-immigrant sentiments after moving to Utah. In the early 1990s, my seventeen-year-old brother drove us to Hardee's for hamburgers and fries in Provo, Utah. On our drive, we were listening to music and feeling blessed to be together as siblings, hanging out and having fun. As soon as we pulled into the Hardee's parking lot, a police squad surrounded our car. I was seated behind my brother when a cop placed his gun on my brother's temple and screamed at my brother not to move or he would shoot him. The cops held us at gunpoint until they decided my brother was not the suspect they were looking for, but he had "fit the profile." The policeman who almost shot my brother was an average-looking white guy, nothing physically demonic about him. In placing his weapon in his holster, preparing to leave, he said to my brother, "I love Polynesians. My girlfriend is Hawaiian." We felt sick to our stomachs because of having to cooperate passively in order to not be killed or harassed further under this extreme threat. We never talked about the terror this experience left branded on our skins and spirits as siblings.

We do not talk about the countless experiences of police and court harassment and abuse we experienced growing up as immigrant, brown Pacific Islander young people in a Mormon white Utah that feared us, new immigrants, in the 1990s. The part of us that needed to discuss our experiences of racism with each other was silenced.

I also experienced intense racism at the schools in Utah I attended. At my first ever Lincoln and Douglas debate tournament, I placed in the top three spots. It was not due to any formal training that it happened. My debate coach never spoke to me and my two fellow Lincoln–Douglas debaters who were from the Philippines. Our class time was spent in a small room by ourselves. She refused to teach and advise us about debate and gave all her attention to the white students. Regardless, I continued to perform very well in tournaments. However, I did not receive any feedback from my teacher on which direction to take my debating and I decided to stop. I could have soared as a debater if I had some support and advice. I was always neglected by my teachers. In my AP history class, all the students raved about how the teacher was so helpful to them. I attended class each day and I wanted to thrive like the other students, but the teacher did not speak to me ever. I felt unseen and I dropped out of the class. I could not succeed in a class where the teacher did not see me as her student. My early years of living in Tonga and Hawaiʻi, where a majority of my peers and teachers looked like me, enabled me to more clearly interpret the treatment I received as a student in Utah as the racism it was.

Learning from the native, indigenous people of Turtle Island, I was also able to articulate the displacement that I lived through and the importance of Tonga as my motherland. As I learned how genocide eradicated indigenous people in Utah, Massachusetts, and California, the places I lived in on Turtle Island, I slowly understood what happened to me as an indigenous Tongan person. I learned in the last few years I have lived in Berkeley, Huichin, the land of the Ohlone Lisjan tribe, from Ohlone Lisjan leader Corrina Gould, that a motherland, a homeland, is sacred. Although Berkeley, next-door town Oakland, and the San Francisco Bay Area are a hub for new, innovative creativity, including cutting-edge tech companies, artist creations, and social justice activism, Corrina Gould reminds us that we must respect the sacredness of the land we live on. The protests at Standing Rock also reminded us to respect the sacred. I feel this is what we have lost as Tongans. To see our motherland as sacred.

Our stories reveal and map why our migration was a forced displacement. They are accounts of what was displaced and what was lost that Western money and better opportunities will never be able to replace. We must tell our stories of migration, which tell of what our ancestors, through us, yearned for, what we lost, what we gained along the way, and what we continue to look for in our displacement from our motherland.

For me as a Tongan Takataapui woman, to write about the environment is to write about my own life experience of being forced to migrate from my homeland of Tonga, the first natural environment that I treasure and hold dearest to my heart. Forced migration and displacement from my homeland and its ramifications is the first environmental fight I experienced. I am Tongan, I am an indigenous person, and my own life story parallels that of other indigenous people who are displaced from their homelands, and our self-determination is undermined by systems outside our own culture and ways of life. I carry my environment in me from my homeland, and this informs all new environments I go to. I also carry the shame, the silence, the rage and grief of forced displacement that, through the years, have tried to silence me. They try to stop me from speaking up for my native environment or joining other indigenous people who ask for support to fight for their lands. Let's start telling our stories, recounting them to our children, to our siblings, our cousins, our parents, and to each other. Let's listen and let's begin to heal so we can learn to articulate what our environment is and reclaim the environmental issues that are most important to us. Let us, as the indigenous people of Turtle Island teach us, reclaim the sacred. Let us put ourselves in the shoes of Tāufaʻāhau and other Tongan chiefs who feared that Tonga would be completely consumed by the colonizing powers, which, I'm claiming it right here, happened. We're in a juncture similar to where our ancestors stood in the seventeenth and eighteenth centuries, when companies and foreign countries, now not only from the West, but also from the East, are vying for power over our sovereignty and self-determination. Let the truth of your story of migration be a banner you proudly show that we will no longer sacrifice our motherland and we will fight for our freedom. Let the stories carry us and let the stories gather strength and resist the powers of domination. And lastly, let our stories reclaim the sacred and let us return together, in our most sacred ways, back to our motherland, Tonga.

fa'ñague / fuh-nyah-ghee/

Danielle P. Williams

1. a person or
    place habitually frequented;

    // a presence entering the
    questioning of your dreams

    // the way the breeze whispers
        through the coconut trees
            in your aunt's backyard

    // the shrieking panic coming from the
        chickens that wake you up at 4 a.m. like clockwork

    // the danger in turning your back to the sea

2. the action or power of being
    haunted;

    // a shadow along the
        lining of my skin

    // where your past and
        present selves begin

    // an attachment; a belonging; a becoming

3. the haunting;

    // the taotaomo'na, aniti; the people before time, the
        spirits of our same name

    // the strength in realizing superstition lives
        the life you're afraid to

4. an awakening;

// when a person returns home to the Guåhan; to
Saipan; to whatever islands are
embedded in their dna they begin
to feel whole again

I couldn't feel you before this, where have you been?

Guam's Place Names Continue to Be Challenged

Peter R. Onedera

Any place on the globe, such as an island, an atoll, a country, a peninsula, a continent, or a vast topography, that shows regions depicting states, countries within a continent, or nations with varying differences of government, a race of people, and distinct languages, customs, creeds, and climate has a name that provides a glimpse of the language defining that place.

On a smaller or perhaps lesser scale, hamlets, towns, cities, settlements, villages, communes, tribal reservations, protectorates, housing areas, clan quarters, and enclaves, as well as communities of people with separate ideologies, are entrenched in the language of usage to describe them.

I bear this in mind because I have long had a fascination for place names not just on my island but I've developed an eye for language use of places among the numerous locales I've visited throughout my life.

Language plays a very important role, as it is depicted in the printed volume of documents, maps, charts, journals, and every known piece of literature, most particular, on which I'm basing this writing, on place names or public signs.

Everyone is lost without a language to call one's own and it is the very first introduction to a visitor to a foreign place anywhere on the globe. For me, signs depicting the name of a certain place are how I know without being exposed to the education of the history, customs, traditions, and practices of a given place that it is the language in use for all to see. It is the first indication of how that language, especially if it is indigenous, introduces me to a place.

My language, CHamoru, has long been on the endangered list. I got wind of it as an adult and I went through my own personal renaissance that included learning an alphabet system, orthography, and grammatical structure and eventually teaching the language to toddlers and up to adults.

I think my memory banks began at a very early age. I'd have vivid memories of events, people, places, and my knowledge and use of CHamoru as my language was in place in those early years. I think I was described as precocious. I was forever inquisitive. Sometimes members of my family would discipline me to shut me up momentarily.

As a toddler, I understood and communicated in CHamoru. I didn't know a word of English until I began my pre-primer days at my village elementary school.

I was born in 1953. The Guam of that era was sort of a rebirth of American English that spelled the beginning of the end of the CHamoru language. The citizens of the island were catapulted into the whitewash American dream brought about by the status that the signing of the Organic Act bestowed in 1950, turning everyone living on the island into US citizens or Americans at best.

And before I ever began my schooling, a sign that was posted everywhere my parents took me had the blazing words in CHamoru that I could read and still know today. The sign said, "Probido Fumino' Chamorro." Simply stated, it came to many in my community in one of three translations: "It is a danger to speak CHamoru," "CHamoru language is forbidden," or "Do not speak CHamoru as it is unlawful." As a youngster, it didn't matter what it meant because I spoke it fluently, among friends and classmates, to members of my family and other relatives, and to my neighbors in the central village of Sinajana.

And that was the only sign I ever saw that was forever present throughout the island. It was there in the only local hospital in Tamuning. It was at the village post office a couple of blocks away from my house, it was on the wall at Torres Store, and it was also on the clinic of the Seventh Day Adventist where my mother went regularly as she was a diabetic. And it was there at Town House and Butler's as well as the small airport that was right near a chain-link fence of what was then US Naval Air Station or locally called NAS Agana. The most indelible distinction was that it was posted on the entrance of my village church of St. Jude Thaddeus, and our religious observance and daily masses were conducted in Latin, the language that went extinct, but I remember litanies and prayers of sorts to this very day.

There were no other signs anywhere. I'm assuming that everyone knew where places were because in many conversations about descriptions of places and how one needed to get there, it was never about crossing a major highway, the name of a street, or the name of anything in the vicinity. Descriptions were always replete with landmarks, a beach, a geological abnormality of a place, a legendary nomenclature, and also-known-as places that expounded the reputation of someone, a person, like *Tun Bu, As Penggao, As Åtdas,* or *Nan CHai'.*

I didn't know about street names, names of buildings, names of government agencies, establishments, and other distinctive attributes of any place on Guam. I didn't even know the name of my elementary school until I think I was in the third grade. I thought how simple life was then, for me, at least.

However, CHamoru as my language became a personal endeavor and I endured through many years of watching denial among local people regarding their place in the indigenous culture. Many shunned the language as well as identity. They felt ashamed. It went on for decades and it was so glaring that nobody seemed to want to bring the matter into discussion. So, it was set aside.

An upheaval, I should say, confronted the CHamoru. Where did one stand as far as the island was concerned? As generations grew so did education, and it wasn't long before people started learning about political status, of an unincorporated territory that no one seemed to be able to explain, indigenous rights, and the downward spiral of the language that was declared as endangered. Finger-pointing and blame suddenly popped up everywhere, but there was no solution. And, it was true, people who claimed CHamoru lineage were actually told that they would never get far if the only language they knew and spoke was CHamoru. English was important and immediately needed to be learned, period.

My only resolve, or so I thought, was that the mother country that was Guam was where CHamoru all began and that the island I called home was where I belonged. Above all, everything that was here was what I called my own, most especially the places where I grew up.

Imagine my shock when I came across a booklet that was published by the University of Guam's Micronesian Area Research Center. It was compiled by retired professor Marjorie G. Driver. It was titled *Guam: A Nomenclatural Chronology.* I perused the book after noting that Professor Driver said that the men who sailed the Pacific in the sixteenth century included captains, pilots, missionaries, sailors, and soldiers, but I missed her inclusion perhaps of whalers, navigators, and explorers.

From their visits to Guam and the Mariana Islands, their findings and eventual names that they affixed began appearing in ships' logs, diaries, letters, manifests, journals, and other documents, many of which were in libraries and institutions all across Europe and other parts of the world. Included in the booklet were maps that were drawn or redrawn by these discoverers. I noted that some of the places I was familiar with, villages or settlements, had names that must have replaced original ones or that they were changed despite different spellings to suit whoever drew the maps. From this, too, I learned that the Spaniards, Portuguese, English, French, Flemings, and Dutch had had a hand in the naming of Guam. Professor Driver also mentioned that several linguistic regions of Spain contributed to many of the names listed.

In history books, I learned of Islas de los Ladrones, Islas de las Latinas, and, of course, Guahan and Guam. The latter two ran neck and neck in the number of documents where they were included and listed in the booklet. There were numerous others, such as Baham, Goaam, Volid, Bacin, Chamures, Y Guan, San Juan, Uan, Guajan, Guabon, Gaum, St. Jean, Iguana, Marianas, Guaham, Guaxan, Gouaham, and San Lazaro. All the names that were listed were given to my island, the island that was my home. Altogether, my count amounted to about one hundred and ninety or so names. It left me puzzled, wondering what was the true name of the island of Guam.

It appeared that it was this way for the countless centuries when the island was discovered over and over again by foreigners who stepped foot on its shores, be it northern Guam or the southern village of Humåtak, notably pillaged by Ferdinand Magellan and his crew in 1521.

Lost in all this was the original name of the island as known and called by the indigenous inhabitants even to the fact that their peoplehood was given the same name as the language. Documents revealed that the word was Spanish in context, meaning, and usage and that it was the conquering Spaniards that relegated the name to the people. Today, there remains the question, what did the indigenous inhabitants call themselves? The name *taotao tåno'*, or people of the land, was what I heard and eventually became popularly used, but that came about just yesterday, the latter part of last century and continuing on to this century too.

I was led to believe that no one ever asked the CHamorus who they were and what was the name they called themselves, much less the name of the language that they spoke. Linguistic studies later revealed that it was Malayo-Polynesian or that it was from the Austronesian family.

Into this web of intricacy, names of places on the island that existed for the four thousand years of its existence were obviously changed many times over, as some of the maps showed spelling inaccuracies derived from European languages or that they were spelled the way they were heard phonetically. As was the practice, the men who were cartographers failed to consult the indigenous people on the correct names of places on the island.

The latest travesty was when the invading forces of Japan conquered the island in the dark days of World War II. They forced the Japanese language on them, punished them for any show of allegiance to Uncle Sam, and renamed their villages. Thus, *Hagåtña* became Akashi, *Hågat* became Showa Mura, *Barigåda* became Haruta Mura, *Sinahånña* became Sinagawa Mura, *Humåtak* became Umada Mura, and next door, the tiny island of *Cocos* was named Nagashima.

And everyone who was from everywhere else came and forged a name on the island's streets, villages, housing areas, major roadways, beaches, cliffsides, ranchland, jungle areas, and schools.

The island's map of today shows names of places that are not CHamoru at all. Many are in English and they made me wonder if there was no imagination left in naming some of these places. There appeared to be puns of a sort, a number that may have bordered on the silly, such as NeverMind Road, Cross Island Road, BPM, Fern Terrace, Swamp Road, and Gun Beach. Then there was the Gill Baza Subdivision, where a community of previously homeless and downtrodden Chuukese lived but had no access to adequate sewer, water, or power lines. This illustrates that original place names have been erased forever, as if they fell off the face of the earth. Judging from comparisons of maps drawn in the past centuries, there was no repetitive consistency of the names of villages, settlements, and even landmarks. It was inconsistently illustrated in what was an attempt to retain from archival sources.

As examples, the following are in today's maps. From the Spaniards came Plaza de Espana, Paseo de Oro, Paseo de Susana, and Fort Santa Agueda. The United States, through its governors and first ladies, contributed Agana Heights, Nimitz Hill, John F. Kennedy High School, Harmon, Skinner Plaza, Gibson Highway, George Washington High School, and through its military forces named places such as NAS Agana, Andersen Air Force Base, Camp Bright, Marbo, Harmon, Captain William B. Price Elementary School, Wettengel

Elementary School, Andersen South, NCTAMS (pronounced *nick tams*), Naval Station, Naval Mag, and Agafa Gumas. Another branch of the US government gave the island GHURA 501, GHURA 502, GHURA 503, and the other GHURA-subsidized housing areas.

The Koreans have their stake in Hyundai Toto and Hyundai Santa Rita. The Philippines, namely the Filipinos originally from many of its provinces, became the second-largest minority group on the island. They were not to be outdone, and names such as Mabini Street, Magsaysay Street, Del Pilar Street, and others in northern Guam as well as Rizal Beach and Camp Rojas to the south were their contribution. The Carolinian Community that eventually settled in Saipan in the Commonwealth of the Northern Marianas left its imprint on the village name of Tamuning and in Orote Point on the southern end of the island that was subsumed in the housing area of military families at Naval Station.

The Catholic Church had a village named in honor of a patroness when the island established a postwar village that resulted from the demise of a centuries-old ancient village of Sumay, which should be spelled Sumai. Its displaced residents were moved into the hills of what became Sånta Rita.

Politics, too, left its mark on the island through two well-known CHamoru gentlemen. The late congressman Ben Blaz introduced in the US Congress the changeover of Orote Point to Morris K. Udall Point. His effort was supported by the signature of former governor Joseph F. Ada. Udall, a former secretary to the Department of the Interior, never visited Guam to at least see his name emblazoned on a memorial plaque at the site.

Commerce, too, should not be forgotten, with contributed names and tracts of land such as Jonestown, Perez Acres, Kaiser in Dededo and Piti, Nimitz Towers, Ypaopao Estates, Perezville, Baza Gardens, and the industrial parks of Tamuning and Harmon.

It wasn't clear, as of this writing, who designated the major roadways of the island known as Route 1 to Route 10, but if it was the government of Guam itself, it could stand for designating these routes with indigenous names like *Kalachucha, Birenghenas, Fanihi,* or *Hilitai,* or something reflective of the island's indigenous flora and fauna.

Even CHamorus had a stake in renaming places on the island that are not even close to CHamoru in language, distinction, or anything cultural. Marine Corps Drive, Purple Heart Highway, and the Vietnam Veterans Memorial Highway resulted from this renaming effort. The island has long been regarded as a US military island since under the governance of the United States, one-third of the island was taken over by the military. Some tracts were eventually returned to their original landowners but that took place several decades later. US Marines and their families will be relocated to Guam from Okinawa, and a huge housing development on primal land in the northern part of the island was set aside for construction of dwellings to accommodate about five thousand people.

Several years ago, a Japanese multibillionaire developed the Leo Palace Resort on the outskirts of the village of Yona. As it neared completion, he, without consultation from anyone, took it upon himself to rename acres and acres of land to Miyama Hills. His reason was that the place where the resort now stood was once a huge concentration camp to which CHamorus were forced to walk and where they lived in squalor and deprivation. The camp was established by the Japanese military forces in the waning days of World War II. The name of the place was Manenggon, and according to cultural lore, it existed for centuries, in name and its terrain. He felt that it would be a tremendous detriment to trying to entice Japanese investors, visitors, and hotel guests to patronize the place because of the reputed distinction of the area. The Guam Place Name Commission challenged the developer and overturned his attempt, thereby retaining the original name of the place. If the commission did not object, that place would have had a new name today.

I needed to make mention of the nearly accidental renaming of Manenggon to Miyama Hills. Manenggon was huge. It spanned miles and miles of acreage that included a surging river spilling into nearby tributaries that fed nine waterfalls, swampland, habitats for wildlife, and soil that was ideal for subsistence farming in olden Guam. Because of its significance in the war, the area also became a historical site, and yearly pilgrimages occur with the annual Liberation Day observance. This one incident was luckily caught by the commission, but the previous listing of names of places on Guam either escaped its attention or development was happening simultaneously all over and no one took the time to notice that a grave injustice was happening underneath the noses of the island's government leaders. The plausible explanation given was that a commission was not established until some politician took notice and decided to enact legislation that would put a stop to the renaming of places. At the cost of progress, perhaps, it happened just a wee bit late.

In summary, the Guam Place Name Commission in 1994 also gave the public an opportunity to provide input when it embarked on a program of bringing to the community original names of villages, outskirts, and well-known places, their definitions and the need to correct them with the mandated CHamoru alphabet in place. Public hearings were held for more than three months in every village community center.

Although they may have appeared original, the fact that spelling had always been in contention for decades throughout the nearly four hundred years of existence of maps made them a bit confusing. As an example, the capital city of Hagåtña appeared as Agana but variations of spelling ranged from Hagatna to Agaña as well as Agadña. To date, the capital city is the only name that resulted from introduced legislation in the Guam Legislature that spelled it correctly. None of the others ever went through similar proposals. Villages such as Malesso' appeared as Merigo and Merizo; Inalåhan appeared as Inarajan or sometimes Narajan; Hågat was Agat; Dededu was also Dededo; Sinahånña was Sinajana, and young, mischievous individuals played on the word with their own version, calling the village Sin City. Other names were more modern and were attributed to some cultural folklore like Yo'ña in reference to the ownership of huge parcels of land by a noted village leader; the three central villages of Mongmong, To'to, and Maite' derived their names from the physical features of a mythical god; Yigu, appearing as Yigo, referred to the yoke of the karabao, which wasn't even an indigenous beast of burden on the island; Humåtak also appeared as Umatac and was, about two centuries ago, the previous capital of the island. There are many conflicts that confront the placement of names on the island of Guam. Attempts have been made to make some sort of correction, but there never seemed to be a consensus as the community would be torn between correct and proper spelling, pronunciation, and the English contrasting alphabetic system and that of CHamoru. There are many examples still in limbo; for example, Ypao should be Ipao.

Agana Heights was a nineteenth-century name that sprung up when the wives of naval governors gave the place where an official government house was erected its name, establishing it as the home of the naval governor and his family. When communicating with people on the mainland, they gave the place its air of distinction as their newfound status catapulted them into an affluent community of white up-and-coming wealthy socialites, likening it to the city overlooking the capital of the island; hence, Heights was added to the capital name, which was Agana, although municipally it was located in the next village, which was nestled in the hills. The original place name of Tutuhan was contested by residents themselves because the name is now relegated to just a section in today's village proper. Tamuning is the only village that was not an original CHamoru name. Credit was given to the community of Carolinians who peopled the area that was once known as Maria Christina and Okka. Like Agana Heights, Okka became a section of the village in Tamuning, while Maria Christina disappeared some time ago and was no longer included on maps. Others desperately need spelling adjustments, such as Asan, Barrigada, Chalan Pago, Maina, and Talofofo. Others like Tumon was Tomhom or sometimes just Tommom; Apotguan was Aporgan and sometimes appeared as Apotgguang, Apporgan, or Aporgant; Adelup was Adilok and, at one point, as a pun, became Ada Loop under the name of the new governor; Anigua was Aniguak; and Harmon, now an official village in the municipality of Tamuning and Tumon, was a name that came about because of a military officer. There are numerous places on the island with a misspelling or misuse of some word, like the classic example of Agafa Gumas, which actually stood as an acronym of a gun placement ordinance area established by the military, but it has stood as the official name of an as-yet-to-be-established municipality. The area has expanded to a size that was comparable to some villages in population and distance from personal, private, and government properties. The place already has a parish church and an elementary school, and businesses are sprouting up throughout the area. The place adjoins the new place set aside for the new housing development of soon-to-be-transferred US Marines and their families from Okinawa.

Place names on Guam needed to be fully addressed. Names continue to be included on maps with hardly any major changes in spelling and distinction. These names would get tossed about and changed by new mayors that get elected every four years. A government agency that had jurisdiction on major thoroughfares also gave input when establishing names for direction purposes, but nevertheless their changes, such as Routes 1 to 10, appeared on maps. Another government agency had the authority to establish a name for a school upon the construction of a new campus. A Territorial Land Use Commission, through every change in government administration, oversaw development proposals. Introduced by planners and developers, their new housing construction proposals also included a name.

The last, the Guam Place Name Commission, was one of the major responsibilities assigned to the CHamoru Language Commission, which recently underwent a name change, too, by the current governor. With an expanded role, the Commission on the CHamoru Language and the Teaching of the History and Culture of the Indigenous People of Guam replaced the previous one, which was established in 1965. A body of nine members appointed by the governor are supposedly conversant, knowledgeable, and trained in CHamoru language, history, and orthography. As a government of Guam agency, the commission was often underfunded, regularly challenged by the community, and never treated as a priority by the powers that be.

Many times, these five government entities clash with one another, as all have claimed to have jurisdiction and authority in naming public places on Guam. Not mentioned here is that the US military installations, too, were notorious for overturning and renaming jurisdictions on land that comprises what they administered.

For the size of the island of Guam, at thirty miles in length and about six miles in its widest near-center of the topography, it is small and a simple matter, as place names could not be resolved. To me, this oversight continued through generations and generations of indigenous people and so maps leave much to be desired in terms of ownership of the land. Land to all indigenous people is precious and its cultural significance must be preserved and maintained for posterity. The name of the place must also be perpetuated for time immemorial.

I compared my island's usage of CHamoru on places everywhere on Guam. As I indicated early on in this writing, a majority of places on the island have no CHamoru language or cultural significance. Many places that were named or renamed reflect representation of the different groups that make up the population of the island.

The countries that I observed with their place names took great pride in making sure that their connection to the land through their language showed genuine care for their history, customs, beliefs, traditions, heritage, and people. Many stood alone in native or indigenous language use, especially in countries like Japan, Germany, Cook Islands, Taiwan, South Korea, Indonesia, the Philippines, Solomon Islands, and the islands of Micronesia such as Palau, Marshalls, Chuuk, Pohnpei, and Yap. Hawai'i impressed me in that being the fiftieth state of the union, great pains were taken to ensure that place names reflected Hawaiian throughout.

The only country where I saw a duality system in place was New Zealand, where both Maori as the indigenous language and English as the immigrant language were official, and their place name signs reflected this. This also holds true for Guam, as both CHamoru and English are official. In the Commonwealth of the Northern Mariana Islands, there are three official languages: English, Chamorro, and Carolinian.

My sense of place wanted to know the dominance or prominence of the languages of each visited place in terms of whether they've been in use for centuries. Because language continually evolves, I also wondered whether place names, their usage and familiarity continued from one generation of maps to another or did what I saw in signs show a replacement of original place names somewhere in time.

To me, the personality of the place spoke volumes in terms of their names. Knowing the meaning of a word that was applied to a place name was history altogether. A place could also have been named to honor an indigenous citizen whose contributions were so deep and profound that government or civic leaders warranted the name of that person to be carried to posterity in its locale. Such names have been given to schools, buildings, government offices, parks, and battlefields.

I've long desired to do a complete makeover of Guam's place names. I once assigned my CHamoru language class at the university to look at the current map that was in place in 2009. The entire semester was devoted to researching places on the island to see if there was any historical significance such as a battleground of the Spanish-CHamoru Wars; an epidemic such as the smallpox that totally wiped out a settlement; the prevalence of diseases such as leprosy, locally called *nasarinu* or *lasarinu;* amyotrophic lateral sclerosis (ALS), locally called *litiku;* and Parkinsonism-dementia, called *boddek;* a distinctive landmark; the prevalence of native flora or fauna; a connection to families who've lived there for several generations and whether their also-known-as names held significance to the place; analyzing soil and vegetation such as the abundance of herbs, roots, and plants used in herbal healing; nearness to the beach where harvesting of fish and other sea creatures provided sustenance or navigation with the flying proa defined that particular place; a place purportedly a site of spirits of the ancient ones or where a legend was born; and the current name of the place and its CHamoru meaning, if it had any.

The semester project included public hearings, visits to senior citizen centers, and interviews with elderly and prominent village personalities, and a website was also created; the massive publicity that it generated allowed the public to let the students know of thoughts, feelings, knowledge, and opinions of the project at hand. A wealth of information and people of all ages came to meetings, panel discussions, press conferences, and workshops. Many shared important information on many of the places, including genealogy, chronological events of great magnitude, generations of families, and the social upheaval that modern living brought about, such as crime, drugs, alcohol, domestic violence, and social ills.

The students catalogued their findings, collected archival copies of documents that showed some sort of history of a given place, and proposed possible names of places over the entire island. The voluminous document was handed over to the Guam Legislature in the person of one prominent senator. The students proposed their findings as legislation to enact and have justice given to the names of places on Guam.

It got nowhere. It sat on the desk of the senator, and the proposed legislation never reached the hands of other colleagues. This particular branch of government never got a chance to review the work of the students.

Ten years have passed since the work was done, and the current map of the island remains the same. Gone, too, is the senator that the document was handed to. Although the students have since graduated and have moved on with their lives, many that I met up with would share with me that their conscience to do justice to the island's place names never left their souls.

I hope that someday, another thoughtful individual will spearhead another drive, another effort, another task, of seeing something like this project to fruition.

The task of Guam's place names and using CHamoru rests in the hands of a new generation.

makua smiles back

leilani portillo

what would you hear makua say?
    before contact
    kapa beaters make rhythm under rising suns
        beat beat beating wauke thin, smooth, soft
    stone against kalo against wood mixed with water
        reverberate valleys
    the streams flow, kiss ocean, for
        abundant fish
    but now
    she screams leftover shrapnel
        —holes they dug into her flesh
    she cries basins of unexploded ordnances
        toxins seeping into her core
    gates ropes fences bridge kapu
        to keep hawaiians at bay, her silent

what would you see in makua?
    before contact
    kanaka work lo'i kalo
        throw net in water
        feed families mauka to makai
    keiki would play streams
        keep their parents company
        fill air with laughter
    kū dictates war
        lono brings harvest
        hina controls bodies
    kaula loops generations
        weaves keiki with kūpuna with mākua
        waiting for mo'opuna
    but now
    ka makani blows against alien greens
        kiawe roots deep in her,
        spread by british cattle

two times a month kanaka are allowed
to visit ʻahu and pōhaku
but can't leave hoʻokupu
(unless it's on the itinerary)
yellow ropes bind
inaccessible gravel paths,
separating artifact from kin
archaeologists decide what is historical
what we leave, what we touch
and how we love our ʻāina

what parts do you wish to share with makua?
i ask makua to receive my unknown genealogies
my kūpuna from the philippines
my kūpuna from japan
my kūpuna from honduras
and my kūpuna from hawaiʻi
i share with her my tears
breathe her in as
she holds my ea close
feel her breath beneath my feet
i bear her ʻeha in my bones

what do you wish to carry from makua?
i carry the mist that descended from the valley
caressing my skin as
she soaks in the leo of her ʻōiwi
i hold her histories
when i enter her waters
feel free as
makua smiles back

Absorb the maunga

Courtney Sina Meredith

Whisking egg whites surveying urbanity
what attitude does longitude have towards longing? Or is it forwards implying
only one of us will move?

Inferred state
let the rest be obtained
let the glow dissipate

clouds arrange my longing
stay away stay alone
eventually outnumbered

we all come from space
we all reappear

predictably cyclic. Float apart absorb the maunga
umbra penumbra antumbra.

Wistful Thinking

Monique Storie

In 1976, my family moved into the newly constructed Latte Heights Estates at the top of Macheche Hill. Our old house in Kaiser Dededo was the three-bedroom home where we watched our air conditioner literally get sucked through the louvers during the height of Typhoon Pamela and where we shouted into the storm after my father ran outside to plug it back into the gaping hole in the kids' bedroom window. One afternoon, while trying to escape the monotony of the windless post-typhoon days, we drove up the hill to tour the new subdivision and ended up staying. In contrast to our modest Kaiser home, the houses in Latte Heights were bright white with glass-louvered windows and new owners had a choice of a lemon yellow–, burnt orange–, or avocado green–colored kitchen. When we moved in, I was so proud that we owned one of the most modern houses on island and that our streets looked like we belonged on television.

Although I liked my new home, I loved our view even more. At the base of the hill was a large valley filled with coconut trees. Morning times in this valley were just magical. During the rainy season, the valley would be blanketed in fog so thick that you could barely even see the island below. During the dry season, the coconut grove's dense canopy provided shade to all who passed (even those who were in cars). In the just-in-between times, the valley would be covered in an otherworldly mist that would lower the valley's temperature to incredibly cool. On those days, my dad would yell out the window of our car as we descended into the valley: "Look at the trees! Look at the fog! It can't be more than fifty-eight degrees outside!" On those days, we would stick our arms out of the windows, allowing our hands to ride the air currents brought on by the moving car and feel the coolness of the valley.

During the next twelve years, I silently wondered how the trees came to be there. "Were they all from one plant that was carried here from another village?" My mind quickly conjured up a Chamorro farmer bringing a coconut sprout from a relative's ranch, planting it, nurturing it, and painstakingly spreading out the seedlings as they began to root until the grove stretched from the base of Macheche Hill out to Marine Drive. "Were they part of an old copra plantation?" I imagined a white-bearded man wearing a white shirt, khaki shorts, and pith helmet staring at the trees counting his coconuts or miles of woven mats with coconut meats laid out to dry. Every day, we would drive past that lush green canopy and I tried to watch life unfold. When I would hear a crash or loud sound, I excitedly searched the grove to see if it was a bird, binådu, or babui, a frond, or a coconut falling to the earth, adding to the growing grove. On rare occasions, I would actually see a frond drop or the grass shake as a fallen coconut settled into the dirt. It was so cool to catch the exact moment that the grove changed.

In 1988, I went off-island for college, but whenever I came back, the coconut grove helped welcome me home. And I would spend the summer driving back and forth through the grove, enjoying how the canopy provided sweet relief from the hot summer sun. Then, one summer, I was greeted by a different type of tree. "Las Palmas" stood where my coconut grove once was. Rows and rows of row houses had replaced my beloved coconut trees. I cried out loud, "If it's called *Las Palmas Condominiums,* why aren't there trees . . . coconut trees or some kind of palm tree?! Why didn't they leave any of the trees?!" Deep down, I knew why. It was the same reason my parents had to buy dirt for our Latte Heights home twelve years earlier: it is more expensive to work around the trees than to bulldoze them down. For the next year, I mourned the loss of my trees, silently wondering, "Did they suffer?" and cursed myself for having to turn down the air. "When did Guam get so warm? Mom used to get so mad that I would wear wool to the fiesta and now I am absolutely melting by the time I drive down the hill." For years after, construction cut and cut and cut away at the coconut grove, taking away the lush tropical view, silencing the coconut grove, and replacing it with urban heat and noise. From the hilltop, I watched this new concrete jungle expand as it stretched from the base of Macheche Hill to Marine Drive, completely replacing the lush green valley of my youth.

I saw my island wither and pale and hoped for a miracle to bring it back. I wished for someone to listen to me when I suggested they let their land remain fallow rather than sell it off to a developer. I wished I could win the lottery so I could buy the land and keep the developers away. I have hoped for someone in power to say no to more buildings and yes to community gardens or to acres of *halom tano'*. I continue to watch, heartbroken, as my green valley turns into a concrete jungle, and I wish to return to the days when coconut groves made the island cool.

Wao / Vao

Karlo Mila

How can we find our way back?

We've entered this forest
of streetlights, skyscrapers
suburbs, streets, fences,
private properties, rentals,
real estate.

We've entered this forest
lost our language
left with another
that names the world
and knows it all,
without knowing the names
of the spirits
that roam the roads,
without knowing the rituals
to keep us safe.

We've entered this forest
no stories to guide us
that tell us where we are.
The only narratives we inherit
are theirs,
already the baddies,
we are Indians, savages
of the south seas,
they are in the cowboy hats,
captains of great ships
spinning silver pistols
the honour of armed forces, armadas
keeping everyone

safe
from us.

We've entered this forest
with only stories that don't
make sense.
No proverbs to warn us
of the dangers that lurk
in the whiteness of its dark.

We've entered this forest
with no elders
to interpret for us
the language of birds, cloud,
wind, insects.
And we've forgotten that the trees
and stones are still alive,
we can't tell which creatures
and plants are our family gods.
In ignorance we eat them.

We've entered this forest
on a Boeing, on a jumbo jet, on a banana boat,
what were our parents thinking?
We are so far from the already interpreted path,
our parents can only point to
books they cannot read.
There is no time for fananga, for mo'olelo,
after the late-shift of the second job.

Then,
a book
at university,
out of print
found in the library stack
held on another campus,
ordered,
waited for,
received.

A proverb
passed down
from one mouth to another
over centuries,

carried, remembered,
recited, passed down,
it breathes to me
unspoken
in the silence
of black typeset
from beyond.

O le gase a ala lalavao.

It enunciates with breath
of an ancestor
spoken in my awkward
English accent
I say it so slowly
but it will not roll
off my emigrant tongue.
My accent is shit.

Brother Herman
has translated it for me,
rendered it, intelligible.

The shade of high trees
will not allow the scrub
to cover your path.

The high trees
are ancestors
always watching
always overlooking
ever-present
ensuring
you find
the pathway
back to yourself.

Yes, they say,
ache in their leaves,
we will ensure
you will find
your way
back to us.

Throughout the Islands

Flora Aurima Devatine

Translated from French by Jean Anderson

Throughout the islands, the land has lost its shorelines, its plains, its valleys, cliffs, mountains, plateaus and hills.
Throughout the islands, the land is being eaten away, from the sides, in every direction, by the cancer of modernisation, globalisation, tax exemptionalisation.
Throughout the islands, the cankered land endures mankind's attacks, more destructive than the weathering of time.

Throughout the islands, the land shows its raw red wounds, the earth slashed open, bled dry in patches.
Throughout the islands, the gashed earth pours out red tears, surging from its bloodied entrails in torrents and cascades.
Throughout the islands, the disfigured land is cut to its very core, its integrity violated, its dignity suffering.

Throughout the islands, the land accuses our silence and denounces our complicity.
Faced with the specter of misery and the desert, both drawing near at supersonic speed.
Throughout the islands, the dying land is murmuring, "How can this be happening?"

And. now.

Shaylin Nicole Salas

My culture has been reimagined for your benefit
Our traditions pushed aside for your betterment
Our land exploited for your settlement

And now I should accept
that we are equals   The past is of the past
And we will move forward
Without reparations
Without revitalization
Without justice . . .

And now I should accept   How you criticize me   How my body has been colonized
My mind created in division   Not fully of me, not fully of you
Lost somewhere in the middle . . .

My culture has been reimagined for your comfort
Our traditions pushed aside by your hand   Our land exploited for your imperial design

And now here I am   A bougainvillea reaching between the cracks of the Tumon promenade
A grain of sand blowing at the edge of Ipan   A coconut crab waiting to be pet at Chamorro Village   And now   here I am

LET THE MOUNTAIN SPEAK

Vilsoni Hereniko

Did you ask me what I want?

Or are you going to speak for me?
I was here before you arrived

And I'll be here today and tomorrow.

Some say I have eyes and teeth,
Others say I'm the perfect mountain,
But have you asked me what I want?

Lay down on the ground!
Feel my truth below your belly button.

Then crawl on your hands and knees
Climb to the top of my summit
Where I wait patiently for your arrival
To break you open!

Now that you're broken open
I will send you down.

Embrace your mothers and your fathers
Your brothers and your sisters
Your aunties and your uncles
Your children
Even your children's children

See enemies with new eyes.

That's when you'll hear
What I want!

From *The Missing King*

Moetai Brotherson

Translated from French by Jean Anderson

. . . I had opted for a hermit's life, far from the world, out there at Te Pari. I had followed the track around the coast that starts at the marina. Every step took me a little further from civilization.

Three years in prison had taken away any desire to be around other human beings. Tihoti was okay. He didn't ask questions, didn't want anything from me. If I offered to help him, he accepted, but he never asked. It had struck me as self-evident that only a hermit's life would bring me peace, that inner peace people are always talking about. I walked for a long time, along the beach, well past the end of the track. The last houses were far behind me at the Aiurua River. Beyond that point there's nothing but nature, wild and untouched. I have to walk carefully, because the beach has given way to rocks that I have to clamber over. From the top of a low hill I can see Fenuaino motu. The last time I came here, with Amadeus, he told me some strange stories, all about tūpāpa'u on the island, which is one of the very few in French Polynesia to have a marae. I pushed on as far as Vaiote River. That was where I chose to spend my life as a hermit.

The phenomenal numbers of mosquitoes make it a very inhospitable place. That's what I'm looking for. A place where no tourist, no tramper, no hunter, would want to stop for a break. Even less to eat or sleep. One of those places people just pass through, because you're never welcome there. I think I must have been repulsive even to the mosquitoes. Or else I was just too lost in my daydreams to feel them biting. I walked up the valley the Vaiote flows down. In front of me, slightly overhanging the river, on the right, there's a hole in a rock. I've just found my home. From my cave to the sea, it's one thousand eight hundred and three paces. On the way back, two thousand and twenty-two. Obviously if it's uphill you take smaller steps. The first week was very tough. The difference between my cell and having this whole valley all to myself was disturbing. And you have to find food. When you've spent too much time in the city, or even worse, in the artificial world of prison, your senses forget what they're for.

Previously published, *The Missing King*, translated by Jean Anderson, Little Island Press, 2012.

I couldn't see. Not far away, the swarm of bees gorged on honey, tucked away in the hollow of a māpē trunk. The big prawns were there, beneath the pebbles in the river. The fat parrotfish threaded their way between my feet, out on the fringing reef. I didn't see them.

I couldn't smell. The scent of the miri, whose leaves are used to soothe toothache. The perfume of wild lemons, roots tucked into the rock, a dozen or so meters above my cave. The invigorating tang of re'a, native ginger, you can crush to give a refreshing juice. I didn't smell them.

I couldn't feel. The stalk of the tī, that becomes brittle when the roots are ready to eat. The flat seaweed on the shady side of the reef, whose sticky surface signals it can be dried. The velvety leaves of 'ape, too young to sting, but edible. I didn't feel them.

I couldn't hear. The sound of a coconut falling to the ground without splitting or cracking. The distant but unmistakable cackle of a wild hen that has just laid an egg. The noisy flapping wings of blackbirds chased from a mango tree by a harrier. I didn't hear them.

So by the end of the week the only taste in my mouth was Tauhiro's miti hue. I had just, very unwillingly, finished the second bottle. And then you adapt. Darwin was right, you adapt. You have to if you're going to survive. I recreated, or remembered, the gestures of our elders and made my first utensils, my first weapons. Oh, not to make war, just for hunting. The childish game of making traps soon became a steady source of food. My senses returned as well. I put to good use the carcass of an umbrella cast up on a beach by the southerly swell. A spear head. Fish hooks, skewers, toothpicks. By paying just a little more attention to the tides and the sun's course I located some little hollows in a big rock that was battered by wind and tides, where salt crystallised naturally. I also learned to tell from the smell of water when it's not safe to drink. Learned to choose the right pūrau bark to make lightweight ropes. Learned to weave coconut fiber to make the strong nape that can be used to catch big fish. Learned so many simple, but forgotten things. Three months went by, and the Vaiote valley finally had a hermit worthy of the name, living in total self-sufficiency.

Over the following year, I came to know the lunar cycle and the limits of the hermit's life. To find your way, it is not enough to cut yourself off from the world. You need an aim in life, even if that aim is to die, for example. But I didn't want to die, not after all my efforts to learn how to live with nothing, nothing but myself and nature.

I-Land-Ness

Sia Figiel

Walking for almost a year
Across Turtle
Island, Mario & i
Were often stunned into
Silence by the number
Of possums, raccoons
Rabbits, snakes
Foxes, porcupines
Deer, turtles
That lay battered
Alongside crosses
Decked with plastic flowers
& teddy bears on
The side of highways
& at the end of each mile
The ocean
That poured
From our skin
Tasted of blood
& bone
As we walked
Or sometimes ran
For our lives
While vans & cars
& SUVs & big trucks
Sped by
(With the occasional driver
Who stopped to give
Us a ride in the middle
Of a thunderstorm
Or a heatwave—though most were)
Oblivious
To our crossings

Or
The movements
Of wildlife stuck
Beneath their impetuous tires

Once we held a funeral for
An Owl in Louisiana
Next to the road
It was Winter
And the cold bit
Into our faces
And fingers
But we could still feel the warmth
Of her heart
& her eyes staring
Straight through us
As we dug a hole
& wrapped her in
Sycamore leaves
Returning her
To the land
With a small prayer for the dead
Ia manuia lau malaga Lulu
While a flock of geese in V formation
Honked across the sheltering sky

From "The Summer Island"

Kristiana Kahakauwila

An excerpt from a novel in progress

Synopsis: In 1904, pregnant and on the run from something or someone she has never named, Mele Wainui arrived at Leitfarm, a ranch on the coast of Washington State owned by Lidi Chapman and Jane Ellison. Prior to arriving in Washington, Mele worked as a domestic servant for the Chapman family, the most powerful sugar cane magnates on the island of Maui, and upon her arrival at Leitfarm she took up the same position for Lidi and Jane. But her relationship with her employers is complicated by the birth of her daughter Lena as well as the mystery of why she left Maui. In this excerpt, Lena reflects on her upbringing far from her mother's ancestral home and her relationship with her hanai aunts.

In those first years after my birth, Aunt Lidi and Aunt Jane lived year-around on the farm. Although they would indulge in weekend jaunts to Seattle, they put off all other travel. Lidi went without seeing Maui for three years, and Jane denied herself a mountaineering adventure in the Alps. Nothing compared to the home they were building, the child they were raising.

In photographs from this time I am glimpsed in a pram pushed by Jane or curled in her arms. In another, taken a few years later, I model a train conductor's hat while seated upon Lidi's shoulders. If my mother appears in these photos, then it is purely by chance. The corner of her skirt. The swirl of a shoulder as she turns away from the camera. Only once do I find her face, tilted toward the sky, laughing. Her hair in a loose bun at the nape of her neck, her teeth big and white. I wonder what made her laugh like that, what allowed her such momentary freedom. I am seated on her knee, my hands clenched around her fingers. A bonnet obscures my face, but I know I am laughing with her, mimicking her every expression.

The year I turned five, Jane and Lidi resumed their seasonal travel. They'd arrive to the farm in March to prepare the soil for planting and remain through harvest. In late September they'd depart for their latest adventure: a hunting safari in Africa, a painting course in Paris, a paleontological dig in Oregon. At some point each winter Lidi and Jane would visit Hawai'i, typically staying in Honolulu with

Lidi's older sister Elise, who welcomed Jane as if she were part of the family. Lidi would then travel alone to Maui to visit the rest of the Chapman clan.

During those winter months my mother ran Leitfarm, monitored the herds in the pastures, and directed the year-around labor in their duties. At some point I was enrolled in a local schoolhouse run by a Finnish man who was married to a Kootenai woman. They had homesteaded in Montana, only to leave there for the coast with their four children: three boys, all older than me, and a daughter, born the same year as I but whose intelligence would never increase past the age of ten. Mr. Jarvinen had taken over the schoolhouse in an attempt to protect his children from being sent away to a boarding school, and he was fortunate that the gambit worked. In fact, the school created a haven not just for his children but for others like his. Even the white children in the area, lacking any other options, were taught by him, and in some years we had up to fourteen students, half of whom were darker toned than me. My mother and Mrs. Jarvinen often assisted in the classroom, so a closeness sprung up, and the Jarvinens became our primary source of socialization when the Aunts were away.

The Jarvinens had, at one point, thought they would homestead on an island a short boat ride from the coast where we lived. They logged the land and then, realizing that their children were at risk even in the middle of the sound, decided that Mr. Jarvinen would apply for his teaching position. They kept the plot on that island, however, and built there a cabin and traditional Finnish sauna. Mr. Jarvinen called it their summer cottage, and as soon as the Aunts departed, he would motor my mother and me to the island to enjoy the final days of sun before the endless Washington rain began.

At Leitfarm, everything belonged to the Aunts. Not just the house or the land or the herds or the fields, but the times of day, the expectations, the rules and ways of being. In the farmhouse my mother and I each had our own room, identical to one other. A wooden bed frame pushed to the far wall, a nightstand, a dresser. I remember still the wool blanket, the itch of it under my chin, how once I awoke from a nightmare and went searching for my mother and found the same rough wool on her bed as was on mine. My feet were cold on that wooden floor and I was shivering, from the night and from my fear. The dream had been violent, my father's body in pieces on the ground. I tugged at my mother's blanket, wished to crawl in beside her, to cuddle into her warmth, the scent of her. But she refused. She led me by the hand back to my bed. She instructed me to sleep. She didn't even lie next to me. Just sat stiffly at the foot of my bed and waited until I closed my eyes.

On some level I knew the dictum to which my mother was responding, how Aunt Lidi believed it was unhealthful for a child to sleep with a parent. It bred illness, a suggestion of the old Hawaiian ways. But that did not prevent me from feeling alone, separated from my mother as if by a wall. Furthermore, in being separated from my mother, I was separated from stories of my father. I knew she and Kaluhea wrote letters to each other, long epistles that she handed to the postman, never allowing the Aunts to mail them on her behalf. But I rarely heard her speak of Kaluhea. Aunt Lidi, on the other hand, had many colorful tales from their childhood together. The time they'd squared off in a one-on-one polo match. The time they'd raced to the summit of Haleakalā. The time he accompanied her and her father to Ke'anae, where they first met my mother. Aunt Lidi spoke of Kaluhea more often and with a greater affection than she did her own brother, and if she didn't quite long to bring Kaluhea to Washington, she did often note the regret she felt that she could not bring me to Maui.

My mother, in her practiced silence, never agreed or disagreed with this sentiment. Occasionally she allowed me to make a drawing for Kaluhea and enclose it with one of her letters. Once, when I was learning to write and added the words "To Father," my mother refused to send the drawing. It was the only time she established a rule of her own. "You will call him 'Uncle,'" she said, "in the Hawaiian way."

Aunt Lidi said my father had been injured in an accident, and my mother had nursed him. That's when they fell in love. He was unable to travel, however, owing to the lasting effects of his injuries. Aunt Lidi claimed that I, to avoid accidents of my own, should never approach a horse from behind, nor play around the thresher, nor swim in the ditches when I was alone. Because disease was bred in close quarters, I should walk daily, even when it was raining. Above all else, a girl like myself should guard my virtue, and so I prepared to be vigilant, against what I didn't know. Here Aunt Jane added that a woman's morals were superior to a man's, and that the time would come when I'd need to remember that. Then she grew misty-eyed and held my cheek in her hand.

Whereas the Aunts were quite vocal with some rules, others I knew without ever being told. I changed into a dress when we went to town, though we wore pants every day on the farm. I never spoke of the third bedroom, equal-sized to my mother's and mine, with a four-post canopied bed trimmed in white lace. At school, if asked who my father was, I was appropriately vague, alluding to an injury that prevented him from leaving Hawai'i. Because my classmates knew as much as I did about that territory—which was to say, nothing at all—my declaration was easy to believe. Hawai'i was so far off. It seemed a miracle anyone traveled there, or back, even if they were in perfect health.

At the Jarvinens' summer island, everything was different. The rules that governed my mother's and my lives did not apply, so that annual vacation became the only time I glimpsed something of who my mother might have been without Lidi or Jane. I remember the first time we visited the island, when I was probably nine or ten. The cabin had two bedrooms, the main with a double bed and the other with bunks for the children. When I went to make a bed in the bunk room, my mother told me it was too much to heat an additional space and not to bother. Instead, that night, with my aunts' voices in my head, I took the outer edge of the double mattress, as far from my mother as I could, and she let me. But in the morning I awoke curled and pressed against the small of her back, and I knew my body had found its way there, had wanted to be as near to her as it could be. She was awake. I recognized the shallow quality of her breathing, the little sips of air she took when she was alert and thinking, but she didn't move and neither did I, and I wanted to weep with the closeness of her.

In the morning we read and drank tea, and in the afternoon we swam. She showed me how the wind wrapped around the island and why the Jarvinens had chosen this side to build their dock—how the trees created a natural windscreen for the small bay. Mr. Jarvinen had shown her a plank of wood he had carved for his boys, a shallow canoe, he had called it, with edges rather than sides. She made me rest my belly on it and she swam beside me, one hand on the port side of the thing, as we made our way beyond the bay. When I paddled I felt like a turtle, my inner arms brushing against the wooden shell. "Lift your elbows more," she told me. "And scoot forward on it, so you're balanced on your stomach and not your chest." When I shifted my weight I could feel my hips and pelvis like a fulcrum. I arched my upper back and dug more deeply into the water with my hands. "That's it!" my mother cheered, letting go of the side of the little plank boat, and I sped ahead of her.

"Come back now," she called after me. But it was too late. I bolted beyond the protection of the bay and into the current. At first it didn't bother me and I thought I could easily turn around, which I did by sinking the lower half of my body in the water and holding the board while motoring my legs. But by the time I faced shore again, I had been pulled by the current and the island was to my right rather than in front of me. I kicked and paddled, trying to push myself in line with the bay, but the more I worked the less I moved.

At home my mother never swam in the ditches, rarely even went barefoot, while the Aunts would sigh with relief to plunge their toes into the sticky waters of the dikes. But now my mother made long, strong strokes. Her brown shoulders rising and falling, sleek as one of the otters who made their burrow above the beach. And as if she were that animal, when she reached me she took the head of the board in her hands and pulled it to her chest, so she was on her back floating and I above her. "Go, go," I urged her.

Instead she smiled at me, slow and calm. "Look," she said. "Watch the ripples on the water. Which way are they moving?" Even as I clung to the board, I did as she said. The ripples moved toward the open ocean for another couple of yards, but then the water went flat again, like in the bay. My mother churned her legs, gently angling us for the smooth surface. When we reached it, the current abruptly stopped tugging. We were far from the island but the smooth cut like a road straight to the outside edge of the beach. She released her hold on the board. "You go first," she said, and I understood that she would not help me. I was to paddle the whole way myself, following this flat strip of water. She stayed beside me, sometimes on her back looking up into the blue sky and sometimes on her stomach, her chin dipped into the sea, in an easy stroke that barely disturbed the water. When we reached the island I swam toward a rock outcropping, but she caught the board and held me back. "You'll cut your feet," she said simply. I followed as she outlined the shore without nearing the rocks. When we were in front of the pebbled beach, I lunged for land, my legs unsteady and trembling, while she calmly heaved the wooden plank from the water.

Then she splayed on the beach, and I followed suit, the stones pressing into my calves and back and shoulder blades, their heat calming my muscles. At home the Aunts were always the ones teaching me, and my mother listening, as if she, too, were learning for the first time. The Aunts showed us how to plant tomatoes, cut asparagus stalks, distribute manure in the fields. The Aunts urged us to take up handicrafts to stay busy in the winter, as if my mother wasn't busy enough with the farm and I with my schoolwork. The Aunts forbid paperback novels, encouraged the study of geography, insisted I write them weekly so they could follow the development of my penmanship. The Aunts. They loved me with an aching need that left no room for any other kind of love, so my mother found her role, acting as if she were also a child in want of their education and knowledge.

Even when the Aunts described my mother's childhood—one I knew they had not witnessed—or when they made claims of the Hawaiian people, my mother listened silently. Sometimes she'd nod in agreement and other times make no perceptible movement at all, the only sign to me that she might have opinions or memories of her own. But now, today, she had shown me a different side of herself, one that she did not allow to come forth on the farm, even when the Aunts were not present. I wasn't surprised that she could get me out of the current—I presumed any caretaker could and would do the same for their charge—but it was the way she swam beside me, how her body moved with ease through the water, and her voice, soft, calling out small suggestions—*use your legs more so you tire less, cup your hands*—that implied a lifetime of knowledge I was not privy to. How had I, her child, never seen this side of her?

A couple years later, just before I was sent to board at the Annie Wright School in Tacoma, I glimpsed something more of this aspect of my mother. We were again at the summer cottage, set to take sauna, which my mother relished. Some years she heated the stones every night of our sojourn. That evening we sealed ourselves in the tiny room and let the heat settle over us.

She ladled water on the stones, and the löyly thickened the air, wrapping first our shoulders, then our chests, then our thighs. "Like being inside an 'imu," she murmured. After thirty minutes or so she let herself out the wooden door. I stayed, determined to last longer in the extreme heat than my mother had, my skin tingling with sweat, my eyes bleary. Then I burst through the little door, ran barefoot to the water, and splashed into the cold. She was there already, in the midst of a gentle breaststroke, waiting for me. I realized with a bolt that she was nude. Her bathing costume in a pile on the stone beach. I had never seen a woman's body before. The Aunts always took care to undress in the bath, to keep a robe wrapped to their neck when they stepped from the steamed room into the hall. Even their nightclothes were thickly layered: a gown, a fastened robe, sometimes a long scarf they braided through their hair and draped down their side. I had the sense that a woman's body was different from mine—wider and with more topographical variation—but otherwise I had no idea of the details.

Now, as my mother and I returned to the flickering light of the sauna, I could see her for the first time. I peeked at her breasts, the dark circles around her nipples, the long wiry hairs. She had hair on the mound of her pubis, and she had hair beneath her armpits, and all of it was dark and kinked. She even had little hairs on her toes, and I stared at my own toes wondering if and when I would grow hair there, too.

She leaned back against the wooden wall, her body expansive in the heat. Her eyes were closed, and as she inhaled I could hear the breath stirring in her throat. "Your body will be changing soon."

I nodded, as if I knew this, and waited for her to tell me more about what was to come.

"Our teachers never told us about these things in school. I think they were afraid of it, really."

When she didn't continue, I whispered, "Afraid of what?"

"Us growing up, becoming women. We'd know if what they taught us was true or not. The things they said about men." She laughed, her whole body shaking with some private humor, but her eyes remained closed. "I realize now that probably none of them had been intimate with a man. None were married. Some never would be." She laughed again.

"What is it like to be with a man?"

She paused, probably trying to guess at the impetus for the question. I wasn't asking about the intricacies of sex. We lived on a farm. I understood how a bull availed himself upon a cow. I more meant for her to tell me what it was like to live with a man, to have a family that included a man. Mr. Jarvinen sat at the head of the table in his house, but so did Lidi in ours. He hoisted his children above his head, raced them, taught them how to pitch and field. But, again, Lidi had done the same with me—would even join Mr. Jarvinen in training up their team of infielders, as they called us. No, there was some other quality of a man that I was misunderstanding. Some duty he served that could not be replicated by a woman, even one as capable as Lidi.

"Can you feel your skin right now?" she asked.

I nodded.

"You can feel, then, how it tingles, how the hairs lift in the first moments of heat, how your muscles after a time loosen and relax. How you can smell the wood and feel the nubs of the towels beneath you. How everything is a little sharper, a little more vibrant."

I closed my eyes and breathed deeply, ran my fingers along the wood edge of the bench, the tiny splinters there scratching my skin. Yes, I knew what she meant.

"This is what it's like to be with someone you love."

"So this is how you felt to be with my father?"

She was silent for a moment before she answered. "This is what I felt the first time I met your aunt."

Papa-tu-a-nuku (Earth Mother)

Hone Tuwhare

We are stroking, caressing the spine
　　of the land.

We are massaging the ricked
　　back of the land

With our sore but ever-loving feet.
　　Hell, she loves it!

Squirming, the land wriggles
　　in delight.

　　We love her.

Previously published, *Making a Fist of It: Poems & Short Stories,* Jackstraw Press, 1978.
This poem refers to the Awakening—the Maori land march that began at Te Hapua, the northernmost settlement of Te Aupouri, on 14 September 1975 and ended at Parliament Buildings, Wellington, on 17 October.

Mother's Chemo Cycles

Donovan Kūhiō Colleps

for Papahānaumoku

I help my mother walk her breast
through clamping hospital doors.

Moʻo have been gathering for weeks
around her chest, clicking, scratching.

At least it's not anchored, they say,
to land, to muscle and bone.

This thread of moons looping
back through the deepest of carvings.

Mōhalu
        Hua
                Akua
                        Hoku
                                Māhealani
                                                Kulua

This horizon is seeping ordnances

                                                Passing
                                Fullness
                        Sunken
                God
        Fruits

Unfolding

I try clearing the edges of her body
lacerated by plastic lei and styrofoam.

We throw down seeds
together in parking lots.

And we smile at the bold flowers
still sprouting from storied crevices.

Still singing from under the lesions
about returning to a sound coherence.

My body, she says, needs
old songs so I can tremble again.

The cardboard ʻuala is no good.
The Milky Way has soured.

I blend ʻōlena and ʻawapuhi
with ripe maiʻa for her nausea.

I watch my mother run hands through her hair
and the last ʻōʻō feathers fall.

Sing about the moon again, she says.
        Sing about fullness.
                Sing until everyone knows all the songs again.

FLOWERS, PLANTS, AND TREES

Plants grow roots and bloom in our writing as signs, symbols, and cultivated layers of meaning that have formed the basis for our island poetics. For as many island plants as there are, there are as many corresponding possibilities from which we shape our poetry, our stories, our specific connections to life cycles in place and in our movements. We craft language for our senses through the lessons we have learned from plant life; our desires and pleasures in sharing meaning bloom across these pages. Plants teach us the responsiveness, precision, and deep specificity of relations, reciprocity, and balance. They live in this section as guides for paying attention to our senses and focusing our sensuality, modeling the processes by which we reach out, sensing the world around us.

Over the course of this section, writers document how we use plants in our everyday lives, how they operate and grow (in) our languages, how they carry place-based memory and meaning. We use them not just to describe, but also to structure, how we define ourselves and our relationships to our environments. We work with and through plants to create medicine and heal ourselves, to remember and carry on stories, and to see what forms of being in the world our stories create when we shape them to bloom, weave, and unfold. Documenting our observations and relationships to plants allows us to pay attention to cycles of life, how we learn to sense and respond to the world, and how the repetition and variation of meaning in symbols grow and shape-shift.

The stories of this section also bring us into close observation and reflection on the nature of roots. What do the life patterns of our island roots teach us? What happens when we move them across oceans? What happens when we must translate our roots in different languages? How do we reclaim roots when our access to traditional planting cycles have been so drastically interrupted, at times directly burned, by processes of colonial expansion and waves of "development"?

The lives of our plants teach us possible answers to these questions in intergenerational lessons around growth, conflict, unburying memory, resilience, cleverness, tenacity, and resistance. Our roots—both in digging deep and moving vast distances—teach us a critical attention to context, specificity of relationships and reciprocity, and understanding of our immediate and intergenerational impact on the world. We trace some of the ways we story and re-story the meanings of our roots—our signs, symbols, and structures of making meaning.

Throughout this section, trace the language of flowers, plants, trees, and what these symbols bring into possibility and fruition. Here, we grow our structures of association and connection through metaphor and our multiple, place- and time-specific poetics. Layers of meaning grow from the appearances and cycles of our plants. In these pages we show pieces of our cultivation practices, storying relationships between the lives of our plant worlds, the language that grows from observations and use of plant life, and how those plants then carry our stories, memory, and layers of meaning across time and distance.

And so it is

Albert Wendt

we want so many things and much
What is real and not? What is the plan?

Our garden is an endless performance
of light and shadow   quick bird and insect palaver

The decisive wisdom of cut basil informs everything
teaches even the black rocks of the back divide to breathe

Blessed are the flowers   herbs and vegetables
Reina has planted in their healing loveliness

The hibiscus blooms want a language to describe their colour
I say the red of fresh blood or birth

A lone monarch butterfly flits from flower to flower
How temporary it all is   how fleeting the attention

The boundary palm with the gigantic Afro is a fecund nest
for the squabble of birds that wake us in the mornings

In two weeks of luscious rain and heat our lawn
is a wild scramble of green that wants no limits

Into the breathless blue sky the pohutukawa
in the corner of our back yard stretches and stretches

Invisible in its foliage a warbler weaves a delicate song
I want to capture and remember like I try to hold

Previously published, *NZ Poetry Shelf*, 2018.

all the people I've loved or love
as they disappear into the space before memory

Yesterday I pulled up the compost lid
to a buffet of delicious decay and fat worms feasting

Soil   earth   is our return   our last need and answer
beyond addictive reason   fear and desire

Despite all else the day will fulfill its cycle of light and dark
and I'll continue to want much and take my chances

Family Trees

Craig Santos Perez

1

Before we enter the jungle, my dad
asks permission of the spirits who dwell
within. He walks slowly, with care,
to teach me, like his father taught him,
how to show respect. Then he stops
and closes his eyes to teach me
how to *listen. Ekungok,* as the winds
exhale and billow the canopy, tremble
the understory, and conduct the wild
orchestra of all breathing things.

2

"Niyok, Lemmai, Ifit, Yoga', Nunu," he chants
in a tone of reverence, calling forth the names
of each tree, each elder, who has provided us
with food and medicine, clothes and tools,
canoes and shelter. Like us, they grew in dark
wombs, sprouted from seeds, were nourished
by the light. Like us, they survived the storms
of conquest. Like us, roots anchor them to this
island, giving breath, giving strength to reach
towards the Pacific sky and blossom.

3

"When you take," my dad says, "take with
gratitude, and never more than what you need."

Written for the 2016 Guam Educators Symposium on Soil and Water Conservation.

He teaches me the phrase "eminent domain,"
which means "theft," means "to turn a place
of abundance into a base of destruction."
The military uprooted trees with bulldozers,
paved the fertile earth with concrete, and planted
toxic chemicals and ordnances in the ground.
Barbed wire fences spread like invasive vines,
whose only fruit are the cancerous tumors
that bloom on every branch of our family tree.

4

Today, the military invites us to collect
plants and trees within areas of the jungle
slated to be cleared for impending
construction. Fill out the appropriate forms
and wait 14 business days for a background
and security check. If we receive their
permission, they'll escort us to the site
so we can mark and claim what we want
delivered to us after removal. They say
this is a benevolent gesture, but why
does it feel like a cruel reaping?

5

Listen, an ancient wind rouses the jungle.
Ekungok, i tronkon Yoga' calls us to stand tall!
Listen, i tronkon Lemmai calls us to spread our arms wide!
Ekungok, i tronkon Nunu calls us to link our hands!
Listen, i tronkon Ifit calls us to be firm!
Ekungok, i tronkon Niyok calls us to never break!
Listen, i halom tano' yan i taotaomo'na call us
to rise, to surround our family of trees and chant,
Ahe'! No! We do not give you permission!

Friend

Hone Tuwhare

Do you remember
that wild stretch of land
with the lone tree guarding the point
from the sharp-tongued sea?

The fort we built out of branches
wrenched from the tree, is dead wood now.
The air that was thick with the whirr of
toetoe spears succumbs at last to the
grey gull's wheel.

Oyster-studded roots
of the mangrove yield no finer feast
of silver-bellied eels, and sea snails
cooked in a rusty can.

Allow me
to mend the broken ends
of shared days:
but I wanted to say
that the tree we climbed
that gave food and drink
to youthful dreams, is no more.
Pursed to the lips her fine-edged
leaves made whistle—now stamp
no silken tracery on the cracked
clay floor.

Friend,
in this drear
dreamless time I clasp

Previously published, *No Ordinary Sun,* Blackwood and Janet Paul, 1964.

your hand if only to reassure
that all our jewelled fantasies were
real and wore splendid rags.

Perhaps the tree
will strike fresh roots again:
give soothing shade to a hurt and
troubled world.

In truth, I have gathered you all from the same garden

Teresia Kieuea Teaiwa

In truth, I have gathered you all from the same garden.

LANGAKALI

Konai Helu Thaman

Langakali!
Have you heard the latest?
The jellyfish at Fanga'uta swim freely in the wastes
Of Vaiola, refuge of our ailing brothers
From the north.
Hangale flowers, we'll pick no more—
Government houses have killed them all.
Yesterday I saw a child "swimming" in a 'umu
I said, "Why don't you go to the sea?"
He just stared at me in silence
Then said, "It's Sunday, can't you see?"

Must we wear this band of progress
Stand in line for the sweat
Of our brothers' brow?
Must we now wear trousers and neckties
To be respectable?
Must you throw this medicinal branch
Out the door?
It will put out roots
And one day the tree will destroy
Your brick house,
You, and your sick son.

Previously published, *Langakali,* Mana Publications, 1981.

langakali (Aglaia saltatorum)—a tree bearing clusters of very small brown odoriferous flowers, commonly used to make garlands, leis and scent Tongan oil. Rarely found today.

Fanga'uta—central lagoon on the main island of Tongatapu

'umu—underground oven

hangale (Lumnitzera littorea)—small tree with small red flowers, commonly found in mangrove forests. Rare today.

tamanu—a type of hardwood, prized for its timber, now almost extinct due to deforestation

Pulotu—the place where the spirits of the dead dwell

Hala Liku—the main road along the upraised coast of Tongatapu

Today I'll polish my son's shoes
For the parade—parliament's closing.
He'll stand on the broken pavement
Drink the sun's heat
But will not hear the proclamation
National airlines, royal tours, the Arabs.

(We need their money but not their religion).
"Stay, help your father carve
Heads from the tamanu,
For your fees and the church."
Must I wear this black garb for another day?
Grandma is probably laughing in her grave,
Her educated son wears leather boots
Even in the house.

Why do you weep Langakali?
Is it because they lied to you?
Or is it because they did not tell you
The whole story?
You see, the Four Winds did send me away
To bathe in the storm clouds;
A commoner with no soul I journeyed
In the grey hair of the sky,
But I heard the song of the sea,
Made my heart strong
That I could still find a place.

Langakali!
Did you begin to wonder
Whether I would ever return?
Would you see me again
Amidst the darkness and soot
Of our burnt-out fale?
They said that burning is good for the soil
But the trees suffer—
They take so long to mature;
Black coconut trunks, a dreadful sight
Headless they scorn the corrupted air.

The old man in the boathouse
Is growing weary.
He told me that he knew
The sea's origin, the moon's, the sky's
And even the sun's;

But he did not know
Why men deceive and women keep on loving them.
It was at Hala Liku that I met him
Alone, he only had the rain and the surf,
The land he gave away
They are building runways, hotels and warehouses
On it.
It was a stormy day
When he paddled away
In a borrowed canoe.

His son, he said, had gone abroad to work
For money.
He paid the Company for airfares
Accommodation and food, and
Came home a poor man.
Now his house belongs to the Development Bank
His boat belongs to the chief, and
He's working on a deal with the taxman
In respect of a sizable "gift";
Too many people are working
For money.

The sound of the conch shell
Haunts me still
Like the cry
Of my unborn child!
I remember his face
Turning away
Trying to hide his grief.
The masters of our land
Have sold our souls
To the new religion, moneylenders,
Experts and the watchdogs of Vegas

Langakali!
No longer do I see your face
Adorn our roads and roaming grooms
Or perfume the evening sea breeze.
Broken beer bottles
Greet the incoming tides
And gravetalk is no more,
For the unblinking eyes of plastic flowers
Stare away visitors from Pulotu,
Home of our warriors and conversationalists.

Pray, give me now a fast canoe
That I may join
The fish of the ocean
And together we will weep
For the works of the night.

Native Species

Dana Naone Hall

One day we went to see Rene,
who is descended from Hawaiians on both sides—
though he bears the French name of a family friend—
and found him at work in the botanical
garden that is full of Hawaiian plants
started from seedlings he grew himself.
We passed the fat black goats in their pen
unlike the ones on Kahoʻolawe
that the Navy has promised to get rid of
or to keep the populations so low
they won't get into the new plants
Rene plans to take to the island
after the first rains of the Makahiki
have settled the dust. Two thousand
to begin with, *all native species.*
When those cover the ground
in thick profusion and the scent
of hinahina is in the air again,
the shrubs will be planted.
Once they're established in native ground
places will be prepared for the tress.
All of this he tells us with his hands
clasped and resting lightly on his stomach
as we stand in the shade of the kukui tree.
Native species listening to talk about native species.
The native plants are disappearing, he says,
they're losing their habitat
and they're prey to ignorance and laziness
as much as to greed.
Out comes the story of the two Hawaiian coconuts
old trees that lived next to a brackish well

Previously published, *Life of the Land: Articulations of a Native Writer,* ʻAi Pōhaku Press, 2017.

along the dry coast at Mākena, near the bay
where the ʻōʻio were once as thick as sand.
Not long ago, someone came along and wanted
the nuts from one of the trees and cut it down.
The other tree is still there
but there won't be any more seedlings.
The male flower always blooms first
and after it dies the female flower blooms.
A single tree cannot make love to itself
and without another nearby of its species
there will be no more young trees.
Then there's the hao, name for Maui,
that he found growing along the same coast.
One of the trees is so old he suspects
it was there when La Pérouse came into the bay—
in the company of his own kind,
among the first white men to lay eyes on Maui.
Sometimes on his walks he comes across
a plant growing in isolation. When that happens
he says he asks himself why is the noni here?

I started thinking I'm living 300 years ago
I get one Malo on.
I'm thinking what I'm doing here
what kind grass is over here I need
for my house down the beach
or my canoe or for my fishing net.
Sometimes I get crazy walking
on the lava thinking about the plants.

By now we're following him around, hot and crazy
in the sun ourselves, walking on the lava,
and then he says

The Hawaiian plants are social plants.
If you go look underneath the Hawaiian tree
there's all kinds of plants that grow under them.
Ferns and vines and shrubs and other kinds of trees.
They all grow together under the Hawaiian tree.
But the nonnative plants are antisocial trees
like kiawe or the eucalyptus or the ironwood.
Go down to the beach sometime he tells us
and look at the ironwood tree, the mature
ironwood tree, nothing grows under there.
They don't like anybody else except
for one species, their own kind.

We figure we know what he's talking about
and we laugh.

I also figure that these plants are still
in the world because Rene knows their names.
He knows where they come from
and how to keep them straight
kolomona, nehe, ʻāwikiwiki, naio.
That's because he knows where he comes from
and he doesn't tell us but we understand
it's up to us to trace
our genealogy through the native species
and to get to know our own kinds.

Blood in the Kava Bowl

Epeli Hau'ofa

In the twilight we sit
drinking kava from the bowl between us.
Who we are we know and need not say
for the soul we share came from Vaihi.
Across the bowl we nod our understanding of the line
that is also our cord brought by Tangaloa from above,
and the professor does not know.
He sees the line but not the cord
for he drinks the kava not tasting its blood.
And the kava has risen, my friend,
drink, and smile the grace of our fathers
at him who says we are oppressed
by you, by me, but it's twilight in Vaihi
and his vision is clouded.

The kava has risen again, dear friend,
take this cup . . .
Ah, yes, that matter of oppression—
from Vaihi it begot in us unspoken knowledge
of our soul and our bondage.
You and I hold the love of that inner mountain
shrouded in mist and spouting ashes spread

Previously published, *We Are the Ocean: Selected Works*, University of Hawai'i Press, 2008 (1976).

Tangaloa and Maui are well-known Polynesian gods, and Vaihi (Hawaiki) is the legendary ancestral homeland. The kahokaho and the kaumeile were long yams sent as first-fruit tributes to the Tu'i Tonga, the semidivine ruler. (Orators refer to the monarch as the "Hau.") Takalaua, the twenty-third Tu'i Tonga, was killed by two men, whom his son caught, took to a special kava ceremony, forced to chew the dry roots of the kava plant for the king's kava bowl, and then had butchered for distribution to the assembled chiefs of the realm. Pulotu, the paradise, was presided over by Hikule'o, the goddess of fertility, whose earthly representative, the Tu'i Tonga, received (on her behalf) the annual first-fruit tribute. To Pulotu (and hence to Hikule'o) went the souls of dead chiefs, and from Pulotu came the great long yams—the sons of Tonga.

by the winds from Ono-i-Lau,
Lakemba, and Lomaloma
over the soils of our land, shaping
those slender kahokaho and kaumeile
we offer in first-fruits to our Hau.
And the kava trees of Tonga grow well,
our foreheads on the royal toes!
The Hau is healthy,
our land's in fine, fat shape for another season.

The professor still talks
of oppression that we both know,
yet he tastes not the blood in the kava
mixed with dry waters that rose to Tangaloa
who gave us the cup from which we drink
the soul and the tears of our land.
Nor has he heard of our brothers who slayed Takalaua
and fled to Niue, Manono, and Futuna
to be caught in Uvea by the tyrant's son
and brought home under the aegis of the priest of Maui
to decorate the royal congregation and to chew for the king
the kava mixed with blood from their mouths,
the mouths of all oppressed Tongans,
in expiation to Hikule'o the inner mountain
with an echo others cannot hear.

And the mountain spouts ancestral ashes
spread by the winds from Ono-i-Lau, Lakemba, and Lomaloma
over the soils of our land, raising fine yams,
symbols of our manhood, of the strength of our nation,
in first-fruits we offer to our Hau.
The mountain also crushes our people,
their blood flowing into the royal ring
for the health of the Victor and of Tonga;
the red waters from the warm springs of Pulotu
only you and I can taste, and live
in ancient understanding begat by Maui in Vaihi.

The kava has risen, my brother,
drink this cup of the soul and the sweat of our people,
and pass me three more mushrooms which grew in Mururoa
on the shit of the cows Captain Cook brought
from the Kings of England and France!

DER TRAUM

Witi Ihimaera

The Man Wakes Abruptly

The man wakes abruptly after having had half a dream.

His dream has been moving in a certain direction that isn't to his liking. Uncertain as to how it will resolve itself he says *No*, very firmly, and forces himself to wake up.

In the dream, the man had been in a small van, perhaps an eight-seater. He was on a tour of the South Island with indigenous friends who were familiar to him but whose names he couldn't recall; as soon as the dream was over, they disappeared from his subconscious. The dream began just as the van was leaving a busy metropolitan market. His friends were all artists, carvers and craftsmen, and among them was a weaver, maybe in her fifties. As the van was waiting at the lights of the busy intersection, she looked back.

Silhouetted against a red sunset was the marketplace with its jumble of stalls. Close by was a flax vendor. *Oh, what beautiful harakeke,* the weaver said. She began to cry, and the sound of her weeping invaded the dream. A tear, like lustrous jade, fell slowly from her left eye.

For some reason, the man felt sorry for the weaver. He called to the driver, *Let the woman go to buy the flax,* and then, immediately, he felt embarrassed. He had overstepped the mark as such a decision to stop was the responsibility of the tour director, a young woman. He apologised to her. It was clear that the young woman was annoyed, *We are running late,* she answered, but she nodded to the driver to let the weaver out.

The weaver ran through the bloodred sunset past the many other traders to the flax vendor. They began to talk, but something went wrong because the vendor began to shake his fist. He called over another person and the arguing escalated. Clearly the weaver was continuing to offend. The anger was menacing. *You don't want to pay?*

I will pay but your price is not a fair one.

The price I quoted is the market price.

The argument rose to a crescendo. The man heard the woman say, *Harakeke should not be sold in the first place.* He thought, *I better step in.* He got out of the van but before he could go any further, the flax seller and the person with him—the manager of the market—approached. They had taken the weaver into custody.

She has offended us, the manager said. *She asked if she could purchase our harakeke and is now objecting to the price. If you wish to have her freed so that she can rejoin you, it will cost 98 dollars.*

The man looked at the tour director, expecting her to take charge of the situation. Instead, the young woman looked at him. At that point, not sure if he wanted to take responsibility, he had decided to wake up.

I Need to Explain

I need to explain a particular circumstance that makes the man's dream somewhat unusual.

The man was in Berlin when he had the dream. He had flown seventeen hours from Auckland to Dubai and then six hours to Germany, with two stopovers of three hours each. One day he had been in the Southern Hemisphere, the next in the Northern.

It also happened to be Easter, a time when the Christian world reflected on its humanity. And as anybody who visits Berlin frequently would tell you, the city at any time was an utterly fragmenting experience: it forced you into personal encounters with a history characterised by constant reinvention. On previous visits, for instance, the man had considered the city to be in self-denial about its past, especially its Nazi history and division into East and West Germany. But now he admired Berlin because, ever since the wall had fallen, it had gained great momentum. The most obliterated country of World War II was now the undoubted leader of the EU.

Let me tell you more about the man's itinerary. He was staying in a well-known hotel just off the Unter den Linden. And yes, he was with a tour group from New Zealand and Australia, some of them artists, one a weaver—and there was indeed a tour director, a young woman, concentrating on the operation of the tour rather than her group. Therefore, reality had certainly coloured the man's dream.

So too had the group's cultural programme. On the first day they had visited the Brandenburg Gate and the Holocaust Memorial, always sufficient to remind him of the city's troublesome histories. Their first evening out had been to see a performance of *Adam's Passion,* a new production by Robert Wilson based on Arvo Pärt's music, *Adam's Lament, Miserere, Tabula Rasa,* and *Sequentia;* after being expelled from the Garden of Eden, Adam anticipates all of mankind's catastrophes, blaming himself for them.

A few days ago, on a tour to Potsdam, the old city of kings and kaisers, flakes of snow had started to fall; the man was reminded, sentimentally, of a snow globe; but there was nothing sentimental about shopping among the expensive shops in the Friedrichstrasse, and there the snow was real and bitter to the taste. In one of the shops the man saw a beautiful shimmering cloak, made entirely of feathers like a Maori cloak, but reconstructed as an haute couture high-end fashion creation. The price tag was exorbitant.

Although the cloak delighted him, the man had sensed something disturbing. *Everything in the world is for sale,* he thought, *even us.*

The night before at the Staatskapelle Berlin the tour group heard Daniel Barenboim conducting Debussy's *Le Martyre de Saint Sébastien.* Last evening, they had been at *Das Wunder der Heliane,* the extraordinary opera about a stranger from a distant land who commits suicide and is then resurrected by his lover.

The sonorities and their dissonance only served to amplify the man's thoughts on life, it's transformation, transfiguration, and, yes, transubstantiation. The change of something natural into something manufactured—a feather into a cloak. The placing of a monetary value on a simple item, like flax, even though the essence had not changed.

And so the man had awakened from his dream at three o'clock—or was it four o'clock?—the change to summertime only adding to his disorientation. He made a cup of tea and watched the grey light seep along the Berlin boulevards. But the dream still disturbed him.

He began to ponder a scenario that might have occurred had he not said, *Stop.*

The Man Heard with Anxiety

The man heard with anxiety the manager's decision, *If you wish to have the woman returned to you . . .*

The situation could quickly spiral out of control and he had to think fast. The manager held the upper hand, he the lower. This was the world as a global marketplace, whereas the man and his colleagues were indigenous visitors. And so the man began to negotiate for the weaver's release by being conciliatory.

I respect your decision, he said in a contrite fashion, an attitude against his nature. *However,* he continued, asserting his own mana, sovereignty, *it has been taken unilaterally, and you present it to me and my fellow companions as a fait accompli.*

Experience had taught the man that sometimes it was better to establish an arena of negotiation as fast as possible, and he was pleased to see the manager take an unconscious step backward; sometimes, negotiation skills from people of colour were unexpected.

Your woman was disrespectful to the principles of our business, the manager rejoined.

Let us see if she was, the man interposed quickly, preferring not to seek permission to proceed from the manager. *After all, both you and I were not witness to the encounter between her and the flax vendor, you being in your office before being attracted by the commotion and me in the van. Shall we talk to the vendor first?*

A large crowd had gathered to observe the proceedings. The manager called the vendor of the harakeke to come forward. *The woman was rude to me,* he said. *She came running to my stall and ordered me about, rummaging through my flax and choosing the best stalks. And when I told her what the price was she refused to pay it.*

The man gestured to the crowd. *Can anyone among you verify the vendor's story?*

An elderly man spoke up. *The woman was certainly in a hurry,* he said, *but perhaps she was less rude and more anxious to finalise her purchase.*

And what price did you charge her? the man asked the flax vendor.

Ninety-eight dollars.

A murmur rustled through the crowd. Clearly, ninety-eight dollars was on the high side. But the flax vendor defended himself. *It's the market price; the stocks are based on supply and demand.*

And, *The woman's offence still stands,* the manager said. *She refused to pay.*

The man paused, wanting the crowd to know that he was pondering the manager's words with care. *But clearly there are mitigating circumstances,* he began, *and we are adjudicating not just on the commercial value you put on the transaction but, at origin, an even larger question to do with custom, not cash. Who owns harakeke?*

The crowd appreciated his observation and there were some nodding heads. The man pressed home his point. *Therefore,* he suggested to the manager, *if we expand the focus of the offence, perhaps the woman's error might be considered against a wider, more informed, background?* After all, cultural context, while a minefield—whether it be Maori or for that matter, Syrian, Palestinian or Turk—was a valid defence.

It was appropriate that the man should direct the question above to the manager because that allowed him to make the judgement and, by it, prove his magnanimity to strangers. It also revealed his essential fairness to the vendors who rented the stalls in the marketplace.

Okay, the manager agreed and, at the words, the man sighed with relief. He wondered why the tour director herself had not joined the debate and realised that such people occupied a curious position in any negotiation. They had their own agenda, in particular the need to continue to maintain their contracts with the market.

This scenario agreed to, the man was happy to add it to his dream. But as he continued to drink his tea, he became irritated about not finding a way to resolve the dream and give it a satisfactory conclusion.

What had caused him to dream the dream in the first place? Certainly I have earlier pointed out the external factors: Berlin, Easter, the resonances from his stay in the city.

There were others.

Sometimes a Dream

Sometimes a dream is a metaphor for what is engaging our brain at the time. In this respect, perhaps I should tell you more about the man. In particular, what he had been thinking about while at sojourn in Berlin.

It had not helped that on his way to Europe via Dubai he read Salman Rushdie's new novel, *The Golden House*. In the book, an uncrowned seventy-something king from a faraway country arrives in New York City with his three motherless sons to take possession of the palace of his exile, behaving as if nothing is wrong with the country or the world or his own story. But clearly there is. With all three. A new president, Barack Obama, is elected at the beginning of the book, and by its end his successor is appointed, whom the protagonist refers to as "the Joker."

Reading Rushdie itself was, for the man, a parabolic experience, especially within these days when the global order was undergoing huge traumatic changes. The world was seeing the return to Great Power politics that were not necessarily only due to the comedian in the White House or to the shape-shifter in the Kremlin. The bewildering nature of the new order had also conjured up the ivory child, shooting off nuclear toys from a Korean palace. Elsewhere, the world was being dictated to by a killer klown in Syria and many others of his ilk.

China had, within all this, become surprisingly the newly appointed moderate broker, the smiling tiger in the world firm. Meanwhile the Lutheran pastor's daughter kept the EU to its cooperative principles as much as she could. Add the chaos of refugee migration, fuelled by wars in the Middle East and Africa, and you had a picture of utter destabilisation.

And, well, the internet Millennial Moguls were putting their own spin on global culture, politics, and finances and creating out of it a new metastasising world order.

It was clear that the existential crisis had had a trickle-down effect, even to the man's dream world; moemoea had always been the place where he could figure out where he and—by extension—indigenous people existed in an international political, economic, and environmental bubble over which they had little control. Coming from islands of Oceania did not secure their safety; they were not immune to what was happening in the rest of the world. Their world was the international world. The global story was their story, the international marketplace their reality.

Like it or not, their own cultures were tradeable commodities, and there was no free pass.

Nor had reading the daily *New York Times* while in Berlin brought the man any joy. An analysis in the international edition of 28 March had caught his eye. Written by Peter S. Goodman under the headline "Global order is assailed by the powers that built it," the man had focused on two sentences.

First: History was not supposed to turn out this way.

And second: In the place of shared approaches to societal problems—whether trade disputes, security or climate change—national interests had become primary.

After decades of promoting cooperation, the globalists were losing. And when they lost, so would indigenous people lose, for once the gates started to close again, they could be shut out of the political and economic endgame.

Was this why the man had dreamt what the Germans would call his *traum*?

And So the Man

And so the man decided to resolve his dream in the following way.

The *traum* had become his deeply unsettling trauma, but once the parameters of the negotiation were agreed upon between the man and the manager of the market, there were enough mitigating circumstances to enable a judgement to be made. The weaver was released.

Everyone began to hongi, press noses, in the sign of respect and conciliation. Emotions were smoothed over. There had been no sale. *Let's get back on the van,* the tour director said. She was pleased that she would be able to bring another tour group back to the market.

And that would have been the end of it except that the man still couldn't let the dream go. Instead, two further questions rolled around in his brain:

First, must all negotiations be based on political considerations, particularly self-interest—on notions of, say, America First, which is really Trump First? Or, second, on economic considerations—the trade deals, say, which have seen self-interest prevail, as witness Mr. Trump bypassing the World Trade Organisation (he calls the organisation a "disaster") with tariffs here and there?

Instead the man decides on an addendum to his dream, which counters that bargaining basis.

Taihoa, he says to the tour director. *Wait.*

He places a gift of ninety-eight dollars on the ground between himself and the manager. As he steps back from the gift he says, *Large animals should not fight, for if they do all the grasses beneath their feet get trampled.* It is an appropriate gnomic utterance that those who are there will interpret how they wish. The interpretation will depend on the hearers' backstories and how they feel at being brought against their wills to the brink, for instance, of environmental collapse.

The manager interprets the utterance his own way. He sends out a representative to pick the money up. But before the representative steps forward, he says, *One moment.* He orders the flax vendor forward to offer the appropriate reciprocal gift.

The harakeke, the flax.

Take whatever moral you want from this story. Regard it as you wish, it only has merit if you think it has. Consider: in the dream, the man has offered the manager a redemptive act, but in the real world, could it or would it ever occur? Or is it simply an act of sentimental wish-fulfilment that the man makes to enable him to feel better—to give him a sense of having some power or hope in a situation over which he has little power?

Be that as it may, never forget: a story is a free gift; it does not need to have merit or meaning. Nor does a dream need to make sense or be consistent, comprising as it does oscillating experiences of hope and terror, pleasure and nightmare, which amount to something . . . or nothing. Sometimes it is better not to remember them at all but to let them fade with the dawning. But the man is not like that. His cross is that he must never forget.

Therefore pity him because he has been truly frightened by the dream. And now, still worrying over it, he is asking himself, *Why ninety-eight dollars?*

Ponder this question with him as he drinks his tea and imagines white-winged angels coming with the day to perch upon the towers of the city.

In Berlin, in the early morning. At Easter, while the workers tread the streets below.

Easter, Berlin, 2018

Lele Nā ʻUhane o Nā ʻOhiʻa

Jessica Carpenter

A ruby heart
Caged in frosty ribs of snow
With each pluck of this soft thorny gem
Falls a crackling flood
A blessing, a cry, a breath of life to wash away drought

A pale opal pearl
Encased in grey, brittle shell
For every fall
A feather dusts the pine below
With the absence of a single pluck
With the silence of a chant
With the stifling of a breath
To put out every fiery cheek

Your crowns fall down
Constant as the rain it causes
And silent as a slap from an axe is brutal
Its quiet, roaring passionate fiery ʻeleu mana
Plummets to a flatline
What used to be a beautiful sunrise
To hōʻike the blossoms of life you laid to birth
Is now shameful exploitation
To the tune of excruciating silence

A dry dark congregation
As each bone laid to rest
After each bud has leaped
Lele nā ʻuhane

lei-making

Ryan Tito Gapelu

tūtū's brittle fingers weave tightly,
story and history into the blood of us
her children over and over writing
that he begot sons and they
begot daughters who bore sons and then
she begot them and they are in
new zealand but they send their love.

we are being written into the song
that tap-tap-taps tatau onto boys
and births men submissive to duty,
that marks towering women
with the mana of chiefs
singing the ink into our tongues until
our very cells sing of dancing
winds agi a luga, agi a lalo, singing of
maui's stolen fire falai-ing corned beef and onions,
threading steel fish hooks that birth
marae, malae, mala'e
binding us to the oceans she crossed
carrying in her belly
the future beating
at the walls of her womb
to be born into the dirt
with our heritage
intact.

she is weaving, weaving tightly
teuila and frangipani with tī leaf or tuberose,
human hair and whale bone,
crimson covered pandanus,
lacquered kukui, ni'ihau shell,
tapa, kapa, siapo, ngatu,
adorning ourselves

in the wealth
of belonging.

tūtū's brittle fingers sing that these
frail things connect you,
you my children
you my children of
havaiki, savai'i, hawaiki,
kaliponia, niu sila, ausetalia
it does not leave your chest
though you wander
as she wandered
on the water following the sky
clasping her hands to her heart praying
that land would sprout
from beneath her massive waka
soaring on the first jet liners
guiding our tupuga further
than their va'a could sail
past amelika off into
the universe dancing in
the circle of places
we had not seen
but sang of
anyway.

tūtū's brittle fingers place it
on your neck and it never leaves
because on its own it is weaving,
weaving, weaving, and you
are never forgotten because
it is singing, singing,
singing, and you are
honored because your lei,
your kahoa,
your ula,
your salusalu
saves you a space
in the memory of us her children,
a part of the constellation that is her
genealogy, in the stories
of the old and new,
in the weaving
of history
of story.

sing and weave and
tap ocean children,
steer and soar and run
ahead from the malae
keep your garlands
to your necks
with them
you are
permanent.

tala

Leora Kava

v., to tell, relate; to state, assert; to tell, command
n., thorn, prickle, spike, barb, or bristle

the movies i loved most as a kid always
had a spike or barb in them

from *Beauty and the Beast* and *Sleeping*
Beauty to *The Secret of NIMH*

stories were *talatala'ia, abounding in*
thorns:

a rose in the way of telling time

briar and thicket, names for protection

the rose bush, a resistance movement

clever and catching onto any unsuspecting
pant leg, t-shirt collar, or soft palm

a story was the sharp thing to tell, relate,
assert, command

what made me pay attention to my hands,
how i would carry and give away each
spike, barb, bristle

What the bush really wanted

Tevachan

Translated from French by Jean Anderson

This is the story of a bush
That wanted to become a tree,
To do this
He needed to be in the earth
So he could spread out his roots
But he was in a pot
Where every year
People would put him into another pot
Always a bigger one
Whereas what he really wants
Is to explore places unknown
Thanks to his roots
And in this way to be linked to Mother Earth.

Trongkon Nunu

Arielle Taitano Lowe

Si Nanå-hu biha, ti komprendi yu',
annai kumuekuentos gi fino'
English.

If I speak in English,
my great grandmother can't understand
what I'm saying.
Her native language,
my native language,
is rooted in this land,
just like the banyan trees,

i trongkon nunu,
connects us to our ancestors,
i taotaomo'na,
the first Chamoru people.

And through
invasion after invasion
conquered by Spain,
captured by America,
occupied by Japan,

Waves of genocide,
colonization,
and imperialist policies,
have tried to cut out our native tongues and
uproot our ancestry.

Spanish and Japanese invasions couldn't
eradicate our birdsong.

But Today,
back in U.S. hands,
re-occupied by America since 1944,

In my generation,
we are told as often as the ring of school bells that
i fino'-ta, our Chamoru language is disappearing.
Dying.

Like the absence of birdsong
  in our trees.

Decaying like a
trongkon nunu
slowly rotting with disease.

On our island, English was
forced upon my grandparents.

My grandma tells me
how she was punished for
speaking Chamoru in elementary school.
I wonder if she knew
an English Only Policy
would spread from the school hallways,
into the school bus,
into our home.

In my family
I come from a second generation of Chamorus
whose first and often only language is English.
In just two generations
our island let this species take hold.

Wake up!
English may be beautiful in its own right,
but it isn't native to this land.

I've been pushing through the leaves of books,
and digging through the roots of my family,
trying to nurture a language
my grandmothers couldn't pass down to me.

And my roots have led me to them.
My grandmothers taught me
what good soil looks like.
That learning
Chamoru
is as easy as asking them questions.

I can't deny
that language revitalization
lies on my tongue.
Buds of banyan flowers
waiting to bloom as red
as my grandmothers' achiote stained hands.

Sen gef pa'go i fino'-ta.
Our language is so beautiful.
My generation may not be flourishing with fluent speakers,
but like my grandmothers say,
we are made of good soil.

Ti sina fumino' yu' perfekto
lao bei hu chagi kada dia para i lina'la-hu.
I may not speak perfectly,
but I will practice each day,
and pass on what I can.

Dumodokko' i simiya gi pecho-ku.
The seed in my chest is growing
with the strength of my ancestors.

Dumodokko' i hale gi simiya,
anai kumuekuentos yu' gi fino' Chamoru.
Roots burst from this seed
with each Chamoru word I speak.

Dumådangkolo i ramas
gi trongkon kanai-hu yan gi petnå-ku
The branches are growing inside my limbs.

Ha chalalapon i hale nunu gi tataotao-hu.
The roots are spreading through my body.

I metgot na håle nunu
sina ha pokka' i simento.

The strongest roots can
crack colonial cement.

Teniki mayamak i simento,
anai kumahulolo' i hale manantigu.
This colonial foundation will crumble
as the roots of our ancestors rise.

Gathered by Plants: Some Decolonial Love Letters

Lia Maria Barcinas and Aiko Yamashiro

To my oldest friend,

We first met in Guagua soil. Placed in a hole by mango loving hands.

You wrapped me in your roots and grounded me to the land. I watched as you grew so much taller and wiser than me. You stay in place, keeping me always home no matter where I travel.

I remember the summer when you shook the mountains with your laughter. Standing strong in the ground as you said to the world "this is me." Laughter hanging on to every branch. I watched as every fruit ripened and danced their way to the ground. A mungge mess of giggles turning the grass to gold, calling our sisters to bring their baskets and carts. They cartwheeled with you. All the trees around you held the laughter too, but it was you that everyone most wanted to taste.

I think about you always from across the ocean. Thankful for how you hold me in the darkest soil and clay. Under the moon, I hold you in my memories you are standing happy beneath the mountain. In my dreams, I watched you dance. I saw fresh woven Guagua overflowing with your laughter. Children arrived and climbed up your branches. All of us laughing together in Guagua. I watched you start to smile as they cartwheeled again and again and again. Your daughters planted with them. All of us golden and pink and placed in Guagua by mango loving hands.

~Lia

My grandparents' home is located below a mountain called Guagua. Gua'gua' in Chamorro is a woven basket. On the mountain there is a river which flows down and wraps around our house. The river makes the soil rich and everything grows more abundantly in the area. It is our family tradition to plant our umbilical cords with mango trees. Growing up we would spend all year talking about and anticipating mango season. My grandparents would talk about all

Previously published, *Ke Ka'upu Hehi 'Ale,* March 6, 2017.

the different varieties they knew of, each of the characteristics and what made each mango so special. They would talk about their grandmothers' mango trees and tell stories of how their mothers would smoke under the tree every day for the mango to bloom. I know a mango tree in Guagua.

"What do you know about bananas?" is how Aiko invited me to the East-West exhibit on Okinawan dance last November. On a Thursday afternoon we watched videos about the Okinawan traditional art of creating banana fabric and clothing. We shared our different stories about the plants our islands share—coconut, niyok, niu, banana, ito-basho, aga', mai'a, stories about how they grow, stories about what threatens them, stories about grandmas and their gardens of friends, how flowers are laughter not luxury.

Stories of hope. We wanted to further explore our families and histories in Guåhan, Okinawa, Hawai'i, but in a different way. We didn't want to connect over our stories of trauma, colonization, militarization, yet again. Instead, we wanted to remember and explore our islands' interconnections through the plants we share and love. What can plants teach us? How can plants carry us through our struggles?

We talked about coconut trees. How they give us everything we need to live. How they too are affected by militarization but also show us connections beyond it. We talked about rhino beetles, how they eat the heart of leaves till they cannot be woven. We talked about the feelings of despair and how when plants are sick we need patience. We talked about Belau, how their women teach us resilience. How when beetles came to their islands they kept planting coconuts and encourage us to do the same. How planting more can be the best medicine.

So much more than a thing in the ground. Plants gift us: sustenance, hold our memory, offer us a connection to places and people lost. Plants are creators of islands. A way to go home and grow home. They are mo'olelo. Medicine and healing, hope and resilience, adaptation and generosity. They are history, a way to remember childhood and family. They teach us navigation. They help guide our paths. They help us hold the connection we need to sustain resistance, the bravery to act.

Our list was long, but it was difficult to write about them while honoring their spirit and the relationships they create for us. We decided to write to them instead, expressing our love, offering gratitude, asking them for help with conflict and pain, for their wisdom, and trusting them in their thousands of years, that they know a better way.

When I pick mango with my Nana she will tell me stories of why they choose to plant everyone their own mango tree; "So no one will fight," she says, "all of you will have mangos to eat and when others come to ask for mango there will be plenty of mango to share."

My favorite thing about both my grandparents and mango trees is that they are sweet and generous. In recent years when I have been able to share mango with friends I now understand that joy and appreciate my grandparents even more for not only teaching us how to be generous but also for growing the mango trees which allow us to practice generosity in abundance.

Our mango trees were the first of many ways that my grandparents taught us to love and appreciate the land. They taught me that when we take care of and love the land it will feed not only ourselves but our loved ones, and our community too. This to me is one of the sweetest forms of love we can experience.

Dear mai'a, dear banana, how often have I stood under the shelter of your arms. You turn the sun's heat into a cool green roof. The neighbor opened all his windows to see you clapping your leaves into thin strips, to better dance with the wind. You were happy and safe enough to grow a family, peeking from under the roof you built. Thank you for yellow yellow hands hands hands hands, teaching us to share sweetness. To bring gifts for ancestors, to leave gifts for descendants, to bring something extra for the unexpected stranger who will help you along the way. Thank you for clean green leaves to imu, umu, to tender wrapping fish, embracing rice. I remember the destruction of moving you—centipedes, wrestling your bodies to the ground. Sap everywhere. Carrying your keiki in buckets of cool wet earth. Planting you again in Kāne'ohe, with prayers for a new start. You begin all my mornings green, reaching for the sky. You begin again, growing a family out of happiness and hope.

~Aiko

I signed up for an Okinawan dance class at the University of Hawai'i at Mānoa, looking for my grandmother somewhere in my hands, my weak wrists, kachashii fingers, strong bones. Yukie Shiroma shinshii had our class attend a visiting textile art exhibit and dance concert. A video with English subtitles taught us about bashofu—the beautiful summer cloth made out of woven banana fibers.

We learned it takes years for bashofu makers to prepare the plants—first pruning and chopping them to soften and straighten their fibers. Then the sticky slaughter for weaving, then boil and soften the fibers, then weaver's knot them carefully into longer lines, then chart out the design. And finally, weave by monsoon weather so the air is damp enough that the fibers won't break. I remember the scene in the video where two people had to stand on either side of a large courtyard, using their entire bodies to stretch the fibers out.

Bashofu taught me that a cultural art form is a way of practicing and remembering loving and committed relationships between people and plants. Bashofu depends on the soil, the air, the rain, the memories of generations of women, the dedication between people and banana to create something.

My father, second/third-generation Okinawan in Hawai'i, will tell me sometimes about the memories his mother didn't want to talk about. The bloodiest battle of World War II left Okinawa devastated. People leaping from cliffs to the sea below, by the thousands. Killing their babies in caves so they wouldn't be raped or murdered by the enemy, so their cries wouldn't give them away. Later being herded into camps by the US military liberators. My grandmother as a young woman, standing in line for food rations for her sister, going back for herself later, being screamed at by a soldier for lying, for asking for more than one person's share.

What happens when silences fall on soil, air, rain, memory. When war. So many stories about being hungry. Grandma's brother catching frogs all night long to eat over the fire. How my dad used to hide in seigo palms to be safe when playing tag or chase. How she told him the stories because he was the only person for her to talk to. Later when he was older and he asked for these silences again she looked at him, asking: how did you remember that?

I am looking for my grandmother in a book by K. Hendrickx called *Bashôfu: Banana-Fibre Cloth and Its Transformations of Usage and Meaning across Boundaries of Place and Time in the Ryukyu Archipelago.* She writes about another grandmother, Toshiko Taira. After the war, US forces cut down many banana plants to avoid the spread of malaria. Because Okinawans wanted to be American, traditional textiles were being lost. At that time, the desire for the crisp lightness of bashofu was fading. Into that silence, Toshiko Taira called women together to become weavers. Women who had lost their husbands during the war. These women wove and wove into a present reality where bashofu is a national treasure, a bolt of cloth something fine and even more precious than before.

When bananas reproduce, the keiki are genetically identical to their mothers. Sometimes I wish for memories and stories to be passed down whole like that, perfect. Instead I try to learn the art of catching glimpses: my grandmother's shadow dancing in the corner of my father's house. Planting banana trees. This is the muddled journey of decolonization.

To the amagosu,

I smelt you in his breath, days before he held you in his hands.

We used to eat your seeds like they were candy. Crack your fruits open just like Grandpa did.

You were my first amot lesson as I nervously followed Uncle Greg to your home in Billie bay. Sitting in the back kitchen with Nana and Papa, it was you that brought us health and practice. We filled up our cups as you gifted us with memories of when you filled Nanan Rita's morning pots. You hold stories of all the mothers and babies who would come to her door. She moves with you as you walk across the yard. Carrying the stories across the island and silently offering healing as you go.

When the moon stayed you called baby Rita to gather your leaves, We joked at how she moved just like her nanan biha. She has always been that way.

On my morning runs you follow me. I find you at Gotña too, growing in protest for the sacred spaces.

From Tagachang to Hagatna all of Grandpa's jungle neni love your seeds. Dark red, slippery sweet, suck then spit—amagosu seeds. I look at my baby cousins who are jumping in the jungle and I ask them if they want to taste. They think you're candy too.

~Lia

My grandparents came from the WWII generation. There were a lot of big changes during the post-WWII era and there was a lot of focus on eliminating our indigenous language and traditional practices. Much of this elimination process was conducted in schools where speaking Chamorro resulted in shame, embarrassment, fees, and physical punishment.

Traditional medicine has always been really interesting to me but growing up I was very nervous to talk to my grandparents about it. Traditional medicine is sometimes seen as a taboo topic (especially in Guam's very Catholic community). I noticed that Chamorro medicine was never something that my grandparents brought into our conversations in the same way they taught us about cooking, planting, weaving, or other traditions.

They would share pieces of knowledge like putting aloe on our cuts and burns, and eating certain foods for their health benefits, but amot was a conversation I felt I had to force out of them. I was afraid to ask them at first, afraid to request it from their silences. I would tiptoe around the question by bringing books about plants of Guam and asking them every question I could think of. I would sit with them for hours working up the courage to ask for the information that I really wanted.

When I did finally ask them to teach me specifically about amot, they had so much information. The medicine was growing all around me. My grandparents had taught us about these plants since we were little kids, knowing that it was medicine but only sharing after we asked. Eventually we made medicine together. They shared stories of their mothers making medicine while they were growing up. All of us drank a little bit of the medicine that day, but the thing that healed us most was to break the silences. I could tell there was a peace for them to finally share their stories and I'm so thankful to have those memories with them.

There is a proverb that says "Maolekna manggagao ya ti mana'i, ki manai ya ti ma agradesi." (It is better to ask and not be given, than to give and not be appreciated.) Whenever there is something I want to know about my culture or language, I try to remember this experience with my grandparents. Amagosu taught me that there is healing in asking.

One belief in traditional medicine is that the plants have a spirit and will grow where they are needed. Medicinal plants are especially found in sacred spaces. A lot of our sacred spaces are also places that are desirable for military and tourism.

The first protest I ever participated in was against a hotel construction at a beach called Gotña. After the ceremony my mom and I ran into some relatives who told us stories about collecting medicine from the area. They expressed their concern around development of the area because of how it grows certain medicines which are place specific. A lot of Guam's medicinal plants only grow in certain conditions, so when new projects are presented our community searches for the medicines of the space. The endangered nature of our medicine has become a way to speak out against new proposals.

When we hold actions or protest, the amot of those places provide us courage and reason to persevere. When we oppose projects that could threaten them, it is giving the plants our commitment to protect them and our sacred relationships to them. Our demonstrations might only last for a few hours, but as long as the medicine is growing our connection to those spaces continues.

The TV is loud enough that my parents don't notice when I come home. I carve the bittermelon into canoes. The seeds packed softly away for the journey: red stories, brown stories. The lines on the outside curving, raised veins, old hands. "Like I told you, the only ones that ate it were me and my father," Dad says. We fight about something else. He is quiet. "If I didn't like you I wouldn't say such things," he says. "The more you cook it, the less bitter it will be," he taught me. "You have to make your own taste," his mother taught him. We both like the bitter, but we have to think about everyone else who is going to eat too. Quietly, one door after another. A lucky night. Nobody forcing, just laying one quiet word at a time into the space between, hoping for a new pattern. "Do you always use fish sauce?" I ask. "No, I never did. At a restaurant, you spend all this time perfecting the perfect taste. But if you're a home cook, you just cook." Today there is fish sauce and tomato. Once there was fish sauce and calamansi. I was proud that day too, making my own taste for the first time.

Today, yesterday, tomorrow, the US-Japan government started construction of a new US military base in Okinawa, in Henoko Bay. Dredging, laying concrete blocks, setting up floating fences and guards to keep out the protestors, who have been guarding the bay for over twenty years. From O'ahu, I watch a video on Facebook posted by Okinawan Independence on February 6, 2017, of a grandfather being bundled and dragged away by police. Please give me the gift of stopping what you are doing, he says. *Itai, itai,* he says. *itai itai. where does it hurt. it must hurt in the memory, in the coral memory beneath the rib cage. where the bay lives. where the fish live. itai itai, where does it hurt. does it hurt all the way across the ocean, here. does it hurt in my grandparents, in their parents. does it hurt in salt water, in sururu, in nets, in dugong mouths. does it hurt behind the riot gear, in gloved hands. itai itai, in fences and patrols. it hurts in the singing, in naked feet. itai, itai, it hurts in the unborn children too. to bind up and drag away this place. it must hurt. it must hurt.* Norman Kaneshiro shinshii of Ukwanshin Kabudan, an O'ahu-based group dedicated to perpetuating Okinawan language and culture, shared with us that we are vessels for our ancestors' emotions, thoughts, memories, to which we add our own. Poems and songs should remind us of the stories we already know in our guts, bones, memories. That week, after uta-sanshin class, we talked about Henoko, and how hard that war generation fought. How they could meet pain with a resolve we can barely imagine. How they could commit their lives to peace. What do we do when we are faced with losing a place we love? I am remembering the lesson we learned from Aunty Pua Case and the Mauna Kea protectors: how we fight with aloha to protect our sacred places. How this fierce commitment to aloha is what will save our own lives too.

I will watch my teachers carve themselves into vessels to carry Henoko Bay. Hump coral mountains, ocean forests of paddleweed, walking goby, mangrove, anchovy and black tern, sailing dugong, moon tides and bright anemone—all of you, rushing forward into our homes, rushing into our families, filling our connections again.

Dear goya, how do I become a good vessel, strong, buoyant? How do I navigate the warships, the unexploded ordinance, the masked faces? How do I set sail by every memory in the sky? I know you are a wa'a to his bright bays, full of fish and clear water. I know you are a wa'a to where his mother is waiting to hold him. I hold your old wise hands, ready for the journey.

~Aiko

You are ancient dreams.

Brother and Sister our Beginning, and Daughter our Rebirth. Pontan Niyok—heavy, brown niyok—our clans begin when you drop.

Ancient canoe plants, voyager and navigator—we are islands. You teach us
that there is honor in migration, that there is innovation in mistakes,
and that we must plant our hopes from the ground up. Ancient mothers
carried you across the ocean to grow our homes away from homes.
Nana says if we have a coconut tree we will have everything we need to live.
You are my first dance teacher. Your spine bends and sways
with full futures, wound with your strongest fibers.
You crash bravely into my world,
breaking open parking lots, car boundaries.
My father used to sit in the car,
sit in front of the TV, and say that trees destroy pipes, walls, houses. I crack open your dreaming
to find a clean white moon, rising,
rising to dance with you in the sky.
Meeting you was like dreaming of an old friend. As if part of me has always
been here waiting with you. You sit in this valley calling
to the mountains, singing a gathering song. You hold and you hold us.
In ancient and sacred space. I feel your resilience and breathe it in.

Thankful. You offer me your ocean in a shell. Waves roll back
and forward. Futures and past.
You gather and you gather us in new patterns,
folding us into aunties' hands, into uncles' laughter.
I hold your fingers and follow you to Waiāhole, to He'eia,
to Kāne'ohe, to Maunalua, to Pauoa,
to Kamoku, to Mānoa.
To bridges, streams, grassy hills and elementary
school classrooms, to Marshallese Consulates.
You fold us into new responsibilities, new relationships.
Pull until the weave is tight,
until all our stories are touching.

Star Pines

Briar Wood

The whanau miss it every solstice,
standing just above the waterline,
felled by a wealthy homeowner.

Now there's a gap in the air where
the tree was chopped down, gratuitously,
a wounded space eyes scrape against.

Just one ordinary tree, but multiply it
a thousand times for every vanished plant
that put down roots to hold the banks

in place, where now erosion seeps sand
with over-reaching waves at each spring tide.
Centenarian tree; at least fifty metres tall.

Landmark, sentinel, a living lighthouse,
that rākau crossed the Pacific to put down roots
to hold the oceanfront with its geometry

and be called Norfolk further along the beach.
The summer after-comers wish it was here.
Green snowflakes on a humid summer day.

To Hear the Mornings

Haunani-Kay Trask

To hear the mornings
    among *hāpu'u:* a purity
of cardinals, cunning bees
    in shell-covered sleeves
        of honeysuckle,
            . . . the aqua undertones
        of cooing doves.

To seek our scarlet
    'apapane, Hōpoe restless
        amongst the liko
            and *'ōlapa* trees,
        shimmering the leaves,
            . . . shush-shush
                of burnt rain
                    sweeping in from Puna.

To watch our lustrous
    volcanic dawn seducing
        'elepaio, speckled beak
    sucking 'ōhelo berries
        oozing sap
            under a crimson sun.

    To breathe the Akua:
        lehua and *makani,*
            pua and *lā'ī,*
                maile and *palai*
                    . . . pungent *kino lau.*

Previously published, *Night Is a Sharkskin Drum,* University of Hawai'i Press, 2002.

To sense the ancients,
ka wā mamua—from time before
slumbering still
amidst the forests
of Ka'ū, within the bosom
of Pele.

To honor and chant,
by the sound
of the *pū,* our
ageless genealogy:
'āina aloha,
'āina hānau,
. . . this generous, native Hawai'i.

Make Rope

Imaikalani Kalahele

get this old man
he live by my house
he just make rope
every day
you see him making rope
if
he not playing ukulele
or
picking up his moʻopuna
he making
rope

and nobody wen ask him
why?
how come?
he always making
rope

morning time . . . making rope
day time . . . making rope
night time . . . making rope
all the time . . . making rope

must got enuf rope
for make hōkūleʻa already

most time
he no talk
too much
to nobody

Previously published, *Kalahele: Poetry & Art*, Kalamakū Press, 2002.

he just sit there
making rope

one day
we was partying by
his house
you know
playing music
talking stink
about the other
guys them

i was just
coming out of the bushes
in back the house
and
there he was
under the mango tree
making rope
and he saw me

all shame
i look at him and said
"aloha papa"
he just look up
one eye
and said
"howzit! what? party?
alright!"

"how come
everyday you make rope
at the bus stop
you making rope
outside mcdonald's drinking coffee
you making rope.
how come?"

he wen
look up again
you know
only the eyes move kine
putting one more
strand of coconut fiber
on to the kaula

he make one
fast twist
and said
"the kaula of our people
is 2,000 years old
boy
some time . . . good
some time . . . bad
some time . . . strong
some time . . . sad
but most time
us guys
just like this rope

one by one
strand by strand
we become
the memory of our people
and
we still growing
so be proud
do good

and
make rope
boy
make rope."

ANIMALS AND MORE-THAN-HUMAN SPECIES

Writing our relationships with animals both centers and decenters our ways of being in the world as humans. The writers in this section pose questions about our positions as humans in relationship to animals, while also narrating specific time- and place-based relations that position us outside of a hierarchy of species and into more nuanced positions within a web of relations. We become students in these relationships. These relationships define our practice of observation and closeness with animal ways of responding to and shaping the environment. We inhabit positions as collaborators, adversaries, facilitators, detractors, listeners, builders, lovers, and villains in our relationships to animals within an infinitely complex, tremendously connected world.

This section documents and navigates multiple forms of being in the world. Coming from very specific Pacific Islander contexts and histories, the stories in this section call us into relations of closeness with animal beings. These relations have been passed down in our languages and cultural protocols of observation. Our practical and existential considerations of our position and responsibilities as a species are encoded in our ancestral, contemporary, and futurist stories that document deep closeness between animals and humans.

One of the ways we demonstrate relations of closeness is in our stories of shape-shifting between what is animal and what is human. Our stories of transformation, of shifting and sharing bodily forms, signal ways of thinking about connection, similarity, and differentiation with animals and our curiosity about form and behavior as beings in the world. In our stories, we transform between animal and human forms; between our roles as guides, adversaries, tricksters, and hunters; between what feeds and what is eaten. We differentiate our forms at times, and become the same forms in others, exploring the meaning in inhabiting bodies that shape and are shaped by our environment and relationship to one another.

This section maps relationships to animals in terms of kinship, descent, conflict, and the intimate links between behavior and environment. Our writers narrate relationships to animals in order to show definitions of, and oscillations between, balance and imbalance. We tell these stories as ways of thinking through survival, ways of making home, and processes of movement. We pose frameworks for paying close attention to our immediate and intergenerational relationships with animals. In doing so, we document and examine our positions as actors within extensive, nuanced, and contested ecological structures of kinship.

Taonga

Tina Makereti

It started with a shell—the perfect, unbroken curve of its lip curled over a flash of iridescent blue-green-purple. Two strange things: the size of it, and the location. It was the wrong stretch of coast for paua. And it was so small. Perfectly formed, but small. Lennon was sniffing all along the tideline, chewing the odd piece of seaweed. He wagged his entire back end as I bent to retrieve the shell, looking expectantly from me to a stick of driftwood nearby. As I placed the shell in my pocket with one hand, I scooped and lobbed the stick with the other. Lennon ran towards the stick and skidded to a stop before grasping it between white teeth. I didn't think too much about the pretty thing in my pocket again until we got home, where I put it on the shelf above the fireplace with all the other beach treasures: driftwood with sinuous curves like sea mammals; shells coiled into flawless spirals; sand dollars; two beach stones we'd painted under the influence of mulled wine; various crab body parts. Anything unusual got its place on the shelf—a habit from childhood. I remembered walking beaches in the Wairarapa as a kid—big, hoary paua shells for miles that we collected until we ran out of reasons to keep taking them. We put them in the garden and tried to make jewellery out of broken fragments and our parents used the biggest ones for ashtrays.

A week after I found the first shell there were dozens—paua of all sizes. I amassed quite a handful before I put them all down again, confused. Each day after that, the number grew more, until they started washing up with flesh still attached, rows of them at the tideline. Lennon sniffed his way along the beach slowly, lifting his paws tentatively at the black rubbery meat of the molluscs. Sometimes I saw one flexing itself, heaving in search of a host to attach its muscle to. The dog would always skirt sideways away from one of the living. I imagined them emitting a low moan.

After they started washing up live, I mentioned it to Spike.

"Yeah, sounds odd," he said, and went on fixing his bike.

"Don't you think someone should be noticing? Is there someone I should tell?"

He didn't look up, "I dunno, maybe the council?"

Then it appeared in the newspapers. "Marine Biologists Investigate Strange Paua Stranding" said one headline. "Where Do Paua Go to Die?" said another.

They talked about algae and poison sea cucumbers. I began taking Lennon to the park instead of the beach for walks, just in case. Gradually the newspapers started running more alarming headlines: "Paua Were Just the Beginning"; "Scientists Recommend Swimming Ban"; "Kaumatua Place Rāhui on Kaimoana."

I stayed away for weeks, using the dog as my excuse to walk in the opposite direction. Spike went down a couple of times and came back quiet and agitated.

"It's getting worse," he said one time, then seeing my expression added, "I'm sure it's a temporary thing—a shellfish bacteria perhaps. Sure it won't last." He didn't go back for a week after that. Rode his bike up into the hills every day. I decided to studiously ignore the whole situation until the news reports improved. There was too much going on in the world. It was not like I could do anything about the situation. But then there was the funny smell. It began to pervade the house, like something in the fridge you slowly become aware of each time you open the door, something gone rotten in a quiet container at the back. If I woke in the night it was there, a taint behind the everyday smells of bedclothes and bodies. Soon even deodorant and shampoo couldn't disguise it.

"It's time," I said.

We left Lennon at home, wore good walking shoes. Our house was only five minutes from the beach walkway, but we went slowly.

"Whatever's going on," Spike reminded me, "it's not the end of the world."

His grip on my hand was tight.

We were at the top of the steps when we saw them. Hundreds of seagulls and other marine birds were circling above the beach, which was now obscured by shells and seaweed and a large number of dead fish. As we got closer, we could see how the carcasses fed out of the water, the waves mounting up new piles with each inward push, the ocean a soupy mess.

We hesitated halfway down. The noise and stench were almost overpowering now.

"We should see," I said, "we should just see." It felt like we were visiting the corpse of a relative at a funeral home. At the bottom, we found Harold, our neighbour with the Scottish terrier. He didn't have Balderdash with him. We couldn't help screwing up our noses as we nodded to him.

"It's not even what you can see," he said, "it's what's beneath. Me and the wife been getting pipis here every summer for twenty-eight years. If you dig down this lot, you'll see 'em. Tried to come up out of the sand before they died. All of them, underneath. Imagine it. Can't even think about the water, what's going on under there."

The fumes from the rotting fish were so strong my eyes stung. I pretended this was the reason for my tears.

"It hasn't even started yet. They're hardly even rotten." Harold was shaking his head, shaking and shaking so that I worried he might injure his neck as he walked away.

We searched the internet for theories and hope. No one knew what was happening or why. Some scientists talked about a chain reaction brought on by global warming and phytoplankton extinctions. Their colleagues chastised them for fearmongering. Journalists and bloggers sparred about conspiracy theories and who to blame. Governments had posted civil defence notices about contingency plans. That night, I couldn't drag myself away from the screen, clicking manically until Spike took the mouse from my hand.

Five days later, the evacuations began.

Our route away from the coast takes us up the steep side of a hill that overlooks the whole curve of the bay where we lived. They say it's a temporary measure, but when we left the house it felt like a last goodbye. I don't think we'll be back. The stench is overwhelming eighty metres from the shore, and freshwater supplies are low. The birdcall that had grown almost deafening died off suddenly in those last days. As Spike drives and Lennon mopes in the back, I look out at the sea—no longer algae blue, but sludge brown. I look hard, but I can't see the sea creatures that litter the stagnant beach from this distance. I only see larger mammals—whales tipped on their sides in the water, like mountains of grief.

That first shell is back in the same pocket of my jacket now. I don't know why I took it when we left, rushing to stuff the van with everything we thought we'd need to get by: camping gear, clothes, nonperishable foods. Like other coastal refugees, we don't know if or where we might settle; the van could be our home indefinitely. I lost all sense of proportion at the end, choosing to bring a photo album instead of the national park guidebook, filling my pockets with mementoes of the life before. A childhood by the beach, piles of shells that were once home to the living, our treasures all lined up above a fireplace—I want to remember everything the way it used to be. But as we swing around a bend away from the ocean, I realise that none of that will bring comfort. I wind down my window, take the small shimmery thing from my pocket, and thrust my hand out. The wind is cool on my fist. I hold it a moment, then open my palm. There is a flash of blue-green, and then it is gone.

Chasing the Sun's Rays

Leilani Tamu

in a sheltered bay
on the island of Fukave
reef sharks chase the Sun's Rays

their flat glistening bodies
dart silently from one breaker
to the next, passing time while the tide

exhales

waiting for the next breath that will carry them
in and under the trench and back to 'Eueiki
where tiny cleaner fish await their return

ready to do their diligence and clean their masters' gills
keeping Tagaloa's house in order while the great god
slumbers awake only   in his dreams

Previously published, *The Art of Excavation*, Anahera Press, 2014.

Kuita and the Flame

Daren Kamali

Cina lured Kuita with her maka feke

Luring him up from his dungeon home
in the deep wasawasa

Kuita pulled Cina
Into the deepness of the Pacific sea

❦ ❦ ❦

The giant mourns in shame

Ta'uvala woven from tentacles

Tentacles that slashed Cina's waist
scarring her belly
with ancestral patterns

❦ ❦ ❦

---

kuita—Fijian for squid/octopus
cina—Fijian for light/glow
ta'uvala—waist belt made from coconut rope
maka feke—Tongan octopus lure
Uvea Mo Futuna—the Pacific Islands of Wallis and Futuna
masi—Fijian tapa cloth
ulumate—warrior wig
bati ni qio—teeth of the shark
Mata Ni Siga—Eyes of the Sun
meke vula—moon dance
vuku—clever/talented
bure—Fijian house
qio—shark

locked in moments of
igniting fires
burnt flesh
smashing hearts

Her maka feke
Distracted his vision
Untangled his arms
Welcoming her into his heart

❧ ❧ ❧

Hard to let go

They melted apart
like the islands of
Uvea Mo Futuna

Kuita released maka feke
He sunk down into his bottomless sea
Cina spiraled up
Escaping his underwater world

❧ ❧ ❧

Au sa soro

I give up

Echoes from the deep

Kuita weaves his chopped tentacles into an ulumate
Scratching the word
Cina
Into his cave walls
Suckers filled with sharp teeth
Scraping sacred symbols
Bati ni qio
Cannibal forks
To sharks' teeth
Running down his spine
Ancestral pathways
Marked with masi designs
Ancestral stories

Marked on skin
Mysterious ocean creature

❦ ❦ ❦

Sinking deeper into the brokenness of his lonely shell
Kuita tracks back
To when Degei let Turukawa go

He cannot believe
Degei allowed her to escape

Kuita cannot believe
He let Cina go

❦ ❦ ❦

Cina surfaced near her waqa
Anchored in the same spot

Canoe surfing waves back to shore

Rinsing her slender body in the wai tui

❦ ❦ ❦

Meke vula on white sand
under the dark moon

❦ ❦ ❦

Back to her bure
Sheltering their son
Qio
A gift from the Mata Ni Siga

Qio
Still a baby shark
Also vuku
He just doesn't know it yet

❦ ❦ ❦

Kāne Kōlea

Jamaica Heolimeleikalani Osorio

He comes to take
His feathers growing
dark silk wraps his marbling sides
leaving
without a thought
to the poʻowai
now dry
the craters carved under his claws
the god choking concrete he leaves behind

He does not cut the mouth
while sucking the last bit of sap from his spurs
I watch, wishing him that scarring lesson

While he departs
whole,
my ʻāina cavernous
summits stolen
rivers dry
and renamed
He leaves, full
having emptied this ʻāina
mauka a makai

---

kōlea—1. nvi. Pacific golden plover (*Pluvialis dominica*), a migratory bird which comes to Hawaiʻi about the end of August and leaves early in May for Siberia and Alaska. *Figuratively*, to repeat, boast; a scornful reference to foreigners (Kel. 70) who come to Hawaiʻi and become prosperous, and then leave with their wealth, just as the plover arrives thin in the fall each year, fattens up, and leaves; a less common figurative reference is to one who claims friendship or kinship that does not exist. Definition from Mary Kawena Pukui and Samuel H. Elbert, *Hawaiian Dictionary: Hawaiian-English English-Hawaiian*, rev. and enl. ed. (Honolulu: University of Hawaiʻi Press, 1986).

we are left with a foreign landscape
unfamiliar to our akua
and
I curse the patience of karma

Fish & Crab

PC Muñoz

The fish is in the ocean
The crab is on the land
I am not a fish or crab
But our dreams go hand in hand

Present-day Kantan

Fish Tickling

Clarissa Mendiola

some might flex permissions
on the reef with bone-tipped spears
and uncle's keen sense of entitlement

women employ patience
dexterity the taste of fish heads
on the wet edges of our tongues

the tips of our fingers dip into salt
water: disguised kelp bulbs drowned
brown insects swollen crumb of bread

waiting eye fixed beyond the surface
then the credulous tug of fish mouth lured

not by line or chum but time
and the sweetness of our fingers

foot-sole against coral shard
barnacled legs stilt a weathered pier

for all that come later to stand
upon our backs

and see flashes of ocean
in the gaps between planks

Fish Girl

Serena Ngaio Simmons

I am from a place
where many of us can trace our whakapapa
all the way to a successful fishing trip
our home being the sacred catch of Māui
the young island
that agreed to the bait the pōtiki threw down
I am of the iwi of Te Ika-a-Māui
whose body lays gently above Te Waipounamu
the island that grows taonga in the bellies of its rivers,
both lands holding stories
mana
people
who have no choice but to know this ocean

So I am part fish
born in Hawai'i
raised on yellow sand and bright blue water
rough feet from walking barefoot to the beach and everywhere else
hapa guppy trying to graduate to dolphin,
it was my mother
who first told me to never turn my back on the ocean
to be respectful of land and sea
to ask permission
even when the walking bottle of SPF 40
waltzes in like royalty, remember
to use manners

He huanui, he huaroa ki te ao
Omaio ki tua e
Karanga ki te waitai e
Haramai e te taitimu
Haramai e te taipari

Nau e Hinemoana
Nau e Tangaroa e

And so 22
older and with less scales
wondering how long it's been
since the invasion
how long it's been since escaping
colonial haze and concrete net
slow and pained, swimming through distance
public education
the bullshit that is *Once Were Warriors*
Alaska winter with an old Georgia gutter punk
diaspora, each
scraping globs of ocean worn skin off
leaving patches here and there, markers
signs
showing the difference in me
talking loud at gatherings, saying proudly now
what moana
awa
hāroto
form the base of my roots
telling of how many years it can take
for some of us to find them
and how lucky we are
if we can at least hold on to the fins

I am back in Aotearoa
when I have the money to be
row there every year in metal waka
and find my world in family
poetry
Rangi kissing orange-yellow onto the water
in Hicks Bay
te papa kāinga
places where tūpuna still walk
taniwha still swim
and Awatere can still flow
places where I can wake up to the current
and not the thousands of bodies that could be disturbing it

It is at home
where the regrowth starts

where the grey on my sweater and face
is taken over by the blooming of bright skin
scaly āniwaniwa
another lost one finding homecoming in the ocean
winter waves though cold
when ringed by mountains are warm
light sunlight and smooth beach,
it's alright, aye?

Just enough to let the fins stretch
sort the gills out
give thanks
pray for this to remain

Excerpt from *Anggadi Tupa: Harvesting the Storm*

John Waromi

Translated from Indonesian by Sarita Newson

Book description: In this contemporary fable, Papuan author John Waromi highlights the struggle of Papuans to preserve their ancestral traditions and protect their sacred environment. Set in the coastal regions of West Papua, this story of the Ambai people and their relationship with nature is told through the friendship of four underwater creatures, whose habitat is threatened by dynamite bomb-fishing.

Prologue

A child calls out as he runs along the beach. "*Aii yee, Daiiee!* Mama, Papa! *Anggadi tupa, anggadi tupa!*—The coconuts are coming! Coconuts coming!"

A man in the distance replies, echoing his call.

"*Tafu ee!* Grandma, Grandpa! *Anggadi tupa, anggadi tupa!*—The coconuts are coming! Coconuts coming!"

A woman appears from the same direction. She stops and stares at them.

Suddenly, they appear through the gaps in the reef. The dark wet shapes float and roll in the whitewash of the waves as they are eventually cast ashore.

The boy and his father scramble for them. They will plant coconuts all along the shore.

One by one the names of the fishes are called out loud, as they are imprinted upon the child's memory. All the names, that is, except that of anggadi, the coconut. One by one he calls out the plant names, then commits them to memory.

. . . all the plants that grow and bloom in the ocean.

. . . all the plants that grow and bear fruit.

Previously published, *Harvesting the Storm,* Monsoon Books, 2019.

Even those that grow in spirals, climbing, blooming, and bearing fruit on the trees.

Their leaves are full of life, they have a voice, and they talk, whisper, and sing.

Their skin sweats, feels, touches, smells, listens, and sees.

There are reptiles of all shapes and sizes; some without hands and feet, others with lots of feet—some as many as eight feet plus a pair of hands, four feet and no hands, two feet complete with a pair of wings.

One by one he counts the flying fowl, then he imprints their names, too, upon the child's memory.

Years change, and centuries pass. The sandy island is in the middle of the atoll, lush and green amidst the blue of the ocean.

1

Greedy

They tell of a time when the underwater world was calm and clear. The morning sun shone brightly.

At the end of a sandy beach bordered by a cliff, Andevavait, the Tide-pool Blenny, was sunbathing. Beyond the water the fat-bellied Toadfish, Bohurai, also known as Porobibi, reclined on a rock, where Andevavait lay in the sun. They were enjoying a chat. As he listened to Andevavait, Bohurai kept his eye on the fruit hanging from the shady trees above the water.

"I can't wait any longer," Bohurai said to Andevavait. "Friend, I can hardly follow our conversation, I'm so distracted by that fruit hanging up there."

Andevavait looked around and said, "What do you mean?"

"Try looking up!"

Pretending not to understand, Andevavait waggled his fin in the direction of the tree. "That one up there?"

"Why, don't you know it?"

"Here we call it anggadi," said Andevavait.

"Can you eat it?"

"Yes, of course you can eat it!"

"*Wah*, that big fruit?"

"You don't eat the whole thing."

"What part of it do you eat?"

"The insides. It's delicious, but the skin is very hard . . ."

There was no further comment from Bohurai of the fat belly. He was disappearing back into the coral as if he had been offended. Andevavait tried to call him back, but Bohurai was already upset, and Andevavait felt like he was talking to himself. Andevavait had no choice but to follow him.

"Dear friend," said Andevavait. "Please come back—I'll tell you the secret of the coconut tree."

Bohurai ignored him.

"I'm going to prove that I wasn't teasing you," said the Blenny.

Suddenly Andevavait disappeared from the surface of the water. A moment later a voice came from high above:

"Hey, Bohurai, come on up."

Hearing his friend calling him from above, Bohurai wanted to climb up, too. He was amazed to see Andevavait way up there, floating at the end of a coconut frond. Suddenly Andevavait plunged toward him. Water splashed everywhere, and the surface of the water was covered in ripples. Bohurai's fat body was flung about by the impact. The circular ripples went all the way to the shore and ended up on the sand. Andevavait was very happy to see his friend rocked by the disturbance and obviously impressed.

"Andev, you're a champion," Bohurai said, once the water had calmed. "But what was that thing you brought down with you??"

"A coconut! That's what you just asked me for."

"You're trying to trick me again."

"It's like this, my friend. There are certain conditions if you want to know the secrets of the coconut."

"I'm not interested in the secrets," said Bohurai. "Just the coconut fruit. I want to try it."

"Oh, I see. Are you really serious?"

"I'm serious. But don't go to a lot of trouble."

"It's no trouble. Listen, my friend. First condition: you must learn to hold your breath."

"And then?"

"The second condition is that you have to learn to put up with a hungry stomach."

"That's easy! Is that all?" said Bohurai.

"Yes. To eat a coconut, my friend, first you must be able to hold your breath and put up with hunger."

"Fine, if that's all, teach me to hold my breath!"

Bohurai started right away on his first lessons, from floating on the surface of the water, to sunbathing under the sun, just as Andevavait did. Eventually, Fatbelly Bohurai passed his breath-holding test. But Andevavait seemed to be in no hurry to bring down a coconut for him.

Bohurai wondered if his friend had been teasing him all along. But he began to be patient and followed Andevavait's advice. Now that he could hold his breath, he could see interesting things above the surface of the water, and enjoy the beauty of a world that, until then, he knew could be visited by only a handful of water creatures. By holding his breath, he could watch the creatures that lived above the water, and appreciate all the compelling beauty of nature.

Now he could watch the changes that took place in nature from the moment the sun came up until it set. The instant it appeared, its gleaming light illuminated all the above-water creatures of the earth. At moments like that, he understood what was happening in his world beneath the sea. Bohurai had thought that this single source of light was close to the world, hovering just above the water. Now he realized that it was far away and unattainable. At last the Toadfish understood why, every morning when the sun was about to rise, Andevavait disappeared up above water level.

He also saw the birds in the trees and heard their song. There were fowl that flew freely in the sky. There were creatures like him, who crept over the land. There were creatures that stood, propped up by two legs. And there were others with four legs.

"Andev, I really want to try that coconut. You can help me, can't you?" the Toadfish begged him again.

"Of course I can," said Andevavait, "but can you fulfill the second condition, my friend? Because this is about controlling personal desire."

"What sort of personal desire?"

"The kind that is never satisfied!"

"What do you mean? Give me an example."

"You know, my friend, I usually adore eating those little prawns," said Andevavait. "I can't eat more than a dozen before I feel full. Now: what if I never felt satisfied, and kept eating till I could hardly breathe? That's what I mean by controlling personal desire."

"Oh, that's what's called being greedy!"

"So you already know what I'm talking about."

"But what does that have to do with the coconut?"

"Some coconut palms grow on their own, but others are planted by people. We need to be aware of that. If the person that planted them is present, then it's not possible to take their fruit."

"Oh, right. I thought they all grew wild, like things do under the sea: they belong to everyone. Whoever is quickest gets them."

"My friend, the world above the water is different. Like the people who live in the villages here: they have their own customs. If they meet another person who wants to take a coconut because he's hungry, then that is allowed. The owner might even climb up to get the coconut himself and present it to his guest. When you want to pick coconuts and the owner isn't present, however, it's important not to take too many and not to forget to say thanks by leaving the coconut shell behind, under the tree. That way, when the owner shows up he won't worry. He'll think it was a friend or relative that left the coconut shell lying on the ground, because only family or friends are allowed to guard the village gardens."

"Oh, in that case I'll leave it up to you," said the Toadfish.

"Good. You wait here and keep an eye out, and if any villagers show up give me a signal. Watch your head."

Soon coconuts could be heard falling into the water.

"Is that enough?" Andevavait shouted down from the treetop. "Or not yet?"

"Not yet, keep going, throw more down! Keep going!"

A bit later: "Is that enough, or not?"

"Not enough!"

"Hey, how many is enough?" Andevavait peeped down through the gaps in the coconut palm fronds.

"It's best you throw down some more. Later on I'll add it up and let you know if it's enough!"

"How many coconuts are down there?" shouted Andevavait.

"Andev, they've all drifted away!"

"Drifted? How could that happen?"

"Just throw some more down, there's still plenty up there."

"My friend, I'm exhausted; I'll throw down three more, and that's it!"

"Fine," said Bohurai. "Three is enough."

Andevavait threw down three more coconuts, and with his last remaining strength climbed down the coconut palm. As he crawled down, he tried to remember exactly what had happened. With his friend's encouragement, he'd thrown down two entire bunches of coconuts. So how did Bohurai manage to save only a couple? When he reached the bottom of the tree, Andevavait leaned back on the trunk of the coconut palm exhausted.

Meanwhile, under the shade of the coconut tree, Bohurai the Fat-Belly was still lying in the water. His eyes felt heavy, and in his two fins he grasped two dry coconuts.

Andevavait was too tired to move. He watched Bohurai, and hoped that the bunch of young coconuts had already sunk to the bottom and were stuck in the coral. But where had the other lot, from the bunch of dry coconuts, drifted off to?

Someone else was also watching Bohurai: the striped Crab, Anggereai. He crawled along the side of the rocks and suddenly scratched Bohurai's ear. The dozing Fat-belly was taken by surprise. Stammering, he called out: "An . . . Andevavait, we need one more coconut, then you can come down!"

Sliding up behind his friend, Andevavait said with a grin, "Are you talking to me?"

Bohurai was astonished to find Andevavait right next to him.

"*Wah,*" said Bohurai. "There are only two dry coconuts here. We need one more."

"I'm exhausted," Andevavait replied. "You can have both those coconuts yourself."

He was amazed at Bohurai's attitude. Like he'd done nothing wrong. And he was so quick to forget someone's hard work. It looked like Anggereai, too, was waiting for Bohurai to explain, but Bohurai ignored him and started to snore.

2

The Tragedy

It was hot that morning and Andevavait had confined himself in a hole in the rock. He was fasting. He tried to go on a fast every low-tide season. It was his normal routine. While fasting, he was careful to keep away from his seawater world. Although he could hold his breath for hours out of the water, Andevavait always had to watch out for enemies. Predators lurked both under the water and above. There were Barracuda and a gang of Flat-tailed Long-toms that liked to chase and prey on little fish like him. Both of these predators often visited this beach and the tip of its peninsula, because that was where the Endracht Hardyhead and Bareback Anchovy lived and bred. Tawaiseng, the Hook-jaw Moray Coral Reef Eel, with his set of sharp teeth, also liked to hang out there. His head would appear from a hole in the reef and he would wait for an opportunity to attack his prey as they passed by. Because of his soft body, Andevavait the Tidepool Blenny was one of Tawaiseng's most favored quarries.

That afternoon the tide was so low the whole coastline was dry. The reef where the fish normally hid was sticking way up out of the water. While fasting in his secret hole, Andevavait heard a groaning sound from the coral nearby. He thought he recognized the voice. Curiosity induced him to peep out at his surroundings. He worried that it might be a predator or kids from the village that could spot him, roll over the rock he was hiding under and capture him. If the grownup people saw him, they would leave Andevavait alone in his hiding place; they considered Andevavait too small to be worth hunting. But the kids thought capturing Andevavait and his kin a test of their dexterity. He was also afraid of predators off the land such as the Kamantifu monitor lizards or Karu mice. And he could not ignore the threat of Kaintani the Kingfisher or Awaingge the Beach Heron.

After confirming that it was safe to venture out, Andevavait happily checked around the rocks to see if he could determine the source of the groaning in the coral wall. It turned out that the voice was that of Raukahi, an injured octopus.

"What's wrong, my friend?" he asked.

Raukahi showed him a fresh wound on the stump of one of his tentacles. "I was swimming, searching for food, when suddenly Tawaiseng the Hook-jaw Moray appeared and bit off one of my tentacles." Now he only had seven tentacles left.

"Why didn't you just hide in your hole and wait for passing prey?" said Andevavait.

"Ah," said the octopus. "My hiding hole at the bottom of the ocean has been blown up by dynamite."

It was lucky the octopus didn't have a bone structure like the fish, whose bones had been cracked by the explosion. The octopus had survived, but the fish world around him had been plunged into terrible grief and mayhem. Raukahi went on to describe the horror.

The fish that were near the blast had died immediately, their backbones instantly shattered. A cloud of sand and reef debris mixed with mud and sulfurous smoke had risen up and was carried by the current—then slowly a pile of dead fish could be seen settling at the bottom of the ocean. The fish that were a bit further away from the center of the explosion also suffered fractured backbones; all they could do was swim in circles on the water's surface. The current dragged the dying fish until they finally expired and sank to the bottom. The radius of the pile of carcasses spread even wider. A few days later the surface of the water was covered in dead fish. On the seashore, all along the waves' breaking point, the normal salty and delicious smell of the froth was now replaced by the stench of rotting fish.

After the trauma of the dynamite explosion that had almost killed him, the octopus didn't feel like taking advantage of the free food, even with thousands of dead and dying fish right there in front of him. He could only watch the feeding frenzy of the other predators—Paimani the Stingray, Tarubain the Trout Cod, and even the Mandohai sharks. He saw all the many members of the crab family out there, including Awein the green Lobster, who, along with his crab friends, preferred to pick out the fishes' eyes before eating their flesh.

Now Raukahi was homeless, without a hiding place. For the time being, he could dodge the ocean predators. But when the tide came in, he would have to speedily seek a safer place.

"Pues adios, Paluma! Esta agupa'!"

Kisha Borja-Quichocho-Calvo

> The loss of birds [on Guam] is believed to be largely a result of habitat alteration and the effects of the introduced brown tree snake.
>
> —*Guampedia*

When we first got out of the airport in Luta
my two-year-old daughter said,
"Mommy, do you hear that? I hear the birds! I want to go see them!"

What an observation for my neni to have made.

At two,
even she could already see the difference between Luta and Guam.

Because on Guam

the only birds we can see are invasive—pigeons and chickens—

the only birdsongs we can hear are those captured by Hans Hornbostel,
recordings on *Guampedia*
and at the Guam National Wildlife Refuge in Litekyan.

But in Luta
we could see birds

thriving

throughout the island—from Sinapalo to Songsong
watch them flying, nesting, feeding

hear them chanting, singing, calling

Everywhere

but especially at I Chenchon Bird Sanctuary
(or "Bird Sanctuary" as the locals call it)

Fagpi apa'ka
Chunge'
Sihek
Aga

White, black, blue, mixed

Different shapes
Different sizes
Different sounds

But all the *same* Beauty—
    Beauty that we noticed
    and kept searching for in Luta

    Beauty that we never get to see on Guam

My daughter
overwhelmed by all of the Beauty
made a friend with one fagpi apa'ka at Bird Sanctuary.

"Annie" she called her.

And each time
my daughter recognized Annie
and the bird's ways with the wind
I thought about how she needed

to learn how to fly.

But I wondered:

How could she learn to fly
when on Guam
our people don't have any birds to teach us how to fly?

If we can't hear the songs of our native birds
then who else will teach us how to sing when we fly?

Who else will show us the ways of the wind,
how to rise up in the midst of the trauma and trials we face?

Who else will teach us to fly when the only birds we see
are those held captive in books, pamphlets, websites
and the articles of foreign researchers—

And those birds
still in the moment
aren't

flying?

[wondering ceases]

As we were leaving Bird Sanctuary
we could hear the birds.
My daughter said, "Mommy, the birds are crying because they want me.
And I'm crying because I want them.
This is so sad."

Even my neni could feel what I felt.

At that moment,
I didn't want her to feel my pain
so I told her:

"Don't be sad. We'll come back again. Tell the birds, 'Pues adios, paluma!'"

"Pues adios, paluma! Esta agupa'," she quietly said.

My heart was sad.
Sad to be going back
to a place where
the only birds we could see were invasive
the only birdsongs we could hear were recorded

and where our people—
many of whom had never seen or heard native birds—

couldn't

even

Fly.

As we drove away from Bird Sanctuary, I said a short prayer to myself:

O Saina,
On Guam, as we brace ourselves for more devastation to our environments
and for more invasive species,
I hope that our people will still be able to strengthen our native wings
and will learn how to fly
and that we will all be more than paintings on walls,
recordings played on Guampedia and YouTube.
Saina ma'åse'.

Red and Yellow

Jessica Carpenter

A servant of gods on Earth
Your only duty to cloak the king in glory
Scarlet and gold draped over the shoulders of history
Ali'i marched into battle with the embrace of an 'ahu'ula 'i'iwi
The song of 'iō and 'o'o and 'i'iwi was the war cry of Hawai'i
Shoulder to heel dripping in the blood of victory
Blood as crimson as the hulu clutching his shoulders
With the end of a war the trees screamed
A weeping a shouting a chirp a cry a peck
The capes of young men grazed shoulder blades
With age their feathers grew to kiss their ankles
A prince walks and displays the beauty and splendor of our rich fertile island
Look we bear rich sweet soils, strong heavy woods
A pregnant sea lush with fish because we only catch in season
It is illegal, kapu, forbidden even to prize an 'opelu
When the winds were high and the air was cold
The cycles of our island are the calendars of our people
Listen here and let it be known that we are teeming in the fruits of a paradise
We worked for our abundance
The land responded with the fruits of our labor
We asked the gods for permission
And listened for harmony after we chanted Kū Nihi Ka Mauna
And turned around if nā Akua showed us we shall not enter
We plucked and planted and cleaned and maintained and hunted
And we chanted back to return the ahu'ula o nā ali'i when they left us for Aotearoa
And when you looked at it
And ogled it and wanted so badly to touch it
And think that the accumulation of this satin glory was a waste
And irresponsible to our environment
Mai poina that we worked

And took a few feathers for decades and let the birds fly back home
But you didn't know that
So you didn't protect them, you expected your manu to always fly back home
Our forest is silent
And the only red and yellow we spot is from an ailing ʻōhiʻa
Why are the colors of nā aliʻi always the subject of threat
It is because you have forgotten our calendars
And have forgotten that our tides don't rise and fall
For your surf and your tanning days
They rise and fall because the moon pulls them up and down
Trying to remind us when Makahiki is
And when the seasons of Kū and Lono and Kāne are
And we chant e ala e as if we are awakening the yellow crimson orange sun
And it is loud and we cheer and clap
Because we did not forget that we knew what we had
And we will cry for you ʻiʻiwi because you remind us of our once prized ʻāina
We view you in a glass case at a quiet museum
And only some of us can hear you cry
As our aliʻi were buried, the forest grew somber
And yet the cries are still there in the backs of our minds and we did not forget
And will never forget your red and yellow majesty

Fanihi

Desiree Taimanglo Ventura

I gently coax a dukduk from its shell when an unfamiliar sound, somewhere between the chirping of birds and the squeaking of mice, erupts above me, gentle calls floating over salty air. The sweet sound releases a melody over calm water, harmonizing with the lapping tide and a barely audible rustle of hagon niyok. It echoes off of limestone cliffs, wrapping around me. I whip my head around, searching for its maker. It's a sound I have never heard, but somehow, it feels familiar. My body responds knowingly. As my head tilts up, my five-year-old heart stops, unaware that the precious dukduk I worked so tirelessly to steal from beneath wet sand had fallen and scampered away. I hold my breath as black wings fan above me. "Fanihi," I whisper. I am too overwhelmed to breathe. They are dancing, falling toward and away from each other amidst high pitched calls. My eyes widen at the contrast of black wings against warm orange and rosy pink. I think of ice cream: Baskin-Robbins rainbow sherbet that can only be found within the Air Force base's concession area. I should blink, but I do not. I cannot bear to miss a single second before the colors are stolen by night's deep purple.

---

hagon niyok—coconut leaves
dukduk—hermit crab
fanihi—indigenous Chamoru word for the endangered Marianas fruit bat. The fanihi leave their colonies to forage for several hours around sunset. They search for lemmai, papaya, fadang, figs, kafu, talisai, kapok flowers, coconut, and gaogao, all of which are less plentiful on Guam due to development, invasive species (the brown tree snake), and military activity. Marianas fruit bats do not live in caves. They dwell deep in jungles, hanging upside down on trees. This was once a common sight for older Chamorus. With the clearing of jungles and spraying of DDT (a pesticide to prevent mosquitoes near base housing areas), much of their resting places have disappeared.
Talagi—northern beach and site of ancient Chamoru villages, burials, and artifacts. A once popular hunting ground for Chamoru fanihi peskadot. A beach that once provided access to the ancestral lands of the San Nicolas, Perez, Castro, and Artero families (among others). Currently recreational space for military families on Anderson Air Force Base. Sponsorship from a resident with military identification is required for access.
sirenu—night air
Yigo—northernmost village of Guam where fanihi were once plentiful

I watch as they swoop down only to rise again. I sway my body left then right before ducking up and down, mimicking their dramatic curves and angles. They take turns chirping. Sometimes seeming to call out to each other before crying out in groups. I think of a school of dolphin I once saw while riding in my uncle's boat. My heart is full inside, erupting with something I do not yet have the words for. My young mind races through its forming collection of vocabulary words, trying to describe the sight above me. *Very good. Awesome. So nice. Pretty. Favorite. Love. God.* I cannot find a word. Only one word works. *Magic.* I lift my hands in the air. They are too high to touch, but I reach anyway. Can they see me? I am desperate for them to see me. "See me," I chant over and over within my head. The moment is moving by too quickly. I am panicking, terrified of its end. They are returning to their colonies after foraging before the end of sunset, but I do not know that. All I know is they are quickly descending back into wherever they emerged from, somewhere along Talagi's limestone forests and green jungles. "No. No, wait." I whisper silent pleas and a new feeling is knotting up inside me, right between my throat and chest. It hurts. I do not know what to do with the pain and respond to it with heavy tears. I will learn, with time, that there are names for this pain: *heartbreak, loss,* and *mourning.* I try to stretch seconds into hours. As the last fanihi disappears, I am left in silence. The neglected dukduk has found its way back to the small tide pool it had been kidnapped from. My breath returns with a muffled cry. Confused by the aching inside, I swallow, choking as I wipe away liquid dripping from my nose and eyes. I stand still, face tilted up, waiting, hopeful that they will return. The beach is silent, save for the lapping of water against rocks in the tide pool and the steady sound of ocean. I stand so long the dreaded dark purple arrives. My rainbow sherbet melted. My damp bathing suit sends a chill through me. The sirenu is here and I have not changed. My long hair is matted with sand and salt water, in desperate need of washing. "Come back. Come back. Come back," I chant over and over again, searching the darkening sky.

My father's hand gently lands on my shoulder. I have wandered away from the family again. They are worried. They are looking for me. "Neni, what are you doing?" The outline of my small body standing still in the middle of a tide pool startles him. I stare at him, blankly . . . sadly. Fear spreads across his face. What happened to his girl as she wandered alone down this empty beach? "Bats," I whisper. "Fanihi," I clarify, certain that "bat" was not a worthy enough word for the animals I had seen. "I saw fanihi," I tell him, quietly. His eyebrows lift in surprise. He looks up, as if he might get to see them too, but we both know they have left. I point up and let my palms fall and rise again in large, fast curves, imitating the movements of the fanihi. "I want them to come back!" I cry, unable to conceal my devastation. A smile lights up his face as he bends low, placing his hands on my shoulders and pulling my face close to his. "Do you know how lucky you are?" he asks. I am confused, frustrated that he is smiling. "You might never see that again."

The next time I see a fanihi is years later, when I am in graduate school. I am walking through the San Diego Zoo when my stateside boyfriend calls out in excitement. He has found something that will please me. He motions for me to hurry. "Read this!" he points, smiling proudly while pointing at a plaque installed before a glass display case. "It's from Guam! It's from where you're from! It says it's a delicacy for you guys!" I look down at the bolded title: "Pteropus mariannus mariannus: Mariana Fruit Bat, endangered." I press my face up to the glass, making eye contact with the small fuzzy creature. The familiar, painful knot returns and the smile on my haole boy's face falls as he watches. "What are we doing here?" I whisper to it. "Me and you, we belong in Yigo."

Olik

Hermana Ramarui

Te kmo, "A olik a tellatel."
        They say, "Bats are upside down."
Tir a bai tellatel.
        They are upside down, instead.
Le lak ltellatel,
        If they are not upside down,
Ng melemalt a osengir.
        They could see straight.

Te kmo, "Ng diak de melemalt."
        They say, "We (bats) are not straight."
Te kmo, "Kede tellatel."
        They say, "We (bats) are upside down."
Tireke leme er tiang,
        If they come here,
Ng sebechir el uai kid?
        Can they perform as we perform?

Te omdasu el kmo tir a melemalt.
        They think they are straight.
Kede omdasu el kmo kid a melemalt.
        We think we are straight.
Kid me tir a du 'l di melemalt.
        We and they are both right side up.
A bo deuai tir e kede mo tellatel.
        If we be as they are, we'll be upside down.

DA LAST SQUID

Joe Balaz

Willy Boy wen score.

On da mudflat
wheah da reef used to be

he wen speah da buggah—
da last squid, brah.

In da abandoned conservation area

between da industrial park
and da old desalinization plant

he wen find ‘um

dough how any squid
could live ovah deah

I dunno.

Maybe da ting
wuz wun mutant, aah?

And as to how

Willy could go diving in dat spot
next to da effluent outflow

Previously published, *Whetu Moana: Contemporary Polynesian Poems in English,* University of Hawai‘i Press, 2003.

I dunno eidah.

You know wat "effluent" mean, aah?
Dats just wun nice word foa dodo watah.

But still den

Willy wuz all excited
aftah he wen cook dat squid.

Wen he wuz cutting 'um up
he wen tell me,

"Eh, you know wat dis is, aah?
Dis is da last squid, braddah!"

Da last squid—

It's kinnah funny, brah,
wen I tink back

but it really wuz da last squid.

Now by dat same beach
nutting can even live

cause da watah stay all black
and even moa polluted den before.

It's just like tings wen change ovahnight.

But you know
it started long time ago.

Way back wen

I remembah my maddah told me
just before I wuz born

dat dey wuz building wun second city on Oahu
and finishing wun new tunnel on da windward side.

Latah on
wen I wuz growing up

tings wen accelerate

and da whole island
wen just develop out of control

into wun huge monstah city.

By den
had so many adah tunnels too

dat da mountain
wen look like wun honeycomb.

Everyting came different, brah,

cause da island
wen grow so fast

and had so many people.

Maybe good ting Willy Boy wen die early.

He nevah live to see
how tings got even moa worse.

But back den
wen we wuz youngah

he looked so happy
wen he wuz cutting up dat contaminated squid.

I can still hear his words—

"Dis is special, brah.
Dis is da last one."

Wen he wen offah me some

foa lottah reasons
dats hard foa explain

I just told 'um,
"Naah. No need."

But deep inside, brah,

I nevah like be da one to eat
da last squid.

Hawaiians Eat Fish

Wayne Kaumualii Westlake

HAWAIIANS
EAT
FISH
EAT
HAWAIIANS
EAT
FISH
EAT
HAWAIIANS
EAT
FISH
EAT
HAWAIIANS
EAT
FISH

Previously published, *Westlake: Poems by Wayne Kaumualii Westlake (1947–1984)*, University of Hawaiʻi Press, 2009.

Bird of Prayer

Hone Tuwhare

On the skyline
a hawk
languidly typing
a hunting poem
with its wings.

Previously published, *Short Back & Sideways: Poems & Prose*, Godwit, 1992.

Kāhea Before the Approach of Makahiki

D. Keali'i MacKenzie

after Selina Tusitala Marsh

Paukū 'ekahi: Inoa

Pule au nā inoa o ke akua 'O Lono:

Lono-nui-noho-i-kawai (Great Lono living in the water)
Lono-nui-akea (Great Lono in the heavens)
Lono-'opua-kau (Lono whose place is the rain cloud)
Lono-i-kapo (Lono in the night)
Lono-i-ke-ao (Lono in the light or Cloud)
Lono-i-ke-ao'ouli (Lono in the dark black cloud)
Lono-nui-'aniha (Lono the great angry one)
Lono-kuli (Lono the deaf one)
Lono-i-ka-ua-paka-lea (Lono in the spattering rain drops)
Lono-i-ka-ua-loku (Lono in the pouring rain)
Lono-wahine (Lono the woman)
Lono-makua (Lono the Parent, lighter of fire)

Here the season as the rains come,
before the land sighs away its thirst,
before the first new moon
after the rise of Makali'i,

I pray
and await
your return 'O Lonoikamakahiki
Lono the yearly one

Previously published, *From Hunger to Prayer,* Silver Needle Press, 2018.

Paukū ʻelua: Puaʻa

The stiff bristles of a pig
Kamapuaʻa—incarnation of Lono—
whose snout rummaged through
moist earth for all kinds of openings.

This rutting pig
whose exploits exhausted
chiefs, makaʻāinana, and Gods
moved as an insatiable vine across
these islands sprouting here
and there anxious for people
to consume and feed.

I'd take him in
dirty hooves and all,
bid him eat and eat until
ready to burst.
I'd let him have his way
all the while reminding him
how we laugh and poke fun
at his wild excursions.

This divine trouble maker
with hiwa eyes and a sly manner.

I'd pray him, too.

Paukū ʻekolu: Kino lau

ʻUala, Kumara: sweet potato.
Earth sprouted rainbow of

red
pink
yellow
orange
purple
light cream
white

numerous varieties to explore
with vines that grow long
and bright across the land,
a crop to fight famine, sustain
the people.

There are rumors of ʻuala poi,
tubers cooked in coconut milk,
or steamed leaves seasoned with salt . . .

Lono, your body nourishes,

I remain, thankful
aware of the good dirt
beneath my feet.

Paukū ʻehā: e hoʻi hou

Come back.
Return.
Not like Captain Cook
In bloody imitation of Cortez:
a legacy of death, suffering,
diseased horror,
and stomachs turned
dry as empty gourds.

I pray you return to places like Kahoʻolawe, Halawa
Kaneohe, Mākua, Pohakuloa, Waikīkī
places cracked from military
bombs or profit-driven bulldozers
Sweep down

E hoʻi hou
return

as the long cloud
a dark shimmer before heavy rain

return as new growth to break concrete

return as puaʻa to uproot the diseased abscess on the land

E hoʻi hou

return as the one who lights the fires of Pele,
a hot touch before the wood explodes.

Return so fishponds and lo‘i may flourish
and we may be secure in our
source of food.

E ho‘i hou
Return
Return
Return
because we have been waiting so long
afraid our prayers are a hollow gasp on the wind.

My Jesus Is a Monk Seal

Teresia Kieuea Teaiwa

The path to hell
is paved with good intentions,
and I had every intention of going to mass
on Easter Sunday, 2015.
Nothing physical prevented me from walking
the 1.9 miles from the New Otani Kaimana Beach
to St. Augustine by-the-Sea
for the 6 a.m., 8 a.m., 10 a.m., 5 p.m. masses.
So many options for fulfilling this
Holy Day of obligation,
I really had no excuse.
Nothing other than a sneaking suspicion
that my savior was not going to reveal himself to me
as a Middle Eastern man
but as a Hawaiian monk seal.
That's my excuse.
That's my Jesus.
Sure, it's blasphemy according to
Canon Law.
But as my friend Flo says,
laws are made by men,
and therefore can be changed.
Like the law which states
that the body of Christ
can only be represented
by wheat bread,
and his blood only by grape wine.
Church law, therefore,
dictates that the body and blood
of our Savior must always be imported—
shipped or flown in from foreign faraway lands.
In Hawai'i, in Fiji, in Kiribati—
Jesus is always colonizer, tourist, or cargo.

And in good conscience
I feel I must follow Flo.
Our savior was crucified
according to the laws of men.
Change the laws.
Let my Eucharist be
breadfruit and coconut
grown from the lands of
my birth, adoption and ancestry!
Let the sun of God baptize
all us wanderers
on the sidewalks in Waikiki!
And let us all step off the pavement
to worship this majesty.
My faith is being decolonized
and my friend Father Kevin
is concerned about binaries.
"Why either/or?
Can it be and/both?
Universal and particular?
Connected and distinct?"
Settler and native?
Anthropocentric and animistic?
Because history has entangled us,
theology confounds us,
and language shortchanges us.
But memory is what will define us.
And the truth is that
long before there was a me,
a young fisherman at sea
was startled by a creature
that jumped into his outrigger.
It barked. Terrifyingly.
And then dove back into the ocean.
It was no dog. So was it a devil?
The young man paddled back to shore,
and his story became legend.
Until the time came
when he had to exchange his youth
with his eldest son,
who came back from university in Hawai'i
certain he could explain the mystery
of the barking marine being.
"A lost seal," my father told his father,
"A lost seal."

And so the legend continues,
because now I can tell my sons
about the seal I encountered
perfectly at home
among both tourists and locals,
malihini and kama'aina,
haole and kanaka.
And like Jesus after the Resurrection,
he would be taken into heaven.
Except his heaven and mine
is deep undersea.

CLIMATE CHANGE

In this section, the content and form of our stories are shaped out of climate change. They are shaped from our responses to the possibility of a future without our islands. They are shaped out of explaining what existence is, and what our terms of existence are as islanders. They name how histories of annihilation—from colonial invasion to nuclear testing—are directly linked to the structures of power that trivialize, ignore, and erase the impacts of climate change. Our response is to create.

Here is a body of stories.

Here are living, breathing pathways for stewarding this earth.

These stories document our attitudes and definitions of change—how *we* change in response to the health of our environments. We carry these changes in our very bodies, as our bodies are tied to the lives of our islands and ocean. Our bodies are part of this climate. We work through all of our bodies—of water, land, animal, plant, and human—to translate our stories of change into courses of action. To make you see us. To shape how you might listen and know that you are connected to us.

We respond to the immensity and specificity of climate change by documenting how climate change shapes the ways we move and think in the world. The writers in this section share structures of response to change; how we look for and find answers. We draw from ancestral stories, our languages, and our definitions of home and movement. We remember and apply histories of balance and imbalance that have been passed down in our cultural archives living in our names, languages, storytelling, arts, sciences, navigations, social protocols, political histories, and structures of power.

How do we shape terms of change and action?

This section shows our responses to climate change based in our understandings of history. We do not pronounce climate change without speaking the histories of nuclear testing in our ocean, or remembering the impacts of missionization and militarization. We do not speak about climate change outside of histories of disease, epidemics, land dispossession, occupation, or how change has been defined through projects of colonialism in our islands.

We document and define the "front line" of climate change. That it isn't a line.

It's an ocean. It's a sea of islands.

Bodies of water and land.

Your body.

Our body.

This section maps pathways of solidarity, linking our specific responses to the immensity of climate change. We tell these stories of change and movement in order "to build new lives," as Takiora Ingram says in this section. We tell these stories to build possibilities of living in the world in the face of climate change. We bring our island-shaped stories here because this earth is our island body. It is all. We. Have.

More than Just a Blue Passport

Selina Neirok Leem

Looking out my window
There sits my grandparents' and my mama's grave
White rectangle they are closeted in
Its inside
Gray and still
My backyard is
A four-meter history
of waves crashing and breaking
seawalls built with uncles, brothers, and grandpa's sweat
that one great wall
two meters high
my family's only protection from the water
made a mockery
as the water has risen
level with the land
and spilled over human debris weaving
a remnant
a reminder
of human being's greediness

To the developed countries
To the advanced nations
You think you know us
But you know NOTHING—NOTHING
at all

Should I tell you what is happening in my backyard?
What is that?
You think you already know?
You think you know better?

No, no
You have no say
You have had yours

When the man from the military said
Testing nuclear bombs
67 of them
on tiny strips of land
with many parts
barely a meter above sea level
is "For the good of mankind
and to end all world wars"

How many wars have ended now due to nuclear weapons?
How many?
How many innocent lives killed?
Remember March 1, 1954
When they dropped the Bravo bomb in Bikini
Bravo! Bravo!
Ever-famous for leaving their mark behind

Like the mark
on my home
The Marshall Islands
is now a weary mother of
A dome filled with radioactive waste,
all from the bombing, "For the good of mankind"
With a sign that said, "Do not return for 25,000 years"
It has been seventy years
We have 24,930 years left
Until we can go back home to Runit
The land, the island this dome burdens
But now the waters have washed it away
Eroding parts of this dome away
Cracking it
Leaking harmful radiation out into the open
So foreign men who have visited the dome to study it say
the outside is even more contaminated than the inside
and they leave again
with numbers and calculations
No solutions
Not a thought for us

Foreign men, do you think
Do you think about the waters rising
My island ain't got no time for 24,930 years
Scientists have predicted by 2050
We are NO MORE
NO MORE
2016—I am here

My islands got 34 years left
34
But in 24,930 years, we will be able to live on Runit
How far do you think she will be underwater?

Looking out into horizons of waves angry
hungry for redemption
A bubu sits on her plywood
10-inch-high bed
She looks at me
Confusion and sadness in her eyes
"What is wrong with our islands?
I don't ever remember it being like this."
It hits me
She does not know
She does not know what is happening in our islands
Not knowing these waves pounding her shore
are human-induced
but I swear
I will fight for this grandma
I will fight for my family
I will fight for my country's survival

For bigger countries mock us
after they have violated the earth's virginity
with their carbon-filled aphrodisiac
Digging and pumping out fossil fuel
from our mother's womb
Relentlessly
Constantly

Mocking us
At 1.5 degrees
At us
At the risk of my people becoming climate refugees
Becoming stateless
Becoming landless
Becoming just a blue passport
The only identity of this grandmother and me
Will the first three pages of Marshallese stamps
Be the last stamps I get from home?
Will this blue passport be the last one I will ever have from home?

My backyard
is not like your backyard
My backyard is trees, crippled

It is broken bones unearthed from graves
It is nuclear-radiation rich
It is tides with white fangs
It is houses broken down, no more occupants within
It is the land getting smaller
and smaller
My backyard is my bubu, jimma, and mama lying in their graves
It is my grandpa telling me while in pain
"Jibu, I cannot wait to go
I will soon be resting
resting from all this world's chaos
I will now sleep
peacefully"
My backyard is a promise
a promise to let them sleep peacefully
It is we, Marshallese, saying
1.5 is all we got
Mock, be skeptical
1.5 pffft. Impossible. Unattainable.
Again
It is all we got.

Puka-Puka—Taui'anga reva, climate change

Takiora Ingram

Recently Johnny Frisbie
An elder from Puka-Puka asked me
What will happen to my people?
Once, over six hundred lived there
Now only 450 people remain on our island
And migration continues
As atoll living increasingly becomes unsustainable

For centuries
Puka-Pukans survived devastating hurricanes
In 2005, after Cyclone Percy's destruction
Some talked of abandoning their island
But they stayed, rebuilt their homes, their lives
Proved their resilience
To nature's forces
Ata wai wolo, thank you

But now sea level rise
And frequent heavy sea surges
Threaten their survival
When the earth is closest to the sun
King tides sweep over, inundating the motu
Eroding scarce land
Seawater seeps into taro patches
Contaminating soil with salt
Taro crops die
Coconut trees die
Food sources compromised

While global fossil fuel consumption
Continues at an unsustainable rate

And fossil emissions have risen forty percent
These small atolls face inundation, loss, destruction
Puka-Puka, powered by solar energy
A model of natural energy efficiency
Stands at the frontier of climate change
Victim of developed countries' over-consumption

Now, many empty houses
Stand like monuments to a once golden life
As more and more leave
To build new lives
In Rarotonga, Aotearoa, and Australia
People forced to migrate somewhere
Forced to abandon their homes, their sacred motu
For foreign lands
Leaving behind their land, lagoon, lifestyle
But taking with them their language
And the traditions of their tupuna
When will the tide turn? Will Puka-Pukans return?

September 2016

Chief Telematua's Speech to the United Nations

Vilsoni Hereniko

Noa'ia 'e mauri, Ni sa bula, Tampara, Ko na mauri, Malo e lelei, Aloha, Yokwe, Hafa Adai, Kia Ora, and so on and so on . . . Greetings to you all, in our Pacific languages, from our Pacific tongues.

Thank you for this opportunity to address the nations of the world. The United Nations!

My name is Chief Telematua, and I speak on behalf of the people of the Pacific Islands.

One voice for many Voices!

Our islands are sinking, swallowed up by the rising seas. Swallowed up by ways of life in which money and development and fossil fuels and greed have caused the rising seas to overcome us.

Soon, we'll be forced to abandon these beautiful islands of white sandy beaches, coconut palms, blue skies, and dazzling sunsets. What some of you call Paradise!

If we lose our lands, they too might disappear, along with our languages, and our oral traditions. Our world, and yours too, will be a poorer place, don't you think?

Even if you're willing to welcome us to your shores, what about the bones of our ancestors! How can we forget our past, our ways of life? Our heart and our soul?

You ask: how can you help? What can you do?

Here's how. You can be our advocate. Wherever you are!

Spread the word about us. Tell them we are drowning; that we may be forced to give up these islands that have given us life, for thousands of years.

Should we be forced to relocate, our desire is to leave with our dignity intact.

Do not call us climate change refugees. We do not deserve that label. Instead, call us migrants to a new land, where we will rebuild our lives, piece by piece, slowly, but surely.

And when people ask you about us, tell them this one thing: that when you saw us leave, we left with dignity. Our heads held high, as the tears rolled down our eyes.

May God bless you all!

Jacinda Adern goes to the Pacific Forum in Tuvalu and my family colonises her house

Tusiata Avia

It's a nice new two-story house in South Auckland with a village in the backyard

I'm guessing that park doesn't actually belong to Jacinda and her family, but they have full use of it

We've been upstairs in Jacinda's house for a while and we've made a bit of a mess really, it's all the kids

Who can stop them from running around and chucking food on the floor which gets ground into the carpets?

I know Jacinda—who is the prime minister—we're all on first-name basis in this country, which is similar to Tuvalu where their prime minister is sitting on the roof of his house

I know Jacinda is weary, it's hot over there in Tuvalu and tiring because the sea is taking over, so, the only place to play cricket is the airport runway

And the schoolkids have to sit cross-legged in their classrooms up to their waists in seawater, but they still wear their uniforms proudly with that lovely shiny black hair that island kids have

It's a crisis alright, but it's also tiring and Jacinda goes back to her house which she paid for out of her prime minister money

We all know that her partner does a lot of the child-minding, but you can't tell me that it's not tiring to be a prime minister of a whole country and have a baby as well

It must be nearly as tiring as being a Tuvaluan prime minister sitting on his own roof to stop from drowning

I feel sorry for Jacinda because I'm a solo mother and know how tiring working and looking after a baby can be

I want to advise her to get a nanny, I know I'd get a nanny so I could get some sleep, if I had as much money as a prime minister

She's not that angry about my family having colonised her house, but she does look stressed and not like she does on TV

She's trying to think of something to say over the sound of my family—who're talking to each other across the wide spaces, because it's a really big house that she's got here—when she says to me:

Yes, there's something about the Polynesian accent that makes the things you're saying sound really threatening

While I'm trying to come up with the next thing to say, I hear the voices of a whole lot of cuzzies I haven't seen for ages. They're walking around and sitting down and taking over the village. Ihumātao village. Right here in her backyard.

Nice Voice

Kathy Jetñil-Kijiner

When my daughter whines I tell her—
Say what you want in a nice voice.

My nice voice is reserved for meetings with a view, my palm outstretched saying *here. Are our problems.* Legacies rolling out like multicolored marbles. *Don't focus so much on the doom and gloom,* they keep saying. We don't want to depress. Everyone. This is only our survival. *We rely heavily on foreign aid,* I am instructed to say. I am instructed to point out the need for funds to build islands, move families from weto to weto, my mouth a shovel to spade the concrete with but I am just pointing out neediness. So needy. These small. Underdeveloped countries. I feel myself shrinking in the back of the taxi when a diplomat compliments me. How brave for admitting it so openly. The allure of global negotiations dulls. Like the back of a worn spoon.

I lose myself easily in a kemem. Kemem defined as feast. As celebration. A baby's breath endures their first year so we pack hundreds of close bodies under tents, lined up for plates I pass to my cousin, assembly-line style. Plastic gloved hands pluck out barbecue chicken, fried fish, scoop potato salad, droplets of bōb and mā. Someone yells for another container of jajimi. The speaker warbles a keyboarded song. A child inevitably cries. Mine dances in the middle of the party. The MC shouts *Boke ajiri ne nejim jen maan.* The children are obstructing our view. Someone wheels a grandma onto the dance floor, the dance begins now here

is a nice

celebration

of survival.

c entangled letters of the alphabet washing the ocean a mix

Audrey Brown-Pereira

a

b

cc

c   o   p

u   n   f   triple   c   c   c

1.5   (pre-industrial)

~~or   2   degrees(pre-industrial)~~

s i d s   **l m n o b**

q r s 2 (much)   **u v**   **more/ or less**   **g h g**

anthro – what?

anthro – what?   anthro-po-gen-ic

o - u - mean - man - made!

w x (hale)   breathe breathe breathe

y (not)   ***b*** *survivin'*

instead of

z(ee)z(ee)z(ee)   **1st (world)**

2nd (world)

3rd (world)   **time hereafter**

p i c   (t) s

picts picts picts picts c – **level rise**   **c-level r i s e**

c-level risin'   the bet in the alpha

b drownin'   ***i-land***   ***under the ocean***

Surely uncertain

Teweiariki Teaero

Precise science tells us
And we believe its insights
Our lovely isles are sinking
Some of us will go in five or so decades

Vintage history tells us
And we believe its wisdom
We have a past so nice
Longer than forever

Our ardent heart tells us
And we believe its passion
We want to live here
As people proud to be

But paradise is paralysed, well, almost
The isles are bashed by cyclones
They are drowning in rain
They are diving into rising seas
We are melting in intense heat

Now what do I tell them
My elders and ancestors
Who made and moulded me
To hold high their torch?

And what do I tell them
My many hopeful kids
Who I expect to carry on the dreams
Of our collective being?

From the misty past
Through the perilous present
Into the unknown future?

Composed at the hills of Upolu overlooking the area that was struck by the tsunami a year ago today, Samoa. 29th September 2010. First anniversary of the tsunami, *galo afi.*

Homes of Micronesia

Yolanda Joab

From the rolling hills of Yap
To the low shores and landscape of Majuro
To the serenity of Kosrae
To the booming mountains of Pohnpei
To the everlasting lagoon of Chuuk—
I've lived, I've worked
I've taught, I've learned
I've shared and received
And I've listened
To these people, their stories
My people, my stories.

I used to live in Yap
Where the rolling hills bleed red dirt
The same deep red we get from chewing betelnut
But will never see on the clean streets
Where the winding road to Maap sneaks you between unbothered villages
Where the talk is quiet and the boast is scarce
Where thuws are worn in peaceful pride
And colorful vibrant grass skirts swing in the March sun
For hundreds of curious and awed onlookers on their name day
Where life is carried in a basket
Yap was home
Yap is home

I used to live in Majuro
Where the ocean greets you with a blunt first impression
Where the horizon stares you down in the face
And then blesses you with a peace offering of the most glorious sunset
you've ever seen
Where to conquer the highest peak in all the land is to jump off of a
bridge
Where songs are sung in gifted spirit

Always in unison
Always in perfect harmony
As if rehearsed for a lifetime
Where celebration of life is always the celebration of a lifetime
Because it needed to be
Where it still needs to be
Majuro was home
Majuro is home.

I used to live in Kosrae
Where the dewy fog settles you in and nestles you down
Beneath the sleeping lady's bosom
Where the green runs into green and then blends into more green
Only interrupted by the halting blue of the encroaching ocean
Where the days are quiet and the laughter is loud
Where the mangroves form mazes for you to get lost in
Where the pace reminds you
That life is not a race
But to be appreciative
Kosrae was home
Kosrae is home

I used to live in Pohnpei
Where I was born
Where I was born a Lasialapw woman
Taking after my mother's and her mother's and her mother's before hers clan
Where in our municipality only a Lasialapw woman can give birth to a king
Where the mountains boom and demand the sky's attention
Only to surrender back down to the land with waterfalls
As if blessed by the heavens
Where the sakau is strong
And the culture for it stronger
Where the stones of Nan Madol raise up
From where our history and heritage collide
Where my ancestors fought
Where my children will live
Pohnpei was home
Pohnpei is home

I live in Chuuk
Where the lagoon scatters us like stars in an ocean sky
Where the island warrior mentality is ever present
Only to succumb to the humility required of us

Where the women form rainbows of colorful muumuus
And skirts that literally brighten up your day
Where our reputation precedes us in the same way
Every movie you thought you were gonna hate but ended up loving does
Where family is life
And if you come for one of us
You come for all of us—
The hundreds of us
Where if you ever wanted to learn
What "don't judge a book by its cover" literally means
Then I suggest you call up United flight 155 and ask for my in-laws
Yeah, where I found love
Where I found family
Where I found a home
You see
These
Are my homes
Of Micronesia

The common thread of coconut fiber that weaves it all together?
One: In every single one of these places
Our livelihoods, our livelihoods, our livelihoods—
Our names, our history, our legacy, our blood, our bones, our breath—
Is anchored in our oceans and burrowed in our land
Two: For us conservation and sustainability are not just words
That we throw around at meetings and on paper, but lived, every, single, day
Three: It's in the way my grandmother's been able to feed generations
Of her children from the fruit of her own two hands
Four: It's in the way my brothers and uncles negotiate the oceans' catch,
While their mothers beg the oceans' mercy for their safe return home
Five: We can't afford the luxury of denying science
That proves climate change puts all of THIS
Into a ticking time bomb that we have our fingers on
Six: Because for us when we turn a blind eye
We get slapped in the face on the other side with
Seven: King tides that engulfed Majuro and Kosrae
Eight: Relentless back-to-back typhoons
That swept Pohnpei, Chuuk and Ulithi
Nine: Droughts that sucked the life
And water out of all of us
Ten: Creeping sea levels that tap all parents on the shoulder
Like a nightmare that our children haven't even had yet
Ten: I heard one of your presidential candidates
Doesn't believe in climate change

Ten: It doesn't matter how much money he has,
God forbid if elected, he can't afford to ignore this too
Ten: I once said to my students that if our islands are too small
To be seen on a map then you make them see *you*.
Ten: *I'm saying it again.*
Ten: I'll say it for the rest of my life.
Ten: We can't afford to keep counting to eleven
So ten, let's end it here.

Pacific Islanders March for Self-Determination

Fuifuilupe Niumeitolu

Even several years after that historic moment, viewing images of our Pacific Islander (Melanesian, Micronesian, Polynesian) contingent, marching collectively alongside one another and arm in arm with our Native American relatives in the Indigenous Block at the major Climate Change March on Saturday, February 7, 2015, I'm always moved to tears. I'm humbled by the images of us, so many of us, brown-skinned, Pacific Islander bodies that included crying babies, youths and elders, mobilized and marching together, enduring the rain, moving slowly but steadily under the shadows of tall high-rise buildings holding banners and signs that unapologetically tell our struggles. All of us, together, took over the streets of Oakland, California.

These images, whether those shown widely disseminated on social media, or stored within the repository of my memory, tell the story of that day. They are stories of strength and they are stories of healing. One of the banners that resonate in my mind protested the often negative representations of Pacific Islanders in the mainstream media, and also reminded us Pacific people of the importance of our original teachings and our homelands. "Moana is not a Disney Movie, She is our Grandmother, Our Pacific Ocean," it said. This poignant sign was the vision of my younger sister and community leader, Loa Niumeitolu. Like all of the signs that we proudly held that day, this one explicitly renders us visible here in the U.S. by reminding us that we Pacific Islanders are Indigenous peoples from the Moana. We are not API, like the U.S. government classifies us, and we refuse to be silenced within this contemporary racialization that further invisibilizes our communities. Like our Native American relatives that we marched alongside within the Indigenous Block, our connections to our Creator, our ancestors, including our lands and oceans, as well as grandparents and the spirits of children, not yet born, are all vā, or sacred connections, which are central to our identities and our survival as Indigenous peoples from the Pacific. Thus, the many images of our Pacific Islander contingent at the march unabashedly retell stories about ourselves and our Pacific Islander communities that counter the colonial myths deployed to invisibilize and dehumanize us. The images of us from that historic moment remind us that the medicine for our personal healing and our collective healing as a community lies within ourselves and within our communities. The medicine for our wounds lies in the heart of our struggles and our resistances.

The images from that historic moment remind us of the significant gifts that each individual, and each respective Pacific community, shared so generously with each other and with our collective. I am reminded of the important gifts shared by our Marshallese brothers and sisters. They were a large youth group organized by beloved female Marshallese community leaders Rena Abon-Burch and Wakein Deunert. The youth group traveled before sunrise from Sacramento to be part of this march. I remember Rena Abon-Burch texting me on the morning of the march before 6 a.m. to reassure me that her group had started their journey to Oakland. She reminded me that this is the first time that many of the youths have ever left Sacramento, and this is also the first time that many of the youths have ever visited the Bay Area, and many of them were scared, but they were so excited to tell the stories about their Marshallese ancestors and the consequences of climate change on their communities.

At the march, the Marshallese youths marched behind big banners. One beautiful banner stated, "Our Tides are Too High So We Rise for Our Grandchildren." They also offered heart-felt chants and songs in their Indigenous language to empower and motivate us throughout the march. In fact, their generous offerings of songs and prayers were the medicine that led us, compassionately, to the finish line when the rain began to pour. Moreover, at the end of the march when we were wet, tired and ready to fall, our Marshallese brothers and sisters, once again, lifted us up. Marshallese community leader Rena Abon-Burch shared a prayer and the youths offered a closing prayer-song in their Indigenous language on the main stage. The closing prayer-song was an offering shared with the crowds of thousands who attended the march. During their heart-felt message, I observed that they moved the crowds to reverence and many of us to tears. Their prayer-song was medicine for our spirits. At that precise moment, we stood tall, unabashed, and connected to each other and to the spirits of our ancestors. It was a beautiful moment to be alive, to be a Pacific Islander, to be Indigenous and to be part of a movement of Pacific Islanders united not only in our struggles against climate change but united in our struggles for Pacific Islander self-determination.

On that historic day in Oakland, and contrary to the colonial narratives, our beloved Marshallese family took their rightful role as warriors at the forefront of our movement. Our relatives from the Marshall Islands, a nation located within the Micronesian region of the Pacific, who we once held intimately as a close relation, had been unfortunately severed from us as a consequence of Western colonization. Thus, from that separation, the Pacific regions, Micronesia and Melanesia, were designated "other" even within the Pacific Islander community, while Polynesia, although also marginalized by the West, was often privileged and offered more opportunities for visibility. Hence, it is not surprising that Polynesians are often the only population included within the term "Pacific Islander." But out on the streets of Oakland that day, our lives depended on our Marshallese relatives and, in turn, they courageously carried us to the finish line.

Yes, all of these courageous relatives carried us home. This new home we've created is a home that can shelter all of us, especially those of us that have been marginalized or cast aside. This is a new home built on our collective struggles, resistances and inexorable love for our ancestors, and for each other.

The letter of the day

Katerina Teaiwa

following Sesame Street

Dance nearby

Dance faraway

Now clap your hands to the letter of the day!

clap clap

What's the letter?

clap clap

What's the letter?

clap clap clap clap

What's the letter?

What's the letter?

What's the letter, what's the letter, what's the letter?

The letter of the day is C!

Create

Crucify

Christianity

Crusade

Conquer

Colonize

Capitalism

Consume

Coal

Climate

COVID

Calamity

slow clap

The Word of the Day

Penina Ava Taesali

Every Day Is Earth Day

The word of the day could be dreadful or atrocious or lost for the roses root deeper for cleaner water to survive this August. Their petals pealing to blossom our eyes open so we may protect the wild green dawn so we could stop. Let the unexpected tributaries off 14th Street & Madras stream for the mallard and her drake with the seven ducklings paddling through the narrow brook of the First Peoples lands mourning for Mother Earth

and the word of the day tomorrow? Let it not be brutality or money or rifle or my religion or yours let it be leopard or rhinoceros or red abalone or blue whale or Yangtze River dolphin or let the word be African talking drum or Fijian canoe drum or Filipino kulingtang or Appalachian dulcimer or ukulele or slack-key guitar or let it be trombone carried on the confident shoulders of a ten-year-old girl—let us think the where and how and why

we pick-up and play and write and sing and dance so that the Honduran emerald hummingbird the leatherback sea turtle the mountain gorilla the tiger salamander the fender blue butterfly the honeybees the living coral reefs the breathing rainforests in Brazil in Guinea and there in the Sacramento Delta where river otters fish and breed let our word be bigger as in humility as in mountain water tree food sun moon stars for them for them for them

Sunday, April 22, 2018

Previously published, *Take a Stand: Art Against Hate,* Raven Chronicles Press, 2020.

Moa Space Foa Ramble

Joe Balaz

Sell dat beachfront property now
and get as much as you can foa da house.

Wheah you got your plumeria tree
and nice green lawn

going be wun playground foa da fishes.

Methane from da tundra
and CO_2 from smoke stacks and exhaust pipes

going turn all dat melted ice from da poles
into moa watah foa da lobsters and da eels.

Middle of da island
dats da place to go.

Dere's no getting around it
cause da coastline going sink.

Take wun good look at da airport
and da brand new rail—

all of it is moving inland, brah.

Waikiki going be real different too.

Previously published, *Pidgin Eye,* Ala Press, 2019.

Might as well just give it up
cause wun surrounding wall not going help.

Too bad no can build da same kine mega dam
dat dey going make in San Francisco Bay.

Da Golden Gate sure going look different.

Global warming—

Foa da longest time
plenty people wen blow it off as wun myth.

Now Kanaloa going have moa space foa ramble.

Water Remembers

Brandy Nālani McDougall

Waikīkī was once a fertile marshland
ahupua'a, mountain water gushing
from the valleys of Makiki, Mānoa,
Pālolo, Wai'alae, and Wailupe
to meet ocean water. Seeing such
wealth, Kānaka planted hundreds
of fields of kalo, 'uala, 'ulu in the uka,
built fishponds in the muliwai.
Waikīkī fed O'ahu people for generations
so easily that its ocean raised surfers,
hailed the highest of ali'i to its shores.

Waikīkī is now a miasma of concrete
and asphalt, its waters drained
into a canal dividing tourist from resident.
The mountain's springs and waterfalls,
trickle where they are allowed to flow,
and left stagnant elsewhere, pullulate
with staphylococcus. In the uplands,
the fields have long been dismantled,
their rock terraces and heiau looted
to build the walls of multimillion-dollar
houses with panoramic Diamond Head
and/or ocean views. Closer to the ocean,
hotels fester like pustules, the sand
stolen from other 'āina to manufacture
the beaches, seawalls maintained
to keep the sand in, so suntan-oiled
tourists can laze on what never was,
what never should have been. No one
is fed plants and fish from this 'āina now—

its land value has grown so that nothing
but money *can* be grown—its waters unpotable, polluted.

Each year as heavy rainfalls flood the valleys,
spill over gulches, slide the foundations
of overpriced houses, invade sewage pipes
and send brown water runoff to the ocean,
the king tides roll in, higher in its warming,
lingering longer and breaking through
sandbags and barricades, eroding the resorts.

This is not the end of civilization, but
a return to one. Only the water insisting
on what it should always have, spreading
its liniment over infected wounds. Only
the water rising above us, reteaching us
wealth and remembering its name.

Ewi am lomnak

Carlon Zackhras

Ewi am lomnak ilo an maroñ jemlok adwoj
jukjuk im amnak ion aeloñ kein ad.

Lomnak kin an maroñ jemlok am relak im lale
an ro tutu im bok jeramon in malo eo eblue.
Sit under the coconut tree, riaelon kein rej ba
ni im et bwin ko reman im melu.

Ijelok in am roñ an lajimma ba, "ahh iakwe
lijububu" "kwoj tal ñan ia lajibubu." Konej roñ
hello, hi ako mool ijab konan bye ñan
lamoren in an bubu im jimma.

Ijo jikun lijelbabbub im lijabkonira. Jikun
iaikoj eo an timur im jabro. ijo lektañur
kejobelbel wujla eo jinoun tata. Aeloñ ko
letao ear boktok kijek eo jinountata bwe
riaelon kein ren bok jeramon jen e.

Ewi am lomnak. Ilo an maroñ jemlok. Kajin
in ad im manit in ad renaj bed wot ilo, aeloñ
kein ad.

Ewi am lomnak. Mool uaak eo eben ak kin
menin eben lak jen menko reben, uaak eo
am enaj kaben joñon iakwe eo am ñan aeloñ
kein am.

Tāwhaki

Witi Ihimaera

E Ara Mai

I'm dozing in my crew cabin when the video link tells me, "Tāwhaki, wake up."

It's Dad of course. Other people prefer electronic wake-up calls, but I prefer my father's voice and face. "Mōrena," he smiles. "Good morning. E ara mai, rise up."

I pull the sleeping bag around me, yawn, and cock one eye at him. Dark weathered face. Big head and high forehead like mine, but lots of thick black hair whereas I have a military fade. Crooked teeth, one grazing his bottom lip. A quizzical, teasing expression. And he always calls me Tāwhaki even though my name is really Branson. Mum's choice, but it's too up itself, he reckons.

"You haven't got a girl . . . or boy . . . in bed with you?" he teases.

"As if," I give the usual snort. "No room, and nobody I'm attracted to." Would I admit to my father that nobody is attracted to *me?* Hell no.

Dad's face goes into his pretending-to-be-sad look. "You better watch out, son," he says. "You're 23, your gears must be in perfect working order, but they could go rotten."

I turn my back on him.

"Don't roll over and poke your bum in my face. Time for you to do your mahi. Is Pōhutukawa looking beautiful this morning?"

The World in the Sixth Extinction

Pōhutukawa is one of the Māori names for the earth. And it's just like Dad to prefer the Māori description. "Earth" has no beauty to it, being monosyllabic and inert.

I wash and brush my teeth, take a dump into the collection bag and an air current sucks my urine into the waste compartment. I suit up and listen as *Ranginui-14* groans around me, whining like a cantankerous god.

Heigh-ho, it's off to work I go, floating my way through the connecting corridors of the space station to the observation cupola. I'm one of the weather-casters on board. Early morning shift today, so there's only a few military boys at their posts and a couple of fliers chatting up Anahera, one of the shuttle captains. "Mōrena," she grins.

I wink at her, grab what passes for breakfast—coffee to go and a sandwich—and float on by to the lookout to take over from Nigel, my American counterpart.

"Hey," I say to him.

Changeovers of shifts are always monosyllabic and Nigel's in a hurry to get to bed. "Did you change the sheets?" he quips as he vacates the chair.

I strap myself in, do the usual instrument check, and then surrender to the lyrical beauty of a sea of stars. The panoramic vista always takes my breath away. Space is studded with light, twinkling diamonds strewn on a velvet cloth all the way back through the twelve heavens. To Io, God of all Gods, in the topmost bespaced rangi tūhāhā. And further back to Te Pō, the night even before stars, to Te Kore, the nothing before that.

But that's the view in front of me. I pull the visor down across my face and rotate the cupola to the view behind and beneath. The shadow side of an enormous dark globe wearing a corona of radiance. Patch my father back into the comms. He looks eagerly over my shoulder at the world below.

"Yes, Dad," I say, trying to keep the sarcasm from my voice. "There she is! Your beautiful Pōhutukawa! She was once the daughter of Rangi Tāmaku, the eleventh heaven, wasn't she?"

"You remember my old stories?" Dad asks, delighted. "Her other name was Papatūānuku and she married Ranginui, the Sky Father. There was nobody more glorious than she was in all the firmament, moko. Glowing like pounamu, with blue oceans the colour of a whale's dreams."

I turn my father off. "You're too sentimental, old man."

Because below me is the brutal reality. The night is retreating over the Americas—or what is left of it. By the 22nd century, global warming had melted both ice caps and raised the sea levels over 200 feet. In what used to be the USA, the entire Atlantic seaboard, gone. The Rockies as well as the Sierra Nevada and the Appalachian ranges, the primary high dry regions. A cluster of islands where San Francisco was. Further north in Canada, the bare bones of the Canadian Rockies extension, the St. Elias and Laurentian chains. And southward, what was once Central America has been washed away. And the accustomed shorelines of South America have long disappeared. It's people clambering up the stark backbone of the Andes.

Stink, man.

If that hadn't been enough, earth's rising heat made much of the surface uninhabitable. And during the daytime, with the sun at its apex, nobody could survive in the open. No wonder all humankind went underground, working at night and sleeping during the day.

"Tāwhaki," Dad warns. "Pay attention."

The corona has burst a flaming red over Pōhutukawa below. I can't help it, I take a deep breath. It's an unconscious gesture, a flinch against the awesome power of the sun, I want to scream. My instrumentation starts to go crazy, the panel flashing all kinds of signals.

And I start my daily transmissions. "Get underground, people," I warn everyone, "here comes Te Rā." I broadcast the readings to the relay stations below. Count down the sun's advance, "T-minus 10, 9, 8," for the northwest sector. As the ground temperature starts to rise, "T-minus 7, 6, 5," for the central sector. Back to that edge of sun scything through the northeast, "T-minus 4, 3, 2 . . ."

There's the usual adrenaline rush of fear. Uncle Sam is on fire and there's just a few seconds for any stragglers to reach the scattered silos and batten down the hatches. Quick. Now. *Get the kids to safety.*

Ranginui-14 is on a high Earth and geosynchronous orbit. It's in a sweet spot, some 35,000 kilometers above the equator, where the space station can match the rotation of the earth on its axis. From the cupola I have views north and south of the arc.

Behold, the world below, a burning fiery furnace. It's been a long time since anybody lived at 0° latitude. The parts of those countries in Africa, South America and Asia that once straddled the equator had the sun directly overhead and were the first to fall victims to it, pretty much. And Kiribati, Maldives, São Tomé and Principe were among the early island states to succumb to rising sea levels.

The next casualties were *all* the countries between the Tropic of Cancer (latitude approximately 22°27′ north of the equator) and the Tropic of Capricorn (latitude 23°26′22″ south). Once upon a long-ago time the zone between was called the Tropics, holiday destinations associated with waving palm trees, smiling natives, suntans and sex in the sand. Among the countries in the zone were Mexico, Egypt, Saudi Arabia, India, southern China, northern Australia, Chile, southern Brazil and northern South Africa. We call it the Scorch Sector now. Anybody left in the open will be burnt to cinders.

But, hey, my geographical references are coming from the old tattered early-21st-century map pasted on the roof of the cupola. It's like a treasure map to a lost time, because everybody knows that's not the world we live in any longer.

"Satisfied now?" I ask Dad. "What would all your Māori gods of creation think of this? I reckon Io, God of all gods, in his uppermost first heaven would be truly pissed off."

I'm baiting him, pushing the envelope, but he pushes back. "So would Rehua in the third heaven," he says, "and don't refer to the gods with such disrespectful language."

"All their work for nothing!" I mock him. "Not to mention the other creation gods and goddesses of the time-space continuum, eh, like Māhorahora-nui-a-rangi, her husband Te Mangu and their four sons. They kept the wā, the energy of the universe, flowing from the past into the present, and what do we do with it? We abuse the taonga tuku iho, the gifts of life, they gave us."

Dad is getting riled with me. "Are you trying to pick a fight, son?"

"Just saying, Dad. Somebody sure messed up. And it wasn't me or my generation."

He searches for a rejoinder, trying to lighten the mood. "Maybe you can reboot creation for us," he says after a while. "You could do a Māui."

I cock an eyebrow at him and throw my *what do you mean* look at him.

"Don't play the dumbass," he grumbles. "You know full well, the story about how, i nga wā o mua, Te Rā went so fast across the sky that the people didn't have time to work the vegetable gardens. No sooner had the sun come up and they had started planting then, e hika, down he went and it was nighttime already . . ."

Yes, I remembered the story, it had been a favourite when I was a boy and Dad told it to me at bedtime. He was the well-loved supervisor of the engineering team which kept Rarohenga—that's the nickname we have for our very own underground city in New Zealand—operational. You've heard of Rarohenga, haven't you? It lies at the base of Hikurangi Mountain, the first point on the earth's surface to be touched by the new day. If ever you are lost in space, all you need to do is wait until the sun comes up. What would you be waiting for? Why, the flash of sunlight on the sacred mountain! Once you see that sword of light, then you can calibrate your position. Ah, ko Hikurangi, there, and mark.

". . . anyhow, it was up to Māui, the demi-god, to come up with a solution," Dad continues. "He gathered his brothers together, and they travelled to the ends of the earth where Te Rā lived. They wove a magic net and, when he started to rise, Māui trapped him in it. He used a magic jawbone to belabour the sun into submission. And when Te Rā pleaded for clemency, Māui made him promise to go slower across the sky."

"The point being?"

"Maybe it's time for a modern Māui to give Te Rā a hiding but, this time, to make him go faster."

"Yeah, right, well don't look at me, Dad." He's always thought I should rise above my current position forecasting weather. "Māui was half-god, and that story's just a myth. I don't have a magic jawbone either."

I ignore him and get back to my instrumentation. I try to push back on the reality of a China that is now flooded. All Bangladesh gone along with coastal India. What's Cambodia now? Just an island with its Cardamom Mountains the peak.

What happened to their billions of population? Don't ask.

I really don't have time to continue arguing with Dad, as Australia is looming up below. "I'm putting you on hold," I tell him.

The space station starts to judder and groan as corrections are made to adjust its orbit. They bring mathematical focus to the fires that have been burning day and night. Time to broadcast the specific coordinates for the roaring conflagration so people further south can get out of harm's way.

And then I receive a transmission from earth. It's my Auntie Kui, She-Who-Must-Be-Obeyed, Dad's sister.

"Kia ora, Branson," she says.

She looks across my shoulder and sees Dad behind me.

"Still talking to your father, I see. Are you on track for arriving home this weekend?"

"Yes, Auntie." She thinks I'll do a runner. "My leave's been approved." Suck that up.

"So you'll be on the shuttle, arriving home on Saturday? Ka pai."

She's just about to sign off except that she hesitates and looks at me with tenderness.

"You have to let him go someday," she says.

Pōhutukawa, Who Used to Be Blue Once

The shuttle screams like the hōkioi, the fabled bird of prophecy, as it hits the main air of earth's atmosphere.

"Good morning, Vietnam," the captain, Anahera, says. The five grunts in the cabin go ape at the retro affirmation of a safe entry. *Ranginui-14* has a primary military surveillance operation, safeguarding the ANZUS Quadrant. The infantrymen are transferring to comms duties at ground stations in Antarctica.

"Here, bud, have a beer," one of the grunts offers.

I pretend to join in the revelry but I'm not feeling it. I've been living on *Ranginui-14* for an entire year. The bubble up there has been cosy, safe, above the dying planet not in it. But now that the shuttle is descending through the realm of Tāwhirimātea, god of winds, I realise that soon I will have to face the realities of ground zero.

And I can't stop the rage that I was always able to suppress on *Ranginui-14*. Medievalists had defined humanity as *animal rationalis*. What the fuck happened? Jonathan Swift, author of *Gulliver's Travels*, satirically defined us as *animal rationalis capac*, capable of acting rationally—which he didn't actually believe and which the evidence proved devastatingly otherwise. Because in the mid-20th century the Anthropocene epoch arrived and humankind became the defining agent in changing the ecology of the environment. Mass exoduses of humankind out of war-torn Africa and the Middle East due to war had already placed pressure on nations on their perimeters. Then came the climate refugees.

"Hold on tight, boys," Anahera says to us. "We're in for a rocky ride."

The shuttle is being thrown all over the sky. No need for Anahera to generate drag and thereby dissipate speed. Jet streams are smashing against the craft and doing that for us. They are voluminous with thick, dark detritus pelting the bodywork with the shattered bones and cartilage of earth.

"We're through," Anahera says as she angles the descent into something resembling a glide path.

And the world turns a virulent red. This is what hell must look like. The atmosphere swirling with tornadoes and twisters. Lightning strikes close to the shuttle, *let us in, let us in.* The air stinks. Rotten. Below is the sea. It looks as if all the gods of the twelve heavens have vomited their guts out into a bowl. The waves are froths of bilious blood-veined sick.

Oh Pōhutukawa, you used to be blue and green once.

A Kōrero with My Father

I can't help it. I mouth the words to myself, "What have we done to you? What have we done to *us?*"

"You mustn't be so hard on humanity," my father answers, eavesdropping on me as usual.

"The clear signal," I reply angrily, "was the creation of a blanket of definable man-made radioisotopes around the earth. Why didn't humankind see it?"

"You're talking about *them,*" Dad says. "We did take notice, son."

"But you couldn't stop their actions. And when the refugees fled in terror from the Scorch Sector north or south to the Pole sectors, they were turned back. To face certain death."

A massive stasis had occurred in all the world's governments. The situation of the world's dispossessed, the homeless, the starving, became too big to fix. The United States, unapologetic about not signing up to the goals of the 2015 Paris climate agreement, fast-tracked its "America First" policy. Then chaos . . . temperature trends in the troposphere shot into the *red red red* . . . there was ozone depletion . . . massive emissions from the ocean of hydrogen sulfide . . . the destruction of the ceiling above let the sun in . . . and thus began the rise in fatal levels of UV radiation . . . all symptoms of the collapse of the biosphere.

Aue te mamae, there was a confluence of mounting catastrophic events . . . famine . . . severe droughts . . . earthquakes . . . melting ice caps . . . viruses . . . the four horsemen of the Apocalypse came *riding scything souls bring out your dead* . . .

International and trade blockades went *up up up* . . . and the entire system of international cooperation broke *down down down* . . .

In the early 21st century the world population had peaked at almost 8 billion, and it was already overcrowded. By the 22nd century, 5 billion had been wiped off the slate. The human brain cannot contemplate the magnitude of such losses.

Wherever people survived, they were left to sort out a future for themselves. The world writhed in all the agony attendant upon the sixth extinction. Auē, taukiri e . . .

"Stop this," my father says.

He has always been the voice of sanity, bringing everyone back into the room.

"We're still here," he continues. "We've muddled our way through. The old verities are gone, but humanity still holds. No use crying over spilt miraka. Here at the bottom of the world we do not go gently into the night, we go raging at the light."

It's a nice little kōrero, no wonder Dad has always been a leader of men. But I am not about to let his clever turns of phrase divert me. I haven't finished with him yet.

"Dad," I say to him. "The worst is we weren't just killing ourselves. Look at what else humankind destroyed. The only way to see the big whales, cats, lions and cheetahs is to watch them via the feeds that play into our dreamworlds when we sleep. The biomass of birds, the skies are empty. The total mass of insects, gone, and wasn't the state of bugs the state of the world?"

"There's always hope," Dad answers with his usual refrain. "If you can't do a Māui, you might have to do a Tāwhaki. You remember your namesake, don't you?"

"How can I forget? You told me often enough when I was a boy."

My father is persistent, his voice riding through my words. "It was Tāwhaki who climbed from the twelfth heaven through all the rangi tūhāhā to make a special request of Io, God of all gods, in the uppermost level."

Dad is gentling me, calming me down, cutting me off from the terrible pass that I sometimes plunge into. "He was just a young man like you, and he went by way of the aka mātua, the parent vine, climbing through the eleventh, tenth, ninth heavens. He was transformed by the task from corporeal to spiritual, from unschooled to literate, from human to superhuman. Oh, his climb took him a long time, son . . . up the poutama, the stairway, he ascended, eighth, seventh, sixth, fifth . . . and on the way he tested the parameters of life and death, the parameters of creation . . . where did space begin and end? Where did time begin and end? He came to the fourth heaven, the third, the second . . ."

My father's voice rises to a level of heightened ecstasy. He makes me imagine Tāwhaki kneeling before Io.

Tāwhaki has come to ask for three baskets of knowledge, though some people say there were four. In the first basket, Te Kete Aronui, is the knowledge to help all humankind. Te Kete Tuauri, the second basket, contains the ancient rites and ceremonies to ensure the tapu reinforcement of the knowledge of Te Kete Aronui. The third basket, Te Kete Tuatea, has examples of the lessons of history to learn from. Although divisible, the ultimate power of the baskets multiplies exponentially when they are operated together for the benefit of all.

"E Io," Tāwhaki asks. "Humankind seeks enlightenment."

He is surrounded in a dazzle of illumination. The heavens begin to sing.

Let the baskets of knowledge be theirs.

City Beneath the Mountain

A pattern of lightning strikes. Not heavenly song but the screaming sound of a world *in extremis.*

"We're approaching Hikurangi," Anahera tells us. "We'll be at the landing zone in five minutes and counting."

"Tāwhaki had magic karakia to help him, Dad," I say to him as I check my seat belt. "And where would I find the aka mātua in a world like ours?"

Anahera is in a race with the sun. Although we're coming in on the mountain's shadow side, we must drop down into Rarohenga before Te Rā rises above the summit.

Dad snorts. "Don't you know anything? The story of your namesake is a metaphor. You have to find the aka mātua in yourself son, as we all must, and find the way from death back into life."

"Just in time," Anahera says. The deflector shields part, the earth opens up, and she steers the shuttle into the arrival dock. Everything happens quickly after that. Customs and security clearances. Descending by lift into the bowels of the city. When the doors open, Rarohenga blazes with light.

The city carries its military function lightly. Stripped down. Functional. A people who can build a space station surely had the expertise to create an underground complex. And after all, in our mythology there were two primary worlds, one was Te Ao Mārama and the other Rarohenga, the world below. The parents of the demi-god Māui lived there. Like we do now, when the day dawned, down they would go to the cool world beneath.

Around the world there are many underground cities like ours. Built by the survivors of the precipitous decline in the world's populations. But even now there are still too many people for the cities to service. And so while the cities still maintain a quasi-governmental and military function, the society is divided into Essentials on one side and the Non-Essentials (NEs) and Olds (Os) on the other.

"At least at Rarohenga," I say to Dad as we step from the shuttle, "you may be old but you're still essential." In some cities around the world the NEs and Os are in permanent lockdown. Stacked on top of each other in enforced hibernation they are fed dreams of what the world used to be like, a home where the buffalos roam.

"I love you too," Dad says in response to my sarcasm. But his voice is shadowed and his eyes are glowing. "Ah, there's Kui."

And I feel a darkness descending all around me. A huge sense of impending loss.

She waits in the arrival concourse to greet me. My three sisters are with her. I recognise other whānau as belonging to agricultural crews which supply the city with kūmara, the staple food that Rarohenga depends on. They were with Dad and me when . . .

"Nau mai, haere mai ki te wā kainga," Kui smiles. You have arrived, you are here, welcome home. *Home?*

She looks across my shoulder to my father. "E te rangatira . . ."

I follow her gaze. Dad looks at me, tenderly. "This had to happen sometime, Branson."

Why is everyone weeping?

"Goodbye, son."

It happens so quickly. One moment Dad's there. The next moment he is gone. It's the moment I have dreaded. Because I have not only been running away from reality. I have also been running away from this particular moment.

"Thank you for bringing your father back," Aunt Kui says. "I didn't think you would be able to do it."

I am terrorised, gasping. The sense of loss overwhelms me. "I . . . I . . . I . . ."

I am in psychic shock. *Dad, don't leave me.*

And I fall in a faint into my Aunt's arms.

Kete O Te Wānanga

A year ago. I am with Dad and his work crew. It is night and we have driven to the outer perimeter of the plantations to fix some of the sun-filtering shades. Some of the louvres aren't functioning, not closing, and the harsh sun is shrivelling the kūmara below.

It is dark when we leave Rarohenga. When we arrive at the plantations, we see that some of the kaimahi ahuwhenua, the farmers, are working the fields with their wives and a group of small children. Dad goes to greet them. "The women wanted to bring the kids into the fresh air. Have a picnic before we go back. And the tamariki like to play in the cool night."

"Ka pai," Dad answers. "All good." He pats the little ones on the head. "You are the future," he says to them. "Your ancestors came from a place called Hawaiki. You are royal children."

The engineering team work speedily. Overhead, the sky turns, a few scattered stars.

After we've fixed the shades we sit around with the farmers enjoying each other's company. The kids scamper around, enjoying themselves. Someone has brought a guitar, so we sing some of the old songs.

"Me he manurere, aue . . ." That was Mum's favourite before she died. I was still a baby and Aunt Kui brought me up. It's basically been just Dad and me after that, really.

How did it happen that we left our return to Rarohenga too late? The dawn is already lightening the sky, but we think we have time. We travel back to the city in convoy, the two crews, engineers and farmers in four transports. Hikurangi mountain doesn't look too far away.

Then one of the farmers' transports breaks down. "You three go on," Dad tells the others. "You go with them, Tāwhaki."

"No," I answer. "You might need me here."

We watch the other transports as they depart. Then Dad says, "Haere ki te mahi," rolls up his sleeves, and tries to figure out what the problem is. There are fifteen of us waiting around, Dad, two engineers, me, six farmers, two women, three children—two of them are babies being breast-fed.

"We should have put the women and children in the other vehicles," Dad says.

"They didn't want to leave their husbands," one of the farmers says.

"I should have forced them to go. They are my responsibility."

The problem is found and can't be fixed. Three batteries damaged. "I'll radio base," Dad says, "and ask them to send an extraction unit. Not a problem."

And we still think that we're okay except that . . . sometimes it's not the sun you need to be aware of. The rising sun has kick-started the morning wind. Before we know it, the currents are swirling an eviscerating, hot blast of heat. The world becomes an oven and begins to cook us. Before we know it, we are gasping and falling to the ground.

"Tāwhaki," Dad yells, "break out the fire blankets."

The blankets are fire-resistant wingsuits that might win us some time. We huddle beneath, the men forming a protective rim for the women and children in the middle.

Above us, the sound of an extraction unit. "Get the kids to safety," *Dad says to me.*

"What about you?"

"Me and the other men have to keep the blankets up and around you as you leave. The women and children are in your care. Go, son."

Every second counts. Stepping beyond the blankets, we are already burning. The children are screaming. The wind is a fiery maelstrom. We fall into the arms of our rescuers.

"What about my Dad!"

"We have to go." The rescue transport wheels away. The wind whips the blankets away from Dad and the men. Dad raises an arm.

He bursts into flames.

The women, children and me were in the burns unit at Rarohenga for over a month. I embraced the pain of the skin grafts, I felt I should have died with my father. We all recovered and, when I was well enough to return to duty, I applied for transfer to *Ranginui-14* and got it. But I had loved Dad so much that I couldn't let him go. I took his wairua, his spirit, with me, whether he wanted to come or not, whether others wanted me to take him or not.

They could go to hell. He was mine and I would not let anybody have him.

And now, over a year has passed. I have returned for the hura kohatu, the unveiling ceremony for Dad and the other men who died. Unveilings usually take place a year after the tangihanga, the mourning ceremony.

I stand with Aunt Kui and the mourners in front of the memorial stone in the family urupa. It's outside Rarohenga, within a cleft of Hikurangi mountain. Among the attendants are the wives and children who survived with me.

"Shall we begin, nephew?" Aunt Kui asks.

I nod my head and the tributes start. Not only to Dad but also to the other men, the engineers and farmers, who died with him. And, contrary to my expectations, the commemoration is not as sad as I was expecting. In fact, some of the memories are hilarious and others are, well, quite salty. In other words, human. "I didn't know Dad was such a ladies' man," I whisper to Aunt Kui.

She rolls her eyes. "Let's just say my brother's gears never went rotten, and leave it at that."

Everyone begins to sing songs in celebration of the lives that were taken so that we can go on. One cheeky kuia starts doing a hula.

"She was one of your father's er . . ." Aunt Kui begins, leaving me to connect the dots.

Oh, Dad. You were always talking about my namesake Tāwhaki.

I will try to find a way. For the sake of the children, I will climb to the uppermost heaven, yes, I will find the aka mātua, and I will do it. But, Dad, when Tāwhaki brought back the baskets of knowledge the first time, look what humankind did with all those taonga. We trashed them.

My father, we don't deserve a second chance. And the real question is: if we are given it, and if Io grants us the baskets of knowledge again, will we get over our self-destructive nature and obsessions and do better this time?

Will we?

Wellington
3 April 2020

Unity

Selina Tusitala Marsh

Written and performed for Her Majesty Queen Elizabeth II, Westminster Abbey, 2016

> Maluna a'e o nā lāhui apau ke ola ke kanaka
> "Above all nations is humanity"
>
> —Hawaiian proverb

Let's talk about unity
Here, in London's Westminster Abbey

did you know there's a London in Kiribati?
Ocean Island: South Pacific Sea.

We're connected by currents of humanity,
alliances, allegiances, histories

for the salt in the sea, like the salt in our blood
like the dust of our bones, our final return to mud

means while 53 flags fly for our countries
they're stitched from the fabric of our unity

it's called the Vā in Sāmoan philosophy
what you do, affects me

what we do, affects the sea
land, wildlife—take the honeybee

nature's model of unity
pollinating from flower to seed

Previously published, *Tightrope,* Auckland University Press, 2017.

bees thrive in hives keeping their queen
unity keeps them alive, keeps them buzzing

they're key to our fruit and vege supplies
but parasitic attacks and pesticides

threaten the bee, then you, then me
it's all connected—that's unity.

There's a "U" and an "I" in unity
costs the earth and yet it's free.

My grandad's from Tuvalu and to be specific
it's plop bang in the middle of the South Pacific

the smallest of our 53 Commonwealth nations
the largest in terms of reading vast constellations

my ancestors navigated by sky and sea trails
way before Columbus even hoisted his sails!

What we leave behind, matters to those who go before
we face the future with our backs, sailing shore to shore

for we're earning and saving for our common wealth
a common strong body, a common good health

for the salt in the sea, like the salt in our blood
like the dust of our bones, our final return to mud

means saving the ocean, saving the bee
means London's UK seeing London in the South Seas
and sharing our thoughts over a cup of tea.

There's a "U" and an "I" in unity
costs the earth and yet it's free.

Dear Matafele Peinam

Kathy Jetñil-Kijiner

Dear Matafele Peinam,

You are a seven month old sunrise of gummy smiles
you are bald as an egg and bald as the buddha
you are thighs that are thunder and shrieks that are lightning
so excited for bananas, hugs and
our morning walks past the lagoon

Dear Matafele Peinam,

I want to tell you about that lagoon
that lucid, sleepy lagoon lounging against the sunrise

men say that one day
that lagoon will devour you

They say it will gnaw at the shoreline
chew at the roots of your breadfruit trees
gulp down rows of your seawalls
and crunch your island's shattered bones

They say you, your daughter
and your granddaughter, too
will wander rootless
with only a passport to call home

Dear Matafele Peinam,

Don't cry
mommy promises you

Previously published, *Iep Jaltok: Poems from a Marshallese Daughter,* University of Arizona Press, 2017.

no one
will come and devour you

No greedy whale of a company sharking through political seas
no backwater bullying of businesses with broken morals
no blindfolded bureaucracies gonna push
this mother ocean over
the edge

No one's drowning, baby
no one's moving
no one's losing
their homeland
no one's gonna become
a climate change refugee

Or should I say
no one else

To the Carteret Islanders of Papua New Guinea
and to the Taro Islanders of the Solomon Islands
I take this moment
to apologize to you

We are drawing the line here

Because baby we are going to fight
your mommy daddy
bubu jimma your country and president too
we will all fight

And even though there are those
hidden behind platinum titles
who like to pretend
that we don't exist

Who like to pretend
that the Marshall Islands
Tuvalu
Kiribati
Maldives
Typhoon Haiyan in the Philippines
and floods of Algeria, Pakistan, Colombia
and all the earthquakes, hurricanes and tidal waves
didn't exist

Still
there are those
who see us

Hands reaching out
fists raising up
banners unfurling
megaphones booming

and we are
canoes blocking coal ships

we are
the radiance of solar villages

we are
the rich clean soil of the farmer's past

we are
petitions blooming from teenage fingertips

we are
families biking, recycling, reusing,
engineers dreaming, designing, building,
artists painting, dancing, writing
and we are spreading the word

and there are thousands out on the street
marching with signs
hand in hand
chanting for change NOW

and they're marching for you, baby
they're marching for us

Because we deserve to do more than just
survive
we deserve
to thrive

Dear Matafele Peinam,

you are eyes heavy
with drowsy weight

so just close those eyes, baby
and sleep in peace

because we won't let you down

you'll see

ENVIRONMENTAL JUSTICE

What place protects you?

What place is worthy of your protection?

If this earth is our only place, is there anything, anywhere, that is truly disposable?

Our writing and our stories are always shaped by place, in place. As writers who carry islands and ocean within our bodies, languages, memory, and names, we understand that in simply speaking our stories aloud, by placing them in these pages, we are the justice of our islands. We make visible and visceral the places and histories of our ocean and island homes, which have been constructed as invisible, disposable, and empty.

Our stories hold definitions of justice, which we learn, contest, and shape through our relationships to the environment. Reclaiming terms of self-representation as Pacific Islanders has come through the generations of remembering and passing down our stories, speaking and reclaiming our languages, searching out and naming genealogies, and setting the terms of how our histories are told. This reclamation of ourselves—which is always rooted in our connections with and stewardship of our environment—is a process of defining a just world.

The cultural protocols and knowledge we reclaim, use, and shape as Pacific Islanders were grown from lifetimes of knowledge gained from surviving in, growing from, and traveling beyond island and ocean environments. Our histories, languages, stories, and literatures grow from an environmental ethic, generations of knowledge defined by the terms of islands and ocean living. Terms such as learning to work with all parts of your environment to define a life; knowing that distance does not mean isolation; memorizing and holding in your body vast networks of relations and long, long stories of connection.

In this section, writers address the idea that "we are all in this together." We examine this as an attitude, a practice, and a space of examining who defines, and who receives, justice. We address how environmental justice comes with critical attention to indigenous histories, histories of colonialism, movements for Pacific independence and sovereignty. We explore the terms of "we are all in this together" with specific considerations of our contexts, while also translating our stories to connect to wider and wider circles of audiences.

This section therefore documents the global within the everyday because our stories have the responsibility of making those connections. We have to model definitions of environmental justice by operating in realms of the specific and the global simultaneously. In doing so, we define and practice an Oceanic consciousness. This is our practice of environmental justice.

The Broken Gourd

Haunani-Kay Trask

I.

After the last echo
where fingers of light
soft as laua'e
come slowly

toward our aching earth,
a cracked *ipu*
whispers, bloody water
on its broken lip.

Long ago, wise *kānaka*
hauled hand-twined
nets, whole villages shouting
the black flash of fish.

Wāhine u'i
trained to the chant
of roiling surf;
nā keiki sprouted by the sun
of a blazing sky.

Even Hina, tinted
by love, shone gold
across a lover's sea.

Previously published, *Night Is a Sharkskin Drum,* University of Hawai'i Press, 2002.

II.

This night I crawl
into the mossy arms
of upland winds,

an island's moan
welling grief:

Each of us slain
by the white claw
of history: lost
genealogies, propertied
missionaries, diseased
haole.

Now, a poisoned *pae 'āina*
swarming with foreigners

and dying Hawaiians.

III.

A common horizon:
smelly shores
under spidery moons,

pockmarked *maile* vines,
rotting *'ulu* groves,
the brittle *clack*
of broken lava stones.

Out of the east
a damp stench of money
burning at the edges.

Out of the west
the din of divine
violence, triumphal
destruction.

At home, the bladed
reverberations of empire.

Meramu Nafkah Meratapi Lahan

Aleks Giyai

Di kala sinar surya di lapangan langit
Terpancar di sela pepohonan membakar bumi
Ladang hijau pun mengguntingnya

Sunyi nan sepi tertatih menyusuri rimba
Lambaian dedaunan mengiring langkah
Bersama nyanyian burung mengguping
Bagai musik klasic penghibur perjalanan
Menuju kebun alam sumber harta tersimpan

Hitam manis wajah penuh berseri
Tubuhnya yang keriput itu tersengat panas mentari
Mengayungkan tangan perkasanya di pohon
Menokok sagu, meramu berkah, menafkahi hidup

Di atas adonan keranjang menepis ampasan sagu
Air jernih di pematang kayu mengalir menderas
Bagai tangisannya yang penuh deras atas lahan sagunya
Dari serbuan maut tangan-tangan serakah investor sawit

Ladang dan lahan sagu dibumi Cendrawasih
Menjadi binatang buruan kaum kapitalis
Selembar daun merah bernama tuan rupiah
Menyogok raja-raja kecil anak pribumi
Yang bermegah dan bertahta di istana birokrasi
Untuk menutupi telingga dan matanya

Walaupun rakyatnya deru tangis masih menjerit
Merebut lahan-lahan sagu yang di rampas para pemodal
Dengan berbagai syahdu yang melantunkan sebuah nada
Kami bisa hidup tanpa sawit tapi kami tak bisa hidup tanpa sagu

Wahai kaum pemimpin anak pribumi
Yang bertahta berkuasa mengambil kebijakan
Selaraskanlah hukum untuk berkeadilan
Memilah antara hak adat dan hak negara
Melihat mana milik rakyat nan milik pemerintah
Kami hanya haus sebuah keberpihakan dan pengakuan
Kami hanya lapar sebuah keadilan dan kejujuran

Karena inilah kebun kehidupan tempat merambah berkah
Di sanalah Tuhan melimpahkan sumber ekonomi
Di sinilah tempat bersemayam roh para leluhur dan
Generasi akan menyambung nafas seribu tahun lagi
Cukuplah-cukup, kami tak mau meratapi lahan hidup
Wahai kaum serakah perampas nafas kehidupan

Making a Living Mourning the Land

Translated from Indonesian by Bonnie Etherington

When the sun's rays in the sky
Radiate between the trees and burn the earth,
The green fields cut through [the earth] too.

Silently limping through the jungle
Waving leaves accompanying each of his steps,
With the song of an eavesdropping bird
Like classical music, a comforter journeys
Towards a garden of stored treasures.

His face is black and sweet, full and glowing,
His body wrinkled and stung by the sun.
He scoops [sago] from the tree with his mighty hand,
Pounding sago, gathering blessings, making a living.

From the top of the basket of dough he skims sago pulp;
Clear water flows strongly down a timber embankment
Like his heavy cries for his sago land
Because of the deadly invasion of the hands of palm investors.

The sago fields and land of the bird of paradise's earth
Have become prey for the capitalists.
A red leaf named Mr. Rupiah
Bribes the little kings of Indigenous children,
Who boast as they are enthroned in a bureaucratic palace
For closing their ears and eyes.

Even though their people are howling with tears, still screaming,
They seize the sago lands that were confiscated by investors.
With solemn tones, [the people] chant:
We can live without palm oil but we cannot live without sago.

O leaders of Indigenous children
Who are enthroned in power—grasp wisdom,
Harmonize the law for justice.
Sort out customary rights and state rights
To see which belongs to the people and which belongs to the government.
We only thirst for acknowledgment and recognition.
We only hunger for justice and honesty.

Because this is the garden of life, the place where blessings spread.
There the Creator bestowed resources;
Here is where the spirits of the ancestors dwell and
This generation will continue their breath for another thousand years.
Enough is enough, we do not want to mourn the living land,
O greedy people plundering the breath of life!

From *Potiki*

Patricia Grace

Chapter 13: Dollarman

There was in the meeting-house a wood quiet.

It was the quiet of trees that have been brought in out of the wind, whose new-shown limbs reach out, not to the sky but to the people. This is the quiet, still, otherness of trees found by the carver, the shaper, the maker.

It is a watching quiet because the new-limbed trees have been given eyes with which to see. It is a waiting quiet, the ever-patient waiting that wood has, a patience that has not changed since the other tree life. But this tree quiet is an outward quiet only, because within this otherness there is a sounding, a ringing, a beating, a flowing greater than the tree has ever known before.

And the quiet of the house is also the quiet of stalks and vines that no longer jangle at any touch of wind, or bird, or person passing, but which have been laced and bound into new patterns and have been now given new stories to tell. Stories that lace and bind the earthly matters to matters not of earth.

Outside and about the meeting-house there was an early stillness. There was no movement or sound except for that which came from the quiet sliding, sidling of the sea.

But back in the houses, and beyond on the slopes, there was activity. At the houses washing was already out on the lines, morning meals were over and the cleaning up had been done. The vacuum cleaners had been through. Steps had been swept and there was a smell of cooking—of mutton and chicken and fish, watercress and cabbage, bread and pies.

In the hills the saws that had sounded since early morning were now still. Branches had been trimmed from the felled scrub, and the wood stacked and bound. The horse waited, occasionally snorting, stamping, or swinging its tail, but not impatiently. Then the tied wood bundle was attached to the chains coming from the big collar. The horse was led down the scented track under the dark shelves of manuka. Tools were picked up by those who went ahead to make sure the path was clear, while others followed to watch and steady the load.

Previously published, *Potiki,* University of Hawai'i Press 1995 (1986).

At the bottom of the hill the horse and workers emerged from the cool dark into the sharp edges of light. The wood was unhitched at the woodstack. The collar and hames and chains were taken from the horse and put in the shed.

Work was over for the day. The money man was coming, to ask again for the land, and to ask also that the meeting-house and the urupa be moved to another place.

There was in the meeting-house a warmth.

It was the warmth that wood has, but it was also the warmth of people gathered. It was the warmth of past gatherings, and of people that had come and gone, and who gathered now in the memory. It was the warmth of embrace, because the house is a parent, and there was warmth in under the parental backbone, enclosement amongst the patterned ribs. There was warmth and noise in the house as the people waited for Mr. Dolman to speak, Dolman whom they had named "Dollarman" under the breath. Because although he had been officially welcomed he was not in the heart welcome, or at least what he had to say was not.

". . . so that's what it is, development, opportunity, just as I've outlined to you, by letter. First class accommodation, top restaurants, night club, recreation centre with its own golf links—eventually, covered parking facilities . . . and then of course the water amenities. These water amenities will be the best in the country and will attract people from all over the world . . . launch trips, fishing excursions, jet boating, every type of water and boating activity that is possible. Endless possibilities—I've mentioned the marine life areas . . . your shark tanks . . ."

(Plenty of sharks around . . .)

". . . trained whales and seals etcetera. As I've outlined in writing, and as I've discussed with Mr. um . . . here and . . . one or two others. And these water activities, the marine life areas in particular, this is where you get off-season patronage, where we get our families, our school parties at reduced rates. So you see it's not just a tourist thing. It's an amenity . . .'

(An amenity now . . . already . . .)

". . . a much-needed amenity. Well there's this great potential you see, and this million-dollar view to be capitalised on. And I'll mention once again that once we have good access, it's all on, we can get into it. And benefit . . . not only ourselves but everyone, all of you as well. We'll be providing top-level facilities, tourist facilities and so upgrade the industry in this whole region. It'll boom . . ."

"It's good that you have come here to meet us, meet all of us, to discuss what you . . . your company has put forward. Much of this you have outlined in your letters which we have all read and talked about amongst ourselves. We have replied to your letters explaining our feelings on what you have outlined and we have asked you to come here for a discussion. Now you are here which is a good thing. We can meet face to face on it, eyeball one another, and we can give our thoughts and feelings and explanations more fully. As I say we have all discussed this and I have been asked to speak on behalf of all of us.

"This land we are on now—Block J136, the attached blocks where the houses are, and J480 to 489 at the back of the houses, is all ancestral land—the ancestral land of the people here. And there are others too who don't live here now, but this is still home to them. And a lot of them are here today, come home for this meeting.

"Behind us are the hills. That was all once part of it too. Well the hills have gone. A deal went through at a time when people were too poor to hang on. It is something that is regretted.

"But it won't happen . . . to the rest . . . what's left here. Not even in these days of no work. We're working the land. We need what we've got. We will not sell land, nor will access be given. Apart from that, apart from telling you that none of this land here will go, we have to tell you that none of us wants to see any of the things you have outlined. We've talked about it and there's no one, not one of us here, that would give an okay on it. None of those things would be of any advantage to our people here, in fact we know they would be greatly to our disadvantage . . ."

"Well now, you've said that the developments here would be of no advantage to you. I'd like to remind you of what I've already said earlier. It's all job-creative. It'll mean work, well-paid work, right on your doorstep, so to speak. And for the area . . . it'll bring people . . . progress . . ."

"But you see, we already have jobs, we've got progress . . ."

"I understand, perhaps I'm wrong, that you're mostly unemployed?"

"Everything we need is here. This is where our work is."

"And progress? Well it's not . . . obvious."

"Not to you. Not in your eyes. But what we're doing is important. To us. To us that's progress."

"Well maybe our ideas are different. Even so you wouldn't want to stand in the way . . ."

"If we could. That's putting it straight. If we could stand in the way we would. But . . . as we've said, the hills have gone, your company, we believe, now being the owner. We can only repeat what we've said by letter. If you go ahead, which I suppose we can't prevent, then it won't be through the front. Not through here."

"I'll explain about that, about access from behind. Access from behind is . . . not impossible, but almost. Certainly not desirable. We need to get people in, quick . . ."

(Dollarman)

". . . from all parts of the world. Mostly on arranged tours. Every detail taken care of. And need to be able to get them in, get them accommodated, comfortable . . ."

(Minus the dollar)

". . . and they . . . people don't want to be travelling all those extra miles. Costly for them, costly for us. Then when they leave . . . of course we want to be able to move them . . . as conveniently as possible. But apart from all that, and even more important as far as smooth running goes, is services, and workers. This is the main area of concern, why we have to get in and out quickly. It's costly, for people getting to work, for the trucks and vehicles coming in every day. There'd have to be miles of new road. And apart from costs there's time. But with good access, with your say-so we could be into it, in part, next season . . ."

"Well as we've said, these ideas are not welcome to us people here. We can't stop you from setting up . . . what you've outlined, on what is now your land. But, I have to say very strongly, on behalf of us all here—we'll never let this house be moved. Never. Even if we could allow that, then there is the piece of land behind here where our dead are buried, which you would need also. That is a sacred site, as we've said in our letters. Our dead lie there. You will never get anyone to agree to it. No words . . ."

"I hope I've made it clear. There would be no damage. Your hall . . ."

"Whare tipuna. Ancestral house . . ."

". . . would be put on trucks, transported, no cost to you. Set down exactly as it is now. No damage whatever. Two days from start to finish. And your cemetery. There's no real worry, let me assure you. Well it's nothing new, it's been done often enough before. A new site, somewhere nearby. And we've already had a think about this. All laid out, properly lawned, fenced, everything taken care of, everything in place . . ."

(Toe bone connected to your jaw bone . . .)

". . . and you'll be well paid . . ."

(And there's the worry of it all)

". . . for your land."

"Mr. Dolman, no amount of money . . ."

"Well now wait a minute. We have, since our previous communication, had another look at the figures. I'd like to . . ."

"Mr. Dolman, I know we're hurrying you, but it's only fair that you should know. There is nothing you can say, no words, no amount of money . . ."

"But look. I'm not sure that you have fully understood, and this is something I haven't pointed out previously. Your land here would skyrocket. Your value would go right up . . ."

(Dollarman. There's the worry of it all . . .)

"You would have work, plus this prime amenity. On your doorstep, so to speak . . ."

"We already have . . ."

"Work . . ."

"On our doorsteps . . ."

"And a prime amenity which is land . . ."

"Prime amenities of land and sea and people, as well as . . ."

"A million dollar view, so to speak, that . . ."

"Costs nothing."

"Everything we want and need is here."

"Well yes, yes of course. It's a great little spot. But maybe you have not seen its full potential. I'm not talking just about tourists now. I mentioned before the family people. I'm talking about giving families, school children, an opportunity to view our sea life . . ."

"The dolphins come every second summer . . ."

"Maybe so, but not for everyone, and not close, where people can see . . ."

"Close enough to be believed."

"I mean this way the public would have constant access. Our animals could be viewed any time. There would be public performances . . ."

"Every second summer is public enough . . ."

"And the seals . . ."

"One comes now and again, then goes . . ."

"Killer whales. You'd be denying people . . ."

"The chance to watch you lay your head between its jaws. For money . . ."

"Denying people this access, this facility."

"We've never stopped people coming here, never kept anyone out . . ."

"Denying families, and school children, their pleasures."

"We've never told anyone to get off the beach or to stop catching fish. We've never stopped them cooking themselves in the sun, or prevented them from launching their boats. We've always allowed people to come here freely and we've often helped them out in bad weather. And, you know, these people—the families, the campers, the weekend fishing people—they'd back us up on this. They wouldn't like to see it all happen. They wouldn't like it."

"We're not getting very far with this are we? I mean you invited me here and . . . I must say I expected you people to be more accommodating . . ."

"Not so accommodating as to allow the removal of our wharenui, which is our meeting place, our identity, our security. Not so accommodating as to allow the displacement of the dead and the disruption of a sacred site."

"I didn't expect people to be unreasonable . . ."

"Unreasonable? Perhaps it is yourself that is being unreasonable if you think we would want pollution of the water out there, if you think we would want crowds of people, people that can afford caviar and who import salmon, coming here and using up the fish . . ."

"And jobs . . ."

"As we've told you, we have work. You want us to clean your toilets and dig your drains or empty your rubbish bins but we've got more important . . ."

"I didn't say . . . And I wasn't . . . And you're looking back, looking back, all the time."

"Wrong. We're looking to the future. If we sold out to you what would we be in the future?"

"You'd be well off. You could develop land, do anything you want."

"I tell you if we sold to you we would be dust. Blowing in the wind."

"Well I must say I find it difficult to talk sense . . ."

(We notice . . .)

"One puff of the wind and that's it. And who is the first to point the finger then, when our people are seen to be broken and without hope? That's upset all round . . ."

"Not so, not so. I mean I really believe that you people . . . have come a long way . . ."

"Wrong again. We haven't come a long way at all. All we've done, many of us, is helped you, and people like you, get what you want. And we're all left out of it in the end. We've helped build a country, all right. Worked in its factories, helped build its roads, helped educate its kids. We've looked after the sick, and we've helped the breweries and the motor firms to make their profits. We've helped export our crayfish and we've sent our songs and dances overseas. We've committed our crimes, done our good deeds, sat in Parliament, got educated, sung our hymns, scored our tries, fought in wars, splashed our money about . . ."

"And you put all the blame . . ."

"Blaming is a worthless exercise. That would really be looking back. It's now we're interested in. Now, and from now on."

"Well then, that's what I mean. Why the concern with what's gone? It's all done with."

"What we value doesn't change just because we look at ourselves and at the future. What we came from doesn't change. It's your jumping-off place that tells you where you'll land. The past is our future. If we ever had to move our tipuna it would be for our own reasons, some danger to the area, some act of God. It would not be for what you call progress, or for money . . ."

"It's necessary in today's terms, money."

"Nothing wrong with money as long as we remember it's food not God. You eat it, not worship it . . ."

"Better too much than not enough, as they say."

"Either way, too much or too little, you can become a slave."

"Just as you can become a slave to past things. And to superstition . . . and all that . . . hoo-ha."

"We have prepared a meal in the wharekai. You are welcome to eat before you go."

"I'll go then. But I hope you'll all think about what we've discussed here today. There are ways. I'm a man who gets what he wants, and you should think about that. Have a look at the advantages to yourselves, to your children. I mean you've got something we require. We could work on a deal that would be satisfactory to all."

"Something you require, yet you already have land, lots of land . . ."

"We need this corner or the whole thing could fall through."

"We give it to you and we fall through. We're slaves again, when we've only just begun to be free."

A Letter to My Brother

Imaikalani Kalahele

Where does the sun set
Is it here? Is it there?
I know it was somewhere

Perhaps a storm came
and the stream
washed it away?

Perhaps the mountains
came down on us
and covered it all up?

Maybe it was the kai.
Maybe the kai came up
and flooded the valleys
and on its way back
when hāpai everything
and take it all out to sea.

Nah, brah,
it wasn't any of these things.
The storm was greed,
swelling like a dammed up stream
making ready to over run
and wash away.

And the mountains that crumbled
did so because of absence.
Absence from the land.
Absence from the kai.

Previously published, *Kalahele: Poetry & Art*, Kalamakū Press, 2002.

Absence from the people.
Absence from the mana.

And we know what the wave was!
Genocide.
Flooding the valleys
and stripping the limu clean
from the rocks.
Sweeping away the ‘opae
from the streams,
the ulu from the land
and the maoli from the earth.

So . . . ah . . . tell me, brah,
where does the sun set?
Is it here?
Is it there?
Oh . . . ah . . . tell me
where do I take Granpa’s bones?

Looking for Signs

Dana Naone Hall

Aunty Alice said it first
there had been hōʻailona
ever since we took up
trying to keep the old road
from being closed in Mākena
on the island where Māui
caught the sun in his rope.
The foreign owners of a half-built
hotel don't want their guests
to taste the dust
of our ancestors in the road.
They want them to step
from the bright green clash
of hotel grass to sandy beach
and the moon shining on a rocky coast.
The last hukilau in that place
was ten years ago,
but people still remember
the taste of the fish and the limu
that they gathered on the shore.
When tūtū gets sick
the only thing that brings her back
is the taste of the ocean
in soup made from the small
black eyes of the pipipi.
In her dreams ʻopihi
are growing fat on the rocks.
She is old and small now
in her bed above the blue ocean
wrapped in the veil of her dream
like the uhu asleep

Previously published, *Life of the Land: Articulations of a Native Writer,* ʻAi Pōhaku Press, 2017.

after a day of grinding coral into sand.
It was at this house on Sunday
that relatives who stayed home from church
saw a cloud of dragonflies appear
over the ocean and fly through the windows.
Higher up the mountain someone else
dreamed of seeing Pele's canoe
on the water the red sail of Honua'ula
coming toward land.
One weekend the family slept
at another beach along the old road
the old road that is the old trail.
Uncle Charley took us all to the heiau
mauka of the beach.
From the beginning he has said
the road will not be closed.
When we came back,
Ed, one of the boys from Hāna,
was standing in the shallow water
sending the sound of the conch shell
and the winding breath of the nose flute
across the channel to Kaho'olawe
through the ear of Molokini.
Later, we listened
to Uncle Harry joke with the kūpuna.
Tūtū was there and she stayed
all night sleeping in the sand
with the 'aumākua all around.
The mo'o clucked in the kiawe,
while pueo flew through the dark
cutting across the path
of the falling stars,
and manō ate all the fish but one
in the net that Leslie laid.
As for us,
what is our connection to Mākena?
You pointed out that we live on
one of three great rifts out of which
lava poured in ages past
to form the mysterious beauty of Haleakalā.
Two gaps press in on the rim of the mountain
like a pitcher with two spouts.
Ko'olau separates us from Hāna
and Kaupō divides Hāna and Mākena
but there is no gap between us

and Mākena lying at the bottom of
the youngest rift, where the
sweet potato vines covered the ground.
This morning, coming back along the coast,
on our side of the island
where the road bends at Hoʻokipa,
I saw a cloud shaped like a pyramid
and a car driving out of the sun.

HANUABADA

John Kasaipwalova

Hanuabada badana!
Big village, thick village, rusty and grey
Your crowded houses pushing one another
Sit unconcerned on crooked fingers pinching out of mud and water
O Hanuabada! Wan Pis Tru!
Hanuabada, I saw and dreamt you long before my eyes felt you
They told me you were civilized; your iron roofs, timber floors,
  electricity and all
Where the laugh of your girls in their flowing straight pinned hair
Will make my penis water in desperate stiffness
And my eyes turn red from wishful envy
To see your men boasting their lightness
So smartly dressed in trousers, long socks and shoes
So clean, so educated, so rich, so civilized, so new and white
Yes, I saw you and them in my dreams.

O Hanuabada! bada hanua!
Once not so long ago before my skin learnt the shame of nakedness
My heart flamed its desire, my ears lost their sleep
To sit up nakedly listening to the wonders
While the saini bois told me all about you
Yes Hanuabada, my big and beautiful dream village
When the heavy rains broke our rotten grass roof
And made me cold and wetted my sleeping mats
When mud and pigshit smells nearly broke my nose
When mosquitoes bit me and I hit myself for nothing
When robber flies danced aside the swipe of my palm and fingers
To steal again the taste of my two dripping cigarettes from the nose
That's when I wished and dreamt that
One day I will make our grassroofed village like Hanuabada
Iron roofs for grass, timber floors and all.

Previously published, *Hanuabada*, Port Moresby: Papua Pocket Poet Series, volume 31, 1972.

Yet what have they done to you, O Hanuabada!
What have they done to you?
When first my eyes saw you I cried the disappointment of my dreams
One hundred days of waiting expectancy to see the come of nothing!
O Hanuabada, so exciting and elegant in my dreams
What the bloody hell have they done to you!
I heard so big, I wished to see you so much
Now I must turn my head in shame and fear
To see you tucked away beyond the sight of your invaders.
You stand there bulky and imprisoned on that cornered shore
Your houses on their tree posts line up form that tiny beach
Like crowding scavenger sand crabs poised in fear and silence
Lacing their tiny crawling legs for an irate comfort and dignity.
Hanuabada what have they done to you!
Who are these white devils that trample you and use you like a prostitute
Then curse you and forget you as another slummy, dirty native village?
Hanuabada what have they done to you!

When my awkward feet first walked the streets of Moresby
My eyes did not see you in your tight corner
My eyes, my mind and my body counted and followed every car instead
Like a sea gull capsizing up and down in the whirlwind.
How can they be so countless like a flowing stream?
Why the palefaced drivers so stone faced and blind
To the pleading eyes and bare toes of my brother natives covered in dust
As we sullenly walk past Chinese shops toward Koki in the burning sun?
Yes Hanuabada, I did not see you then
My primitive village did not warn me of this new giddiness.
I glued my eyes instead on the long bitumen roads so solid and tearless
I admired the big houses, their water tanks and heaters on top
I stared at the neat green lawns and planted trees
All of them so straight, so huge, so neat and trimmed
Yet somehow my eye felt a strange harshness everywhere
Everywhere I saw a cold silent violence staring hungrily at my flesh and blood.

Yes Hanuabada, the big village, I did not see you then
What I saw in this whirlwind is not a village
But Moresby the whiteman's town!
"Itambu" signs and "No Natives Allowed" snarled at me as if I'm a leper
And savage dogs chained stand ready to strip my flesh.
What can be the meaning of this watchful violence in the midst of this giddiness?
Wire fences around the green lawns to cage the hungry dogs
Wire fences around the windows of these huge houses to shut them in

Like neurotic thieves crazy to protect their stolen loots.
Hanuabada, where are you? Where is that village softness I know?
Even the night brings no sleep and silence in this giddiness
The pale neon lights pull the night insects to their deaths
While my nose kisses the cool clear glass front
To stare enviously at the lighted wealths inside
All of them opening their legs to tease my dry throat
While they mock my empty pockets from the safety of their shelves.

Can this be real or maybe this one another dream?
These monster iron ships, who can build them?
My uncle's big canoe will be a floating match stick beside them
Yes truly I could not believe it
I felt my forehead pain its defeated resignation
I stared and stared at the crates, the cars and all kinds cargo
Lowered from the heavens in rope nets like giant bilum bags
I was silent, I could not speak, still captured silence
But my wantok touch me softly and pointed across the harbour
"Hei wantok, that one over there is Hanuabada! Already you see arh?"
Surrounded by dry winch grinds, smoke from the funnels and cicada
  motors of the fork lifts
I first threw my eyes across the harbour to you Hanuabada
The big village, the village I had seen in my dreams,
Can this really be the punishment of my dreams?
Hanuabada answer me!

Hanuabada answer me! Make your black throat veins swell out their
  answer!
Why are you not what I had always believed you to be
Who has painted you darkgrey and sadly silent
Why do you huddle in shame and keep your black tears covered
Who are these slick invaders whose houses steely and towering
Perch the hills above you like nesting white pigeons on a rocky cliff
While they spit and shit their wastes down to you below
Is this why the colour of your houses from across the harbour
Look like the black clouds of approaching rainy storms
Bada hanua answer me!
Who can name the sad song that runs through your heart and mine
The song of killed yesterday
When Lakatois owned this you harbour
And the voice of Hiri conch shell danced in your vivid sunsets
To make your people walk in dignified pride and to laugh from their
  hearts.
Hanuabada I mourn with you now—your waters is taken!
You and I must crawl and beg in our own "claimed" land.

Open tears like the open raindrops of storms
Beat their fury loud warm and clear
To drench the jungled mountains make a crawling mist along their floors
And river drains clack their rocks in awesome fear
As the brown flood jumps and sings its liveliness.
Yes, the open fury of the open raindrops
Carries life in its waking falling speed
Penetrating the cracked dusty soil to flourish green
And make the browning leaves know again the joy
Of twinkling back to the sun from their soft oiled buds.
But Hanuabada, your tears and mine are not like the open raindrops
Our tears are caged and silenced; turned back into ourselves as beasts
Tearing and eating away our insides in their hateful hunger
Sucking the redness from our blood streams
To leave behind coagulated whitish smelly pus.
Hanuabada, our inward caged tears is our enemy.

I see sad silent women sitting with their beads, pots and baskets
Beside the solid walls of the thief's loot dens
Where counted monies and labelled goods hide behind bars
While the cracked cement pavements outside shake the sound of shoed feet
The women look up a beggar's face to the passing ones
They look down, sneer and walk on to their offices and stores
Leaving the women robbed of pride and blessed with shame
To wait and hope for the next greedy, arrogant passing eye
Hanuabada, SPEAK TO ME!!!
Are these not my black mothers and sisters
Whose veined hands lump around our bony limbs like dry sugar canes
Folded cheeks and foreheads disshaping the tattoos of parched skins
Hanuabada SPEAK TO ME!!!
Why should my black mothers and sisters
Line the pavements like beggars to sell their beads and pots
How long must I endure the bloody hunger of these beastly tears
That drags and flogs the paining skins of my mothers and sisters
To throw them for display on the cold hard cement outside the thief's den.

Hanuabada, the world speaks many tongues
Your silent flesh and blood
Is no sign for your happiness
Now you do not ripple and shriek
Like your angry oceans
Locking your birthing violence
Into pious sentimental goodness

Searching blindly in darkness
Always always hiding your misery in your role playing

Crying only brings me many pains of emptiness
A grey statue with a fixed sad smile
Unmoving lifeless to keep constancy
To avoid hurting grows new shoots
Of poisonous pretences only to weld of steel
Four grey walls of solitary confinement
I have felt the softness of your eyes
Glimpses of moments without words
My fingers poised to embrace and laugh
Turn quickly into nails of crucifixion
Warning guilty to make me the statue.

Pretentious Death
Is more paralysing than the wounds of honest pains
I have ripped apart the house of my soul
To drag before my mirror my naked self
Bloody and shining
Leaping and flowing like a spring
From the depths of misery to the ecstatic heights
There is no stagnant neutrality
To take the unknown jump across the dividing barbed fences
No jeering faces to please
But the pure creation of our naked selves
Beyond the immediate sorrows of good pretences.

HANUABADA your sorrowful begging music
Is not sufficient to tear your pretences apart
Let your sorrows and pains
Run the streets like smashing thunder
Out of whose depths you will find yourself
A River flowing flowing flowing.

bilum, for rosa

No'u Revilla

back and forth bilum carry baby yams and river water.
no government rice because bilum swallows her forehead,
shining brighter than hospital gowns, bilum march for morning star,
knowing on her back bilum bush knives potatoes and fifteen years in prison.

dim-dim afford store-bought string. long-legged, short-skirted
fashionista buy brand name only, baby, the best bilum not knowing
brand bilum bought on the backs of others "eco-ethical" in Paris
"eco-ethical" in Brisbane "eco-ethical" in Waikīkī but no ethics in
West Papua. killing bilum like mosquitoes since 1962.

rosa crossed the border bilum. carry vegetables and referendum.
they want to make her disappear bilum. they want to steal her bow and
arrow throat and machete the sky—that's what happens when Indonesia
owns the right to breathe. meri bilum break your peninsula forehead make
international waters of your hair while islands collect at your neck
bleed black and red bilum. petitions on fire. meri carry the weight of the world.

West Papua. merdeka.

Air Conditioned Minds: The Problem of Climate Control in Guåhan

Leiana San Agustin Naholowa'a

Urban Legend

I asked the guy who hoses water through the filter to clean out gunk from the split a/c unit in my apartment, "Why do people believe that leaving it on all day saves money?"

I've been told by many people that in order to save money on my electricity bill, I need to run my a/c all day long. If I continue to turn the a/c off and on, it will eventually break the unit and worse, make my power bill higher. According to this logic, when the room is hot, the a/c sucks a huge amount of energy through the grid, which leads to high electricity costs. A room left hot becomes needy, and the energy expended to cool that room at its initial start costs more than leaving the a/c unit on all day.

It does not make sense to him as well. He seems like me—he can't afford to buy into this belief system.

We know that using a machine—as loud, as unnaturally climate lowering, as heavily built into windows and walls, as greedy on the power grid that causes load shedding on hot summer days—means that we feel it in our budget and pay for it by economizing elsewhere. With privilege comes anxiety over the temperature of indoor spaces, the ability to refrigerate a house for no one during the day

---

The main title "Air Conditioned Minds" and the first line of the poem are inspired by lines from the poem "Kafe Mulinu" by Cecilia Perez.

During the 2016 Festival of Pacific Arts in Guam, the Guam Literary Arts Delegation, which consisted of committee members in Fashion, History, Indigenous Languages, Oratory, Publications, and Theater, had stayed at Agueda Johnston Middle School with delegates from the Cook Islands, Norfolk Islands, and Samoa.

The 2005 Guam Public Law 28-45, known as the "Every Child Is Entitled to an Adequate Public Education Act," sponsored by Senator Robert Klitzkie, defines "Adequate Public Education" as inclusive of "air conditioned or properly ventilated classrooms in which the sensible air temperature is no greater than 78°F." The room temperatures at Agueda were much lower.

when everyone is at work. Perhaps our collections of store-bought objects rot less, mold less, deteriorate less.

Air conditioning across gender reveals a masculine preference for freezing environments and a menopausal feminine need to extinguish hot flashes.

I find myself aligned with older generations, anxious about financial costs and in pain about even the thought of freezing.

From Fest Pac Climate-Controlled Agueda Johnston Middle School

Air conditioned minds
blanketing
unblanketed siblings,
they buy blankets with money saved for stores cheaper than home.

We blanket them in
blankets we own and blankets we buy, imported not made.

We wrap their rituals
in air conditioning
forcing them to live our own experience of colonization and
the suffering of students "Entitled to an Adequate Public Education"
and 78 degrees and freezing classroom weather.

There is no host here
only ghosts hosts here in that second floor classroom
and bodies that worked an exhausting school year.

There is blanketing,
and no removal of a/c
no lowering of a/c
no changing of
conditions.

On Being Indigenous in a Global Pandemic

Emalani Case

In a global pandemic,
being Indigenous means
the words,
"we're all in this together,"
don't really apply to you
because we're not *really*

all in this together,
not when some of us
have to protect ourselves
and our families
from disease, disappearance,
and disregard

from the threat of war games,
of 25,000 personnel
converging in your waters,
on your land,
promising security,
while putting you at risk,

the military rhetoric really saying,
we're willing to kill you
to save

some

from the threat of infected sailors,
disembarking an infected ship,
staying in hotels,
breaking quarantine rules,

forcing Guåhan to choose,
who to give beds to,

the navy rhetoric really saying,
we have one-third of your island;
we want two-thirds

more

from the threat of construction
on burial sites,
a greedy mayor calling
for non-essential work,
and protectors arriving
in masks, social distancing
from the living, not the dead

the political rhetoric really saying,
pandemic or not, alive or not,
you're still not

worthy

not worthy
of the same protection
extended to some
not extended
to you

because in a global pandemic,
being Indigenous
is like every other day,
struggling to be seen,
only now from

isolation

In a global pandemic,
being Indigenous means

protecting land
when you can't stand on it,

protecting people
when you can't hold their hands,

protecting yourself
when you can't rest,

or take long quarantine naps like others because

colonialism,
capitalism,
militarism,
and racism

are not resting
but working overtime

In a global pandemic
being Indigenous means

waking up realizing,
we've been here before:
ancestral memories
swirling in your veins

corrupt captains
so-called discoverers,
preaching salvation,
bringing disease,

your heartbeats
leaping from your chest
to resuscitate
generations

then
now
and
not yet born

In a global pandemic
being Indigenous
means even the word
"lockdown"
is misplaced
because it implies

we all had the same
freedoms to begin with,

we all have the same resources
to entertain and sustain,

we are all somehow "jailed,"
facing a common enemy

that still impacts
disproportionately

In a global pandemic
being Indigenous means
even this poem
will be attacked
and its author called

insensitive
for wanting to talk about injustice
in a time of global death,

privileged
for having the energy to complain
in a time of global death,

cruel
for cultivating cynicism
in a time of global death,

and maybe even lonely
for retreating to words
in a time of global death

But in a global pandemic
being Indigenous means
writing,
speaking,
crying,
and protesting

your people into existence

because in a global pandemic
being Indigenous means
the very forces
that try to assure you that
"we're all in this together"

are the same forces
that will make the “new norm”
an extension of the old:
a world where being Indigenous
means still having to prove

we’re here

Go Home, Stay Home

Kamele Donaldson and TravisT

What, bra, no can hear?!
What, bra, no like listen?!

I don't care if
round trip tickets to Honolulu were only one hundred and fifteen dollars!
Nearly three million people are sick*
I don't care if
that Airbnb in Lanikai was only $20 a night!
Over two hundred thousand people are dead*
I don't care if
you think this global pandemic is just a hoax by "China and the Democrats"
from Honolulu to New York City
two hundred million people are living under a government imposed stay-at-home order
So go home and stay home!

Tourists
stay home!
College Spring breakers
stay home!
all non-essential workers
stay home!

After all, uninvited outsiders invading Hawaiʻi
has always been non-essential
ever since Kānaka clubbed Captain Cook at Kealakekua Bay
outsiders invading Hawaiʻi has always been about colonization
has always been about capitalist interests
has always been about stealing the land, kicking out Kānaka
and turning our ʻāina into a parking lot and a playground

Statistics reported by the Associated Press as of Monday, April 27th, 2020, were rounded up.

for those willing to pay the price of paradise
But Hawai'i is not your pandemic playground hideaway

Maybe you didn't hear when Governor Ige
encouraged tourists "not to travel to Hawai'i at this time"
Maybe you didn't hear when Mayor Caldwell
encouraged all new arrivals "to self-quarantine for 14 days"
So I am here to make sure you hear me loud and clear as I
encourage you, to go home and stay home!

Excuse me if I seem upset at the image of outsiders landing at Honolulu Airport during a global pandemic
Excuse me if I seem heated at the broadcast of Trump selling lies about Lysol and UV floodlight enemas
Excuse me if I become triggered by CNN at the sight of dead people in body bags stacked two deep on top of ice rinks

As a Kānaka I will tell you when outsiders invade Hawai'i
it is we that have died in the tens of thousands
matter of fact, we died in the hundreds of thousands
and we were not alone
For many Pacific Islanders throughout Oceania
the diseases of progress and travel are all too familiar to us:
1778, syphilis
1804, cholera
1820s, influenza
1839, mumps
1848, measles and whooping cough
1853, smallpox
1869, leprosy
2020, covid-19

In less than a hundred years since the arrival of the West
nearly ninety percent of the native Hawaiian population was make-die-dead
We chanted kanikau and danced hula for the deceased
watching as our ohana cliff-jumped from Hāʻena Point
leaving footprints on the clouds at sunset
disappearing into the horizon with a green flash
joining our kūpuna
But no longer shall we only reserve our voices for grieving the dead
No longer shall we be silenced in the face of another deadly pandemic
No longer shall we listen to "make nice and show aloha"

so Tourists
stay home!

College Spring breakers
stay home!
all uninvited outsiders and non-essential workers
stay home!
and all racist capitalist imperialist globalizers and invaders
throughout Pasifika GO HOME!

you and your kind are not wanted here
and we *strongly encourage you*
to take your sicknesses home with you
and stay there

Kūʻokoʻa: Independence

Noelani Goodyear-Kaʻōpua

I am writing in a time of hulihia. We are living in a time of hulihia.

An overturning. A massive upheaval, so great that when the churning eventually slows, our lives will be permanently altered.

As I write this, Hawaiʻi has seen over 26,000 positive diagnoses since the pandemic began. This past fall, when there were over 8 million cases on the US continent and more than half of all US states were seeing spikes, the settler state government reopened tourism in Hawaiʻi. Although we residents were amid a stay-at-home order and could not gather in groups of more than five people.

An estimated 8–10 thousand tourists arrived on that first day.

Recently Hurricane Laura has tore off roofs, shattered windows, and flooded the Gulf Coast. In May 2020, Typhoon Vongfong destroyed the city of San Policarpo in the Philippines, forcing more than 91,000 from their homes. Six days later, Super Cyclone Amphan ravaged Kolkata in India. Two and a half million people were evacuated in Bangladesh.

Worldwide, storms are intensifying, as the extraction and burning of fossil fuels changes our climate.

In 2019, Hurricane Dorian was the worst natural disaster the Bahamas have ever seen.

The year before, Hurricane Michael devastated the Florida Panhandle.

The year before that, the "unprecedented" category 5 Hurricane Irma brought catastrophe to several Leeward islands of the Caribbean. Two weeks later, Hurricane Maria ravaged Puerto Rico. The US President made light of their hardships, failing to provide urgently needed resources for the recovery. Thousands died.

Earlier version previously published in *The Value of Hawaiʻi 3: Hulihia, the Turning,* University of Hawaiʻi Press, 2020.

Harvey in Texas in 2017. Winston in Fiji and Tonga in 2016. Patricia in Mexico in 2015.

In *Ka Honua Ola,* Dr. Pualani Kanakaʻole Kanahele writes of a distinct group of "Hulihia" chants, describing eruptions so drastic that they make the landscape unrecognizable.

A few days ago, on the US continent, Wisconsin police shot Jacob Blake
seven times in the back, in front of his children—
the most recent instance of state violence against Black lives.
We say their names . . .
George Floyd, Breonna Taylor, Tony McDade, Ahmaud Arbery, David McAtee.
So many names to say.
New iterations of the white supremacy and systemic racism *endemic* to the
founding and expansion of the US continue to deem some less worthy of life,
freedom, and happiness. A summer of protest that has rocked cities—the
largest social movement in US history—is not over.

Hulihia phases are explosive—filled with heat and movement, both devastating and generative.

In the early morning hours of January 6, 2021, Rev. Raphael Warnock was
declared the winner in a hotly-contested election to represent Georgia—the
first African American senator in the 233 years of that state's existence.

Later that same day, the world witnessed an armed coup at the US Capitol.

White nationalists attempted to stop the certification of the US presidential election. Shattered windows, crushed skulls, flaming cameras, nooses, confederate flags.

Signs and t-shirts declaring: "Murder the media," "Civil war," "Camp Auschwitz."

On Jan 6, 2021, about 60 insurrectionists were arrested in DC.

On June 1, 2020 in DC, over 300 Black Lives Matter protestors were arrested in DC. 6,000 law enforcement officers, including ICE, DEA and National Guard, surveilled that BLM protest.

To date, over 465,000 Americans have died.
I open my Twitter feed to see videos of self-proclaimed American patriots
verbally and physically attacking clerks, salespeople, and other workers
just for being asked to wear a simple face mask.
A few square inches of cloth could save lives,
but hyper-individualism must not be inconvenienced.

When new case counts spiked in Hawaiʻi
and the public demanded answers about contact tracing,

the head of State Department of Health deflected criticism by opening a
press briefing with what he called "good news."
The daily numbers were higher because they included over 56 inmates at
OCCC.
Were we supposed to be less alarmed?
Are incarcerated folks somehow less deserving of care?
Over 40% of OCCC inmates tested positive.
Where is the good news in that?

Summer 2020, US President Trump had peaceful protestors teargassed,
clearing the way for his photo-op in front of St. John's Episcopal church.
"Dominate the streets," he told the National Guard.
America is "the greatest country in the world," he said,
holding prop Bible upside down
calling demonstrators "disgraceful," instead of defending free speech.
We see more than incompetence.
We see an empire made brittle by its own supposed exceptionalism.

The US spends more on defense than China, India, Russia, Saudi Arabia,
France, Germany, United Kingdom, Japan, South Korea,
and Brazil combined.
The 2020 appropriations bill contained $738 billion for military spending.
If dollars were seconds, that would be 23,401 years.
All for "national security"
though most folks in and under US empire are far from secure.

The number of incarcerated US citizens and houseless folks
has mushroomed over the last few decades.
This is not a policing and military problem. It's an inequality problem.
Injustice creates precarity and insecurity.

Quaking earth.   Rivers of lava.   Leaping fire and ash.   Clouds of steam.
Whole sections of land rising,   falling,   extending,   disappearing.
Hulihia, a transformative change. Things do not go back to normal.

It is my first day teaching fall classes on Zoom at UH Mānoa.
I ask the students to share where they are, and what they are grappling with
in this time. The first one introduces themself, then—
"What am I grappling with? I don't want to go back.
I'm asking myself, what can I do with these next few months of lockdown so
we don't have to go back to the old '*normal*'?"

Dr. Kanahele tells us hulihia chants are inspired by continuous cycles of the living ʻāina's own renewal. Overturning the assumed normal makes way for new life.

We are writing in a time of hulihia. We are living in a time of hulihia.

Nothing lives forever. Empires are not permanent fixtures. A time will come—like it or not—when US empire recedes, crumbles, and transforms. Or collapses. In my lifetime, the deterioration of US empire has never been more plainly observable.

No matter how we feel about the US occupation of Hawai'i, or whether we celebrate or mourn the American empire's decline, the people of Hawai'i must prepare to be more independent. Such preparation will be good for us, regardless of our future relationships with foreign powers across the ocean.

Many take for granted that Hawai'i is the "50th state"; it's all most adults living in the islands today have ever known. But, the Kānaka who came before exercised political independence here long before the dawn of American empire. And, these islands will be independent again.

In 2014, I watched the Scottish independence referendum with great interest. As the historic vote unfolded, I was intrigued by how different the debates were from those regarding Hawaiian sovereignty in the past thirty years.

In a nutshell—

Instead of focusing on historical or legal justifications, the Scottish National Party explained how independence could make the lives of everyday people better. The party offered a vision of "a greener Scotland," which would provide rural areas with greater support. Of "a smarter Scotland," with free, high-quality public education from pre-school through university. Parliamentary representatives in London were seen as too distant to be accountable, and out of step with Scottish values held dear.

Smaller but well-networked groups such as the Radical Independence Campaign saw independence as a way to oppose UK wars, social austerity, and privatization that benefits corporations rather than everyday people. Such groups called for an end to poverty-level wages. They also urged Scots to raise their expectations, and exercise their imaginations. The possibility of independent government opened space to envision the kind of society they wanted to build.

The referendum's result did not lead to Scotland's departure from the United Kingdom. But as advocate Adam Ramsay put it, "the possibility of independence, and the ensuing debates, brought about a popular mobilisation for radical social change unlike anything we have seen in these islands for a generation."

What I propose is straightforwardly simple and infinitely complex. Let us talk regularly and vigorously about enacting *Hawaiian political independence* once again. E ho'okū'oko'a, e ko Hawai'i. This tumultuous phase of hulihia, when what is above is falling and what is below is upwelling, is the perfect time to generate as many ideas as possible about what twenty-first century Hawaiian independence could look like.

How could independence improve the health of our waters and lands? How could it help us adapt to a changing climate and kick fossil fuel addiction? We need to regularly discuss and debate how Hawai'i could function more successfully as an independent country, once again.

Kanak leader Jean Marie Tjibaou once said that independence is about having the power to negotiate one's interdependencies. How could political independence improve the health of our waters and lands? How could Hawaiian independence give us the space to adapt to a changing climate and kick fossil fuel addiction? How could Hawaiian independence make ordinary people's lives better?

What could independence mean for folks working low-paying service jobs in the tourism industry? What could it mean for students who want to apply their degrees to restoring and maintaining Indigenous and local food systems? What could it mean for families dealing with substance abuse and houselessness? What could it mean for multilingual kids and their families? Or for retired kūpuna who need regular care and support to stay healthy? How can we craft visions for independence that *start* with these people?

Inspired by the natural process of a hulihia, imagining new possibilities can be the best consequence of this undeniable phase of massive disruption and overturning of the assumed normal.

Before the rock begins to harden once again, may four hundred, four thousand, forty thousand, four hundred thousand visions for Hawaiian independence burst forth.

A meditation on pain, solidarity and 2020

Katerina Teaiwa

Yoga prompt:

On dividing attention evenly.
When we look at the left arm, does the right arm fade?
Can we sense not only the place that causes us discomfort,
but the place where we seem to feel nothing?

. . .

"In this together" (National Reconciliation Week, Australia)

"Standing together in solidarity" (Global protests over the death of George Floyd)

On Climate Change:

On COVID-19:

"We're all in this together"

"In this together" is not possible without equality.

"In this together" is not possible without justice.

"In this together" is not possible unless you make space.

Your discomfort does not lead to your death.

And if I strive to be in the place where I feel nothing

there is no more we

or together

or equality or solidarity or justice.

There will just be I.

Pain free.

Muri Lagoon—Te Tai Roto o Muri, Rarotonga

Takiora Ingram

Muri, our lagoon
I mua ake nei, Mei mua mai
I te tuatau o to tatou tupuna
Mei mua mai to matou no'o'anga ki runga i teia enua
Te tuatau o te Tai roto ruperupe
Tai roto manea
I teia nei, kua ngaro

Since the beginning of time
From early days, from long ago until today
Our ancestors settled this land
Sustainably occupied this sacred place
Protected our pristine lagoon
A time of bountiful marine life
Now lost to our people

I teia nei
Te mate nei te kaoa
Te mate nei te ika
Kua kerekere te one tea
Kua kerekere te tai roto
Te ea te onu, te kanae, te pakati?
Kua mate, kua ngaro

Now, corals are dying
Fish, shellfish are dying
Once white sand turned black
Now shades of black, green, grey algae
Darkening the lagoon
Where are our turtles, mullet, parrotfish?

They are dead, lost from our lagoon

Our lagoon
I remember childhood days
Before hotels, before tourists
Sharing stories, swimming, playing
In our pristine *tai roto*
Now, hotel owners' corporate greed
Kills our lagoon for personal profit
Black algae blankets lagoon floor, *Remu kerekere*
Putrid smells, *aunga kino*
Corals dying fish now poisonous
Lagoon desecration

Our lagoon
No hotel sewage treatment plants
Cesspools overflowing
Raw sewage unnatural nutrients
Seep into the lagoon
Poisoning fish
Non-compliance no standards
Big business controlling politicians
Heads buried in the sand
Government inaction, community fear

Our lagoon
Senseless degradation of our precious resource
Undermining our livelihoods
When will they be made to pay?
When will they be forced to clean up
Restore our once pristine lagoon
To its natural state

Our lagoon
When will they wake up
From their million-dollar dreams
To realize, understand
They are killing our golden egg
When will the abuse stop?
When will government take action?

Our lagoon
Respect our people's Indigenous rights to a clean lagoon
Our sacred lagoon

Passed on to us by our ancestors
Protect the livelihood of our children
Sustain future generations
Greed, environmental irresponsibility, complacency
Are killing our children's natural heritage
Our future.

August 2016

O le Pese A So'ogafai

Doug Poole

I lo'u fanua i Tula'ele. Na iai le fale e ono potu, o le fale popo, umukuka, ma le fale Samoa. Na fa'atoa uma lava ona fai ae tupu loa ma le taua.

Na matou o ese ina ua amata le tu'iina o matou e fana fanua—o i Sogi, Apia, ma nonofo ai se'ia uma le taua.

Ua fa'aleaga uma mea, e o'o i ipu. Ou te leiloa pe fia; pau lava lena. Laulau ma nofoa; ou te le manatua pe fia. Tasi le fa'ata tele, pe lua uati tetele, ma isi lava mau mea; a ua galo ia te a'u.

Ua na o le atigi fale; ua fa'aleaga le fale popo, o isi pou ua tatipi ma le fola ua talepe. Ua susunu le fale Samoa. O meaola uma ua leai. Ioe; o pua'a o moa—ou te leiloa pe fia; pe tolu pe fa povi, ma solofanua.

Leai. Ua ou le toe manatua se mea.

So'ogafai's Song II (A Translation)

On my land at Tula'ele. A dwelling house of about six rooms, a copra house, kitchen, and a Samoan house. We had just finished it before the war broke out.

We left as soon as the bombardment started—went to Sogi, Apia, and stayed there until the war was over.

It was all lying about broken and destroyed, and so was the crockery. I don't remember how many; that's all. Tables and chairs; don't

Previously published, *Storyboard: A Journal of Pacific Imagery*, 2014.

This poem was written from the evidence given by my great-great-grandmother, So'ogofai de Carmel Ulberg, to the US State Department and Joseph Richardsen Baker with regards to the claims of American citizens in Apia after the bombing of Apia and surrounding villages in 1899 by the US and British Navy's illegal act of war against Mata'afa and his supporters and the citizens of Samoa.

remember how many. One big mirror, about two big clocks, and a lot of other things; but I have forgotten.

Just the empty house; the copra house was broken—some of the posts were cut off and the floor smashed. The Samoan house was burned. All the livestock was gone. Yes; pigs and fowls—don't remember how many; three or four cows, some horses.

No; I don't remember anything more.

To Pōhakuloa

Emalani Case

I found you between mountains. I was a little girl, stumbling in long grass, nostrils rimmed in red dirt, hair tossed by the wind. My father pointed to you, made sure I could see you. I was disheveled and silly. But the sight of you quieted my giggles, stilled my hands, steadied my stare. You left me wordless.

I watched you from the road, sitting in my father's old, green truck. You seemed to move in pain, each breath a struggle. Something was wrong. I wanted to greet you, to talk to you, to know your story. But my father wouldn't let me get too close. You were dangerous, he said. You could hurt me. It was best to know you from a distance, to be aware of you, to be cautious.

So I left you to save myself, to keep my heart from feeling you, to keep my heart from being broken. And I vowed to stay away.

Years passed. I grew and moved and you stayed there, lying between mountains, arms stretched wide, exposed. You waited for me. You waited for me to come back to you: waited while I attempted to explore the world and my place in it; waited while I learned and taught, entered temples and classrooms; waited while I swam in oceans and moonlight, only to find my way back to you.

One night I settled under the covers of my childhood home, closed my eyes to the night, and heard you. You were screaming. You were in pain and I cried for you. I cried for all of the years I neglected you and sent a long prayer into the darkness. It was a night for prayers. He pō haku loa.

I hoped and cried for your freedom.

You were taken from me years ago, taken from all of us, locked up and abused. You were imprisoned, contained by threat and violence, made to suffer a life

---

Pōhakuloa, literally meaning "long stone," is a land division saddled between Mauna Kea and Mauna Loa on the Big Island of Hawai'i. Some have interpreted Pōhakuloa as "pō haku loa," meaning "the night of long prayer." It is said to be a sacred space, nestled between high points of mana, or spiritual power. Despite its cultural significance, this area has been used as a military training site for the United States since World War II. More than a million live rounds are said to be fired there each year, with various other types of weapons—some even reported to contain toxic chemicals—being used on the land. Those who oppose the military training and bombing call it sacrilegious. This letter was written in response to the pain experienced at, with, and because of Pōhakuloa. For more information, visit http://malu-aina.org/?p=4536.

where you could see mountains but were forbidden to climb them, where you could see stars, but were anchored by stones, long stones. He mau pōhaku loa. You were made a casualty of someone else's war. And when my father warned me about getting too close, it was because he knew I'd try to save you. Saving you would mean stepping *into* you, getting so close that I could be hurt *with* you, destroyed at your side.

But I'm not a little girl anymore, still disheveled and silly, hair still tossed by the wind, but no longer willing, no longer able, to stay away.

I learned your story through those who know you, those who took the time to sit with you between mountains. I learned about how you were stolen, used to train for death, becoming the target of hate, of bombs carrying nothing but destruction. I learned about how your captors tried to fool us, to tell us that they needed you, that you were going to save us all, that sacrificing you was for the world. I learned of their lies.

So I wrote to them. I asked them to stop; I told them of your pain, or *our* pain. And they laughed at me. They wanted proof. They wanted evidence. They threw reports at me, evaluations stating that nothing was wrong with you, that you were fine, that *we* were fine. They gave me numbers and citations. They saw me as nothing more than that silly little girl, breathing red dirt, stumbling in long grass, a girl to be silenced.

But behind every giggle and after every stumble is a word, a word that will be used to free you, to speak to you, to sing for you, to pray for your escape. I will even eat stones if I have to, many pōhaku loa, to feel you, to know you, to taste your pain *and* our liberation.

My dear Pōhakuloa, my stronghold, my anchor, standing between mountains, you are my access to the summit of my potential, of our potential. You are our pathway to ea. Through you, I will keep breathing, with purpose, with passion, sending my breaths out in prayers, long prayers.

Until you are released—no longer held captive, no longer beaten and abused—we will never be free.

As my father warned, as my father predicted, I've fallen in love with you and now there is no staying away.

Bombs in Paradise

Victoria-Lola M. Leon Guerrero

(1)

Inatan and I are sitting at our kitchen table working on his pre-school homework. He is trying to concentrate on drawing five pictures of words that begin with the letter x.

"X-ray, Mommy!"

"That's right."

The sliding door behind him starts to rattle and the curtain blows up against the back of his chair.

"It's the bombs again, Mommy. Why are there so many bombs?"

How do you explain colonization to a four-year-old, whose big eyes are now squinting shut in frustration? He covers his ears with his hands, attempting to silence the roaring jets rudely interrupting an otherwise peaceful evening. This shouldn't be happening here. We live in picturesque paradise. Just outside the sliding door the sky is inventing new shades of fire as the sun sets over the green valley in the distance. Our house is bordered by abundant trees—the musky ylangylang fills the air at this spirit hour and the pink light kisses good night the mulberries, bilembines, lemmai, alageta, and bright orange manha that feed our family.

"They are bombers, my son," I correct him. "The military said there will be 180 of them here for the next two weeks."

"How come, Mommy?"

"They do this every year. It's called 'Operation Valiant Shield.' They bring bombers, and big ships and thousands of people here to practice for war."

"Are they at war with, what's it called, Belly Shield?"

"No, Valiant Shield is what they are calling their practice."

"Then who are they at war with?"

"Everyone."

"Even us?

"It feels like it."

The sliding door starts to rattle again and Inatan's hands fly up to his ears. This time he shakes his head from side to side and tsks.

"Again?!" he exclaims. "Why is it so loud? What do these bombers even do?"

"They drop bombs on places to blow them up."

"Are there people there?"

"Yes. It's terrible and I wish we had nothing to do with it."

"Is someone going to bomb *us?*"

"I really hope not, my baby."

I left Guam when I was eighteen to go to college in San Francisco, but I always knew I wanted to come home when I was finished school, because my island was the only place in the world I wanted to raise a family in. And here I am, back home, raising a family and wondering if I made the best decision. The truth is, we have been bombed before and we may be bombed again. But this time, would we survive? Living here in this colony, whose sole purpose to the U.S. is to test its weapons, bury its waste, station its troops and sharpen its spear (as they like to remind us), war is ever present and we have no power to stop any of it. The one place we belong to in the world no longer belongs to us.

(2)

"Inatan, when your Uncle John was little, he found a bomb when he was playing outside at Nåna's house."

"Really. Did it blow up? Did he get hurt?"

"No. Tåta called the police and a bomb squad came to the house to get it. I was your age, so I don't remember much except that we had to go down to Grandma Deding's house and wait for them to finish what they were doing."

"Did Tåta put the bomb there?"

"No, son, it was buried there during World War II."

"What's that?"

"When Grandma Deding was in high school, Guam was attacked by the Japanese. They were fighting with the Americans, and the Americans left Guam. It was a really hard time for our people."

"How come?"

"War is ugly. A lot of people get killed for no reason. On Guam, our people had to suffer for a war they had nothing to do with."

"Do you know any of the mans that were killed?"

"I was named after Grandma Deding's sister who died in the war."

"Were you sad when she died?"

"I wasn't alive yet, but Grandma Deding was very sad."

"I'm sorry Mommy. You have a nice name."

My grandmother's property is on a list of contaminated sites that the Army Corp of Engineers has yet to clean up since World War II. After the war, the

U.S. buried weapons, vehicles and chemicals throughout the island, and most prominently in the villages of Mongmong and Toto, where I am from.

In 2008, sixty-four years after this war waste had been buried in our land, the Army Corps of Engineers finally came to assess our property and document what was there. In 2011, a public meeting was held at our mayor's office, where our family was informed that the following chemicals were discovered in our property, "total petroleum hydrocarbons as oil, benzo(a)pyrene, arsenic, lead, mercury, pesticides, and PCBs in surface soil; and metals and pesticides in subsurface soil." It was also reported that our water was contaminated with TPH (Diesel, Oil), VOCs (Bromodichloromethane and Dibromochloromethane), Pesticides (Dieldrin), and Metals (Lead and Selenium). We asked for the specific levels of contamination, how much of each contaminant was found, what the volume of toxicity was, and what health risks were associated with these toxins. We still have not been provided this information. The Army Corps of Engineers began unearthing and clearing drums of chemicals the following summer from my Grandma Deding's brother Uncle Ben's yard, which is right below our property. But they ran out of money midway through the project and left gaping, shipping-container-sized pits in his yard that he eventually refilled with topsoil. They never returned to finish the job.

When I was a kid, I would walk through a small jungle trail that led to Uncle Ben's outside kitchen. We would sit around the table and enjoy the fresh fish he caught with creamy avocados soaked in fina'denne'. They were my favorite alageta! Now I wonder if these fruits from his yard were loaded with those chemicals, too. I researched them and found that each chemical has been known to cause serious health problems and cancers. I think about Uncle Ben's children who have battled cancer and wonder what their lives would have been like if only the military had told them what they had done to our family's land sooner.

(3)

"Did you see the PDN this morning?" A teacher at Inatan's school asks when I drop him off. "A Navy commander was arrested for rape."

"I haven't seen the paper yet, but I'm not surprised."

"I know, right? It's been so crazy lately. It feels like things on Guam are only getting worse."

"Tell me about it," I say. "Last night when we were eating dinner three bombers flew over the house. Then when I was getting in the shower at midnight, I could still hear them flying right outside the window. Who the hell do they think they are? We still live here. Why do they think it is okay to test bombers during our dinner and bedtime? It's like my kids are becoming desensitized to the noise and what it means."

"I know!" Another parent who is listening to our conversation chimes in. "We live up north, so it's worse for us! Last night, I can't even count how many jets we heard. I told my husband, 'That's it, we need to go home, we need to move back to Rota. Guam is not safe. It's like we're asking to get bombed.' I realized that if North Korea or China really did attack us, we wouldn't even know it was happening until the bomb dropped because we are so used to this sound."

"I live near Naval Hospital," the teacher adds. "And we've been hearing a lot of helicopters. There were so many that I seriously called 911 and asked if there was a fugitive on the loose and if everything was okay. They said, 'Oh, don't worry about it, ma'am, it's just the military. Everything is going to be okay.' But it's so loud. I'm really tired of it."

When Guam was attacked by Japan on December 8, 1941, our people were caught unawares. Most of the island was attending Catholic Mass in honor of our patron saint and rushed into hiding when they heard the bombs. Just two days prior, Guam's naval governor had been in his office frantically shredding military papers and classified documents. He knew the invasion was coming and did nothing to warn our people. Is history repeating itself?

(4)

"Mommy, Mommy, Mommy . . ." Inatan excitedly wants to tell me something as we lie in his bed.

"Yes, Inatan."

"Mommy, there were robots today, at my school, there were robots."

"Robots. What kind of robots?"

"They were all doing the same thing, Mommy, and they were wearing costumes. They all looked the same."

"Babe, do you know what Inatan's talking about?" I ask my husband, who is sitting beside the bed. "There were robots at his school?"

"He means the ROTC."

"Ooooohhhhh. I get it. Robots. Do you want to be a robot, son?"

"No, I want to be a boy."

"Well, tell me about the robots."

"I saw the America flag, Mommy."

"On their uniform?"

"No, one of them was holding it. The America flag is bad, but not the 'Fanohge Chamoru,' right?"

"You mean the Guam flag?"

"Yes, Mommy, the one when you sing the 'Fanohge Chamoru.' The America flag one, you sing a different song."

"Do you like that song?"

"No. I like the song from Ma'isa."

"Yeah, me, too. But why is the American flag bad, son?"

"Cause they do bad things."

"Like what?"

"They don't listen."

I guess I don't have to explain what it means to live in a colony. He said it better than I ever could. It's true, they simply don't listen.

(5)

I open the newspaper, and the teacher is right, a Navy commander has been accused of rape. In other news, the U.S. launched two bombers from Guam yesterday to fly over South Korea because North Korea recently conducted nuclear testing. The U.S. claims this is dangerous and poses an "unacceptable threat."

This tit-for-tat is as childish as tic-tac-toe, and while it continues to threaten our lives, you wouldn't think it was a problem if you read about it in Guam's newspapers. For days last month, our local media posted videos and photos of what they called an unprecedented event. The U.S. Air Force brought three types of bombers to Guam at the same time—the B-52 Stratofortress, B-1B Lancer and B-2 Spirit bomber. The articles and videos only quoted military officials and seemed to celebrate this as something we should all be proud of.

"It's a very unique opportunity for all of our country's bombers to train together . . . that's really tough to do back in the states," Lt. Col. Keith Butler brags. "Wider open air space out over the ocean . . . will allow us to flex our muscles, if you will."

"We have an open ocean . . . hundreds of millions of miles of . . . a playground essentially," First Lt. Ruben Labrador adds. "Whereas, if we are on land, we have restrictions that we have to abide by."

"It's just the natural course," explains Lt. Col. Jeremy Holmes. "It's a great opportunity to assure our regional partners and allies while deterring potential adversaries."

The natural course? There is nothing natural about bombers flying over my home. The next day, North Korea and China do not appear deterred.

North Korea says this is "sinister strategy" on behalf of the U.S. to "maintain its military hegemony in the region," and "Guam will face ruin in the face of all-out and substantial attack." China sees the bombers as a challenge.

"Well, that's just something we can shelve," the morning host of Guam's local talk radio show says after reporting on our potential "ruin." "No one is going to mess with the U.S." She laughs.

"But they will mess with Guam to get at the U.S.," I scream at my car radio. "Why are we so stupid?"

"What, Mommy?" Inatan asks from the back seat. "How come you're mad?"

"Because I don't want Guam to get bombed."

"How come?"

"Because I want you to live a long and happy life. You know, son, our ancestors did not believe in killing a lot of people. They weren't perfect. They had their battles, but they would stop before too many people died. If one or two people were killed, the fighting ended and everyone went home."

"How come?"

"Because they believed that people who died in battle would become restless souls."

"What's that?"

"Their spirits would not be happy and they would bother everyone. Sometimes I wonder if the restless souls of people who were killed during World War II here are haunting us."

"Who was killed?"

"My boy, thousands of Japanese and American soldiers killed each other on Guam. They say the ocean was pink and red from their blood. A lot of our own people were killed during the war, too."

"Mommy, that's scary."

"I know, but that's what war is. I don't ever want you to see that. I wish Guam could just stop being so proud of the military and focus on who we could be without them."

"Like our ancestors, Mommy? I like our ancestors."

"Me, too, Inatan. Me, too."

No ordinary sun

Hone Tuwhare

Tree let your arms fall:
raise them not sharply in supplication
to the bright enhaloed cloud.
Let your arms lack toughness and
resilience for this is no mere axe
to blunt nor fire to smother.

Your sap shall not rise again
to the moon's pull.
No more incline a deferential head
to the wind's talk, or stir
to the tickle of coursing rain.

Your former shagginess shall not be
wreathed with the delightful flight
of birds nor shield
nor cool the ardour of unheeding
lovers from the monstrous sun.

Tree let your naked arms fall
nor extend vain entreaties to the radiant ball.
This is no gallant monsoon's flash,
no dashing trade wind's blast.
The fading green of your magic
emanations shall not make pure again
these polluted skies . . . for this
is no ordinary sun.

O tree
in the shadowless mountains
the white plains and
the drab sea floor
your end at last is written.

Previously published, *No Ordinary Sun,* Longman Paul, 1964.

Poem for March 1st—Commemoration of the U.S. Bombing of Bikini Island

D. Keali'i MacKenzie

We are gathered here . . .

Because arrogant people feel the need
to dominate the lands of our ancestors

Because decades of bombardment
cracked the aquifer of an island
letting life leach into the ocean

Because atoms were split open
in a torrent to blind the sun

Because the small men never
felt the full weight of their own
humanity when dictating the lives
of others

Because sea and sky,
land and family
have always meant more to us
than the shallow struggles of empires

Because
we
still
live

and with our survivors
our warriors
our beloved

stand firm
against the ragged future
others would give to us.

We are gathered
to breathe new life
into places we are linked to

through voyaging
through occupation
through colonization

through protest and shared
struggle against
militarization
and nuclearization

but more importantly
places we are linked to
through the vast, expanding
ocean

We are gathered,
and in your presence
I say the names of our islands,
abused, scarred, near broken
not to commemorate tragedy

but so these beautiful and storied spaces
may live again

E hoʻōla hou

Kahoʻolawe
Hiroshima
Nagasaki
Bikini
Enewetak
Rongelap
Kwajalein
Moruroa
Fangataufa
Guåhan
Tinian
Alamagan

Okinawa
Kanaky
West Papua
E hoʻōla hou

Live, again

Monster

Kathy Jetñil-Kijiner

Sometimes I wonder if Marshallese women are the chosen ones.

I wonder if someone selected us from a stack. Drew us out slow. Methodical. Then, issued the order:

Give birth to nightmares. Show the world what happens. When the sun explodes inside you.

How many stories of nuclear war are hidden in our bodies?

574—the number of stillbirths and miscarriages after the bombs of 1951. Before the bombs? 52.

Bella Compoj told the UN she could no longer have children. That she saw her friends give birth to ugly things.

Nerik gave birth to something resembling the eggs of a sea turtle and Flora gave birth to something like the intestines.

She told this to a committee of men who washed their hands of this sin—these women who bore unholy things—created from exploding spit and ugly things.

And how these women buried their nightmares. Beneath a coconut tree. Pretended it never happened. Sinister. Hideous. Monster. More jellyfish than child.

And yet. They could see the chest inhale. Exhale. Could it be

human?

Nerik gave birth to something resembling the eggs of a sea turtle and Flora gave birth to something like intestines.

In our legends lives a monster. Mejenkwaad. Woman demons—unhinged jaws swallowing canoes, men, babies. Whole. Shark teeth in the backs of their head.

Necks that stretch around an entire island, bloodthirsty. Hungry for babies and pregnant women. Monsters.

My three-year-old likes to hunt for monsters in our closet. We use the light of my cell phone. A blue glow in the dark. We whisper to each other—did you hear that?

Did I hear what?

The silence of my dreams is severed by her screaming nightmares. And I am a mewling mess turned monster huddled in the corner wide-eyed, wild haired, unable to touch, unable to care, unable to bear the exhaustion, anxiety clawing away at my chest. Am I even

human? Postpartum—easier to diagnose after the fact. Two years later those memories haunt me. When I became the bump in the night. When I realized I needed to protect her. From me.

Did you hear that?

Nerik gave birth to something resembling the eggs of a sea turtle and Flora gave birth to something like intestines.

In our legends lives a monster. Woman demons, unhinged jaws. Swallowing their own babies. Driven mad. Turned flesh rotten. Blood through their eyes their teeth their nose.

Were the women who gave birth to nightmares considered monsters? Were they driven mad by these unholy things that came from their bodies? Were they sick with the feeling of horror that perhaps there was something

wrong. With them.

My three-year-old sleeps next to me. I have lost my fangs and ugly dreams. I watch her chest inhale. Exhale. Know that she is real, she is mine. I try to write forgiveness and healing into our story. Into myself.

In legends lives a woman. Turned monster from loneliness. Turned monster from agony and suns exploding in her chest. She gives birth to a child that is not so much a child but too much a jellyfish. The child is struggling for breath. Struggling in pain. She wants to bring the child peace. Bring her home. Her first home. Inside her body.

It is an embrace. It is only. An embrace. She kneels next to the body.

And inhales.

Yellow the cradle

Chantal T. Spitz

Translated from French by Jean Anderson

yellow, the cradle
because this is a human being
because this is our child
because we love our child
whatever the sex

and the yellow cradle in our bedroom
because we want our child near
because we want to sense to see our child
because we want to sleep with our child
because we love our child

we didn't want the ultrasound
sweet surprise
neither pink nor blue
our child
growing inside me
awaited with impatient patience
like something urgent
head full of images
heart full of tenderness
colors of eternity renewed

red red red
red warning red panic red collapse
blood red
red tides of shipwreck
red tears of disaster
red tragedies of total undoing

red bewildering red storming red raging
red distressing red ravaging red flaming

and the pulpy mass of slimy flesh
that was your body
and that heap of soggy bones
escaping from my body
and what was us
you and I
reduced to a chaotic unmaking

and the hole in my belly
full of all the laughter the joy the delight
aborted in a fire of lancing pain
and the hole in my belly
full of all the futures the horizons the possibilities
cast out into a night of raw ruins
and the hole in my belly
fetid obscene vile
full of all the never-never-evers

and in the hospital corridors
a muffled buzz that denounces
black memories that reveal
black black black
black fetus cast-out monsters
black fetus deformed snatched away
black fetus twisted genetics
black fetus nuclear inheritance

and in the hospital corridors
fifty years after the first nuclear test
they tell their stories
the misshapen bodies monstrous inhuman
genetics run amok
and in the valleys the atolls the towns the plains
fifty years after the first nuclear test
they drag themselves along
the bodies of women stripped of their dreams
hollowed by Nature itself
heritage mutating
human offering to the megalomaniac alienation
of a man who wanted
himself and his country
to be all powerful among the powerful

and throughout the country
red red red

black black black
spontaneous abortions
of atomic monsters

silent carnage
voiceless sufferings

To Tamatahi
To Ludivine
To Vaiokena and Hinara'i

To all those who didn't have the time
to be named

We Are Called

Cita N. Morei

Written two years after Palau's independence, October 1, 1994

From every corner of our lineages,
Through every curve of our villages,
We are called to walk the path
        At Nature's Trail
With the spirit of our ancestors.

We must rise, rise, rise up,
As people of conscience,
People with confidence
As we walk in Harmony with Creation.

We rise, rise as people who care
        Who search for solutions,
Brave enough to ask serious questions.
We hear, we heed the call to be One.

We do not fear to challenge,
The big and the powerful,
We fear not, the ruthless
And the greedy.

We rise, rise, rise up to stand
Together for what must be done
For we are called to be the Hope
And the dream of our children.

Afterword

Kathy Jetñil-Kijiner

Environmentalism is a clunky word to describe the ways in which Pacific Islanders fight for land, ocean, air. Poem after story after article in this collection have sought to explore that connection, that relationship that Albert Wendt once described as "the space between us," the garden we must cultivate. Writing gives us the ability to cultivate this relationship, to till this soil.

I did not come to the work of environmentalism through science, or because of particularly powerful memories in a lush setting. I consider myself a city girl in all honesty. I am most comfortable in an urban island setting—Suva's hectic streets reminded me of concrete high-rises in Honolulu, which echoed the slow inch of cars in Majuro, and in each setting I felt more at home than in the outer islands, a shameful thing for a rimajel to admit. To be comfortable in commodity, in Westernization, rather than in the simplicity and tradition of outer-island living. But we are full of contradictions, no doubt. No, I came to the work of environmentalism because of my cousins, because of my family who told me stories of their connections, because of legends and myths of reef formations that still stand in Aur to this day. It began in curiosity. It continued because of fear.

I have a strong memory of the first king tide I experienced, because it was less than a decade ago. I tell the story at every presentation I give. How I woke up from dreams of our family cooking and eating a shark, the ominous feeling I had when I woke up. My mother and I wandering outside, in a daze, to see the water across the streets, filled with trash the ocean regurgitated. My mother telling me she'd never seen anything like it.

I've been climate envoy for less than a year, a director for Jo-Jikum for eight years, and I've been writing poetry for more than twelve years. I work between anti-plastic community campaigns, meetings with our national government ministries to develop a national adaptation plan, and sitting in on international negotiations on climate, usually one of the few young, brown faces in the room.

I love the work that I do—the challenge of understanding the various alliances and regional groups, the subtle between-the-lines messaging of ambassador statements. I love coaching a youth through his first outreach, giving feedback on a climate poem, coming up with classes and fliers that I think our community will enjoy. But poetry is and always will be my first love, the first thing to root me in the movement. In poetry, I draw the lines across the sand asking everyone—do you see it? Do you see the connections?

This collection is being compiled at a time when the world is in a major upheaval, the likes of which none of us have ever experienced or seen. The global pandemic has slowed down the entire world to a crunching halt. Planes are not flying, trains and cars are not running. The rivers and oceans are cleaner. Emissions have finally started to inch their way down.

When this first was happening, I found myself confused, and unable to understand what my role as a climate change envoy, campaigner, organizer, and artist was in response to COVID-19. This is not the crisis I was prepared for, not exactly. And I saw all the social media posts, the tweets, celebrating the unintended environmental impacts of COVID—"We are the virus." Meanwhile, elders were passing away, alone, with no family around them, my immunocompromised friends were fighting to be heard, fighting for supplies that were being hoarded, and politicians were making awful statements about letting grandparents make the sacrifice.

But this isn't what climate justice is about. Eco-fascism is a political model that forgets the importance of the community, that doesn't value individual lives. Our culture reminds us, though, that every life counts. Our ties and practices that continue to tie us to one another are beyond politics and come from deep time, one that has coral polyp memories.

As I read the work in this anthology, I am reminded of the importance of our stories. How they can reconnect us to feeling, to empathy.

This collection remembers to feel. It remembers West Papua, Waikīkī before, it remembers the birdsongs that have vanished from Guåhan. It remembers Teresia Teaiwa, who really did gather us all from the same garden.

I read this collection after fighting my way through a science stock-take report that detailed the stark reality of what's to come for our island in ten years. The words between these pages were a soothing balm after the harsh numbers and graphs depicting our demise. Science reports, movements, negotiations—all of these have shorter memory than the sharp rock formation rising out of the reef in Aur. I turn back to poetry again and again—not for escape, or for luxury. But to remind me that the emotions beneath the surface of the work are necessary, deeply necessary, to sustain myself and our communities. That there is something beneath us all, that extends beyond each of us, that has survived, and will continue to survive.

Contributors

Jean Anderson taught French language and literature for more than thirty years in Canada and New Zealand. In 2006 she developed an interest in literary translation, with a focus on francophone Pacific writing. She founded the New Zealand Centre for Literary Translation at Victoria University of Wellington / Te Herenga Waka in 2007. She has also co-translated into French seven books by leading New Zealand Indigenous writer Patricia Grace.

Flora Aurima Devatine is a pillar of French Polynesian literature. A founding member of the Tahitian Academy (Te Fare Va'a, 1972) and of the literary review *Littérama'ohi* (2002–), she is a widely acknowledged theorist of "oraliture" (*Tergiversations et rêveries de l'écriture orale* [Meanderings and Daydreams of Oral Writing], 1992) and an award-winning poet (French Academy Hérédia Prize, 2017, for *Au vent de la piroguière—Tifaifai*).

Tusiata Avia is an internationally acclaimed poet, performer, and writer. She has published the collections *Wild Dogs under My Skirt, Bloodclot, Fale Aitu / Spirit House,* and *The Savage Coloniser Book.* Her children's books are *Mele and the Fofo, The Song,* and *Rat and Octopus.* The theater production of *Wild Dogs under My Skirt* garnered the 2019 Outstanding Production of the Year at Soho Playhouse, New York City. Avia most recently received a 2020 Arts Foundation Laureate and became a member of the New Zealand Order of Merit.

Joe Balaz, born and raised in Wahiawa on the island of O'ahu, is of Hawaiian, Slovakian, and Irish ancestry. He is the author of multiple books of poetry in English and pidgin, as well as the editor of *Ho'omanoa: An Anthology of Contemporary Hawaiian Literature.* His most recent book is *Pidgin Eye* (2019), and he received the Elliot Cades Award from the Hawai'i Literary Arts Council in 2020.

Lia Maria Barcinas is a lifelong student of coconut trees. She is a daughter of the Marianas Islands from the village of Malesso'. She is thankful to Aiko for this opportunity to remember and explore our island connections that are deeper than military fences and base relocations. She is thankful for all the plants that have gathered them in this space.

Serie Barford was born in Aotearoa to a German-Samoan mother and a Palagi father. She is widely published in anthologies. Serie was the recipient of a 2018

Pasifika Residency at the Michael King Writers' Centre, Tāmaki Makaurau. She promoted her collections *Tapa Talk* and *Entangled Islands* at the 2019 International Arsenal Book Festival in Kiev. Her latest poetry collection is *Sleeping with Stones* (2021).

Kisha Borja-Quichocho-Calvo is a CHamoru mother, educator, activist, and poet from Mangilao, Guåhan. She is a PhD candidate in the political science program (with a specialization in Indigenous Politics) at the University of Hawai'i at Mānoa and an instructor at the University of Guam. Her research and writing interests are grounded in Guåhan, focusing on CHamoru culture, history, and education, as well as the impacts of US militarization in Guåhan.

Moetai Brotherson trained as a computer engineer and worked in IT before pursuing a career in politics. He has served as a municipal councillor for Faa'a and was elected as representative of the Windward Islands to the Assembly of French Polynesia in 2018. His novel *Le Roi absent* (2008, 2020), a sweeping epic of the Pacific, is available in English (*The Missing King*, 2012).

Audrey Brown-Pereira, born in the Cook Islands and raised in New Zealand, now lives in Samoa with her family. Her collections include *Threads of Tivaevae: Kaleidoskope of Kolours* (2002) and *Passages in Between I(s)lands* (2014). She has pieces featured in several anthologies, journals, and performances including *UPU*, a celebration of Oceanic literature performed by Maori and Pacific actors for the Auckland Arts Festival in 2020.

Jessica Carpenter was born and raised in Pālolo Valley, O'ahu. After attending Kamehameha Schools Kapālama, she received degrees in literature and ethnic studies at the University of Hawai'i at Mānoa. Her time in these valleys, near these streams, fostered a reverence for the relationship between indigenous peoples and the Earth.

Emalani Case is a lecturer in Pacific studies at Te Herenga Waka–Victoria University of Wellington. As a Kanaka Maoli woman, activist, and writer, she is deeply engaged in issues of Indigenous rights, decolonization, and environmental and social justice. Her work is motivated by a desire to strengthen trans-indigenous solidarities across the Pacific. She is from Waimea, Hawai'i.

Donovan Kūhiō Colleps is a Kanaka Maoli (Native Hawaiian) poet, editor, and scholar. He was born in Honolulu and lives in Pu'uloa, 'Ewa, on the island of O'ahu. He has studied creative writing and Pacific literatures at the University of Hawai'i at Mānoa. He is the author of *Proposed Additions* (2014), and his work has been published in national and international journals and anthologies.

J.A. Dela Cruz-Smith is a Chamoru-Filipino, queer poet living in Seattle. His family is from Dededo and Chalan Pago, Guåhan. He received an MFA in creative writing from the Rainier Writing Workshop and works as a TV and film critic for *Yolk*. He is co-founder of the contemporary art house From Typhoon.

Kamele Donaldson was raised in the Pacific Northwest as a Kanaka in diaspora. She currently attends the University of Hawai'i at Mānoa, where she is pursuing her bachelor's degree in 'Ōlelo Hawai'i. She is a regular contributor to the Honolulu spoken-word poetry community.

Bonnie Etherington earned her PhD in English from Northwestern University. Her first novel, *The Earth Cries Out* (2017), was short-listed for the William Saroyan Prize and long-listed for the New Zealand Book Awards. Bonnie was born in Aotearoa New Zealand and raised in West Papua.

A mother of two sons, **Sia Figiel** is a poet, writer, and translator. Her first novel, *where we once belonged*, won multiple awards. She is also the author of *To a Young Artist in Contemplation*, *The Girl in the Moon Circle*, *They Who Do Not Grieve*, and *Freelove*. Sia appeared on the amplified poetry CD *Terenesia* with poet and scholar Dr. Teresia Teaiwa. She recently translated Maualaivao Albert Wendt's seminal novel *Pouliuli* to the Samoan language.

Evelyn Flores is a CHamoru writer and a professor of Pacific Island literatures and CHamoru studies at the University of Guam. She dedicates her research and creative activities to preserving and publishing the stories of the indigenous people of Guam as well as the broader geographic area of Micronesia. She is one of the two editors of *An Anthology of Indigenous Literatures from Micronesia* (2018).

Ryan Tito Gapelu is a queer Samoan poet and writer based in Honolulu, Hawai'i. He is pursuing a graduate degree in creative writing at the University of Hawai'i at Mānoa and is currently editing his first poetry chapbook, *Splitting Storms*. Gapelu writes to provide more representation of queer experiences in the diasporic Pasifika community and the intersections of culture, identity, sexuality, and ecology.

Waej Genin-Juni was born in Lifou, New Caledonia, and educated in Nouméa and in Paris (master's in modern letters, Sorbonne-IV, 1989). After working initially as a freelance radio journalist, she took up a position teaching literature in Lifou. She has published short stories and poetry, notably in anthologies (e.g., *Lifou sous la pluie* [Lifou in the Rain], 2019).

William Nu'utupu Giles is a Samoan-American poet from Hawai'i. They are an International Poetry Slam Champion as well as a Kundiman Poetry Fellow. Their work explores mental health issues emerging out of modern colonization, how we change to chase diaspora, and the waters that connect us.

Aleks Giyai was born in an Onago village in the mountains of Papua. He has worked as a manager and administrator for KoSaPa, a collective for the Papuan literary community. In April 2017, he published his first book in Bahasa Indonesia, *Tetesan Embun Inspirasi Dari Papua* (*A Dewdrop of Inspiration from Papua*), and he has won several local poetry and short story competitions. He is at work on three more collections of poetry.

Noelani Goodyear-Ka'ōpua is a professor in the Political Science Department at the University of Hawai'i at Mānoa, where she teaches Hawaiian and Indigenous politics. Her books include *The Seeds We Planted, A Nation Rising,* and *Nā Wāhine Koa.*

The first Kanak woman to publish literary works, **Déwé Gorodé** is known for her poetry and short story collections as well as the groundbreaking 2005 novel *L'Epave* (*The Wreck,* 2011), which deals with the trauma of sexual violence as cultural practice. A leading independentist politician, she served as vice president of the government of New Caledonia from 2001 to 2009. Two further novels, *Graines de pin colonnaire* and *Tâdo, Tâdo, wéé!,* appeared in 2009 and 2012, respectively.

Patricia Grace is an award-winning novelist, short story writer, and writer of books for children. She is of Ngati Toa, Ngati Raukawa, and Te Ati Awa descent. In 2007, she received a Distinguished Companion of the New Zealand Order of Merit for her services to literature. Her books include *Waiariki* (1975), *Mutuwhenua: The Moon Sleeps* (1978), *Potiki* (1986), *Cousins* (1992), *The Sky People* (1994), *Baby No-Eyes* (1998), *Dogside Story* (2001), and *Tu* (2004), among others.

Dana Naone Hall's poetry has appeared in numerous anthologies and publications beginning with *Carriers of the Dream Wheel.* She shaped and edited the first four issues of *Hawai'i Review* and went on to edit *Malama: Hawaiian Land and Water* for Bamboo Ridge Press. She is a recipient of the Elliot Cades Award for Literature and more recently, her book, *Life of the Land: Articulations of a Native Writer,* is a winner of an American Book Award.

A daughter of Guåhan (Guam), **Mary Therese Perez Hattori** is one of nine children of Paul Mitsuo Hattori, who was originally of Kalihi, Hawai'i, and Fermina Leon Guerrero Perez (familian Titang), of Chalan Pago, Guam. Dr. Hattori is acting director of the Pacific Islands Development Program in the East-West Center and is affiliate faculty for the University of Hawai'i.

Epeli Hau'ofa (1939–2009) was a Tongan writer, scholar, and anthropologist. He earned a PhD in social anthropology from the Australian National University. He taught at the University of the South Pacific and founded the Oceania Centre for Arts and Culture. His works include *Mekeo: Inequality and Ambivalence in a Village Society* (1981), *Tales of the Tikongs* (1983), *Kisses in the Nederends* (1987), and *We Are the Ocean: Selected Works* (2008). He co-edited *A New*

Oceania: Rediscovering Our Sea of Islands (1993). His work continues to inspire generations of Pacific Islanders.

Originally from Rotuma, **Vilsoni Hereniko** is an award-winning playwright, scholar, and filmmaker. He received his PhD from the University of the South Pacific, where he went on to serve as the director of the Oceania Centre for Arts, Culture and Pacific Studies. He is currently a professor at the Academy for Creative Media at the University of Hawai'i at Mānoa, where he has also served as the director of the Center for Pacific Islands Studies.

Witi Ihimaera is an internationally renowned and award-winning Māori (Te Aitanga-a-Māhaki) author, editor, and educator. He has written many best-selling novels, collections of short stories, and works for children, including *Pounamu, Pounamu* (1972); *Tangi* (1973); *The Matriarch* (1986); *The Whale Rider* (1987); *Nights in the Garden of Spain* (1996); *The Uncle's Story* (2000); and *Māori Boy: A Memoir of Childhood* (2014). He has also edited and written several books on the arts, literature, and Māori culture, such as *Navigating the Stars: Māori Creation Myths* (2020). In 2004 he became a Distinguished Companion of the Order of New Zealand. He has been a professor of English and Distinguished Creative Fellow in Māori Literature at Auckland University.

Dr. **Takiora Ingram**, born and raised in Rarotonga, Cook Islands, is an award-winning academic writer, poet, and freelance journalist. She co-founded the Pacific Writers' Connection, served on the Creative New Zealand's National Arts Board, chaired the Pacific Arts Committee for the New Zealand government (1997–2000), and established the Pacific Wave Festival in Sydney (2002). She's the first Cook Islander to graduate with a PhD in management and public policy from Massey University, New Zealand, in 1992.

Grace Iwashita-Taylor, breathing bloodlines of Samoa, England, and Japan. She received the CNZ Emerging Pacific Artist 2014 and the Auckland Mayoral Writers Grant 2016. She was a visiting writer at the University of Hawai'i (2018), co-founder of Rising Voices (the first youth poetry slam in Aotearoa), and the South Auckland Poets Collective. She is the author of *Afakasi Speaks* (2013), *Full Broken Bloom* (2017), and the play *My Own Darling*, and the curator of *UPU* (Auckland Arts Festival, 2020).

Kathy Jetñil-Kijiner is a Marshallese poet, born in the Marshall Islands and raised in Hawai'i. She is the author of *Iep Jāltok: Poems from a Marshallese Daughter* (2017). She has performed and exhibited her artwork around the world. In 2019, she was selected as an Obama Asia Pacific Leader Fellow and MIT Director's Media Lab Fellow. She received her master's in Pacific Island studies from the University of Hawai'i and is currently a PhD student at Australia National University. She serves as climate envoy for the Republic of the Marshall Islands and as director for the environmental nonprofit Jo-Jikum.

Yolanda Joab was born and raised in Pohnpei. She helps run the Climate Change Adaptation, Disaster Risk Reduction and Education Program (CADRE) in schools and communities in the Federated States of Micronesia and the Republic of the Marshall Islands at the International Organization for Migration (IOM) Micronesia. She lives in Chuuk with her husband, son, and family.

Kristiana Kahakauwila is a hapa writer of Kanaka Maoli, German, and Norwegian descent. Her first book, *This Is Paradise: Stories* (2013), takes as its heart the people and landscapes of contemporary Hawai'i. She has taught creative writing at Western Washington University and the Institute of American Indian Arts and now teaches in the English Department at the University of Hawai'i at Mānoa. She is currently at work on a historical novel.

Imaikalani Kalahele is a Kanaka Maoli (Native Hawaiian) poet, artist, philosopher, and musician whose work has appeared in many journals and anthologies. His book, *Kalahele* (2002), collected poetry and art in a polyphonic performance of English, pidgin, and Hawaiian. He is also a scholar and practitioner of Hawaiian culture who lives and works in his mountain studio in upper Kalihi Valley.

Daren Kamali, a Fijian-born New Zealander, is a poet/performer and Heritage Pacific Advisor for Auckland Libraries. He is the author of *Tales, Poems and Songs from the Underwater World* (2011); *Squid Out of Water: The Evolution* (2014); and *Vunimaqo and Me: Mango Tree Collections* (2021). He has released two albums, *Immigrant Story* (2000) and *Keep It Real* (2005). He is a former Fulbright–Creative New Zealand Pacific Writer at the University of Hawai'i and at the International Writers Programme, University of Iowa.

John Kasaipwalova is one of Papua New Guinea's most prominent poets and playwrights. He attended the University of Queensland and the University of Papua New Guinea. He has served on the National Cultural Commission, the Council of the University of Papua New Guinea, and the Kiriwina Council of Chiefs. He is the author of the poetry collections *Reluctant Flame* (1971) and *Hanuabada* (1972). He co-authored the folk opera *Sail the Midnight Sun* (1980) and collaborated with Jutta Malnic on the volume *Kula: Myth and Magic in the Trobriand Islands* (1998).

Leora Kava is a hafekasi poet and musician of Tongan descent who received her PhD in creative writing from the University of Hawai'i at Mānoa. She is the founder of the Nuku'alofa-based Pacific Verse project, a music- and poetry-writing workshop series. She is an assistant professor of Critical Pacific Islands and Oceania studies at San Francisco State University.

Emelihter Kihleng completed her PhD in Va'aomanū Pasifika, Pacific studies from Victoria University of Wellington in Aotearoa New Zealand. She was the Fall 2015 Distinguished Writer in Residence at the University of Hawai'i. She is the author of *My Urohs* (2008). She served as the cultural anthropologist for the Pohnpei Historic Preservation Program and most recently worked as the first curatorial research fellow, Oceania at the MARKK Museum am Rothenbaum in Hamburg, Germany.

Selina Neirok Leem is from the Republic of the Marshall Islands. She is a graduate of the international school UWC Robert Bosch College in Freiburg, Germany. Leem is a youth warrior from the Marshall Islands against climate change and abuse against women. She spoke at the COP21 in Paris, France, where she addressed world leaders and urged them on this fight against climate change.

Victoria-Lola M. Leon Guerrero is the managing editor of the University of Guam Press. She has an MFA in creative writing from Mills College and a BA in politics from the University of San Francisco. She has authored a children's book, several short stories, essays, and the play *Pågat;* co-edited an anthology of Chamoru writers; and edited *Storyboard: A Journal of Pacific Imagery.* She is the co-chairperson of Independent Guåhan and a member of the Commission on Decolonization.

Arielle Taitano Lowe is a Chamoru poet born and raised on the island of Guam. She started writing spoken-word poetry at George Washington High School. She competed and placed in poetry slam competitions locally and competed at Brave New Voices International Poetry Slam Festival as part of Team Guam. Since then, Arielle has expanded her genres to include documentary poetry, creative nonfiction, and memoir.

D. Keali'i MacKenzie is the author of the chapbook *From Hunger to Prayer.* A queer poet of Kanaka Maoli, European, and Chinese descent, his work appears in, or is forthcoming from, *Home (Is)lands: New Art & Writing from Guahan & Hawai'i, homology lit,* and *Foglifter.* A Pushcart nominee and past member of the Worcester Poetry Slam team, he received an MA in Pacific Islands studies and an MLISc, from the University of Hawai'i at Mānoa.

Tina Makereti's books include the novels *The Imaginary Lives of James Pōneke* (2018) and *Where the Rēkohu Bone Sings* (2014); an anthology of Māori and Pasifika fiction she co-edited with Witi Ihimaera, titled *Black Marks on the White Page* (2017); and a short story collection, *Once Upon a Time in Aotearoa* (2010). In 2016 she won the Commonwealth Short Pacific Regional Story Prize for her story "Black Milk." Tina has a PhD in creative writing from Victoria University of Wellington, New Zealand, where she also teaches.

Jully Makini was born in Gizo in the Solomon Islands. She graduated from the University of the South Pacific and attended the Solomon Island Women Writers' Workshop. Her books include *Civilized Girl* (1981), *Praying Parents* (1986), and *Flotsam and Jetsam* (2007). She co-edited the first anthology of Solomon

Islands women's writing, *Mi Mere* (1983). In 2017, she received the International Women of Courage Award from the US secretary of state for her work in promoting women's rights in the Solomon Islands.

Selina Tusitala Marsh (ONZM, FRSNZ) is the former Commonwealth Poet, New Zealand Poet Laureate, and an acclaimed performer and author. She was made an Officer of the New Zealand Order of Merit and inducted as a Fellow of the Royal Society of New Zealand. An associate professor in the English Department at the University of Auckland, Selina teaches Maori and Pacific literature and creative writing. Selina has performed for primary schoolers and presidents (Obama), queers and queens (HRH Elizabeth II). Her award-winning poetry books include *Fast Talking PI* (2009), *Dark Sparring* (2013), and *Tightrope* (2017). She also authored the award-winning graphic memoir *Mophead* (2019) and its sequel, *Mophead TU: The Queen's Poem*.

Brandy Nālani McDougall is a poet and educator who weaves the Hawaiian language with English to create a complex, bilingual texture. She earned her MFA from the University of Oregon and is a PhD candidate at the University of Hawai'i at Mānoa, where she currently teaches in the American Studies department. She is the author of *The Salt-Wind / Ka Makani Pa'akai* (2008) and the scholarly monograph *Finding Meaning: Kaona and Contemporary Hawaiian Literature* (2016).

Dan Taulapapa McMullin is a Fa'afafine artist and poet from Sāmoa i Sasa'e. Their work is described by *Hyperallergic Magazine* as "a poetic corrective to the West's violent appropriations and erasures." Their art has shown at the Metropolitan Museum, De Young Museum, Auckland Art Gallery, and Musée du quai Branly. Their collected poems *Coconut Milk* was on the American Library Association Rainbow List Top Ten Books of the Year.

Clarissa Mendiola (familian Månnok yan Vincentico) is a mother and poet who lives in San Francisco. As a CHamoru woman raised off island, poetry is the method by which she bridges the distance between her home island and where she stands. She was a 2011 Hedgebrook Writer in Residence and currently teaches creative writing camps and workshops at a San Francisco high school where she also serves as a communications writer.

Courtney Sina Meredith is a poet, playwright, fiction writer, and musician. Her play *Rushing Dolls* (2010) won a number of awards and was published by Playmarket in 2012. She is the author of *Tail of the Taniwha* (Beatnik) and *Brown Girls in Bright Red Lipstick* (Beatnik). She held the LiteraturRaum Blebitreu Berlin residency in 2011, and she was New Zealand's representative for the International Writing Program's Fall Residency at the University of Iowa in August 2016. She is of Samoan, Mangaian, and Irish descent.

Karlo Mila (MNZM) was born in Rotorua, New Zealand. She earned her BA from Massey University and worked for ten years in labor organizing and health research before earning her PhD in sociology. Mila is of Tongan, Samoan, and European descent. Her books include *Dream Fish Floating* (2006), *A Well Written Body* (2008), and *Goddess Muscle* (2020). Mila is the recipient of a Fulbright–Creative New Zealand Pacific Writer's Residency and represented Tonga at the 2012 Cultural Olympiad event Poetry Parnassus Festival in London. She is the mother of three boys and lives in Auckland.

Grace Mera Molisa (1946–2002) was a Ni-Vanuatu politician, poet, and campaigner for women's equality in Vanuatu. She earned her BA from the University of the South Pacific, and she served as spokeswoman for the prime minister and the secretary of the Ministry of Social Affairs. She was involved in founding Vanuatu's National Arts Festival and Vanuatu Women in Politics. Her poetry collections include *Black Stone* (1983), *Colonised People: Poems* (1987), *Black Stone II* (1989), and *Pasifik paradaes* (1995). She published the voices of indigenous Pacific women through her press, Blackstone Publishing.

Serena Morales is a queer Kanaka Maoli and Latinx poet from the Queendom of Hawai'i, currently based in Canarsee/Lenape lands (colonially known as Brooklyn, New York). Serena works at Books Are Magic, where she champions the works of underrepresented authors. In 2020, she was awarded the inaugural Duende-Word BIPOC Bookseller Award in the category of Activism.

Cita N. Morei is a women's liberation and anti–nuclear weapons activist and writer. She is a member of the Belauan women's organization Otil a Beluad and author of "Belau Be Brave," "Planting the Mustard Seed of World Peace," and many other works. Morei is an active campaigner for the preservation of the land in the Pacific island of Palau.

PC Muñoz is a Chamoru recording artist and writer based in San Francisco. Muñoz's work bridges the gap between pop songcraft, experimental literature, musique concrète, and the insistent rhythms of funk and hip-hop. He is a current Mosaic Silicon Valley Artist Fellow and a former board governor for the San Francisco chapter of the Recording Academy/Grammys.

Leiana San Agustin Naholowa'a is from Dededo, Guam, and she was a Publications and Literary Arts committee member and delegate representing Guam at the Festival of Pacific Arts (2016). She specializes in CHamoru women and gender studies, orality, myths, legends, and folklore. She supports regional publications in the Pacific, and she is one of the founding members of Ta Tuge' Mo'na, a nonprofit that supports literary communities in Guam.

Sarita Newson, originally from New Zealand, has lived in Bali since 1975. She started publishing books under the company name Saritaksu Editions in the early eighties as a sideline to her main business, a graphic design studio. She has translated and published more than fifty books, including novels, pictorial art and coffee table books, nonfiction, and children's books.

Fuifuilupe Niumeitolu is a Tongan scholar, storyteller, and community organizer. She received her doctorate from the Comparative Ethnic Studies department at the University of California, Berkeley, and a UC President's Postdoctoral Fellow at the Department of Native American Studies at the University of California, Davis. She is on the founding committee of the Moana Nui Pacific Islander Climate Justice Project and Oceania Coalition of Northern California. She is part of the Sogorea Te Land Trust, an Indigenous women–led organization in California.

Loa Niumeitolu is a Tongan poet, grounding into her Indigenous auntie role in her community. Her ongoing work for Mother Earth includes organizing more than two hundred Pacific Islanders as a contingent for the global Rise for Climate March in San Francisco in 2018; and, currently, growing food and learning together with youth and elders, with particular joy in farming with BIPOC queer and nonbinary folx, while following Lisjan Ohlone leadership on Ohlone Territory.

Peter R. Onedera is a CHamoru playwright, author, master storyteller, and language educator. He received his master of arts degree from the University of Guam, where he also taught CHamoru language. His many books and plays include *Ai Haga-hu!* (1997), *Nasarinu* (1999), *Nå'an Lugåt Siha gi ya Guåhan: Guam Place Names* (1989), *Fafa Na 'Gue Yan Hinengge Siha* (*Ghosts and Superstitious Beliefs*) (1994), *Cheffla gi i Manglo: Whistle in the Wind* (2006), *Gi I Tilu Gradu* (*In the Third Grade*) (2009), *Wednesday's Child* (2016), and *Taimanu na Ini* (2018).

Dr. **Jamaica Heolimeleikalani Osorio** is a Kanaka Maoli wahine artist/activist/scholar born and raised in Pālolo Valley to parents Jonathan and Mary Osorio. Heoli is an assistant professor of Indigenous and Native Hawaiian politics at the University of Hawai'i at Mānoa. She is a three-time national poetry champion, poetry mentor, and author of *Remembering Our Intimacies: Mo'olelo, Aloha 'Āina, and Ea* (2021).

Jay Pascua is a poet, a writer, an actor, and a Chamorro chanter—a storyteller. Jay told numerous stories in his fifteen-year career as a journalist but now passionately shares stories of his culture. His work has appeared in books published on Guam, print and online poetry magazines, a poetry book published in the UK, and BBC Radio 4. He hopes his stories inspire other Chamorros to embrace and perpetuate their heritage.

Craig Santos Perez is a CHamoru from Guåhan (Guam). He is the author of five books of poetry and the co-editor of five anthologies. He is a professor in the English Department at the University of Hawai'i at Mānoa.

Mahealani Perez-Wendt is a Native Hawaiian author who lives on the island of Maui. She was a recipient of the Elliot Cades Award for Literature in 1993, and her work has been published in many literary journals and anthologies. She is the author of the poetry collection *Uluhaimālama* (2008) and the co-editor of *Hoʻolauleʻa: Celebrating 10 Years of Pacific Writing* (2012). Her poem "Voyage" appears in the preface to the law textbook *Native Hawaiian Law: A Treatise* (2015). She recently retired as the executive director of the Native Hawaiian Legal Corporation, where she worked for more than thirty years.

Kiri Piahana-Wong is a poet, editor, and publisher from Aotearoa New Zealand. She is of Māori (Ngāti Ranginui), Chinese, and Pākehā (English) ancestry. Kiri founded the small-press publishing company Anahera Press in 2011. Her poems have appeared in more than fifty journals and anthologies, and she has one full-length collection, *Night Swimming* (2013). Her second book, *Give Me an Ordinary Day,* is forthcoming. Kiri lives in Auckland with her family.

Doug Poole is of Samoan (Ulberg Aiga of Tulaʻele, Apia, ʻUpolo) and European descent. He is the publisher and editor of the poetry e-zine *Blackmail Press.* His work has been published in many literary journals and anthologies. He produced the performance poetry show *Polynation* (2008) and co-produced *Atarangi Whenua–Shadow Land* (2009), a touring exhibition of paintings and poetry, with New Zealand painter Penny Howard.

leilani portillo is a queer Kanaka ʻŌiwi poet, potter, and artist born and raised on occupied Ohlone Territory. She moved to Hawaiʻi in 2012 for school and has since been reconnecting to her roots and exploring her kuleana as a diasporic Kanaka. She is currently pursuing her PhD at the University of Hawaiʻi at Mānoa in English with a focus on creative writing.

John Puhiatau Pule was born in Niue. A self-taught artist, he is poet and writer as well as painter and printmaker, often combining the different forms. He has been included in three Asia Pacific triennials at the Queensland Gallery of Modern Art. Since 2015 he has been living in the village of Liku in Niue and to mark his return staged a solo exhibition in Liku in 2016. He also maintains a studio in Auckland.

Michael Puleloa, PhD, was born on Majuro in the Marshall Islands and raised on Molokaʻi and Oʻahu in Hawaiʻi. He has taught composition at Kapiʻolani Community College and the University of Hawaiʻi at Mānoa. He is currently an English teacher at Kamehameha Schools, Kapālama (his alma mater). His story here is the companion piece to "Man Underwater," which can be found in *Bamboo Ridge: Journal of Hawaiʻi Literature and Arts,* no. 118 (2020).

Tagi Qolouvaki is Fijian-Tongan via her mother's people in Fiji—resilient coastal and river delta people from Sawana, Vanua Balavu in Lau, and Lomanikoro,

Rewa on Viti Levu—and German, Irish, and English American through her father. Born and raised in Fiji, she currently lives in occupied Hawai'i. Her poetry is the work of a queer, indigenous Pacific woman remembering her ancestors in body, spirit, language, and loloma.

Hermana Ramarui received a BA in English from the University of Guam in 1970, and she has worked in Guam and Palau as an elementary and high school teacher, director of bilingual projects, student services coordinator, and Palauan language teacher. Her book, *Palauan Perspectives,* was originally published in 1984.

No'u Revilla is a queer 'Ōiwi poet, educator, and aloha 'āina. She taught poetry at Pu'uhuluhulu University in the summer of 2019 and is an assistant professor at the University of Hawai'i at Mānoa, where she teaches creative writing, decolonial poetics, and Native Hawaiian literature. Her most recent chapbook, *Permission to Make Digging Sounds,* was published in *Effigies III* in 2019.

Shaylin Nicole Salas is a CHamoru artist and researcher. She lives on Guåhan, where she likes to spend her time with family and/or playing in the ocean waves. She does agricultural studies for the Unibetsedåt Guåhan (University of Guam), while writing and drawing in her free time.

Terisa Siagatonu is a queer Sāmoan award-winning poet, speaker, educator, and organizer from the Bay Area. A President Obama's Champion of Change recipient and 2019 YBCA 100 List honoree, her work has been published in *Poetry Magazine* and has been featured in *Academy of American Poets, Button Poetry, CNN, NBC News, NPR, Huffington Post,* and *Buzzfeed.*

Serena Ngaio Simmons (Ngāti Porou) (she/her, he/him) is a takatāpui writer and performer born and raised on the island of O'ahu. She has a BA in English from the University of Hawai'i at Mānoa. Much of his work is concerned with themes such as diaspora, identity conflict, queer/takatāpui identity, mana wāhine, and home.

Peter Sipeli is an arts manager and supporter of the spoken-word arts movement in Fiji. Peter founded the online arts magazine *ARTtalk, Fiji,* as well as the Poetry Shop, Fiji. He works as a gay activist using storytelling as advocacy. In 2016, Peter was among seven presenters who participated in the inaugural TEDx Suva, in which he spoke on storytelling for advocacy.

Chantal T. Spitz lives on Huahine, French Polynesia. She published the first novel by an Indigenous Tahitian writer, *L'Île des rêves écrasés,* in 1991 (*Island of Shattered Dreams,* 2007). A founding member of the literary journal *Littérama'ohi,* following a career in teaching, she has published several other books, including *Hombo, transcription d'une biographia* (2002), *Elles, Terre d'enfance* (2011), and *Cartes postales* (2015).

Monique Storie earned a BS in Spanish from Arizona State University, an MA in library science, and a PhD in language, reading, and culture, also from the University of Arizona. Dr. Storie has worked at the Richard Flores Taitano Micronesian Area Research Center since 1995, serving as the Guam and Micronesia Reference Collection librarian and more recently as interim director. She helped to restart MARC's Familian Chamorro Genealogy Program, which began in the early 1980s with MARC librarians, including the late Al Williams.

Robert Sullivan is a member of the Māori tribes Ngāpuhi and Kāi Tahu. His seven collections of poetry include *Captain Cook in the Underworld, Shout Ha! to the Sky,* and the bestselling *Star Waka.* He co-edited three major anthologies of Pacific and Māori poetry. For more information see the Academy of New Zealand Literature page: https://www.anzliterature.com/member/robert-sullivan/.

Penina Ava Taesali is a Samoan poet, educator, and cultural arts activist. Taesali is published in literary journals and anthologies around the world. Her first collection of poetry, *Sourcing Siapo,* was published in 2016. Her chapbook *Summons: Love Letters for the People* was published in 2018. Taesali earned her MFA in writing from Mills College in 2012. She lives in Salem, Oregon.

Virginie H. Tafilagi-Takala, a teacher by profession, was born in 'Uvea (Wallis) and is active in preserving and promoting 'Uvean language (faka'uvea) and culture. She is a member of the traditional dance group Wallis Mako. Her first poetry collection is forthcoming.

Lehua M. Taitano is a queer CHamoru writer and interdisciplinary artist from Yigu, Guåhan (Guam), and co-founder of Art 25: Art in the Twenty-Fifth Century. She is the author of two volumes of poetry: *Inside Me an Island* and *A Bell Made of Stones.* Taitano's work investigates modern indigeneity, decolonization, and cultural identity in the context of diaspora.

Born in Aotearoa New Zealand, **Leilani Tamu** published her first book of poetry, *The Art of Excavation,* in 2014. A daughter of Te Moana nui a Kiwa (the great ocean of Kiwa, the Pacific), Tamu's ancestral and marital connections are to the islands of Samoa, Tonga, and Niue.

Teweiariki Teaero (1962–2021) was known to friends as Tevi. He was a senior and active member of the Kiribati Writers Association. He was previously a senior academic at the University of the South Pacific, where he taught for more than two decades. In 2019, he was awarded the National Order of Kiribati medal. He has three anthologies of poetry to his credit and contributed to many collections.

Katerina Teaiwa is of Tabiteuean, Banaban, and African American descent and mama to two girls. She is a full professor in Pacific studies and a deputy director in the School of Culture, History and Language, College of Asia and the Pacific, Australian National University. She is author of *Consuming Ocean Island: Stories of People and Phosphate from Banaba* (2015) and a visual artist who has toured her work *Project Banaba* in Australia, Aotearoa New Zealand, and Hong Kong. Katerina is currently vice president of the Australian Association for Pacific Studies and arts editor of *The Contemporary Pacific.*

Teresia Kieuea Teaiwa (1968–2017) was a leading, and much loved, Pacific studies scholar, teacher, activist, feminist, and poet. She was born in Honolulu, raised in Fiji, and was of Tabiteuean, Banaban, and African American descent. She was founder and director of the Pacific Studies program at Victoria University of Wellington in Aotearoa New Zealand. Her words "we sweat and cry salt water, so that we know that the ocean is really in our blood" have been quoted in countless artistic and scholarly contexts. She was married to Sean Mallon and had two sons—Manoa and Vaitoa. *Sweat and Salt Water: Selected Works* was published by the University of Hawai'i Press in 2021.

Tevachan (David Teva Chan) was born in Tahiti and educated there and in France. A keen chess player and practitioner of martial arts, he has published online and in the French Polynesian literary journal *Littérama'ohi.*

Konai Helu Thaman is from Nuku'alofa, Tonga. She is the author of five collections of poetry: *You, the Choice of My Parents* (1974); *Langakali* (1981); *Hingano* (1987); *Kakala* (1993); and *Songs of Love: New and Selected Poems* (1999). She earned a BA from the University of Auckland; an MA in international education from the University of California, Santa Barbara; and a PhD in education from the University of the South Pacific, where she taught for many years as a professor of Pacific education and culture. Thaman was a fellow of the Asia-Pacific Programme of Educational Innovation for Development and has served as the UNESCO chairperson in Teacher Education and Culture.

TravisT (Travis Kaulula'au Thompson) is an award-winning Kanaka Korean spoken-word poet and touring teaching artist from Kalihi, Honolulu, O'ahu, Hawai'i. As the only child of activist educators, he began performing his poetry at protest rallies and political demonstrations. He was a co-founder of the re:VERSES Poetry Collective; co-founder and director for Youth Speaks Hawai'i, Pacific Tongues; and is currently a founding member of HI Poets Society.

Haunani-Kay Trask (1949–2021) was a Native Hawaiian scholar, poet, educator, political scientist, and professor emeritus at the University of Hawai'i at Mānoa, where she was the founding director of the Center for Hawaiian Studies. She authored two monographs, *Eros and Power: The Promise of Feminist Theory* (1984) and *From a Native Daughter: Colonialism and Sovereignty in Hawai'i* (1993), as well as two collections of poetry, *Night Is a Sharkskin Drum* (1994) and *Light in the Crevice Never Seen* (1999). She also co-wrote and co-produced the award-winning documentary *Act of War: The Overthrow of the Hawaiian Nation.*

Hone Tuwhare (1922–2008) was a boilermaker/welder by trade, a trade union delegate, a member of J Force to Japan (1946), and internationally renowned author. He was an organizer of the first Maori Writers and Artists hui at Te Kaha and walked in the Maori Land March in 1975. Over his career, he published more than a dozen collections of poems, short stories, and plays. He received many awards and fellowships, including a Scholarship in Letters by the Queen Elizabeth II Arts Council of New Zealand, and the Inaugural Prime Minister's Award for literary achievement. He never had secondary school education, but he received double honorary doctorates of literature from Auckland and Otago Universities. He was named New Zealand's Te Mata Poet Laureate (1999) and one of New Zealand's ten greatest living artists (2003). A posthumous collection of his writing, *Small Holes in the Silence: Collected Works,* was published in 2011.

Dr. **Frances C. Koya Vaka'uta** is team leader, culture for development at the Pacific Community in Suva, Fiji. Prior to joining the Pacific Community, she was associate professor and director of the Oceania Centre for Arts, Culture and Pacific Studies at the University of the South Pacific. A poet and artist performing under the pseudonym 1angrynative, her work explores contemporary Pacific issues and Pacific heritage.

Desiree Taimanglo Ventura is an educator and author from Yigo, Guam (familian Alamasak). She has taught communications and composition at the University of Guam and the Guam Community College. She currently works to author and edit local publications that center the CHamoru experience. She holds an MA in rhetoric and writing studies from San Diego State University and a BA in English from Chaminade University in Hawai'i.

John Waromi was born in 1960 in West Papua. After studying law at Cenderawasih University, he moved to Jakarta and joined the dramatic troupe Rendra's Bengkel Teater. As an actor he performed throughout Indonesia as well as touring New York, Japan, and Korea. He now lives and writes in his home province.

Jahra Wasasala is of Fijian/Euro origin, based in Aotearoa New Zealand. Wasasala is a cross-disciplinary artist utilizing her training within performance activation, contemporary dance technique, and poetry to investigate ancestral attunement, transformation, and visceral character work through her art. Jahra has toured across her home of Aotearoa as well as Australia, Hawai'i, New York, Berlin, Guåhan, and Canada.

Maualaivao **Albert Wendt** is an award-winning Sāmoan poet, novelist, playwright, artist, scholar, and educator. He has published more than a dozen novels and short story collections, including *Sons for the Return Home* (1973), *Pouliuli* (1977), *Leaves of the Banyan Tree* (1979), *The Book of the Black Star* (2002), *Adventures of Vela* (2009), and more. He edited several anthologies of

Pacific literature, including *Lali* (1980) and *Nuanua* (1995), among others. Wendt has taught at Samoa College, the University of the South Pacific, the University of Hawai'i, and the University of Auckland. In 2013, he became a member of the Order of New Zealand.

Wayne Kaumualii Westlake (1947–1984) was a Hawaiian poet, journalist, educator, artist, scholar, and activist born on Maui and raised on O'ahu. He earned his BA in Chinese studies at the University of Hawai'i. Before his tragic death, Westlake wrote innovative poetry and translated Japanese literature. The posthumous collection *Westlake: Poems by Wayne Kaumualii Westlake* (2009) was edited by Mei-Li M. Siy and Richard Hamasaki.

Danielle P. Williams is a Pushcart-nominated poet, essayist, and spoken-word artist from Columbia, South Carolina. She is an MFA candidate in poetry at George Mason University. Danielle strives to give voice to her Black and Chamorro cultures. Her poems were selected for the 2020 Literary Award in Poetry from *Ninth Letter*.

Steven Edmund Winduo is a Papua New Guinean writer and scholar. He earned an MA from the University of Canterbury and a PhD in English from the University of Minnesota. His books include *Lomo'ha I am, in Spirits' Voice I Call* (1991), *Hembemba: Rivers of the Forest* (2000), *A Rower's Song* (2009), *Detwan How? Poems in Tok Pisin and English* (2012), and *The Unpainted Mask* (2010). He was the founding editor of *Savanna Flames: A Papua New Guinea Journal of Literature, Language, and Culture*. Winduo lectures in literature at the University of Papua New Guinea and is director of Melanesian and Pacific Studies in the School of Humanities and Social Sciences.

Briar Wood grew up in South Auckland and currently lives in Te Hiku-o-te-ika—Northland, Aotearoa New Zealand. She has lived and worked in Britain, where she has published poetry, fiction, and essays, as well as teaching Pacific literature. Her Te Hikutū ki Hokianga, Ngāpuhi Nui whakapaka connects her with ecological concerns that emerge in recent poetry collections *Rāwāhi* (2017) and *Welcome Beltane* (2012).

Aiko Yamashiro is a proud descendant of Okinawan farmers, mechanics, dancers, cooks, and storytellers. She is so grateful to Lia for deepening her relationship with ancestors and their green green leaves, and for all the friendship and adventure grown out of this weaving. She is so grateful to the plants for their decolonial lessons of healing, compassion, and resilience. You can find more of Aiko's writing on the online blog *Ke Ka'upu Hehi 'Ale*.

Carlon Zackhras is a nineteen-year-old youth climate activist currently studying liberal arts in the College of the Marshall Islands.